THE KILBURN TALE

BOOKS BY ERNEST RAYMOND

Novels :

WE, THE ACCUSED
THE MARSH
A SONG OF THE TIDE
FOR THEM THAT TRESPASS
THE FIVE SONS OF LE FABER
THE LAST TO REST
WAS THERE LOVE ONCE ?
THE CORPORAL OF THE GUARD
TELL ENGLAND
A FAMILY THAT WAS
THE JESTING ARMY
MARY LEITH
NEWTIMBER LANE
THE MIRACLE OF BREAN
CHILD OF NORMAN'S END
ROSSENAL
DAMASCUS GATE
WANDERLIGHT
DAPHNE BRUNO I
DAPHNE BRUNO II
THE OLD TREE BLOSSOMED
MORRIS IN THE DANCE
DON JOHN'S MOUNTAIN HOME

Trilogy :

ONCE IN ENGLAND
 comprising definitive editions of
  A FAMILY THAT WAS
  THE JESTING ARMY
  MARY LEITH

Biography :

IN THE STEPS OF ST. FRANCIS

Essays, &c. :

THROUGH LITERATURE TO LIFE
THE SHOUT OF THE KING
 With Patrick Raymond :
BACK TO HUMANITY

Plays :

THE BERG
THE MULTABELLO ROAD

THE KILBURN TALE

by

ERNEST RAYMOND

CASSELL AND COMPANY LTD.
London, Toronto, Melbourne
and Sydney

First Published 1947

Reprinted 1967 by Cedric Chivers Ltd., Portway, Bath,
at the request of
The London & Home Counties Branch of The Library Association
ECM - ANTON HAIN K.G.
Printed in Germany

THE KILBURN TALE

CHAPTER ONE

" I CAN'T go on with it, and I'm not going on with it,"
said Mr. Rostrum, striding up and down his room.

His arms behind his back and his right wrist lying in the
convulsive grasp of his left hand, he strode between door
and window ; and the door was sternly closed upon his
family, and, indeed, upon the whole family of mankind.

" It's no good ; no good," he said ; and he paused and
beat his toe upon the carpet, while his head hung forward,
weighted with misery. And, sixty though he was, he told
himself the truth. " I should like to cry." To which, a
second later, he added an untruth. " I should like to die."

> I could lie down like a tired child
> And weep away the life of care

He began walking again. " It would be better if he had
never been born. Yes, I mean it. It'd be better if he'd
never been born. I wish he'd never been born. I do,
really. I can stand it no longer, and I won't. If there's
going to be trouble with Mildred and the children, there's
going to be. That's all I can say. There's going to be
trouble." Now his underlip thrust itself forward and pressed
up his mouth into a thin, incised arc ; and his lean face
with its fine nose and receding, obstinate chin was the very
portrait and mask of determination. But the lip slipped
back into position, and it became the mask of tragedy.

So often a receding chin goes with lean features, a thin
neck, and a long body ; and Mr. Rostrum was a long-
drawn figure like this. In his inmost heart he could have
wished himself a little broader in shoulder and chest, but
he was proud of his height, very proud. " Yes, I am over
six foot in my shoes," he would say, when people to his

pleasure inquired his height ; and this was exactly true, for his height was five foot eleven and a half inches, and his shoe's heel was the better part of an inch. His body was adequately built but thin ; his shoulders were a little rounded, and his head a little projecting. The head seemed to run forward to the fine, shapely, high-bridged nose. (He was very proud of his nose.) His brow was a splendid summit, high, wide, and shining ; his dun brown hair was thick on the back and sides of the white porcelain scalp and sprang away from it like horsehair escaping from the sides of a sofa ; his eyebrows were thick too, and one of them had a splash of silver (of which he was proud). So far a handsome face. Whoever in the blue-print offices of heaven had drawn the plan for Mr. Rostrum's profile had begun like a man inspired : his hand had drawn fine lines for crown and brow and nose. But at this point it had tired : when it came to the mouth and chin, its enthusiasm and strength had gone from it ; and when it dropped to the neck and shoulders it had straggled weakly and apparently forgotten what it was at.

The room in which Mr. Rostrum was padding like a jaguar in pain or (as he foresaw contention with the family) like a dramatist excogitating a scene of wrath with some good lines for the hero and possibly a strong exit—this shut and explosive room was a little like Mr. Rostrum in that it too was high and rather narrow. It was furnished in part as a study and in part as a work-room. Easy chairs, shabby and comfortable, turned their feet towards the fireplace ; bookshelves filled the recesses at the sides of the chimney breast ; and an Indian rug, somewhat stained, muted the padding of Mr. Rostrum's feet. This much of it was a study. But against the wall beneath the larger window was a long working bench ; and beside it a sink ; and on the bench were some of the appliances of an expert photographer : a vertical enlarger, a spirit vapour lamp, an electric Nernst lamp, a Bradley trimmer, two roller squeegees, and a squeegee pad. A modern eye would have seen at once that these appliances were of old-fashioned design, though still serviceable, and had probably been in use for twenty years or more. In the sink were some developing dishes and some glass measures of various sizes. Above the bench on a narrow shelf stood bottles and cartons and envelopes of a photo-

2

grapher's chemicals ; and in a corner stood two large frames on which travelled black and red blinds. They were exactly the size of the windows and when fixed in front of the sashes converted the room from a study into a photographer's dark-room. Between the working side of the room and the relaxing side stood an oval table, and on it, appropriately blending work and rest, were some dusty copies of the *British Journal of Photography*, the *Miniature Camera Magazine*, and *Photograms of the Year*, and some old novels and newspapers. The room, so equipped, was the home room and evening habitat, the refuge, shelter, and hermit shell, of Mr. Alexander Rostrum, proprietor of Rostrum and Eve's, Photographers, an old-established and much respected business in Kilburn High Road.

§

The house that held this room, so charged and explosive just now, was a large, grey, double-fronted, corner house in Nunsbury Road, Kilburn. It was almost a mansion, and it was Mr. Rostrum's own, though he lived only on its ground floor and in its semi-basement, and let the upper half as a maisonette. Everything about it was large, because it belonged to the large days of Queen Victoria : it had large windows, a large door, and twelve steps up to a large Ionic portico before the door. Tall trees stood before it, behind a low, grey wall : three lime trees, an ash, a plane, and an acacia. Planted when the house was built, they were now as tall as the house itself; the acacia which stood at the corner of the shallow garden and hung its tresses over the pavements of both Nunsbury and Withycombe Roads was a singularly fine tree and the delight of Mr. Rostrum's heart.

It is important to stroll up and down before this house, No. 25 Nunsbury Road, and see behind the trees the windows of the entrance floor and the barred windows of the basement under the steps, and to place Mr. Rostrum, Mrs. Rostrum, and their children in their right rooms. The room on the right of the Ionic columns is Mr. Rostrum's study, and it is behind that closed window that he is padding to and fro. The room on the left is Mr. and Mrs. Rostrum's bedroom. Behind Mr. Rostrum's study is the drawing-room

—you can see its large bay-window at the side. Behind the parents' bedroom is the small bedroom of Julian, their eldest child. That barred basement window on the right of the steps is the living-room, and the barred window on the other side is the beloved bedroom, the refuge, shelter, and hermit shell, of Brenda, their elder daughter. Behind it, immediately under Julian's room, is the little room of Joanie, their younger daughter. Sixty, seventy, years ago, when the house was new, and its grey bricks were white, and its trees were saplings, Brenda's bedroom was a house-keeper's room or servants' hall, Mr. Rostrum's narrow study was a part of the huge drawing-room, Mr. and Mrs. Rostrum's bedroom was a breakfast-room, and Julian's little cell was some small office or gentleman's closet. One can think of the house, and of every such house, as a massive grey mausoleum behind its London trees, with its old, dead memories lying, one above another, on its various shelves ; while, without, its grey brick and stucco, its pillars and quoins and cornice, have become a vesture of slow decay. Do the ghosts of the old memories slip along the passages and round the doors of the several rooms like draughts of cold air ? Mr. Rostrum, a fanciful and wonder-ing man, and a great lover of the house because he had bought it, liked to imagine that he was " psychic "—though " only in a small way," as he would say in modesty to his friends—and could apprehend on occasion a strange atmo-sphere in some of its rooms and on its basement stairs, as if the ancient emotions experienced here had gone out in power to impregnate the walls and now came issuing forth to touch him as he passed ; but it was all sentimental and self-exhibiting talk, for he had never really seen or felt any-thing. The house kept its secrets from him ; and it keeps to this day certain other secrets which shall now be told.

§

It was Sunday morning, and that was why Mr. Rostrum was in his room behind the closed window and the curtains. The Sunday silence in Nunsbury Road knew nothing of the crisis behind those curtains. The trees moved their crests in the softest of breezes, but not so as to make a whisper

4

and still less a sigh ; and the faded leaves in the gutters (for though it was only June the leaves can drop early in a London street) stirred in their humiliation and sank to the dust asleep again. There was hardly a sound in the street, except the visiting murmur from the High Road, because it still wanted three minutes to half-past ten, and the church bells of Kilburn had not yet begun to ring.

The crisis in the room had a name, and the name was Dudley. Dudley was Mr. Rostrum's youngest child. He had four children : Julian, a tall boy of twenty-two ; Brenda, a tall girl of twenty-one ; Joanie, a shorter, plumper child of seventeen ; and Dudley, who was not, as you might imagine, a lean-shanked schoolboy of fifteen or thirteen, but a pink and round-limbed infant of three. Three years and nine months, to be exact, and more full of vitality than his small body could contain—or Mr. Rostrum could stand. Dudley had been born when his mother was forty-six, and her time at hand. He had rushed into the world while there was still one minute left ; he had slipped into the family circle, triumphant and smiling, just as the door was about to close.

" To rack and ruin ; to splinters and ribbons," said Mr. Rostrum, who was now standing quite still, as if his bitterness had turned him into a pillar of salt. " Rack and ruin. Splinters and ribbons."

This was not an exact statement of fact : his house was not being reduced to rack and ruin—to be sure, he was not very clear what " rack " was. It was merely a lyrical rendering of his indignation at the minor lesions which his small boy was inflicting upon the structure and the furniture : at the scribblings on the walls and the scratches on the bureaux and the rents in the curtains and the stains on the carpets. It was, in a word, music : a pattern in sound, expressive of grief. He had been so proud of his large rooms and of the furniture with which, through the years, he had adorned them ; and now Dudley was " reducing them all to rack and ruin." The springs of the beds were in danger of being broken by the trampoline act which he liked to perform on them ; the handles of the W.C. door were loose upon their axis, because he must always be swinging in and out on the door ; the walls and the loose-covers were patterned with the imprint of his coal-black palm ; the keys were gone from the locks because he could never resist a key ; and, worst of all, the handle of every cupboard, drawer, or chamber door was sticky and glutinous from the manipulation of his fingers. And every one of these impairments to his well-loved home rasped Mr. Rostrum's nerves. Scratch his furniture, and Mr. Rostrum bled.

And the noise since Dudley joined the family group ! In his excitement he would shout at people though they were only ten inches away ; in an excess of high spirits he would stand and scream in the living-room like a locomotive under a terminus roof, his face red with the effort and his eyes strained and staring ; in hours of well-being he sang a loud, tuneless, and continuing song ; and in moments of sudden and unjust pain he bawled a cadenza that affronted the neighbourhood and shivered his parents' sensibility, and filled them with alarm for their good name. There had been times when Mr. Rostrum envied his lifelong friend, Jock Aldin, who had died last year of angina pectoris, and found his peace.

But this was not the whole of Dudley's impact upon Mr. Rostrum. He smote upon him in another way that was in complete conflict with this one. He smote upon his heart as well as upon his nerves. The same *fortissimo* exuberance which could drive Mr. Rostrum to a sweet dream of death could sometimes raise in him an exultation, a delighted assent, that could only be described as worship. Dudley tossed him on the twin horns of exasperation and exultation, so that sometimes he experienced both horns at once. Dudley was quite beautiful—or so his father thought. He had darkening gold hair, and gold rings round the pupils of his eyes, turning them from blue to hazel, and long brown lashes, and cheeks so pink and soft that Mr. Rostrum could hardly keep his fingers—or his lips—from them. And he had charming ways—as well as maddening ones. When he saw his father in the distance he would cry out, " My daddy ! " and, running to greet him, would clasp him round a knee ; and in such moments his father's heart was shaken with joy. And the sound of his loud singing when he was happy (and when Mr. Rostrum was not working but disposed to be happy too) and of his gay, impudent, imperious

6

commands to all, even to his father, could be as exhilarating as a breeze on the hills or a draught of good wine. In brief, Mr. Rostrum exulted in and worshipped the abounding life in his little boy, and loathed it.

This morning he loathed it. " I am being martyred," he said. " Martyred . . . Rack and ruin. Splinters and ribbons."

He was middle-aged now (even at sixty he would not allow that he was elderly) and he wanted some peace. Other men at sixty had come into harbour and were resting at anchor on calm or gentle waters. Not he. Not he. Consider what had happened this morning. There were only the four bedrooms in the house, and it had been his desire and happiness to provide his elder children with rooms of their own. For years now Julian and Brenda and Joanie had had their own rooms and learned to love them, and neither he nor Mildred, when Dudley joined the family, had had the heart to disturb this arrangement, so they had kept Dudley's cot in their own large bedroom. For the first three years this had not seriously incommoded them, because a child so consistently healthy had been an easy sleeper, but now he awoke with the birds and longed to start the business of the day. This morning—a Sunday morning when both Mr. Rostrum and Mildred had hoped to lie late in bed—he had sounded the reveille at fifteen minutes past five. He had called " Mummy " a score of times, and, when she declined to hear, he had sung a few flat and tuneless measures and then chanted like a litany, continuously, monotonously, " Mummy, I want to get up. . . . Mummy, I want to get up. . . ." This suffrage eliciting no visible or audible response from on high, any more than does the litany in church, he changed it to one that never failed to get his mother out of bed : " Mummy, I want to do some duty."

Mr. Rostrum had tossed and muttered and blasphemed, while his brain reiterated stupidly :

> There's no more sleep
> With the sun's first peep,
> For he's sounded the old Revally.

He had risen with his temper at the boil. He had gone down to breakfast in the basement living-room, determined

7

to teach that child some consideration for others. He had sat himself at the head of the table, Brenda and Dudley on his right, Joanie on his left, and Mildred before him. He had put on his spectacles, which he needed for the close work of eating, and, behind those spectacles, he had watched and waited, watched and waited, for Dudley to do something that would justify an angry lesson in consideration. And if you wanted a *casus belli* with Dudley at the breakfast table, you were not likely to be kept waiting long.

" 'Morning, all." Julian had entered, " 'Morning, Mum. 'Morning, Dad. 'Morning, Brenda. 'Morning, Joanie. 'Morning, Small Boy."

" Good morn-ang." Dudley, having a powerful sense of the ridiculous, liked to pronounce things wrong.

Julian sat himself at Joanie's side. " Brenda, pass me toast. Joanie, give me butter. Mummie, give me bacon. Dudley, be a good boy. Be excellent." This tall, good-looking lad of twenty-two was the humorist of the family (though, in happier hours, Mr. Rostrum himself had some claim to the title, and Dudley was fast becoming a strong competitor for it).

" I want bacon like Julian and Brenda," said Dudley.

" You'll have nothing till you've eaten your porridge," said his mother.

" But I want it."

" Well, you won't have it till you've finished your porridge. That's final."

Dudley turned sullen and just played with the porridge. After a time, his sense of ill-treatment having been enlarged by brooding, he said loudly, " No."

" No what ? " inquired his mother.

" No nothing. Just no."

Julian, Brenda, and Joanie laughed, and Dudley, perceiving that his remark had been a success, brooded a little longer and said, " Not."

" Not what ? Whatever do you mean ? "

" Not nothing. Just not."

" Don't talk to your mother like that ! " barked his father, deciding that this was his opening—not one of the best, but sufficient. He looked sternly at the little boy over the top of his spectacles. " I won't have it."

8

Dudley looked up, as if surprised at these sudden hostilities.

"I mean it. I won't have it. It's rude. You'll learn some consideration for others."

Now, if Dudley was rebuked too sharply, or in a way that wounded his self-love, he would instantly disappear beneath the table like a submarine submerging and lie on the floor among the family's legs. And on this deep bottom he would remain in silence, refusing to surface. He submerged now—instantly—as a lesson to his father.

"Oh, come up and get on with your breakfast," pleaded his mother. "Come up and don't be silly."

"Don't *talk to him.*" Mr. Rostrum, bereft of his first target, projected his anger upon his wife. "Don't take any notice of him. Isn't that the one thing that encourages him? Isn't an audience exactly what he wants? It's no wonder he's like what he is, the way you give in to him and humour him." And irascibly he pushed back the spectacles which had slid forward on his nose.

"But he must eat something. Don't be ridiculous, Alec. And don't snap at me. I don't like it." Mildred, though fifty now, and more than matronly in figure, and the mother of three adult children, was as easily hurt by a rebuke as Dudley at three—or her husband at sixty. The Rostrums, in fact, were a very sensitive family. And Mildred could be as histrionic when aggrieved as Dudley. Let her consider herself unjustly corrected, and after a very brief brooding, after a few moments of fervid and pulsing creation, she had a scene all ready to stage. She was ready to ring up the curtain on a *scene à faire.* Her resentment *had* to issue in a dramatic performance, and she was her own best audience for such a performance, with a keen appreciation of the speeches she had composed for herself, the power with which she delivered them, and her accompanying "business" with cups and cutlery and what-have-you-at-hand. Often her words affected her so poignantly that the tears gushed. When she was a child, and mother or mistress rebuked her, she used to contemplate sinking to the floor in a faint that they might stand ashamed at their unfairness, sickened by their cruelty, and perturbed at its consequences. This pattern of behaviour remained with her at fifty, and she

9

produced it now. " I must get him to eat, mustn't I ? Am I not his mother ? If he doesn't eat, he will die. Do you want him to die ? " Julian threw a glance of resignation at Brenda and Joanie. They knew what the glance meant, and smiled back despairingly. It meant, " Oh lord, oh lord, we're in for it now, children. She's about to create." And Mildred created. She created some excellent drama. " He must eat his breakfast now or not at all," she began. " I can't be feeding him all day. I've all the work of the house to do. And it's Sunday, and I did so want to go to church. No one ever lets me go to church. Get up, Dudley. Get up at once."

" Leave him alone, I tell you ! I'm not going to have him rude or inconsiderate to anybody."

" Don't worry, Mum," Julian soothed. " He'll have to come up to breathe."

" But he's eaten nothing. He must eat. And it's all getting cold."

" Don't *talk* about him, I say ! The one thing he wants is to make an impression. He's listening to you all the time down there. At this rate we shall have a horrible little tyrant in the house."

" Oh, dear, whatever I do is wrong. Whatever I do is always wrong." Her self-pity and her sense of injustice swelled, and she expounded in a long speech, which she emphasized with sharp, angry movements of plates and spoons, that she had brought up three other children, and they didn't seem to be such complete failures. On the contrary people were always saying how successful she had been with them. Was Julian a tyrant ? (" Not at all," supplied Julian.) Was Brenda a tyrant ? Was Joanie a tyrant ? . . . " I don't see that I've been such a failure as a mother. I don't, really. I don't see that I'm as bad as you all make out. . . ." She felt for her handkerchief to wipe her eyes, since her words had pierced to the spring of tears. " Come up at once, Dudley. I don't care what any of them say. It's a mother's duty to see that you're fed. Come up, I tell you."

But all the time Dudley remained silent under the table. At last Mildred fell silent too ; and for a long, uncomfortable minute no one spoke. Mr. Rostrum ate glumly.

Brenda and Joanie sat and ate like an audience of two, detached from the quarrel, but silenced by it. Then Julian decided that the heavy atmosphere must be lightened with a few pleasantries.

"Brenda," he said, "I trust you will go to your holy church and pray for us all, especially the Awful Little Boy. Joanie, I trust that you will see your way to taking him out, so that your mother can have a little peace. And, Daddy, I trust that you will go to church too. I, unfortunately, shall be otherwise engaged. And by lunch time I hope we shall all be loving each other again."

And Julian, having finished his breakfast, lit up his pipe. His father, glancing at him over the spectacles, thought how curious, how almost comic, it was that a boy who only yesterday, as it seemed, was at school, should now be rising from the table behind a pipe and a cloud of smoke.

A minute later he too rose and went from the table. Unable to speak to anybody, he walked indecisively to the door of the room and went slowly and sorrowfully up the basement stairs. Wandering into his study, he shut its door and locked it. He locked it because it was more than likely that Dudley, his breakfast over, his bib removed, and his heart unencumbered by any sense of a recent quarrel, would come rushing up to the room, shouting, "My daddy!" And he couldn't cope with or show any affection to Dudley now. He was better alone. Alone.

§

"I can't go on with it," he repeated to the locked room as he paced up and down. "I can't."

One thing was certain; quite certain: he'd have Dudley in his bedroom no more. Dudley's cot should go into one of the children's rooms. It hurt his heart not a little—it hurt it more than he could have believed—to think that he must spoil his gift of a room to each of them; but what else could he do? Could he perhaps build on a new room somewhere? He had some capital. (He was very proud of his capital.) Should he spend a few hundred pounds on a new room? Or could he rent a room for himself outside? No, he had only to ask himself this to realize what his house—

the house which was his own—and his bed and his wardrobe, and Mildred and the children meant to him. He wanted his house, with the family in it, to be around him even when he slept.

No, there was nothing for it but to put Dudley in one of the children's rooms. One or other of the children must take him in. "I've worked and slaved and sacrificed myself for them——"

Steps in the garden, and a loud, tuneless singing. The sounds, like an elastic, drew him to the window. It was Joanie and Dudley. Sankey, her dog, followed behind. She was taking them both for a walk in Queen's Park, and she called, "*Will* you come on!" to the dog. "*Sankey*, do you hear me? *Come* on! San-*key!*" Dudley was on his tricycle, and, as usual, was clowning. He pedalled as if in a race, singing at the top of his voice and shouting "Shuh, shuh," when he was an engine and "Prr'pp, prr'pp" when he was a motor. And because it was Sunday he was dressed in a clean yellow shirt and newly washed blue shorts, and his golden hair waved away from a clean, straight parting. He was quite lovely, and pride leapt in Mr. Rostrum's heart.

But he shook his head as he watched. It was no good. "I don't love him. I no longer love him." It sank his heart to say it, but he was trying to speak the truth this morning. "I wish he had never been born."

His eyes fell on Sankey, the dog. Sankey in the main was a dachshund, but surely his long body was rounder and his legs shorter than any normal dachshund's. With his legs so short, his breast so near to the ground, his sleek body so fattened, and his hide so black, he looked like a prize bull from Lilliput. He ran into the coarse grass of the garden and now, with the brief legs hidden, he looked like a wandering vegetable marrow in a seal-skin coat or a fat black crocodile, newly wet from the water, wallowing among the reeds. Because he was of such a full habit, and so black and silky, and his two little forelegs might be described as bandy, Mr. Rostrum had named him Sankey after Archdeacon Sankey, the Vicar of All Hallows, Kilburn Park, who also was round and sleek and wore a black coat and had sleek little legs in black gaiters. But Sankey, unlike the

Archdeacon, had a tan breast and, under his black tail, a tan groove with a tan area around it, which gave Julian opportunities to be funny, for the Archdeacon wore a black coat with a tail.

Sankey had run into the grass this morning because its invitation was too much for him. There was a suggestion in the grass to which he yielded himself at once and willingly. Turning round to face his mistress and Dudley, he lowered his hindquarters and straightened his forelegs and, keeping an eye upon Joanie, responded to the invitation in the grass with a strained and worried look. Before the response could be successfully completed he had now and again to advance his forelegs a pace or two and drag his hindquarters after him. Dudley stood astride his tricycle and watched the performance with an undetachable interest. Joanie, swinging her dog whip, waited for its consummation.

Now, at last, Sankey had concluded the difficult operation with some success and was waddling through the gate. Dudley, this incident closed, turned his tricycle and raced it through the gate too ; he bumped it down the step and began to drive it savagely, teeth set, along the pavement. Mrs. Kemp, at the window of No. 23, called, " Good morning, Dudley," and he shouted, " Good morn-ang," and pedalled on so rapidly that only Sankey, and not Joanie, could keep up with him. Sankey, indeed, was every whit as enthusiastic about this advance as Dudley : so much so that he ran a yard in front of it, on its right flank, and kept turning his head to see that the main body, the mechanized infantry, was coming along properly. There was no such ambivalence to this operation, no such hesitation and conflict and strain, as there had been to the one he had just concluded in the garden.

Mr. Rostrum, watching the small boy, might not be loving him any more ; he might be regretting the day he was born ; but some detached and dispassionate part of him could only bow in worship of such vivacity. This surge of life in the little boy was the initial zest and creative force of the cosmos, and therefore divine. It was in the trees and the birds, it was in galloping chargers and greyhounds straining at the leash—and most notably it abounded, it burst forth, it gushed, it shouted, in Dudley. Purely academically—purely as a matter of theory this morning—Mr. Rostrum watched it and worshipped.

But before Dudley, Sankey and Joanie were out of sight he had forgotten them. He had forgotten them because all his thoughts were concentrated upon his right foot. It ached ; it was warm ; and there was a stinging about its toes. Only a mild discomfort, but more than was natural, surely, after only an hour of pacing and standing. Flat foot ? Age creeping on ? Faculties failing ? The idea leapt upon him like a footpad. It scattered all memory of the morning's threats. He must satisfy himself that this horrid little fear was unjustified before he resumed consideration of anything external to himself. He pressed on the foot to produce more pain. He kicked off his slipper, stood on the foot, and studied its arch. The arch certainly looked depressed. It was unusually low, was it not ? " A depressed area "—and as he said this, he thought it would be a nice little joke to offer the family when he was on friendly terms with them again. A darned good joke—really excellent— " my right foot, children, is a depressed area "—but it must wait for some happier time. He compared his right arch with his left arch, and was not satisfied. He thought of an experiment and, having thought of it, was without ease till it was accomplished. The door ? Locked. Good. He went to the sink by his work-bench, removed his sock, lifted up his foot and pressed it on the wet bottom of the sink, and then pressed it on the cork mat below : much as a man will press a rubber address-stamp first upon an ink-pad and then upon a sheet of paper. He lifted the foot to see what sort of pattern it had left upon the mat. It had left a perfect pattern—a pattern of which one could be proud—and he was comforted and dressed the foot again quickly.

No, perhaps he wouldn't, even in joke, mention a pain in his foot to the family. He had spoken only yesterday of a pain in his ear, and asked what were the symptoms of mastoid disease ; and only a day or two before he had discussed an ache in his finger joints that might be osteoarthritis. He must curb his desire to discuss these small symptoms, if only because he was always so impatient with other people who were " full of aches and pains," and most of all with his wife. Mildred, it seemed to him, had a new pain every day. It was tedious. He would have liked to be sympathetic with her (and to be applauded for his compassionate nature) and so he would have been, if she'd had a new pain, say, every three months, but since she produced one almost every day, he had a task to hide his impatience behind formal words of compassion. It always irritated him to see her taking pills from this bottle, capsules from that tin, or liniment from that jar. Not but what he, when he was feeling ill, tried everything that was suitable in the house.

Another reason for keeping his pains to himself, at least for long intervals, was the fact that he so often reminded the family that he had an iron constitution and hadn't spent ten pounds on a doctor in sixty years. " I'm the only one of the family who's never ill," he would boast. " I haven't had a serious illness since I had measles as a boy half a century ago. I wasn't born with a silver spoon in my mouth, but I *was* born, thank God, with a constitution of iron." His pride in this constitution could generally be relied upon to outweigh his desire to discuss a new pain. But not always. Not if the pain increased.

Steps in the garden again—and he hurried to the window. Brenda this time. Brenda, his second child, and nearly as tall as Julian, nearly as tall as himself; Brenda with her childish face at the top of her tall body, and her eyes that were so often sad as if she sorrowed that she should be so tall ; Brenda too defiant and austere to have a wave in her hair or paint on her face like Joanie ; Brenda setting out for St. Augustine's, Kilburn, her very high church, with her Anglo-Catholic manuals in her large red childish hands. (For the first time, as he saw those little black books, he heard the church bells ringing.) Brenda, the most quiet and reserved of his children ; the one of whom he knew least ; and yet the one who, because she was a daughter ; because she was so like him in figure and face, reproducing his features in a small feminine shape ; because she was at once so self-enclosed and self-sacrificing, trying always to help others ; because she was the most sensitive of them all, flushing from temples to throat if chided or disparaged ; because she was so silent, pensive and mysterious, and sometimes so wilful and rude—held so much of his heart. Julian, because he was a gay, good-natured, satirical youth, one could not but like ; Joanie, because she was placid, laughing, and easy, and withal very pretty, one must love ; but neither touched his heart like Brenda. Brenda, he would tell himself, he could have loved most of all. She was in every way the most like him, and should have been the nearest to him. Instead she had gone furthest away. His heart went with her, and with the black manuals, through the gate and along the pavement. As always she walked quickly, almost passionately, through the world, indifferent to other people and with her own private cloud around her.

She was gone—and of a sudden he felt completely alone—more alone than he had ever felt in his life. Strange, sad thoughts came upon him, as he stood by the window and looked in the direction in which Brenda had gone. It came upon him, for instance, that, however healthy and strong he might feel, he was, in simple fact, slowly dying. Time, in slow motion, was grinding him down to nothing. He was dying upon his feet. " Yes, I am getting old . . . old . . . and that is only another way of saying that I am already in the throes of death." Four children had somehow dropped from him and were wandering about the world, and all their faces were mysteries. Each face guarded a mystery, and Brenda's was the most silent and guarded of all. He too. Just as he stood in a locked room, alone, so his real self stood for ever in a lonely, locked room, shut away from Mildred, shut away from his children, awaiting extinction like a criminal, and given no answer, nor ever likely to be given one, to the riddles that perplexed him. Life . . . its irrepressible uprush in little children . . . its growth in beauty . . . its bloom on Joanie's cheek . . . its hourly efflux in Julian's laughter and fooling . . . its triumph in the voices of young men singing, or in a great chorus of voices, men's and women's, blent together, co-operating, integrated, as they sang their glees in harmony . . . its slow decay in old trees and in men of sixty . . . and the heedless, illimitable sky, which was not subject to mortality, crowning and surrounding the world of men and scorning their question from the beginning and for ever.

This little room of his was at the centre of Immensities, and he was alone in it, and knew nothing. There was no answer in the clean, transparent sky. Not even the church bells this morning, tumbling their tale beneath the wide, blue heaven, gave him any answer that was final and satisfying. Ring on ; tell your tale ; sing your sermon ; but what can you know ; *how* can you know; how can you *know* that you know ? Ring on and comfort whom you may. To-morrow perhaps I shall believe again, as Mildred believes and Brenda believes. It is happier to believe.

Ah, well, since no answer could come, it was useless to ponder the great riddles any more. Best return to the small, immediate problem, What to do about Dudley. He turned from the window and walked the room with this question again.

CHAPTER TWO

THE children fell into their places around the table for the Sunday dinner : Julian and Brenda, Joanie and Dudley ; all in a lively mood and unaware that an apple of discord was on the menu. Mildred, occupied with much serving, was unaware of it too. Mr. Rostrum sat silently, with his family to left and right of him, and the apple, so to say, on his lap. As the head of a churchgoing family he bent his head forward and said grace : " For what we are about to receive may the Lord make us truly thankful."

On the surface he was calm, but a ground swell was running strongly ; and very soon, all being served, he spoke.

" Listen. One or other of you children has got to take Dudley into their room."

" What ? To sleep ? " demanded Julian.

" Certainly."

" Oh my God, no ! Oh, no, no, and likewise Come, come. Why, by five o'clock in the morning his cot stinks like the Gents."

" It doesn't," protested Mildred. " He's been perfectly dry for a year."

" Please, Julian, please." Mr. Rostrum believed in humour, and held a high opinion of his own, but Julian, in his view, sometimes went too far.

" I hoped it was funny," sighed Julian.

" No, no. We must preserve some standards. I like jokes —no man more—but I see nothing funny in pure obscenity."

" *I* do. I get a colossal kick out of it."

" Well, that's where we differ. That's where we very definitely differ. As I was saying, you children must choose between you. I've quite made up my mind that I can't have him in my room any more. If I get no sleep, I can't do any work, and you all depend on my work. Besides, I'm older than any of you and need some peace. One or other of you's got to take him into their room."

" Into his or her room," Brenda corrected him. As a schoolmistress who had passed examinations in English Literature, she was quick to correct the family's grammar. " One is singular. So is other."

Mr. Rostrum hated these corrections by his daughter. Before Brenda had begun to reconstruct his grammar like this he had prided himself on his English, and especially the English of his business letters. " That's nonsense. One or other is at least two. And in this case three."

" It certainly isn't. It's one person, whichever of us it is. One or other can't take anyone into *their* room. And in any case it ought to be ' their *rooms*.' ' Their room ' implies a room held in common."

" Oh, stop it ! Don't be for ever teaching me my grammar. I'm not one of your pupils. And none of this is to the point. The point is that one or other of you's got to take Dudley into their—into his—into one or other of your damned rooms. What about you, Julian ? "

" Hell, no ! Not in a thousand years."

" He's getting big now. Two boys can well dig in together."

" Oh, no, I protest. I protest most fluently. I didn't give birth to him. I protest that in that business I had no hand at all."

" Julian ! Please. That's enough." Mr. Rostrum, needing his spectacles only for his plate, looked over the top of them at his son. " The little boy is your brother. Don't you love him ? "

" I don't think so." Julian gave further thought to this matter and answered, " No."

" Daddy wakened me up," said Dudley, who had been

listening to it all, while he drew on the table with a pencil instead of eating his dinner.

"I did not. Good lord, I——"

"Daddy 'sturbed me," persisted Dudley; and, pressing hard on the pencil, he broke the lead. "Oh, damn and blast it."

"Dudley!" rebuked his father. "You're not to say 'damn'. Or 'blast'."

Dudley, disliking his father's corrections as much as his father disliked his daughter's, asserted his freedom to speak as he chose. "This blasted pencil," he said softly.

"Do get on with your dinner," begged his mother, more interested at this stage in his body's condition than his soul's. "Please eat it up, darling heart . . . *please*."

"Your technique is utterly wrong, Mummy," explained Brenda. "That despairing 'please' of yours is simply loaded with the conviction that he won't do what you ask. It's a most powerful suggestion to him *not* to do it. I've never heard so much hopelessness in a single word before."

"Dudley, *EAT IT UP!*" roared Julian, as illustrating a different technique.

"That's no way to deal with him either," said Brenda.

"You do what your daughter suggests, Mum," sighed Julian. "She alone possesses the truth about everything."

Meanwhile Dudley continued his engraving with the stub of the pencil.

Mildred filled a spoon and put it to his mouth. "Come on, my treasure. You said you were hungry."

"The hungry's gone," expounded Dudley, and ejected all the substances she had put in his mouth. They dropped to his plate like mince from a mincing machine.

"*Dudley!*" This time it was Mr. Rostrum who roared at him, and the roar made Dudley start. "You're not to do that."

Dudley was not disposed to have everyone shouting at him. "I'll do it if I want to."

"*You will not!*"

Dudley laid down his pencil and submerged beneath the table.

Mildred sighed. "Oh, no, no—oh, what am I to do?— oh, please come up, my loveykin. Don't do that."

" Take no notice of him," ordered Mr. Rostrum.

No sound came from the places under the table where Dudley lay among the feet of his family like a submarine among the sea-bed reeds.

" Exit the Awful Little Boy," said Julian.

" Leave him alone. Leave him there. We can now have some peace. We've got to settle this question about where he's to sleep. It lies between Brenda and Julian. Joanie's room is much too small."

" Hear, hear," said Joanie. " I'd have him like a shot . . . I'd love to . . . but there's no room." She was delighted to express her goodwill and helpfulness now that it was clear she would not be asked to put them into practice. " I shouldn't mind having him at all. He wouldn't wake me up. Nothing wakes me up."

" Too true," said Brenda. " Can't we park him in the passage ? "

" I only wish I could do something," continued Joanie, " but I can't."

" Genial Joanie." Julian had decided that his position in this debate was no more than that of a commentator. " Plump and pleasant child."

" But you *could* do something," submitted Mr. Rostrum to Joanie. " You could go and sleep with your mother, and I could have your little room."

" Oh. . . ."

" Yes, I think that's an excellent idea," said Julian.

" You shut up," adjured his sister.

" I will arbitrate." Julian, having nearly completed his five years as a solicitor's articled clerk, liked to burlesque the rôle of a wise, impassible, soft-voiced lawyer. " There is no need for all this heat. I can see two admirable solutions. All that is needed is an atmosphere of scientific calm. One : we shove the Awful Little Boy into Joanie's small room and put Joanie in Brenda's. Two nice girls together. Or two : we give Joanie's little room to Brenda and put Joanie and the Awful Little Boy into Brenda's large room. Two kids together."

Mr. Rostrum shook his head. " Brenda is a young woman now. She should have her own room, and a nice room too."

"I don't agree. Brenda's the one to take up the cross. She's High Church, isn't she?"

"I hope we're all church people."

Julian raised a bland hand to silence his father. "Hasn't she just come from High Mass? Isn't her room full of holy pictures? And crucifixes? They might be a good influence on the little boy. Furthermore she's fond of children. Isn't she devoting her life to a lot of snotty kids in Marylebone? Well, here's an unwanted child for her to take in——"

"Don't strain yourself, Julian," interrupted Brenda. "A little less effort, and you may one day say something funny."

"Hell, the woman gets more of a schoolmarm every day."

"I don't! I don't!" The crimson dye had rushed over Brenda's face and throat, and her words had sounded like an offended child's. The tears were filling up beneath her eyes. Julian by calling her a schoolmarm had touched upon a thorn deep-seated in her flesh. His words had flung back the years and changed her from a sarcastic young woman into a hurt and passionate child. Her hot denial was little different from one of Dudley's.

"She does nothing of the sort," declared her father, who had seen the swelling beneath her eyes. "She's as much right to be sarcastic as you."

His gentleness did nothing to stanch her tears.

Mr. Rostrum had found the clue to Brenda's secrecies, her quickness to criticize, her piety, and her longing for self-sacrifice, when he attributed them to her disappointment at being so tall. Because she was too tall to be loved as Joanie and other girls were loved, because she was twenty-one and no man had looked at her a second time, she refused to put a wave in her hair, paint and powder on her face, or cream on her large red hands. Instead she parted her hair in the middle and dragged it severely to the nape and there twisted it into something that was less a chignon than a swirl of defiance. Such asceticism was a pity because her face with its finely formed nose (the small feminine version of her father's), its wide brow, and large soft eyes, might have been made into something that was more than pretty— something beautiful, something noble, something far more striking than Joanie's round, pleasing, but ordinary face. But what would be the good of such a face at the top of

21

a figure as tall as a man's? Did she want to look like a painted maypole? She did not; and she accordingly withdrew from all competition with Joanie and her like on the playgrounds of love, and determined to give herself to the Church (by which she meant the extreme Anglo-Catholic Church, because her father, mother, and Joanie were Low Church, and Julian was little better than a heathen) and to her work among the children of the poor. Her religion and her work were going to be all her life.

And now she was in a conflict; she was a battleground for good and evil, because they were suggesting that Dudley should be moved into her room. Her room which was so precious to her! It was everything to her. There was a key in its door which she could turn on the world. In it was her long, comfortable bed where she could lie content and warm, because she had escaped from the world into her thoughts. In it was her *prie-dieu*, with crucifix and candlesticks and vases of flowers upon it; forming another gateway out of the world into the serene and shining emptiness where God was all. On its walls hung her large coloured copy of El Greco's tormented canvas, *The Agony in the Garden*, and her smaller pictures of Sœur Thérèse of Lisieux and Santa Chiara of San Damiano, who were perhaps the two people she really worshipped. On its shelves were her books, and very learned (at least in Literature) they seemed; very much a lesson in culture to Julian and Joanie. Why, some of them were even little volumes of French poets, largely chosen and loved because they were the gods of the knowing ones, and because Julian and Joanie had never heard of them, and because Brenda had passed her School Certificate with distinction in French, and because to speak of the Parnassians, the Symbolists, and the Surrealists, was to lay a rich taste upon the tongue. Look along the white shelves, and you saw Gautier, Rimbaud, Verlaine, Mallarmé, and Laforgue. Strange, perhaps, to see *Les Fleurs du Mal* so near to the crucifix and Sœur Thérèse of Lisieux; but that was Brenda. Her room expressed the contents and privacy of her soul.

You could almost say that it had its own private entrance from the street. Under the twelve stone steps that led to the portico was a door which had once been the tradesmen's entrance, and through this Brenda could slip quietly into her room when she returned from church or school and didn't want the family to hear her for a little or break in upon her thoughts.

She loved the room, and the thought of its invasion by Dudley produced a revulsion as instant as the shrinking of the leaf of the sensitive plant when it is touched by an alien hand. But just because it would be a mortification and she loved the sweetness of self-sacrifice (and because such a self-sacrifice would be a punishing lesson to the family) she longed to say, " *I'll* take him." Two such motives in alliance were certain to carry Brenda's will, and she said, " When you've all done quarrelling, you can call the incident closed. This correspondence may now cease. *I'll* have the little boy in my room."

" Oh, no, dear," said Mr. Rostrum, his conscience vexing him. " No, I don't think I like that. If anyone should have a room of their own—her own—it's you."

" I don't like——" Brenda was just about to say, " I don't like it either, but I'll do it for your sake and Mummy's," when her conscience, even quicker on the draw than her father's, flung before her the words, " When thou fastest, anoint thy head and wash thy face that thou appear not unto men to fast," and, triumphing over herself, she uttered instead a lie that was a virtue : " I don't mind. I'd quite like to have him."

Julian had listened with admiration. " When I'm dead," he said, " I shall rely on Brenda getting me into heaven."

" Don't be daft," said Brenda, blushing. And she added, since, if one is going to scourge oneself, one should do it properly : " I obviously ought to have him. Mine is the largest room."

" There, Joanie." Julian turned to his other sister. " I hope that's a lesson to you."

All this time the subject of this debate had remained in his private retreat below the table, as quiet and uncommunicative as an anchorite vowed to silence.

" Well, well," sighed Mr. Rostrum, not very happy about this decision, or about his own behaviour which had encompassed it. " We can try it, I suppose, and see how it works. And perhaps I shall be able to take him back one day."

23

Mr. Rostrum stood by his window again, with his doubts and difficulties still seated in his eyes. And suddenly he noticed that the wind was brushing through the trees, so that the leaves of the poplars scintillated like sequins in the sun The ashes and the tall acacia were waving their feathery branches, and they too made a scintillation but a paler one, as they uplifted the ash-grey undersides of their leaves. The yellow leaves were astir in the gutters, and great full-bosomed masses of white cloud were breasting into the blue of the sky.

And directly he saw that wind he saw a picture. It was a picture behind his gazing eyes. The eyes were empty now of all except this picture. He saw a sheet of water with green slopes descending to it, and willows and lindens and tall, broad planes standing around it, and the wind blowing wide crimped wakes across it, so that it looked like a sheet of grey, watered silk. White sails, wind-curved and slanting, moved in the midst of it, leaving long wakes behind them. Some of the sails were very small, but some were as tall as the boys and the men who stood on the margins of the water, watching them.

In Mr. Rostrum, and, it may be surmised, in every man in London, where the grey streets go on for ever, there were the eyes of a Gainsborough or a Constable, and sometimes even the eyes of a Rubens, a Claude, or a Ruysdael, dimmed by the greyness but not yet sterile, which longed to look upon green places and coloured skies and quiet water, and in some way to make a picture of so much poetry and store it in his heart. The picture which he had drawn from his store and was before him now started a craving in his throat like that of an addict for his drug. His bodily eyes, not the eyes of his mind, swung from the window towards a book-stand on the top of which stood an object on which he delighted just as Brenda delighted in her shelf of poets and the brass ornaments on her *prie-dieu*. It was a model yacht, rigged with mainsail and jib, and painted a dark royal blue from gunwale to water-line and copper from water-line to keel. If you asked him what kind of yacht it was (and you could do him no greater kindness) he would tell you that

24

it was a scale-model of a ten-metre-class racer, with an overall length of thirty-five inches and a beam of seven inches ; that it was Bermuda rigged, which meant that it had a mainsail and jib but no topsail or gaff ; and that its hull weight was only eight ounces, though the bronze keel weighed two and a half pounds. He loved to hear himself explaining these details in the correct terms of a yachtsman. He would ask you if her lines were not beautiful, and when you answered in simple truth that they were (for there must be a poet in you, too) he was almost as happy as when someone praised Julian or Brenda or Joanie.

He had seen a vision and must answer its call. It cried to him to escape from the oppression of houses and streets into the peace, the exquisite peace, that was always his when he was alone in this place of descending green slopes and cupped water, of shapely, brooding trees and mellow air, and engaged upon a pastime that enthralled him as much as the private game of a child.

The craving had its way without further ado. He took the boat from its place ; he unshipped its mast and sails ; he folded and stowed them along its deck ; he wrapped the dismasted boat in a canvas carrier, and took his long pole from the corner by the door. With this canvas load in one hand and the staff in the other he might have been a pilgrim bound for a sacred place—and this perhaps is just what he was, for the emotion that he was carrying to the trees and the water, and to the goodness of God that shone therein, was not less than worship.

For a minute he stood still, with an ear directed towards the door. He did not want to meet anybody as he went down the steps with this gear and tackle in his hands ; not that he was ashamed of what he was about to do, but because he wanted to do it alone.

And as he stood there listening, he heard a shrill voice shouting, " Chitchah . . . chitchah . . ." and " Ting-ting." Dudley. The one person who must not see him with the boat, or he would certainly clamour to come too. He went to the window. Dudley on his tricycle was racing hither and thither in the small space of garden. And it was clear from his " Chitchah " and his " Ting-ting " that he was not sure whether he was on a locomotive or a real " man's

25

bicycle," and that he was equally happy on either. He raced at fearless speed, saving himself from crashing into the garden wall by braking with the soles of his shoes on the ground. He had but the briefest area on which to race his engine (whatever it was) and yet he was a king of infinite space. He was as care-free as a foal in a pasture because all memory of a rift between him and his father, involving a prompt disappearance beneath the table, had fallen from him, and all resentment.

Pride occupied Mr. Rostrum's heart as he watched, and pity too. Pride that his child should be such a supercharge of energy; and pity that he should be so royally content with this confined and flinty playground. At the same time, ever and again, the harsh grating of the shoe-soles on the flints grated on his nerves, for children's shoes were dear. It was a question which emotion stood uppermost : the pride, the pity, or the ever-repeated distress as the shoes tore along the ground.

Now Mr. Rostrum, when his emotions were breaking upon one another like the waves of a wind-fretted sea, was subject to sudden impulses. They were as sudden as a change in the wind. They seemed to have no causal connection with what had gone before ; indeed they were often the opposite of what had gone before. Two impulses would leap upon him like this, an impulse to a self-sacrificing action, and an impulse to gaiety ; and often these two merged into one irresistible drive. Such a double impulse seized him now.

He flung open the window. " Dudley come sailing with Daddy ? "

Dudley left his tricycle where it was, in the midst of the garden. He rushed indoors, shouting, " I'm going sailing with my daddy."

Mr. Rostrum, rejoicing in his attack of goodness, hurried out of the room and down the stairs ot Mildred. " Hallo, ducks," he cried gaily. " I'll take the Awful Little Boy out for the afternoon, and you can have a little peace. See ? " The impulse ordered him to kiss her. Half ashamed of the kiss, he turned to Dudley. " Come along, you silly little coot. Get your hat."

" Oh, will you really, Alec ? Oh, that'll be wonderful."

" Yes, yes. . . ." He was now a little ashamed of his

26

goodness. " I expect you're a bit worn out. Time you had a rest."

" Isn't that lovely of Daddy ? Won't you have a lovely time ? Hurry up, my lamby-kin." Mildred had a gift for the creation of new, affectionate names. They fell from her like blossoms from an almond tree when its time is passing. " Let Mummy dress you, my treasure and heart."

" Will I go on a bus, Mummy ? "

" Yes. Keep still a minute, my pet. Do you want to——" and Mildred, with bashful lips and inquiring eyebrows, framed the words that describe Man's recurring humiliation ; but the impatient Dudley forswore any such need, till such time as wisdom, begotten of his excitement, came in power upon him, and he consented to be led away.

So Dudley was led away to be put in order inwardly as well as outwardly ; and when he was tidy in both parts, he and his father set out, Mr. Rostrum carrying the boat and the pole, and Dudley running at his side.

In Kilburn High Road they mounted a bus, ascending, at Dudley's urgent demand, to the upper deck, and here, on a back seat was their neighbour, Mrs. Stroud, a large, kindly, effusive woman.

" Hallo, Dudley," she exclaimed. " And how's my Dudley this afternoon ? "

Dudley did not answer. He had contracted himself into a shell of shyness, like a snail when its horns are touched.

" Say something to Mrs. Stroud," encouraged his father. " She's asking you how you are."

" Good morn-ang," said Dudley.

" Good *what ?* " cried Mrs. Stroud.

" That's his idea of humour," Mr. Rostrum apologized. " Like all our family's, it's of rather a low order."

" I'm going sailing with my daddy," Dudley volunteered ; now out of his shell again.

" Well, now, isn't that nice ? And where's your dear Mummy ? "

" She's having her peace," said Dudley.

Dudley minted much of his own language as he walked through the world, and often it was as living and potent as the stock phraseology of tamed and educated adults was worn out and lifeless. But, unaware that he had delivered

27

himself of a statement that was as apt as it was brief, he only inquired, "Why did that lady laugh, Daddy?"

From this bus they transferred themselves to another, which carried them between miles of pavements, and through long files of grey, unthriving homes, till at last it put them down by the trees at the foot of a rolling heath. Walking fast between the trees, for both were impatient to come at the ponds, they went up and over the green ridges; not always side by side, because Dudley must often stop to study objects of interest—a dog, another child, a fallen twig, or a pair of lovers in the grass (who were the most interesting of all)—and then Mr. Rostrum, turning his head, would watch the little boy, as, realizing all of a sudden that he was alone, he looked everywhere for his father and, descrying him at last, shouted, "Dad-eye, Dad-eye" (which he thought funny) and came running after him, glad to have found him again; and then there was a slight swelling of Mr. Rostrum's heart. Walking on, Mr. Rostrum looked at other men, quite as old as he, who were strolling on the heath with their dogs for companions. These dogs behaved in precisely the same way as Dudley, halting and loitering before objects of interest, and then racing after their masters —and he told himself, for he was feeling at peace with all the world (which is ever the fruit of a self-sacrificing act), that a small boy was at least as good a companion as a dog, and possibly a better one.

And now they reached the summit of the last ridge and saw the yacht pond beneath them like a shield of silver among the trees, and the yachts aslant upon it, taking the wind with beauty. The sight of the grey and glistening water and the small white sails made them walk even faster, and they came to the water's brink, and Mr. Rostrum, squatting upon his heels, unpacked his boat, erected his spectacles for important work, then stepped the mast, rigged the sails, and adjusted the steering gear. And all the time Dudley, wanting to help, cried, "Let me. Let me;" and there was some slight irritability here to flaw the perfections of this virtue-brightened afternoon. As Mr. Rostrum worked on the sheets and shrouds, a ring of boys surrounded him, for the yacht was a lovely thing, as even the smallest boys could see; and this pleased him well, because he liked an audience.

They plied him with questions, and he was happy answering them in the language of good seamen.

"Yes, if you want to scud before the wind, you must slacken all sails abaft the foremast, whatever your rig. Yes, it's a good rule, whether you're scudding or reaching or beating to windward, to sail your boat with sheets as slack as she'll take them. I shall keep her reaching. I don't want her to work up into the wind."

"She's a smasher, isn't she?" said one of the older boys.

"Yes, she's a pretty piece of work. Lovely lines, don't you think? It's a Bermuda rig. And she's a flyer on her day. She'll do her five knots, running before the wind."

"My *gum!*" The boy breathed it low, in his admiration. "Five knots!"

"This is my daddy," said Dudley proudly.

When the boat was trimmed, Mr. Rostrum walked with it to the edge of the water, the crowd following. He laid it on the water; and the crowd, enlarged now, and including males of all ages from seven to seventy, watched in silence. The boat found the breeze, heeled over, extended her sails in two lovely curves, and swept forward upon her course.

"She moves! She moves!" cried Mr. Rostrum. "She holds her course. She holds her course. Look, Dudley, she's beginning to fly. She's going faster than any other boat on the pond. Four and a half knots, I shouldn't wonder. Four and a half knots."

Mr. Rostrum's mouth was open as he watched, but he did not know it. He was not really standing by the margin on the water: he was on the deck of the boat, standing by the mast. Mr. Rostrum had never stood on a real yacht in his life, nor had he travelled over the sea farther than to the harbours of Dieppe, Calais, and Boulogne; he had been immured since birth in the maze of high houses that was Kilburn; but, together with the eyes of the frustrate artist, there was a deep instinct in him, a half-conscious longing, to revert to the habits of old, unknown ancestors who lived with nature in simpler days; and this hunger was satisfied to a height not far from ecstasy when he escaped from the terraced houses to the sham countryside of Hampstead Heath and put his boat out on the iron-bound water of a Highgate pond. Somehow he was made whole for a little, somehow he broke prison as the boat heeled over in the wind and ran before it, cutting the water as a draper's scissors tear through calico, and drawing her long wake behind.

" Come on, Dudley ! She travels ! She travels ! Come on, or she'll be at the other side before us ! " Dudley had been throwing twigs into the water and getting a happiness similar to his father's as he watched them drifting out to sea. " Come on, old boy, or she'll make it before we do. Gawlummy, she's *hurtling* along ! "

And with his eyes on the flying boat, and his pole in his hand, he ran—raced—round the verge of the pond, Dudley running a long way behind and imploring, " Wait for me, Daddy. Wait for me."

" Can't wait. Can't wait. She mustn't crash against the side. God, she's just hare-ing ! "

It was the most enjoyable afternoon he had spent for weeks. And once or twice, as he and Dudley stood on the brink of the pond, both watching the boat in the far distance, he considered a revelation that had come to him as a result of his self-conquest an hour or two ago and his determination to be kind to the little boy instead of angry with him. " That was a test for me," he thought. " It was a Tremendous Test. And I passed it. And what's the result. I am happy. When I was angry, I felt sour and horrid ; now that I am loving him again and trying to give him a good time, I feel clean, somehow, and happy. You're never happy if you're thinking of yourself all the time. I don't think I've ever seen that quite so clearly."

When he got home that evening, he was enthusiastic about everything : about the boat and its behaviour, about Dudley and his behaviour, and about the revelation that came to him at the water's edge. " He's an absolutely perfect little companion," he declared to Mildred, following her from room to room. " I want no one better as a companion. I loved having him. You know, I'm ever so much happier when I like him. One's always happier when one's liking someone instead of disliking them ; especially if it's one of the family. Especially if it's one's own child." And at some length he discussed this truth, which might seem trite, he said, but had to be experienced to be realized in full.

30

" Yes, I did a lot of thinking by the pond," he added as a last word, walking slowly away from the kitchen to return to his own room.

CHAPTER THREE

IT was ten in the morning, and the family of the Rostrums was dispersed over London. One after another they had gone from the house : first Brenda to her school in Marylebone ; than Joanie to the Public Library in Willesden where she was a junior assistant ; then Julian to the offices of Messrs. Roscommon, Saffery, and Duhamel, Solicitors, at Temple Bar ; then Mildred, with Dudley trailing behind, to the stalls and counters of Kilburn High Road to do the day's marketing ; and lastly Mr. Rostrum to the shop and studio of Rostrum and Eve's, Photographers, in the same crowded and bustling thoroughfare.

Mr. Rostrum went last this morning because he wanted, before leaving the house, to continue the spotting of an enlargement, one of a dozen photographs that he was sending to the Professional Photographers' Association Exhibition and to the London Salon of Photography. He thought of himself now more as an artist than a tradesman and enjoyed this kind of pictorial and commercial work much more than the too-familiar portraiture in his studio. And it was not necessary for him to be punctual at the studio because he had a most able receptionist in Miss Fletcher, who could open the premises and begin the business of the day. Miss Fletcher had been his receptionist, retoucher, and saleswoman for twenty-four years, and his assistant operator for twenty-three of them.

So Mr. Rostrum was sitting near his window and working with his fine-pointed pencil at his retouching desk, when he heard the steps of Mildred and Dudley in the garden and the rattle of wooden wheels on the path. Immediately he stood up to knock his pencil on the pane and wave to Dudley, because Dudley liked to be waved to from a window and to wave back with inordinate vigour. But this morning for some reason—perhaps a desire for variety—Dudley declined to wave. He said, " No," and refused even to turn his head. Mildred exhorted him, " Wave to Daddy, my blessing ; " but he remained resolute and repeated, " No." She appealed to him, knowing that his father would be hurt, but it was useless ; he desired variety ; and he went out through the gate, dragging his large Noah's ark on a string and keeping his eyes inflexibly before him. Mr. Rostrum at the window could not understand, because the child was plainly in a good temper since he insisted on jumping off the step on to the pavement and off the kerb into the gutter. He stood watching with a little pellet of pain in his heart.

Sankey, Joanie's dog, padded after them through the gate. He delayed to investigate some object in the gutter, then, fearful of being left behind, ran speedily after them, like a small black-satin bolster, or long, black toy balloon, his breast hardly an inch from the ground and his brief legs twinkling. Mr. Rostrum watched them, Mildred, Dudley, and the long, waddling dog, till they were out of sight and then sank back sadly into his chair.

§

And Mildred, Dudley, and the dog went on along Nunsbury Road. Mildred was a woman of medium height with fat limbs : her arms were fat enough to form a baby's creases at her wrists, and her hands fat enough to embed her wedding ring deep in her finger. Her hair was grey, parted in the middle, and twisted into a bun at the neck ; her features were small and pleasing, but the whole skin of her face was red and shiny—stove-burned after thirty years in the kitchen. It was even, at times, rather purple, like the complexion of a weary and ageing woman who sought comfort in drink— which was something that Mildred certainly didn't do, being a religious woman and a teetotaller for ninety-nine days in a hundred. However, this lie in her complexion was well contradicted by the clear blue eyes and her simple and kindly expression. Walking along with Dudley, she might well have been his grandmother or his elderly and comfortable nurse.

And now they were in Kilburn High Road. Kilburn High Road, that grand canal, with its streaming buses, lorries, cabs, cycles, and pedestrians, had roared through Mr. Rostrum's life for sixty years and through Mildred's for thirty. Always their home had been on one side of it and their place of week-day business and their Sunday church on the other. It was the thread on which their lives and the lives of their children were hung. Or, because they were never far from its noise, one might liken it to a roaring, vibrating workshop in a house of quiet domesticities. To-day, at ten in the morning, it was full of sunlight and dissonant noises : the hum of cars, the song of fast vans, the heart-beat of heavy lorries, the back-firing and machine-gunning of motor cycles, the blare of jazz from a radio shop, the spieling of costers at their barrows, and the yelping of dogs. Mildred was so accustomed to it that she never really saw it ; never troubled to interpret it. She did not see that it was an inharmonious blend of late Victorian façades and modern shop-fronts ; a continuing disorder of cinemas, chain stores, private shops, and costers' stands ; a vast canvas with Man's cupidity written and painted all over it and especially in the huge, competing advertisements that defaced the house-fronts and made hideous the railway viaducts that shot across its wide lacuna. Nor did she observe this morning, as she turned towards her shops, that the sun-blinds were down on both sides of the throbbing highway and gave to its long vista, in the bright June sunlight, some likeness to an Eastern bazaar. She had not the knowledge to think that only a London Canaletto could have painted that long, receding, sunlit scene, nor the vision to know that it was bathed with beauty only when God rubbed out from it most of Man's handiwork and yet laid a light upon it, at dawn and in the last tinted moments of the day.

Her walk along it, as usual, was an uneven and fragmented process, for she had to halt a score of times and call, " Oh, *do* come on, my sweetest. Come ON ! " to Dudley who was visiting every entry to see what was within or standing to stare at interesting children or pausing to study some article in a shop window and inquire if he could have it. Moreover he was retarded in his journey by the limited speed of the Noah's ark, which overturned and travelled on its side directly the revolutions of its wheels exceeded a certain rate ; and after a time he was calling to her in a monotonous repetition and in the hearing of all, " Oh, Mummy, will you carry this blasted nawzark ? " Her shopping was a succession of heart attacks : now he was touching a kerb-side bicycle so that she feared its collapse ; now he was playing with the weights and scales on a counter ; now he was running towards a crossing so that she had to run after him, though her heart was nearly dead with dismay ; and now, abetted by Sankey, he had turned about and was looking backwards so that he was a permanent and unpopular obstruction to an eddy of shoppers on the pavement.

In this punctuated and broken fashion Mrs. Rostrum, a fat and heavy mother among the slim, young ones, managed to get from dairy to greengrocer's, from greengrocer's to cake shop, and into Woolworth's and along its parallel counters ; and always Dudley and the ark followed behind. By flattery, bribery, corruption and lies she tried to persuade him, against nature, to be obedient and good and do all that she wanted. " Come on, my chicken, you *are* so good," she would say to him when his head was hanging and his mouth was sullen ; " You've been awfully good. I'm very pleased with you. Nobody could have a better little boy ; " and " Come along. You are enjoying it, aren't you ? Isn't it fun ? " when he was palpably hating it.

But it was not only Dudley who punctuated and broke up the walk. Mildred was a garrulous woman. She was garrulous to others in words and to herself in dreams ; which meant that she was either continuously fluent or continuously silent ; and this morning she was silent and abstracted when she walked only with Dudley and the dog, but exceedingly talkative when she met a friend on the pavement or in a shop. With any such friend she exchanged a volume of words, her chatter and interest being only checked by snatches at Dudley who was escaping into the roadway or out of the shop.

It was his unattended exit from Sudbury's, the provision shop, that gave a special distinction to this day's performance by adding to it a fine dramatic scene. The motors on the quaking highway were appealing to him more than the chattering housewives at the counters, and he was standing in the midst of the shop's threshold with the ark on its string (and on its side) behind him, when a robust and laden

34

woman of much the same age and shape as Mildred, leaving the shop, became entangled in the string and, later, with the ark. Much exasperated, she disengaged herself, kicked the toy away, and, turning round to elicit sympathy and indignation, addressed a woman behind her who had muttered, "Tst! Tst!" as if distressed. How should she divine that this fat and rubicund woman, fifty at least, was the mother of the little boy?

"I do think mothers ought to keep their children in some sort of control," she said. "They take no trouble with them at all."

After a morning of strenuous pursuit and education of Dudley this was more than Mildred could stomach. Her blood warmed, and she feared what she might do or say. She feared for her self-control. She feared that her passion for high-pitched drama might drive her, within the next minute or two, to create an admirable Act with full climax and grand curtain.

"He wasn't doing any harm to anybody," she began tentatively. "Poor little mite."

Still the woman did not realize that this was the mother, and she was annoyed that her attempt to share her indignation should have met with disapproval. To be treated as the offender when she was the offended was intolerable.

"Not doing any harm! Why, I was nearly thrown on to my face. I might have been killed. Whoever his mother is, she should teach him some consideration for others. A child of his age! Mothers don't seem to care how their children behave nowadays."

As we have said, Mildred was as sensitive to criticism as Dudley himself—or as her husband—or as Brenda. And when, not only her child, but herself was admonished, it was as if she had been struck on two raw and irritable places at once. Her temper flamed up and, as she had feared, became inspiration. It lit up the lines of a thrilling and explosive scene in which she and Dudley could play pathetic, even tragic, parts. It was exactly inspiration, because it filled her with creative power.

"What d'you mean : a child of his age? He's only a tiny. He's not yet four. And what real harm was he doing? What harm? Just standing there. He must stand somewhere.

He can't stand in the middle of the air. I should have thought it was rather for a person of your age to have some understanding and patience with children. There's not a better little boy anywhere. Kicking his toy away ! It's behaving like a child yourself. He's full of consideration for others. He's the most considerate child I know. Come along, my piccaninny. If your toy's broken, Mummy'll get you a new one."

"What did that lady say, Mummy ? "

"Never you mind what the lady said. She was very rude. She said things she shouldn't ought to have said, not in public and before everybody—in a shop where I've dealt for twenty years and am respected. It's no way of talking, to my way of thinking."

"I wasn't rude at all," declared the woman.

"Oh, weren't you ? Perhaps you don't know when you're rude. Perhaps it just seems natural to you. Perhaps a few lessons in manners wouldn't come amiss to you. Come along, my lovey-lamb. Getting me a bad name ! She doesn't like you, darling. She's one of those who seem to think that people shouldn't have children at all—though how the world would go on if people didn't have children, I can't imagine. But some people care only for themselves, and what happens after they're dead doesn't matter." She turned upon the woman. "I suppose you were a child yourself once, weren't you ? If your mother hadn't had any children, you'd never have been here ; and I'm not sure that that'd have been any great loss, either. No, indeed I'm not." Mildred, when she was in the full torrent of creation, was not hampered by any austere self-criticism. The torrent swept all criticism aside. "I can't stand people who can't stand children. They show what they are if they're unkind to children. Poor little tots : they've got to live, haven't they ? " The idea of their not living filled her eyes with tears. It caused her to shout at the woman who could be so wicked as to hold such an idea. "Perhaps you'd like to kill them all off. Perhaps you'd like him to commit suicide. Perhaps you'd like to see them all dead at your feet. Is that what you want ? "

"How was I to know she was his mother ? " The woman, her cheeks heated and her eyes aflame, appealed to the other shoppers who had paused in their traffic to watch the conflict. One interested watcher was Sankey, the dog. "She looks more like his grandmother. She must be old enough to be his grandmother."

"And what do you look like? And what do you think you look like? You don't look as though you were born yesterday. Or the day before, for that matter."

"If she's his mother, that accounts for everything. You can see where he gets his behaviour from. That explains everything."

But Mildred was quite ready to address the jury too. "She's probably never had a chance to have children herself. If you ask me, that's the explanation. Yes, I expect that's it. Sour grapes."

This public suggestion that her virginity was intact was a calumny that the woman must instantly rebut. "If you want to know, I've had four children. So there!"

"Well, I'm sorry for them, that's all I can say. Come on, Dudley. Don't just stand there staring. You come home. We've more important things to do than to stand here and listen to rudeness. Come away. It's a thoroughly bad example for you when people set you an example of rudeness like that. I don't like you to see it. It's not nice. Oh, where on earth's that dog? Where on earth does he get to? You come along too, or she'll be falling over you and kicking you away, and you won't like that. Just out-and-out bad temper and disgraceful rudeness." She dragged Dudley away by the hand, savagely, rapidly, so that the Noah's ark went bumping behind them on its side. She was impatient with him because she was ashamed of herself. "Come on home at once. You know I've told you a hundred times not to stand in people's way. They don't like it. Where are your manners? There are other people in the world to think of beside yourself. You can just come home."

"But I don't want to go home," complained Dudley. "I want to go some more further."

"You're not going any further. You're a naughty boy. You stood in the shop door and got me into trouble with that woman." Her shame was rising so high that it was ready to fall down in a cataract of tears, and she could find relief only by muttering aloud her disgust with herself, as she hurried the child along. " Behaving like a fishwife. . . . Oh, why do I fire up so and make scenes like that, and in a shop where I'm known ? . . . Why do I behave so ? It's not that I think it's right. It's not that I think it's clever. In fact, it's no way of behaving at all, to my way of thinking. And yet I just don't seem able to help it sometimes. It's like a common woman in the street. Yes, that's what it is : like a common woman in the street."

§

The day graduated into afternoon ; the afternoon declined ; and in the low, broad light of evening the children began to come home. Deep down below the daylight Brenda sat in an Underground train which was crowded with workers returning to their homes in Kilburn and Willesden and Wembley. She sat with her back erect, her large hands at rest on the handbag in her lap, and her long feet drawn in beneath her, so closely packed were the passengers standing in the gangway. There were many working girls seated or standing in that coach, but Brenda was the tallest. Most of the girls had red-pencilled lips and rouged cheeks and hair waved and curled ; and Brenda's face and lips seemed pale compared with theirs, and the set of her hair old-fashioned. Some of them had engagement rings on their fingers, and whenever a girl had such a ring, Brenda noticed it. It was often the first thing she noticed about a girl.

Her expression as she sat there was sad but gentle. It was the expression of one whose eyes were turned inward upon her own thoughts, and whose thoughts were of the sad, heavy cast that makes one feel gentle towards other people. There was that beside her which had driven this heaviness into her heart, for in the seat on her left was a girl of no more than seventeen—of Joanie's age, and with much of Joanie's soft, round prettiness—and she was holding the hand of a young man who stood before her swaying on his strap and often pressed against her knees. A young man with a pleasant face, he was perhaps four years older than she ; and all the time as the train roared through the tunnels,

38

from Marylebone to Edgware Road, and from Edgware Road to Paddington, he gazed down into her eyes, occasionally smiling. And the girl stared up into his eyes and gave, though more diffidently, smile for smile. The love of early youth was pressing upon Brenda with a spear in its hand.

Though she pretended not to be looking at them, she was really studying them all the time. She was fascinated by the thing that hurt her. Like the rabbit which does not run when the weasel stalks it but waits for the bite, she sat there considering the thing which could murder her heart. She pretended to be looking down at her folded hands ; she pretended to turn and look through the window at the names of the stations ; but really she was looking slantwise at the girl that she might be stabbed by the love in her upraised eyes and in her incomplete smile.

At Paddington the standing people became a crushing multitude, and the young man was unable to sustain his place before the knees of the girl. He was forced from her to the front of Brenda, and beyond, and for a second their linked hands, unwilling to part, were lying along Brenda's breast. Immediately the young man smiled an apology and dropped the girl's hand. The two were parted and smiled at each other a temporary farewell.

And then an impulse seized Brenda ; just such an impulse as would seize her father ; an abrupt impulse towards kindness and the savour of self-sacrifice. She waited a few moments ; she let the train go deep into the tunnel ; and then she rose and without a smile, but with a blush of embarrassment that flooded her face and neck and breast, said to the young man, " Do have my seat. I'm getting out at the next station." It was not true ; there were two more stations before Kilburn Park, but she intended to work her way to the crowd by the doors where she would be obscured from his sight and quickly forgotten.

" Oh, no, no," the young man demurred. " Don't trouble."

" Oh, but I want to get near the door." Her blush extended, and a small deficient smile appeared at her lips, but she avoided his face. Her shyness made her more often avoid a person's face, when speaking, than look into it. " I must get near the door, or I shall never get out."

"Well, it's awfully kind of you," said the young man. "Thank you very much;" and he dropped into the seat by his girl's side. Slowly, inconspicuously, they slid their fingers into each other's and sat there, silently happy.

Brenda threaded her way to the doors, advancing from strap to strap; and in the gangway by the doors she stood among a press of men, as tall as most, and taller than some.

§

She did not know that while she was watching the young lovers somebody had been watching her. She had had no eyes for the passenger seated on her other side; but this passenger was a long-legged young man, hatless, with untidy black hair, and wearing the dress of freedom: a grey polo-necked jumper, brown sports jacket, grey flannel trousers, grey socks, and brown suède brogues; and he had been playing much the same game as she. While pretending to read his evening paper, he had really been studying her, the girl on his left. He was of the type that looks at every girl and, if she is worth more than this first glance, looks at her again. And directly Brenda had taken the seat beside him, he had been attracted by her grave, childish face and interested by her upright and discouraging posture. He found her much more interesting than the younger girl beyond, who was like a thousand other round-faced and fluffy-haired girls. Again and again he glanced surreptitiously at her fine, sad profile, her youthful breast, her large red hands, and her large, long feet. He rarely looked at a girl a second time without considering her as a bedfellow, and he now devoted some pleasant minutes to this considera-tion. In a hot, overcrowded, and smoke-hazed railway coach, hammering through the tunnels and blinded by them, there were few pleasanter avenues of escape than the way of an erotic dream. In the dream there was an ingredient that was less ignoble than mere self-gratification, for he felt a real pity, a tenderness that was oddly pleasing, for this with-drawn and silent girl. Given that grave, childish face be-neath his lips, and feeling this rather sweet pity, and with that long, too slim, but not angular body pressing upon him

40

its eager love—yes, he could desire her. He could desire her, not for always, but for a little while. The desire, heightening in his mind, distended his throat and lifted his breast. With sidelong glances he looked at her whenever he could, and the more he looked the more the warm fancies quickened. And when of a sudden she got up and gave her seat to the young man, speaking in a low, contralto voice which, because of her quietness, she managed beautifully ; when she hid herself among the crowd at the doors ; and when she did *not* get out at the next station, he was touched by the unselfishness of her act and guessed, not incorrectly, at its secret root in her heart.

Nor did she get out at the station after that. Strange. Interesting. The train ran into Kilburn Park, and now she descended. At once he rose and descended too. He should have gone on to Queen's Park, but habit took command, the habit of lounging with a dream for company after any girl who interested him, and he hurried after Brenda out of the station. It would be easy enough to walk from Kilburn to his home in Kensal Rise.

Brenda did not know that in the quiet respectability of Cambridge Avenue, and along the noisy channel of Kilburn High Road, she was being followed, fifty yards behind, by a tall, hatless young man in *négligé* garments. She did not know that he stood at the corner of Nunsbury Road and watched her till she disappeared into her home.

§

Soon after Brenda, Mr. Rostrum returned along Nunsbury Road. He was returning early because the artist in him, so much happier a creature than the tradesman, was longing to get back to the spotting of his enlargements for the Salon and the P.P.A. Of some of these prints he had the greatest hopes : he dreamed of seeing them hung in places of honour and of being invited to send one or more for inclusion in the almanac of the *British Journal of Photography*. He might even send some of them to America, to the Chicago International Exhibition, and hope for inclusion in the *American Annual of Photography*.

Reaching his gate, he stood still and looked up at the house. Thirty years ago he and Mildred had begun their married life in a tiny villa little better than a working-class dwelling, so it was always a keen, though clandestine, pleasure to look up at this fine mansion which was his own property. He had done well enough in his life, he thought, as he looked up at the pillars of his portico, the large windows with their stucco architraves, and the quoins framing the lofty walls. The improvements in his earnings had come when, thanks to new plates, new films, and new techniques, portrait studies became a simple business that an assistant could discharge, and he was free to adventure into commercial work. Such work—the photographing, say, of antique furniture for a dealer's catalogue, the photographing of new blocks of flats for an estate agent's window, or the photographing of a factory and the enlarging of the pictures into mural decorations for a stall at the British Industries Fair—such work brought in much larger money than the making of portrait studies in Kilburn High Road or the photographing of wedding groups in the homes of the people. The good money had enabled him to buy this house twelve years ago. Twelve years, and still he could not return to it in the evening without pausing to look up at it with pride. He could not look at the tall trees, and especially at the gracious and feathery acacia at the corner, tall as the house, without thinking that they were his own. He was a landed proprietor, if only of a few square yards of London, and there was timber standing on his land.

This was the home which he had made for Mildred and the children. He had not failed the girl who had consented to marry him nor the children he had brought into the world. " Yes, I'm glad I've been able to make a nice home for them," he said, as he pushed open his gate and walked like a proprietor up his steps.

Letting himself into the hall, he listened. " Anyone in ? Anyone in ? "

" Only me. Only Brenda." Brenda's voice from her bedroom downstairs.

" Where's Mummy, darling ? "

" Out to tea. There's a note on the hall table."

" Oh, yes."

He picked up the slip of paper; read " Gone to tea with Sylvia and Ken; " and experienced an acute satisfaction. He could be alone for an hour or more. Mildred and Dudley were out of the house, and he could work on the enlargements in silence and peace. Sylvia Trimming was a young mother, twenty-five years younger than Mildred, but she had a boy, Ken, of the same age as Dudley and his best playmate. Both children were less trouble when they played together than when they hung about their mothers' skirts; so Mildred and young Sylvia sought often each other's company and at this time were probably gossiping the hours away in the Trimmings' small parlour, while Ken and Dudley shouted and sported in the back garden. There would be quiet in his house for a good hour; the trouble, if any, was Sylvia Trimming's. He went into his study and sat himself on the chair before his retouching desk—that happy and enchanted seat which annihilated time.

The hour passed in what seemed a few minutes, and he was surprised to hear a voice in the road that was surely Dudley's. It was upraised in lamentations and protest. Mr. Rostrum half rose from the enchanted chair—so that his knees were at an angle—and, snatching off his spectacles, peeped through the window. Yes, Mildred was towing Dudley by the hand. The child came as easily as a towed dinghy on the mid-stream ebb, but not without bellowing his disapproval at the world which he was passing. Mildred was not upbraiding him or even registering distress on her face. She was, he perceived, past caring. She had reached, as near as might be, a state of insensibility.

" Oh, God . . . God ! " Mr. Rostrum sighed and tapped on the window severely to silence the uproar.

Dudley heard the tapping; he was interested; he stopped crying, while he peered through the tree trunks for a face at the window. Seeing his father, he waved to him out of habit, and then, remembering that he was offended, resumed his clamour.

They came up the steps, the mother indifferent, the child loudly sustaining his protests. Mr. Rostrum heard their entry into the hall and the rush of Dudley's feet towards his study door. The door handle rattled as the small fingers twisted it, and the door was pushed open, and Dudley rushed to his side.

"Been naughty boy," he reported.

It was a detached, impartial report, as of an interesting episode. It was so dispassionate, indeed, that it seemed like a third party's report. The large eyes stared up into Mr. Rostrum's that they might observe the natural interest there. Dudley's pink and perfect little face had a wide range of expression : it could portray anything from a reproduction of the Infant Samuel's when he was saying, " Speak, Lord, for thy servant heareth " to an imitation of Napoleon's when he had been disobeyed and was steeped in wrath ; and this evening it was the face of a friend eager to share a tale of conflict and commotion. It was not the face of one who was interested in the rights and wrongs of the case but only in an accurate record of the events. He was taking, it seemed, no sides.

" Oh, no, Dudley ! Not naughty. No, no ! "

Dudley nodded. There must be no tampering with the news ; no editing or softening of it. " Yes. Said ' Don't want Mummy '."

" Oh, Dudley, no ! Not to your Mummy who's so good to you ! "

Dudley nodded again ; and there was apparently more to come. " Smacked Mummy."

" Oh, Dudley ! You mustn't. You must never hurt anyone. Never, never, never. But it was good of you to come and tell me."

" Smacked Mummy," repeated Dudley, who was more interested in the fact than the comments.

Mildred was now in the room. She had flopped into an easy chair, a heavy, hot, exhausted woman, whose only comment was a sigh.

" What's been the trouble ? I won't have him smacking you."

" He didn't want to come away. He was so happy, playing with Ken. Oh, Alec. . . . There was trouble the minute I suggested he must come home. Trouble with both of them. I left Ken bawling to heaven and Sylvia trying to pacify him."

" Ken cried too," Dudley endorsed.

Mr. Rostrum rose and paced the room. " It's no good. I can't have you worn out. I *won't* have you worn out.

44

I must get a nurse or someone to look after him. If necessary, I'll take out some of my capital."

"Oh, but wait, darling. I've got news for you."

He stopped in his walk. "What's that?"

"It's almost too good to be true. Sylvia and John are going to Hayling for three weeks and taking Ken. And they want to take Dudley too."

"They *what?*"

"They want to take Dudley too."

"Are they mad?"

"No, Sylvia thinks it'd be less trouble with two than with one."

"She's not doing it out of kindness?"

"She says she's doing it purely out of selfishness."

But this statement he hardly heard. He was staring at Mildred but not seeing her. He was seeing a picture. The Gainsborough or the Constable who sat imprisoned within him had painted it at once; and in all its haunting beauty it stood between him and Mildred. A lake; not the iron-bound oval among the asphalt paths of a London heath, but a mile of natural water with wooded islands afloat on it, and pine trees crowding along its brink and brooding on their wrinkled reflections below them, and the great hills of Westmorland marching in a herd beside it towards a depth of amber sky. There was a dewy freshness in the air above the lake, and a pale saffron bloom on the eastern hills where the sunrays touched them.

"My dear! . . ." he began, "my dear! . . ." There was a craving in his throat like the craving which had sent him out last Sunday to the Highgate ponds. "We could have a holiday together . . . the first for five years . . . the first since Dudley was born. . . ." And he uttered a single name; but what a name! A name that painted a hundred landscapes for him: pictures of long, empty lanes between hedgerows besprinkled with blue speedwell, white stitchwort, and red campion; of fields more yellow than green because washed with buttercups and hawkweed and charlock; of footpaths up bracken-fledged hills and of the patterned world outspread below as you walked their ridges in the rude, clean air. "Callerdale."

Mildred, who had risen to snatch Dudley's hand from

45

among his father's tools, sank back on to the edge of her chair. She stared at her husband. Three weeks free from shopping, from cooking meals for six people, from washing up four times a day, from scavenging and cleaning behind Dudley, and from never sitting down till nine o'clock at night. . . . Three weeks of being able to sleep on in the morning ; to walk in the sun, no longer split between her dreams and the demands of a child, but whole and intact and herself ; to sit and read at any time of the day, or perhaps just to sit at peace without the fear that Dudley was breaking something somewhere ; to sit down to meals which she hadn't cooked at a steaming stove ; to get into a bed which someone else had made ; and to fall asleep without fear of a child's cry.

" Oh, Alec ! Would it be possible ? "

" It's going to be possible. I'm going to write to Mrs. Edmonson at once."

Mrs. Edmonson. A farmhouse at the foot of a hill ; a walled path running towards it, all rounded stones and rich-smelling dung ; a farmyard before its door, all cobbles and flags and cowpats ; and on its threshold, Mrs. Edmonson, forty and weather-dyed and work-worn, but smiling to welcome them in.

Dudley disturbed the vision. " Can I go out into the garden ? Can I, Daddy ? Can I ? "

The sheep being brought down from the hill, bleating in full chorus, with three shepherds and six dogs behind ; the sheep leaping towards the walls to feed on the herbage that sprouted from their stones, and the dogs herding them on ; the sheep-bells clanging——

" Can I go into the garden, Mummy ? Can I ? "

" No, no. It's all clouded over now."

" Oh, it hasn't. It's quite fine. It's going to sunshine out."

" Nonsense. It's much too late now. And it's turning cold."

" It's not. It's boiling. It's boiling, Mummy." There was no finer advocate than Dudley when it came to expounding before his father or mother, those Licensing Justices, the case for doing exactly what he wanted to do. His eyes wide, he would explain the exceeding wisdom of doing now

46

and at once exactly what he wanted to do. He would show that there was no argument in reason for doing anything else. Any such argument was merely frivolous, merely contumacious, a waste of the court's time. " Can I, Mummy ? I won't 'sturb anyone."

" Be quiet. Oh, Alec, do you think we could afford it ? "

" We're going to afford it. If necessary, I'll spend some of my capital. I'll write to Mrs. Edmonson to-night. It's still only June, so she ought to be able to take us in. She'll take us in, if she can. She loves us."

" Oh, Alec ! "

" *Mummy ! Mummy !*" This cry was not from Dudley ; it was from Joanie who had run up the steps and into the hall with something of the desperation of an assassin who runs to an altar for sanctuary. " *Mummy !* "

" Yes, darling, what is it ? " Mildred turned an ear towards the child.

" Oh, Mummy, do come."

" Oh, whatever's the matter now ? I must go to her."

Mr. Rostrum tut-tutted and sighed. Always one child or another irrupted into some interesting talk and laid it in ruins. " It's probably nothing. She's just having one of her ' states '."

" I'd better go and see."

And Mildred hurried out, and Dudley followed her, as ready as his mother to learn Joanie's trouble but otherwise unworried by it. The principle guiding Dudley's life was " Two things stand like stone : Courage in another's trouble, Kindness in your own."

§

Joanie, though she had always been the most placid and " easy " of the children—the happy child with no history— was yet given to what she called " states," and these states, however fretting to her in their brief spell of high fever, were a family joke of the Rostrums. The position was really this : Joanie, having no major troubles to worry about, would get into an " anxiety state "—she had picked up this phrase in her Library—about the most trifling incident, and always the anxiety state was wholly irrational, having no

47

possible justification in fact. She would have a "state" that she had offended someone ; that she had made a fool of herself at a literary meeting ; that she had stayed too long at a party ; that she had said an indecent thing ; that she had talked too much—talked without stopping, and everyone had wearied of her ; that she had made a public exhibition of herself in the street ; that someone was cutting her or disliking her ; or, worse, that she had accidentally cut someone in Kilburn High Road. She would rush with such a state to her mother who had to untie it for her, and often it was a long business, an hour of counsel, consolation and debate, before Mildred had sufficiently disentangled it.

This evening Mr. Rostrum, his talk in ruins, began to think that he too would like to learn the nature of Joanie's alarm, and he went down to the living-room where Mildred and Joanie were in conference—the inevitable conference that always formed the last scene, the *dénouement*, the resolution of the conflict, in one of these quick, short dramas of Joanie's. He found Mildred washing a lettuce in a bowl while she laboured on the child's trouble, Joanie striding up and down in agitation (just as he did), Sankey running and barking at her side, and, to his surprise, Julian, who must have entered unseen by the basement door, standing with his hands in pockets and making merry over the whole episode.

"What is it ? For God's sake what is it now ? "

"Oh, Daddy . . ."

"It's nothing. Nothing at all," said Mildred over her bowl.

"Oh, it is. It's awful. Oh, Daddy. . . ."

"Is it a ' state ' ? "

"Of course it is," Mildred sighed.

"It's a smashing yarn." Julian bobbed up and down on his toes in his delight. "I find it vastly diverting. Gosh, it's tremendous."

"Oh, you shut up," Joanie snapped at him. "It was all your fault, anyway."

"But what is it ? Tell me. Tell me."

Between them they told him. It seemed that Joanie in her Library this afternoon had said an indecent thing to the senior assistant, Nancy Hills, when tidying her section of the shelves, and the Deputy Librarian, Mr. Hewitt, must have heard her since he was standing, unperceived by her, only a few yards away. Feeling a little irritable with Nancy, who had been above herself for some time, she had meant to exclaim, when Nancy demanded that she should loiter a little less and come and help her at the issuing desk, that she was sick of being " badgered about," but instead of " badgered " her tongue had uttered a similar sounding word that was often on the lips of Julian. Somehow, in her pique, the vowel had broadened and the " g " hardened, and it was all Julian's fault because he was always using this expression. One slipped into it unwittingly ; one repeated it like an echo. The damned phrase had said itself. And Mr. Hewitt must have heard her, he just must, since he was only two yards away. And Mummy had only made the matter worse because, on first being told of the mischance, she had exclaimed, " Oh, I think that's rather terrible in a girl ! " which had plunged Joanie into the lowest circle of her present inferno.

And now Mr. Rostrum himself was unwise enough to say, " Oh, but it *is* rather dreadful, ducky. You mustn't say such things. I don't even like it when Julian says it ; " and Joanie was plunged back into the inferno, down into its darkest circle, just after Mildred had extricated her ; and Mildred was complaining, " Oh, why on earth did you say a thing like that to her ? You've undone all the good I did. Now she's in the depths of gloom again. You know what she is ; " and Julian had thrown his head back and was bellowing at the ceiling an unnecessarily loud and protracted laugh, like the neighing of a horse ; and Joanie was adjuring him not to be a perfect fool and telling him that such idiocy " didn't help anybody any " ; that, on the contrary, it stank ; and Julian, in the full tide of his enjoyment, was repeating the performance ; and Mr. Rostrum was declaring that he'd leave them to it ; that it would obviously be an hour before Joanie was in order again, and he'd important work on hand ; that Mildred must cope with the situation because it was entirely beyond him ; that he wished her all success ; that Julian had better quit the room and not make his mother's task more difficult ; and that perhaps they would tell him when the storm was over so that he could come and see them all again.

49

And he went from the room, leaving Mildred to resume her labour of cleaning the last stain from Joanie's memory and smoothing out the last wrinkle.

And up in his study he addressed himself to the exquisite task of writing to Mrs. Edmonson at her farmhouse in Callerdale. To write the letter was to see the lambs in the pasture and to smell the midden in the yard ; to see the lake meandering along for a mile with the wooded islands reflected in its still water and the hills rolling along beside it ; to see the blue-green grass beneath the bare purple rock on the summits, and a ground mist floating like smoke across the water meadows, and a sky, as the sun weakened, of faded pastel crimsons, blanching fawns, and bright, flood-lit blue. More than once he paused and laid the pen down that he might see these things and yield himself to the keen, quick breathlessness of desire.

CHAPTER FOUR

In a few days the great hope had become a certainty : Dudley was going to Hayling Island with the Trimmings ; Mr. Rostrum, Mildred, and Joanie, who had applied for a holiday at the same time as her parents, were going to Callerdale ; Brenda and Julian were remaining at home. There was a disorderly excitement in the hearts of the four who were going away, and a quiet content in the hearts of the two who were staying.

" It'll be as good as a holiday for me," said Julian, " if Joanie and Dudley are out of the house. Those two kids get on my nerves. Brenda will look after me as a good sister should. She'll make me nice meals and see that I'm comfortable. In fact, she'll be able to devote herself exclusively to my comfort. And she'll keep herself to herself. Unlike all the rest of the family Brenda doesn't talk her head off. There'll be peace in the house for once. I'm looking forward to it a lot."

After Dudley's, Joanie's excitement was the most demonstrative, for though she was seventeen she still had much of the leaping and whooping puppyishness of a child of twelve.

She was the one most teased and chaffed by the family; and of late an inexhaustible source for raillery had been the young man, Stephen Emery, who was what Mr. Rostrum called her " follower " and Julian her " gentleman friend." Returning books to the Lending Library, Stephen had seen her at her issuing desk, and stared at her while he waited, and thereafter come to exchange books day after day. It was a safe presumption that the books were seldom read: how could he have studied and digested them in the space of a single evening? A few more of these encounters over the issuing desk, and they were openly in love, and Joanie was spilling the whole story to the family with her eyes alight and her face on fire. Mr. and Mrs. Rostrum were pleased, Julian was entertained, and Brenda instructed herself to rejoice, and did so. Joanie's conquest of Stephen Emery was something of a triumph, both for Joanie and for the family, because he was a " public school boy," as Mr. Rostrum was careful to tell his neighbours in the shops of Kilburn High Road : yes, public school and university too. The son of a man high in the Research Department of a famous firm of electric clock makers, he had gone to University College School and was now doing a four years' course in engineering at University College, London, where he had already passed the Intermediate and the first part of his Finals for his B.Sc. (Engineering). He was taking the second part in a month, and as he would certainly pass, and as Joanie would then be eighteen, Mr. and Mrs. Rostrum saw no reason why the two young people should not become engaged.

" What, I ask you, is our Joanie going to do without her Steve Emery for three weeks? " Julian inquired at the breakfast table, the morning when everything was settled by a letter from Mrs. Edmonson welcoming them to the farm. " She'll pine away."

" Extraordinary how some people think they're witty and aren't," said Joanie.

" I agree," said Brenda.

" Thank you." Julian bowed. " But, be that as it may —a damn silly phrase, I always think, children—but, be that as it may, my question remains unanswered. How will our Joanie survive three weeks without her Steve Emery? "

51

Mr. Rostrum looked from one of his children to another. His lips trembled. When he was happy in the midst of his family, he delighted to shock them with puns, and the worse the pun, the better. " I like our Steve Emery," he announced. " I think he's emery-thing a follower should be."

Most ostentatiously the family maintained a silence and continued eating its breakfast. It was a silence loaded with reprobation. Mr. Rostrum's smile, compressed within tight lips, showed his pleasure in this reception.

" An exceedingly nice lad. I'm sure emery-body agrees." Silence again.

" Pass the butter, Joanie," said Julian. " Thank God it's a fine day."

" Not one of my successes," sighed Mr. Rostrum. " A flop, I'm afraid."

" What I was saying when I was interrupted," said Julian, most pointedly addressing everybody but his father, " was that Joanie will certainly have the megrims, or a distemper, after a week away from her gentleman friend. After two she'll probably develop a carbuncle. She was a pimply child ; and I tell you I'm really anxious about her. And the lad himself ; what's going to happen to him ? "

" All right," continued Mr. Rostrum to himself, speaking with finality. " I shan't cast my pearls before——"

" I'm anxious about him, too ; very anxious. Can anyone tell me what he'll do ? "

" He says he's going to write to me every day," explained Joanie, to whom all talk about Steve gave happiness.

" Good lord ! " muttered Mr. Rostrum, though cast out from the community. " Every day ? That means we shall be snowed under with emery paper."

This was so prompt (as a matter of fact, Mr. Rostrum had seen it as a possibility some days before) that the family was taken at a disadvantage, and Joanie, trying to suppress her laughter, let it burst forth from her nose and lips, with a sound of trumpets, and Brenda had to laugh at this fanfare, and Dudley, catching the infection, screamed his delight, though in what he was delighting he had no idea, and even Julian had let a smile peep at his lips before he could stop it.

Mr. Rostrum nodded happily to himself. " Definitely one of my successes," he said.

But no one was considering him, who was in disgrace ; all were staring at Joanie, Julian even bending his head low to look up into her face, for her lips were shaping soundless words to herself, and this was a certain symptom that she was struggling, by a process of trial and rejection, to mould a pun that should be worse than her father's.

"Don't all stare at me !" she cried, the blood of confusion rushing over her face.

"Come on. Out with it," commanded Julian. "We'd better have it and get it over."

"Have what ? I don't know what you're talking about."

"Oh, yes, you do. Out with it."

"Out with *what ?*" She raised her eyebrows and tried to look innocent.

"The ghastly pun you're at work on."

"I'm not at work on any pun."

"Oh, yes, you are."

"I was only thinking "—Joanie looked down on the table, blushing for the blush that spread guilt on her face—" that if Daddy goes on making bad puns about Steve, we must 'eave a brick at him."

"My God !" murmured Julian in despair ; and Mildred protested, "Really, Joanie !"

But her father nodded several times in approval. "Not bad," he allowed, "but not quite, I think, up to my standard."

"I think Steve's sweet," said Brenda.

This, seriously uttered, was so out of accord with the buffoonery that had preceded it that it needs some explanation. It was prompted by Brenda's ever-present need to show that she was not jealous of her younger sister. Ever since Stephen appeared Brenda had been showing this. She lost no chance of supporting and encouraging Joanie in her love affair. When father and mother were out for the evening, she would stay at home with Dudley and Sankey that Joanie might get to her lover. She would help her dress for the meeting, lending her a scarf or a necklace of her own ; she would be careful to ask all about it when Joanie came home ; and on Sundays she would pray for Joanie's happiness at Low Mass, High Mass, and Evensong.

It was not only to the family but to herself that she had to prove that the approach of Stephen Emery had not hurt her ; and she pressed her bosom upon the sword.

§

Yes, the Rostrum family was in ebullient spirits on the eve of the holiday. In Mr. Rostrum the craving for the lanes and the curled bracken and the lake among the hills was almost like the craving of a man for a woman. The certainty that in a few days he was going to possess these things made a voluptuous excitation in heart and throat. The excitation visited him as he walked to his shop or worked in his " finishing-room " there or in the studio.

But the obverse of the bright promise was a considerable fear. Would something happen to prevent its fulfilment ? A few days ago, before any mention had been made of this holiday, Mr. Rostrum, feeling a pain in his foot, was worried for a minute, examined the foot, did a few exercises along the carpet, and forgot it. Now the pain, or a similar one, was a stab of fright and a continuing anxiety. On the Wednesday morning of this joyful week he was walking with his miniature camera slung on his breast, like the field-glasses of a commander, to the Dobie Paper Mills in Cricklewood, of whose machines and men he had been commissioned to make a series of photographs ; and after two miles along the pavements he began to feel an ache in his left hock. After only two miles ? A fear gripped his heart and gradually constricted it. Did this mean that he wasn't going to be able to climb the bracken-covered hills and walk for miles along their grassy ridges ? Did it mean that his dream of doing ten or fifteen miles a day along the heaving hill-tops would have to be abandoned ? The more he asked himself this, the more he directed attention to the ache in his hock; and the more he directed attention to it—listened to it, as it were—the more it hurt. And, hurting unmistakably, it awoke the memories of other pains, and these memories, in their turn, started their associated pains going. Of late when spotting with his fine pencil he had noticed an ache in the joints of his forefinger. Osteoarthritis ? This

54

ache in his hock, and that ache in his finger—were they the same thing? Failing circulation now that he was sixty? Waste products retained in the blood? And that burning the other day in the transverse arch of his right foot: was it there now? No, thank God, no—but yes . . . yes, it was; and the more he thought it was, the more he felt it there. Was incipient arthritis going to spoil his holiday; or, failing arthritis, was flat foot going to do it? To dwell upon such doubts was to recall other pains—in fact, the bright, the too-well-illumined promise started them all up, just as a lighted match, applied to a fuse, will set off a whole chain of explosions. There was that faint, grumbling pain, low down on the right side of his abdomen? Appendicitis? Or that niggling pain in the centre of his chest after a meal. Sometimes it was more than a niggling; it was like a knife driven into his chest and coming out beneath his shoulder blade. Heartburn? Congestion of the lungs? Or those very private symptoms that suggested either enlargement of the prostate or prostatitis, or both. It would not be too much to say that, as he walked on along the heartless pavements, all these pains were in being, if only slightly and intermittently. When he turned into the yard of the Dobie Paper Mills he was carrying, not only the miniature camera on the outside of his breast, but a miniature box of jangling cares within it.

The ache in his hock, being a new trouble, was the one that exercised him most. He felt he must know, once and for all, if it was going to prevent him climbing and walking on his holiday. He must put the matter to the test; and to-morrow. He would not be perfectly happy till he had put it to the test. And so the next afternoon, which was Thursday and Early Closing Day, he left his shop and began the test. Alone and surreptitiously he began an eight-mile walk along the exigent and unsparing pavements—down Maida Vale and Edgware Road to Park Lane and Piccadilly and so home again. He started briskly, really enjoying himself; any experiment is interesting and, because interesting, enjoyable. All the way, every step of it, he waited for the pain in his hock; he focused his attention on that area; and often he turned an ear down towards it as if listening for the pain.

55

No, he had done two good miles now; and there was no pain, not a trace; three, and still none—this was excellent, and what a fool he had been! His holiday was not going to be ruined. But now—wait—listen—was it beginning? Yes . . . yes. . . . It began in Piccadilly. Not much of a pain, but definitely an ache. It grew no worse, but there was certainly an ache there, and it was with him all the way as he walked sadly home, his hopes of the hill-tops receding.

§

When Mr. Rostrum was heavy in heart, he turned always to Truppy. Truppy he would describe as his " one real friend." And since a man likes to think the best of his possessions, and to display them, he would dilate to others on Little Truppy's quality as a friend. At every crisis of his life, he would say, Little Truppy'd been there. He was there, in his frock coat and top hat, the day he married Mildred. He was there at their door when Mr. Rostrum's old father died so suddenly, and he was at his side, in the same frock coat and top hat, when he laid the old man in his grave. He was there at the same spot, four years later, when Mildred and he laid his dear mother to rest. When Mildred was so ill after Joanie was born, it was Truppy who brought a cab to the hospital door and helped bring her home. Yes, in any great joy or sorrow he could be certain that Truppy'd be there. He felt sure that if he got into disgrace and his name was a byword among men, old Truppy'd stand by him. He often thought that if he had to serve a long sentence in prison, the first person he'd see at the gate when he came out would be Truppy. He'd be there at Mildred's side with a taxi. . . .

Edward Truepenny, Stationer and Tobacconist, had the shop next door to Rostrum and Eve's. It was plainly a shop of a different class from the photographer's. It stood like a black-coated worker in worn garments beside a gentleman in fine clothes. Mr. Rostrum, making good money, had lately gratified an old ambition and put up a modern shop-front, all plate glass and chromium and black glass panels. At the back of this glass box black curtains formed an effective background for a few specimen photographs, tastefully disposed, six of them being portraits of young children and babies ; for Mr. Rostrum not only described himself as a Specialist in Child Photography, but thought himself an artist in it and a man with a wonderful way with children. The shop of E. F. Truepenny, on the other hand, was of so outmoded a pattern in Kilburn High Road as to seem almost rural. His window was no single sheet of plate glass but a triptych of three lights, with wooden glazing bars whose brown paint was eroded and blistered. The fascia board above announced " Stationery, Toys, Tobacco, and Cigarettes," and in an arc of white letters on the windows were the words of a caption which Mr. Truepenny himself had invented and thought extremely clever : " Hospital for Fountain Pens." The " F " of this legend had long since fallen, and its place had never been filled. The dressing of the window belonged, in fashion at least, to the same date as its erection. Time-soiled notepaper boxes stood on end among ink bottles, pencil boxes, paint boxes, cash-ruled and feint-ruled foolscap books, box files, balls of string, and sheets of foreign stamps. Next to this stationery stood pyramids of dummy cigarette cartons, and behind them the display cards provided by their manufacturers. Picture postcards of London's buildings hung in vertical chains down the corners of the windows, and if in an idle minute you studied these postcards in detail, you noticed that the skirts of the women in the London streets and the hats of the men obeyed the fashions of a world that was dead. There was nothing in this ancestral window that might not have been there in the beginning of the century, and if you half closed your eyes, you could imagine among the faded postcards some glossy portraits of Marie Studholme, Mabel Love, Lily Brayton, and other celebrated and lovely actresses of that unvexed and smiling era.

Since all dressing, whether of one's body, one's room, or one's shop window, is an expression of the man within, it was inevitable that the difference between these two shopfronts should be a fairly accurate expression of the difference between Mr. Rostrum and Mr. Truepenny. One reason why Mr. Rostrum was so happy with his friend, Mr. Truepenny, was that he felt superior to him in every way. He was much taller ; Truppy being a little bandy man with the legs of a jockey and the face of a Baptist minister : small nose, small, crisp, grey moustache, and mild, earnest eyes behind gold spectacles. Mr. Rostrum felt big, almost enormous, with Truppy, a Tower of Strength. He looked like a Tower at his side and felt like a Tower. He was more successful in his business : his income must have exceeded Truppy's by two or three hundred. He was more intellectual and better informed : indeed he thought himself as much more sophisticated than Truppy as Julian thought himself more sophisticated than his father, and just as Julian liked to shock his father with an irreverence or a bawdy jest, so Mr. Rostrum delighted to shock little Truppy. Often, after having recovered from one of Julian's riskier remarks, and got inured to it, he discharged it at the mild and serious Truppy and affected a surprise that he should be disturbed by it. If Julian proffered an argument that seemed dangerously socialistic, Mr. Rostrum at first recoiled from it, then took and partly digested it, and finally expounded it as his own to Truppy, with an agreeable sense of superiority and compassion. Books and authors and modern movements which Brenda mentioned, very deliberately, in her talk— especially such fine-sounding names as Baudelaire, Mallarmé, the Parnassians and the Symbolists—he mentioned as soon as possible to Truppy, and noticed thereupon, and pitied, the bewildered crease in his brow. Corrections in his grammar which Brenda made at meals he made at the first possible oportunity in Truppy's grammar, as they walked together. In brief, he walked on a soft carpet, such as is spread for a distinguished guest, when he walked with Truppy.

And Truppy was happy walking with Mr. Rostrum, because he believed in Mr. Rostrum's brains and knowledge, and longed to learn at sixty-five what intellectual people were thinking and to have his own intellect improved. " Old Alec's talk is an education in itself," he would say to Florrie, his wife, when he got home. Florrie, little, smiling, and grey, was as naïve and uncritical as himself ; and he had no irreverent children to unseat his faith in his friend.

As we have told, Mr. Rostrum could not discuss his pains at all satisfactorily with Mildred, because he wanted to be impatient with her when she mentioned hers, but he did not hesitate to discuss any one of them, or all of them together, with Truppy, for Truppy would just be interested, and, having no critical ability, would never, even in thought, pronounce him a valetudinarian. He got a warmer, cosier satisfaction from his talks with Truppy on this subject than on any other—except Sex and the Eternities. "There is nothing Truppy and I can't discuss together," he would say ; and it was rare for their talk not to modulate sooner or later into Sex. And once in that subject they found it difficult to modulate out of it. If they modulated out of it at all, it was into the Eternities.

After his disappointment in Piccadilly the anxiety about his holiday throbbed so persistently that it demanded the salve of a talk with Truppy. And the next evening he walked into Truppy's shop and inquired, "Hallo, young Ed. Game for a walk after supper to-night ? "

" Yes, all right, Alec. Yes, old man."

" Good. Right. It's weeks since we had a good yarn."

" How are you, old Alec ? "

" I'm fine, thanks."

And, impatient for the luxury of describing the pain in his hock, he hastened over his supper that night and hurried round to Kilburn High Road where Truppy lived above his shop, and found him waiting for him. They walked northward along the High Road and Shoot-Up Hill towards Cricklewood : two men in the dark clothes of respectable tradesmen ; a tall one, stooping a little as he talked earnestly, and a small one whose brief bandy legs seemed to walk enthusiastically and with great interest ; the small one wearing a bowler hat (which is just what Truppy would wear) and the tall one in a hat that deserves a careful and studied portrait.

Mr. Rostrum's hat was somehow as characteristic as Truppy's bowler. It was of black felt with a depression in the crown like a trilby's, but its brim was as firm and narrow and formal as a bowler, and its sheen was the sheen of a bowler's. It was as if a bowler had softened and compromised to the extent of allowing a valley in its crown but had refused to yield an inch in the matter of its brim's severity ; and that stiff, curled brim, narrow in any view, looked much too narrow at the top of Mr. Rostrum's height. There was something ceremonial about the hat, despite the concession in the crown ; you guessed that its wearer considered a photographer to be Someone, a professional man and not an ordinary tradesman, and that, just as he should wear a sacerdotal black coat in his studio, so he should wear a hat of some solemnity and formality in the street. One has seen such hats, black and shining, above the beards and frock coats of rabbis in the streets of a ghetto.

"There's one thing worrying me, old man," Mr. Rostrum was saying, as he gazed before him down the long road. "I haven't told it to anyone else, because I hate to be always mentioning my aches and pains—I've no use for the sort of person who's for ever discussing his aches and pains —but with you, old man, as you know, I just think aloud."

Truppy, flattered, urged him to go on ; and for a wholly delightful ten minutes Mr. Rostrum expounded the new strange pains behind his knee and in his knuckle which were spoiling the bright prospect of his holiday. "It's only a mild ache, of course, but it worries me. It's worrying just before a holiday. What do you think it is ? "

"Uric acid." Truppy spoke with conviction. Like many little men he often spoke dogmatically and as one who knew ; and it was a firm persuasion of his that most of the pains of later life could be traced to uric acid. He rehearsed and elucidated the effects of uric acid, and Mr. Rostrum listened with a concentrated personal interest. Truppy's descriptions reminded him, rather unhappily, of those symptoms of prostatic enlargement which had perturbed him of late, and, directly his turn came to speak, he submitted them to Truppy for his interpretation. To his disappointment Truppy, instead of attributing them to uric acid, was convinced that they meant trouble with the prostate. "It's very common at our time of life, you know," he insisted. "We're not getting any younger, alas. We're both getting a bit long in the tooth."

This wounded Mr. Rostrum, for he was five years younger than Truppy and suffered when Truppy spoke of them as contemporaries ; furthermore, he was of opinion that, in anything but a purely arithmetical measurement, he was— and looked—ten years younger. "Confound it, old man, I'm only just sixty."

"But sixty's no chicken."

" It depends on what sort of sixty. I reckon I'm a pretty good sixty. I mean, I haven't a grey hair in my head, I haven't an ounce of superfluous flesh on me, and I feel in my prime. I can walk twenty miles without tiring, any day. I feel about thirty. And do you know, old man, I didn't have a false tooth in my head till I was fifty-five. That was pretty good, eh ? And have I trace of middle-aged spread ? None. (Nor have you, old boy.) And I'll tell you another thing : I'm never ill. I'm the only one of my family who never goes to the doctor. All the others have been really ill at one time or another, but never me. Little ailments, of course, but nothing serious in sixty years. Yes, without bragging, I think I can say I have the constitution of an ox. I'll guarantee to walk any young man, half my age, off his feet. That's why this sudden ache in my hock has frightened me a little. I had set my heart on walking miles and miles over the fields and up the hills and round the lake. It's hurting a little now. God, it's worrying just before a holiday."

" Seen anyone about it ? "

" No. And I'm not going to." It was a prompt and certain answer—all the more emphatic because Mr. Rostrum wasn't sure that it was sincere. " I pride myself on never going to doctors."

" Well, I think that's just stupid."

Mr. Rostrum didn't at all like being called " just stupid " by Truppy. Feeling so much wiser than he, he took, in secret, great exception to being called stupid by Truppy.

" I don't think it's stupid at all. Everybody knows nowadays that nine-tenths of our bodily troubles are mental. Get the right psychological attitude towards your trouble and it disappears."

" And *I* say that's all rubbish."

This was too much. The dogmatism of the ignorant and the unread ! What did Truppy know about it ? What books on psychology had he ever opened ? Had he read *The Home Psychotherapist* or *Mind Therapy* or *The Mental Basis of Illness* ? Mr. Rostrum had—or he had read parts of them. He never came upon a book of psychology without dipping into it in search of some explanation of his own mental states, and as a result he now considered himself something of an

61

expert and wanted other people to think him a great deal of an expert. Vexed with Truppy, he resolved to overthrow him and roll him flat with some very heavy material.

"But what right have you to say it's rubbish? Have you ever really studied the matter? One needs to have made a profound study of psychology before presuming to lay down the law like that. Ever read any Kretschmer, f'rinstance?"

"Any what?"

"Kretschmer. He's a great man on psychology."

"Never heard of him," snapped Truppy. He snapped out the admission because he was not too pleased with it.

"No." Mr. Rostrum had too much consideration for Truppy to add, "I thought not," and too much for himself to mention that he had only encountered this imposing name a day or two before.

"Well, who is he?"

"Kretschmer?" Mr. Rostrum didn't quite know, so he said, "He's a very great man. The Last Word on the subject. His stuff's difficult to read, I don't mind telling you. Actually I first met it in a book of Brenda's on *Psychology in the Classroom*. She's a brilliant girl in her way and reads a lot of these sort of books. And Julian knows quite a lot about the subject too. They discuss it a lot together." Just as well to load the family up on to the steam-roller. "It's fascinating stuff to read, old boy."

"Well, tell me something about it. Tell me what it's about."

"It's damned fascinating stuff."

Mr. Rostrum had been fascinated by Kretschmer because the two of his works that were quoted at length in Brenda's book were *Physique and Character* and *Psychology of Men of Genius*, and he had pored over these quotations in the hope of relating them to himself. He was always interested in his physique, and he wanted to know if he had genius.

"As far as I can see, old boy, he divides people into two classes, cycloids and schizoids. There are hypomanic cycloid types and depressive cycloid types." The steam-roller was going well over Truppy now. "I'm a schizoid, I feel pretty sure. Yes, I'm afraid there's no dodging it. It seems obvious to me that I was a schizothymic child, which is a pity in some ways, because it doesn't make for happiness ; it's the cyclothymic children who tend to be happier. But you could argue that the schizothymic types are more likely to do big things in the world of art and so on, just because they are more sensitive and solitary and tend to suffer more. You are schizoid too, I think."

" What's a schizoid ? " Truppy, thus defined, was now interested. He seemed to walk faster in his eagerness to hear about himself.

" Well, let's deal with the cycloids first ; then I think you'll understand. The hypomanic cycloids are the energetic, sanguine, hot-headed, fiery tempered chaps with no nerves or shyness. Hearty, clubbable, *bon viveur* sort of people, like old Chock Bailey, for example. Well, that doesn't describe either you or me, does it ? Cycloids generally, he says, have a particularly well orientated emotional life, alternating between cheerfulness and sadness in deep, smooth, rounded curves. I don't feel that's me. And I don't feel it's you. And it's certainly not Brenda. Joanie and Julian are the cycloids in my family. And of course the little boy."

" But what are the schizoids ? " repeated Truppy, more interested in his own class.

" He divided the schizoids into two types, same as the cycloids. There are the hyper-æsthetic schizoids and the anæsthetic."

" Which are you ? "

" Oh, definitely a hyper-æsthetic. Brenda and I are both hyper-æsthetic schizoids. I guess you are too."

" Why ? "

" Well, the hyper-æsthetic schizoids are shy, sensitive, nervous and rather excitable people, but they have fine feelings, he says, and a great love of nature and books. I think we could fairly say that's true of us, don't you ? "

" Oh, yes. Yes, I think so."

Truppy was satisfied. He was pleased to be a hyper-æsthetic schizoid. And Mr. Rostrum, after describing the schizoids further, became more and more impressed by his learning, the vigour of his mind, and the opulence of his vocabulary, and felt sore again that Truppy should have called him old.

" These things interest me. I should like to make a much

63

greater study of them than I have time for. I'm at heart
a student, you know. You say I'm getting old, but really,
old chap, I can't help feeling that my readiness to assimilate
new ideas—my *passion* for ideas, if you like—and the ease,
the really consummate ease, with which I find myself understanding most of them, are some proof that my mind at any
rate is still pretty young. And if it comes to that—I don't
want to talk sex, old boy, but you and I don't mind what
we say to each other, do we ?—I can't see that there's any
trace of my natural creative force abating—you get what I
mean, I take it ? Extraordinary thing, sex—don't you think
so, Ed ?—quite amazing——" and so, by the simplest of
turns, he had diverged into this familiar street, Truppy his
faithful companion, and it was unlikely that they would
turn out of it again for a considerable time.

He gave himself completely to this new subject. He said
everything that came into his head, and some of the things
were good and some very silly. He expatiated on this im-
measurable and ever-impelling power that was stored in
the frail body of a man ; on its strange excess over the
uses to which it could be put and on the consequent temptations and struggles in which it involved a man ; on his
own confusions and conflicts when he was young, and on
Truppy's ; on his readiness, when he remembered his own
youth, to forgive any young man who was driven astray
by its urgency ; on his intolerance of those who were merely
intolerant of the sins of the young ; on the difference of
this urgency in men and women—and so he came to a
most interesting and confidential fact—which he had con-
fided to Truppy twenty times before, but why worry about
that when its reiteration was so pleasant ?—the fact that
Mildred, fifty though she was, " was still, for all practical
purposes, as pure as a young girl." Becoming lyrical about
Mildred's purity, for he could be as melodramatic as he
liked with Truppy, he declared with much emphasis that,
despite her production of Julian, Brenda, Joanie and Dudley,
she was still, in everything that mattered, as pure as the
driven snow. She disliked all Julian's indecorous jokes and,
believe it or not, didn't understand most of them ; and
he must say that, though he sometimes made such jokes
himself, he respected her for it. (Proud of many things—

his health, his children, his knowledge, his skill with a camera or a model yacht, his sense of humour—he was equally proud of his wife's purity and, in contrast with that, of his own coarseness.) Take her for all in all, he said, Mildred was a Pretty Good Piece of Work. He might have his tiffs with her, and she might have her tantrums, but he looked up to her as Something Nobler than Himself. Nobler in every way. He went to church and tried to be a Christian of sorts, but he wasn't half the Christian that she was. She was the Real Thing. She really Lived the Life. Her life, all said and done, was one long sacrifice for others.

These topics, vital first and then ethical, led them to discourse of God and His purpose in the universe, and of the mystery of the stars in the unimaginable spaces of the sky (for it was now night) and this last discourse so thrilled them that they walked on and on, along the broad, undeviating highway, past Cricklewood, Brent Bridge, and Burnt Oak, to the outskirts of Edgware.

§

But this talk with Truppy, delectable though it was, had not stopped the small ache in his leg. In the next days this ache asserted itself whenever he remembered it, though not, curiously enough, at other times ; and he decided at last that there could be no real peace for him till he'd been given an authoritative opinion about it. He'd go and see the doctor—in secret. And now this visit to the doctor, firmly resolved upon, began to look even more desirable than the talk with Truppy. He could mention in the same context as the ache those other symptoms which might, or might not, be associated with it, and so get some information about them all. Normally he would have called the doctor to his house, now that he was a man of some substance, but, not wishing the family to know anything of this weak longing for reassurance, he decided instead to call upon the doctor in his surgery hour.

Dr. Soden's surgery hour was from five to six, and the next evening, having said nothing to Miss Fletcher at her reception desk any more than to the family, he issued somewhat guiltily from his shop and walked towards the doctor's tall, grey, double-fronted house in Priory Road. He walked quickly and pleasurably, since a visit to a doctor is so personally interesting that it can never be quite empty of pleasure. The doctor's waiting-room was a large front room, bare of furniture except for a small table in the centre and a miscellaneous parade of chairs around the walls. He found every chair occupied except one. That one hard-backed chair might have been waiting for him. Fourteen people sat against the walls : six solitary women, three mothers each with a fidgety child, three bent old men with moist nostrils and troublesome coughs, and one pale young girl. Mr. Rostrum sat himself among them, against the wall, his professional black hat upon his knees. He felt the only gentleman in the room. More, he felt the only healthy person in the room.

For three-quarters of an hour he sat there, so many were those who had to go in to the doctor before him. He heard young Dr. Soden's voice in the consulting-room across the passage ; he heard it in the hall when the doctor came with a patient a little way from his room. Three-quarters of an hour, while other sick and solitary people wandered into the waiting-room and took the chairs which their predecessors had vacated. Then of a sudden, tired of this long wait, ashamed of his visit, and persuaded that most of these people were really ill while his own pains were imaginary, he got up and, the course being clear, hurried out of the room and out of the house. No one, not his family, nor Miss Fletcher, nor Dr. Soden himself, should ever know of his long session in that room.

§

At home in these days Mildred walked about her household tasks, keeping the thought in her head, as one keeps a sweet in the mouth, that after next Wednesday and for three whole weeks she would have no housekeeping to do, no catering, no cooking, no washing up—nothing to do but to sit about and read, or wander out and enjoy the sunshine, or get into a bed which someone else had made. Three whole weeks of it. The last time she had been to Callerdale with Alec—five years ago, before Dudley was born—it had been so lovely. Such quiet happiness. The memory of it enabled her to realize their fusion in each other after thirty years. Yes, they might get hot and snappy with each other sometimes, but she had only to imagine a visit to Callerdale without him to know that it wouldn't be the same thing at all ; it would be a thing so different that she would hardly desire it. Callerdale meant her and Alec there together, walking the rough country road or climbing the turfy slopes ; not her alone, or her and someone else. How many times had they been there together ? Five ; but this would be the first time they had been there for three whole weeks. Oh, it was wonderful to think they were going there again. Callerdale . . . the farm . . . the sheep on the hill behind the farm. . . .

And then the second molar in her lower jaw began to ache. Only a little—indeed hardly at all—but panic leapt within her. Oh, no, the holiday, the lovely holiday, must not be ruined by toothache. No, *no !* . . . But rubbish ! Nonsense ! At any other time she wouldn't have given a second thought to such a tiny ache. She wasn't even sure that it *was* aching. Forget it. She tried to forget it and for long intervals succeeded, but then she would recall that moment of panic and would stand quite still, on the stairs or in the kitchen, to ascertain if it was aching now. Much as Mr. Rostrum had done, she would turn her head downwards and sideways as if listening for the ache. And once or twice in response to this inquiry it did give a little throb, and each throb was like a little death in her heart. And as her heart died, the neighbouring teeth began to throb, including a few of the false ones. Oh, it was no good : she must get some peace of mind about this. There might be nothing the matter, really, but she wouldn't be happy now till an authoritative voice had told her so. Alec and the children needn't know anything about what she was going to do now, but it had got to be done. Straightway she ran upstairs to the telephone in Alec's study, dialled her dentist's number, and arranged an appointment for to-morrow. And the next afternoon she slipped from the house and hurried with a swelling interest towards the dentist's tall grey house in Cambridge Avenue.

The dentist found nothing amiss or out of joint, and she apologized to him and came home, exulting. So happy was she that she sang about her work all the rest of the day.

But next morning Dudley sneezed. He sneezed all over her pastry just after they had returned from shopping. She looked at him and, to her horror, he sneezed a second time. Again there was a little death in her heart.

Oh, no, no, he mustn't start a cold. That would put an end to everything. It would be unfair to the Trimmings and to little Ken to send him away with them if he had a cold. It would ruin *their* holiday. Panic took command again. Panic, like a long-beaked gadfly, drove her to the medicine cupboard in the bathroom. Cold and Cough Mixture. Nasal Compound. Camphorated Oil. Returning with these to the kitchen, she gave Dudley two spoonfuls of the cold and cough mixture, pumped drops of the nasal compound up each nostril (an operation which he resisted with declamations and despairs), rubbed camphorated oil on his chest and scattered eucalyptus on his handkerchief, so that he walked about the house, stinking. He stank of several different ingredients. With every medicament she had slightly exceeded the prescribed dose in the hope that a little extra would make the prevention, or the cure, more certain. Later in the day, panic still plaguing her, she went into the bathroom and gargled with glycerine and thymol, and squeezed some of the nasal compound—it consisted of ephedrine, camphor, menthol, and eucalyptol—up her own nose, and stank too.

A night and a day passed, and no symptoms of a cold appeared either in Dudley or herself, a fact which she attributed rather to the nasal compound, her favourite remedy in such cases, than to the non-existence of any infection in either of them. " Oh, it's going to be all right ; it's going to be all right," she thought, as she made the beds, washed up, and prepared the meals. and she thanked God, and thanked Him again. Her visions of the farmhouse and the lanes which, like the prospect in a mirror, had been dimmed by Dudley's sneeze, were now as bright and clear as before ; and she sang again as she worked.

Joanie was suffering quietly too in these days. She was making her life a misery lest she shouldn't enjoy her holiday ; and the only difference between her and her parents was that she had more of these " states " and had them worse, and did not keep them to herself but required her mother to unravel them for her in haggard and disputatious parleys that might endure for hours. Quite a few of these states dealt with what *might* be in the future rather than what was menacing now. Joanie could work herself into a breathless agitation about some mischance that might, in certain conditions and one day, befall her : she could die the death before any enemy had been reported ; and accordingly, on her way to her Library, she was now crossing the roads very carefully lest she should be run over before she could get into that train for Callerdale ; she was walking very carefully on wet roads lest she fell and broke her leg ; and she was keeping away from the edge of the platform in the Undergound lest she went suddenly mad and flung herself in front of the train. These were fears that had no basis in fact but only in themselves ; they created themselves spontaneously. She had more justification when, returning home one evening and perceiving at once that her mother and Dudley stank of camphor, menthol and eucalyptus, she promptly applied the nasal mixture to her own nostrils, and applied it abundantly.

A worse state, and one that ravaged a dozen hours, sprang in the beginning from a slight anxiety about her left eye. She imagined one morning, as she walked to the station, that this eye was not focusing the street as well as usual and therefore would not be able to see the view from the tops of the Callerdale hills, and to allay this small alarm she kept closing her right eye to learn what the left was doing. This was an interesting experiment, and one part of her quite enjoyed it ; but it produced a shocking situation in the Underground train—in a word, the small original " state " begat a daughter state twice as big as herself— when, shutting the right eye to see how the other was focusing the compartment, she became possessed by the fear that the smiling man opposite her had supposed she was winking at him. Joanie never had a worse five minutes than in the train that morning between Kilburn Park and Willesden Junction. It embroiled her mother in hours of wordy assuagement later that evening. Hitherto she had always been disturbed lest she had cut somebody in the street; now she was afraid that she had issued an open invitation to a man she might meet every day.

CHAPTER FIVE

BRENDA and the tall, hatless young man were walking together towards Nunsbury Road and her home. It was the young man with the untidy black hair and sports jacket who had watched her in the Underground train; and his name, he had told her, was Lawrence Blythe. He had added, smiling, "Everyone calls me Larry," but she had not accepted this hint and called him Larry; she had avoided calling him anything. They walked slowly as if to delay parting. And they laughed together as they walked; at least Larry laughed and Brenda, something flustered, glanced up at him with brief smiles and looked away.

They turned out of Cambridge Avenue into Kilburn High Road.

"This is not really your way home," said Brenda, giving him her sidelong glance.

"Don't you think so?"

"Well, if you say it is, I suppose it is."

"Doubt if that's a sound argument. You don't know *me*."

"Well, *is* it?"

"It's one way home."

"Where do you really live?"

"Kensal Rise."

"Good gracious, but that's miles away. Why didn't you go on in the train to Kensal Green?"

"Why didn't I?"

"Yes."

"I should have thought that was obvious."

" It's not at all obvious. It seems to me rather absurd."

" You know quite well why I didn't."

" I'm sure I don't."

" I didn't because I wanted to walk home with you."

It takes the whole of a summer for the colour to steal into pear or plum ; it took less than a second for the rich bloom to sweep over Brenda's face.

" Thank you. That was very nicely said."

" It was the truth. If you're not careful, young woman, you're going to have me rather seriously in love with you."

" Don't be absurd."

" I'm trying not to be. But it's not much good. I'm already half in love with you."

" You're being absolutely ridiculous. We've only met three times."

" What does that matter ? Do you mind my being in love with you ? "

She did not answer.

" Perhaps there's someone else in love with you. Is there ? Is your number engaged ? If so, there's nothing for it : you must give me the intermittent, high-pitched buzz, and I'll ring off . . . with a sigh. One hell of a sigh. Do I hear the high-pitched buzz ? Are there heaps of people in love with you ? "

" No . . ." she faltered. " No. . . ."

" But there's one ? Just one who has the whole of your heart, the swine ? "

" No. . . ."

" Gosh, that's a relief. I was afraid I was going to get the buzz. Do you know why I feel I must be falling for you ? "

" No."

" Because I so want to kiss you. I want to so terribly."

Brenda could only meet this with silence, her eyes avoiding him ; and there was nothing in her manner to reveal the shattering, sweet agitation which his words, like a sudden wind on a land-locked sea, had raised in her heart.

This was the third time he had walked home with her, but on the two previous occasions he had kept his talk behind the fence of a charming courtliness. Only to-day had it jumped the paling and run loose in these lively fields. The day after his first sight of her he had waited on the

Marylebone platform till she arrived, and then stepped into the train just behind her and, after indicating a seat to her, had smiled and stood before her (rather like that other young man before his lover) and begun a courteous but merry conversation. The next evening he was again on the platform ; and again he got in behind her and opened a conversation ; and this time he descended with her at Kilburn Park and walked at her side as far as Nunsbury Road. The following evening he had done the same, but this time he had accompanied her a little way along Nunsbury Road and asked her where she lived. When she pointed out her house but a little distance away, he slowed his pace and, three steps later, parted from her with a smile. Brenda liked to think that he who was so courteous and considerate had done this for her sake, that her family might not see him and tease and embarrass her. To-day, the third time, they were like familiar friends, and the string of his tongue was loosed, and he spake plain.

" No, let's go on a little further," he pleaded, as they reached the corner of Nunsbury Road. " Let me have you for a little longer. Don't ration a starving man."

" I've a fancy you don't starve very often or very long," she said with her half-smile and sidelong glance ; and, though she had not answered " Yes " to his request, she walked on at his side. She felt that by crossing Nunsbury Road and going on along the High Road she had crossed a boundary and was walking, not without fear, in a new, strange, and perhaps hostile land. But it was still the same High Road, with the same cluttering and chattering people and the same hurrying, droning, hammering traffic.

Larry's silence increased the strangeness. He was glancing a little furtively this way and that, and she guessed that he was seeking some access to privacy and quiet. They walked on in silence, and their feet brought them to a tranquil square with a church in the middle of it. He glanced into the square and then whispered like a conspirator, " Let's go along here," and, as he said it, slid his fingers into hers. She did not draw hers away, but neither, when he pressed them and toyed with them, did she respond. She was now being led along by him ; and his hand brought her to the porch of the church beneath its steepled tower. No place so quiet as a church porch in Kilburn between Sunday and Sunday. They passed between the stone jambs of its archway and into its captured and dusty twilight as into the emptiness of a sepulchre. Over the iron-studded doors of church, behind the grimed fanlight, was a browning and damp-stained text, "Seek ye First the Kingdom of God." It seemed to sit uneasily on those heavy and bolted doors. Doubt and guilt had been quivering in Brenda, and the sight of that text troubled them further, but the temptation, the craving for an experience she had never known, was stronger than any entangling shackles, and she swung her eyes from those cautionary words and let herself be led onward. The porch was wider than the pointed arch of the doorway, and thus there was a shadowy angle between the clustered columns of the arch and the dust-brown window of the porch. Here he gathered her gently into his arms and kissed her softly, reverently. She trembled ; and her trembling inflamed him, and he began to kiss her harshly and with passion. She did not resist but neither did she respond.

"Now I know that I love you," he said, for his wilfully engendered passion had carried him beyond prudence and self-command.

She only stared up at him with frightened eyes.

"Listen, darling ; you're going to let me take you out sometimes, aren't you ? "

"I'd love to go out with you sometimes," she answered seriously.

"Well, when shall it be ? "

"I don't think it's going to be easy. You see, Daddy and Mummy and Joanie are all going off for a holiday. To Westmorland," she added, for she thought this sounded expensive and would impress him. "And I shall have to look after Julian and get him his supper."

"You could come out with me after you'd fed him. Somewhere near. I know ! Queen's Park. It's just about half way between us. Shall we ? "

"Yes. Yes, if you like."

"Oh, good ! We'll have some wonderful times."

They came away, hand-in-hand, Brenda thinking that their fingers were intertwined like those of the two lovers in the Underground train.

73

When they were back at the corner of Nunsbury Road, he unlinked his fingers ; and as he approached her home he widened the space between their shoulders, that no watching eyes might suppose them lovers. While the trees still hid them from the windows of her house, he asked her, " Which is your room ? "

She pointed to the barred semi-basement window on the left of the hall-door steps. " That one there."

" Aren't you frightened, sleeping down there ? "

" No. Joanie sleeps in the room just behind."

" But she'll be away on her holiday soon. How then ? "

" Oh, I shall be all right. I don't think I'm afraid. Those bars on the window are quite comforting, and there'll be Julian upstairs."

" But if he's anything like me, he'll sleep through anything."

" He won't sleep if I need any help, I promise you. No one will for a mile around."

" I wish I could come and save you from some masked and murderous ruffian."

" Well, I'm afraid I can't manage that for you. But you needn't be anxious about me. If I feel frightened down there, I can always go up and sleep in Mummy and Daddy's room."

" No, don't do that. I want to imagine you in your own room. One day you must let me peep into it so that I can really picture you there." She did not answer this, but looked away ; and he went on, " Perhaps one day I'll come with a guitar and serenade you outside your window. Look out sometimes, and you may see me passing by. I feel that even if you can't come out I shall want to be near you. And now good-bye. Till to-morrow, when you'll kiss me in the porch again. A good porch. I have a great love for it now."

" Good-bye, my dear."

She let her smile follow him for a few steps as he returned towards the High Road ; then she turned abruptly, very abruptly, and with her quick, haughty walk, as if indifferent to all, she hastened into the house, entering by the door beneath the steps. She hurried into her room and shut the door upon herself and turned its key. Shut in here, she flung herself upon the bed and sobbed. The end of loneliness and hunger, the unlocking of her prison gate, was more than she could bear.

§

Larry reached the corner of Nunsbury Road, halted, loitered, and turned back. He walked back slowly towards the house. To walk slowly was to walk more quietly, and it gave him time to consider the house as he approached and passed it. He studied it with the side of his eye. He was studying it as Brenda sobbed upon her bed. A large house; and to Larry who had been reared in a much smaller one, and in a narrower and greyer street, it was an unexpectedly imposing residence for the family of an elementary school teacher. Brenda had let fall that the house was her father's property (she had done it on purpose, to impress him); and one effect of this new knowledge that her family was quite prosperous (had not Brenda also told him that her brother would soon be a solicitor?) was to add a little to her desirability. The conquest of the daughter of a large house was an enterprise more inviting, slightly more voluptuous, than the conquest of a girl who was poorer than himself. Having passed the house once, he turned and passed it again, resting his eyes this time on the window of her room. And to think of her in that room was, for Larry Blythe, who was but twenty-four and very lonely in London, to think of her in her bed. And to picture her thus was to think of himself beside her. He wandered on and out of the road with this high-seasoned and sweetly troubling thought in his mind.

Larry, whose young perceptions were keen, especially when his hungers directed them, had divined a great deal about Brenda. He had known, when she gave up her seat in the train to the young lovers, that no one had ever made love to *her*. He knew, as he walked with her to-day, that his words of love were the first she had heard. That kiss in the church porch was the first that any man had pressed upon her lips. She might haughtily pretend to be indifferent to men, and to scorn the tricks by which other girls tried to capture their admiration, but a sadness that occupied her face when she imagined she was alone and unseen was

75

the truer expression of her thoughts. She was hungry in secret; and just as she had come with him into the church porch, not consenting with a word, but not resisting; just as she had agreed to come to him in the park where she knew he would embrace her again and as harshly as before, so she would come further and further—even perhaps—even perhaps the whole way. She would think as he drew her on, " This perhaps will be my only chance, and I shall take it." She was ripe to fall from her high branch into the first hand that touched her.

Strolling along the High Road, he diverted himself with the sweetly-troubling dream. Where, if it was to be, could he have his way with Brenda? Not in that house, with her sister sleeping in the room behind, and her father, mother, and brother in the rooms above. That brother, twenty-two, and probably as tall and strong as himself, was a shadow in the background that was best forgotten. One could wish he did not exist. One could wish him miles away. And the old father, what of him? One could wish he were dead, and his wife a widow. But even as he thought these things he remembered (had she not said it only this evening?) that her father, mother, and sister were going for a holiday the very next week, and that only she and her brother would be in that house. She in her front base-ment room; he in his back room on the floor above. The memory arrested his steps, and he stood still in the road.

Then he walked on. When she mentioned that holiday this evening two pleasant thoughts had stirred in him. The first was that, since she could not come out to him till she had given her brother a meal, he would not have to spend money on her in restaurants and cinemas but would be able to stage their flirtation in the free places of the neigh-bouring park. This was a real relief to him, and not because he was mean but because he was poor. Larry had better qualities than those of a mean seducer, unwilling to pay for his pleasures; he was full of gaiety and good fellowship and enjoyed being kind; and had he been earning good money, he would have liked to buy gifts, entertainment, and laughter for Brenda, and to be admired by her as a lavish young man. The second pleasing thought was similar to that which the large house had given him: if her father could afford a three weeks' holiday for three of them, and in Westmorland, which sounded far away and expensive, he must indeed be well off; and this made Brenda more desirable, and any increase in his desire was pleasant. And now came this third thought, the most pleasant of all, and one that trapped his breath and shook his heart; in a few days from now, and for three long weeks, her brother, after a certain time in the night, would be out of the way in his room upstairs, and she would be lying in her basement parts alone.

He turned round and walked back past the house and considered it again.

CHAPTER SIX

" GOOD MORNING, Dudley." Mr. Rostrum walked into the living-room and up to the breakfast table with purposefulness and speed in his feet. He was in the humour to be amusing and entertain Dudley. The morning was fresh and full of bird-song, and his spirits were high because he had been seeing the Callerdale lake and the hills beside it as he shaved and dressed. He shook Dudley's hand. " Good morning, Sankey." He shook the dog's paw. " Good morning, Joanie." He shook Joanie's hand. " Good morning, Brenda." He shook Brenda's hand. " Good morning, Mummy." He shook Mildred's hand. " Good morning, Daddy." And he shook his own left hand with his right. Then he went to his place at the head of the table, well pleased with his performance, which was now closed.

It had been a success with Dudley, who was now shaking his own hand over his porridge and saying, " Good morning, Dudley." It had been a success with Brenda, who had exclaimed, " Oh gosh, Family, he's in one of those moods, is he ? " which he much appreciated. There was some doubt as to whether it had been a success with Joanie, who had submitted with a certain indifference to the handshake and continued reading a long letter from Stephen Emery. And there was no doubt that it had failed with Mildred. Her face had been unsmiling as he said his good morning, and it was unsmiling now. Her hand had been as limp as a corpse's when he shook it. She was silent as Brenda spoke.

Possessed by this present mischievous mood, Mr. Rostrum bent his head almost to the level of the dishes and stared up into her face scanning it for some trace of a smile. " Oh," he sighed in resignation. " It's like that, is it ? "

" *Don't !* " commanded Mildred angrily. " Don't stare at me."

" Ah ! " He withdrew his head from under her face. " I see. Well. There it is. There you are. It was not a good time for a little joke. I chose my moment badly. A flop. Definitely a flop."

" *I* thought it rather funny," comforted Brenda. " Not very, but rather."

" Thank you, child."

Mildred remained silent. Joanie read her letter ; and read it again. Dudley, having shaken his own hand, began as usual to draw on the table with a prong of his fork.

" It's an awful close atmosphere this morning, Bren. A general lack of happiness and love. What is it ? Has the Small Boy been bad ? "

" I should say so ! There was trouble about dressing him. Surely you heard it. He offered resistances. Spirited resistances. There was a frightful row."

" Oh, was there ? " Mr. Rostrum looked at Dudley whose rounded pink cheeks and treacle-gold head were bent over his drawings ; whose rose-tipped ears—so complete, his application—were hearing nothing. " Well, it's a good thing he's beautiful. It'd have been terrible if he'd been ugly in addition to being bad. Where's Julian, Brenny ? "

" Need you ask ? Ten minutes ago he was still in bed."

" Well, since you're all so unfriendly, I'll read my letters. . . . A dreadfully chill reception for my few facetiæ. . . . Still, let us bear with disappointment as best we may. What's this ? "

He picked up first a business letter. On its envelope was printed the name of an engineering firm for whom he was hoping to do some advertising work. As he read the letter Julian came in. He walked in as briskly as his father, and it looked as if he was in the same mood.

" Good morning, neighbours. 'Morning, honey." This

to Brenda. "Are you sweet this morning? 'Morning, little Joanie. 'Morning, Small Boy. Ditto, Mum. God, it's a tough life."

"What's a tough life?"

"Getting up at this hour of the day. It's barely eight o'clock. Is everybody sunny?"

"Emphatically not," declared his father. "Only me and Brenda."

"Only Brenda and I," corrected Brenda.

"Oh, well, to the devil with that. There's been unpleasantness with the Small Boy, and I met with a very chill reception from your mother . . . yes . . . *Way-ho!*" He was reading a second letter and now looked over the top of his spectacles at the family. "Way-ho, children all! General Inspection to-morrow."

"What do you mean?" asked Mildred, looking at him in some alarm.

"The Inspector's coming."

"Damn!" said Julian.

"Oh, damn and blast it," said Dudley, delighted to follow his brother's example.

"Dudley, you're *not* to use words like that," his mother threw at him. "Do you *hear*?"

"*You* said it the other day a long time ago," Dudley reminded her. "Don't you remember?"

"I'm sure I didn't. But even if I did, you're not to."

"What is it does when I say it?"

"Never you mind. Julian, why do you say such things in front of him?"

"That's nothing, Mum. He says much worse things than that."

"Bloody," provided Dudley.

"Dudley!" roared Julian. "You're *not* to say that. You're *not* to say 'Bubbly'." This he said on the principle that the one way to ensure that Dudley said something was to tell him not to, and if he was bound to utter a forbidden word, it had better be an innocuous one. "It's very wrong of you to say 'Bubbly'."

"Bubbly," said Dudley.

"Enough," commanded Mr. Rostrum, who wanted to get on with his joke. "All that is a small matter compared

with the danger which is now upon us. The Widow Leicester
will be upon us to-morrow. She writes to say she'll be here
for tea. Julian, while the Widow is here, you will kindly
refrain from indecencies. And keep off politics. Brenda,
you will keep off religion, for the Lord's sake. Alec dear—"
this to himself—" you will keep off art, *please*. Joanie, you
will refrain from being impudent with your father. The
Widow doesn't hold with that sort of thing. And, Dudley,
none of your comedy turns, *if* you please. Just you make a
pretence of being an obedient child while your auntie's here,
or you'll have your head bitten off. And do you good."

" You needn't worry about me," announced Julian. " I
shall make a point of being out."

" So shall I," said Joanie.

" Oh, no, no," begged Mildred. " Some of you must
be here."

" It's best that I should go, Mum," explained Julian.
" If I am here, she and I may have Words. And it's always
a pity when there are Words."

" Oh, rubbish. You must be here for a part of the time,
or she'll say it's rude."

" Sorry, Mum, but my nerves won't stand it. I am not
naturally a nervous type, I think, but the Widow Leicester
leaves me a wreck. I confess it."

" And that goes for Sis too," said Joanie.

" Oh, but you *must* be here, some of you, to help me with
her. I can't cope with her alone."

" I entirely agree with your mother," said Mr. Rostrum,
beaming over his spectacles, because of his very fine humour.
" The Widow is a strong mixture and needs diluting."

Brenda spoke. " I'll be there, Mummy. I'll see you
through," she said, and was about to add, " But let no one
think I *want* to be there. Let all understand that I'm sacri-
ficing myself. I'm always ready to sacrifice myself, but only
if it's observed and appreciated ; " but before she could
say this, her conscience quoted to her, "When thou fastest, see
that thou appear not unto men to fast," and persuaded her
that silence would be nobler than humour. The words
were not said. Her moralism was for ever hobbling and
limiting her humour like this. " I'll come back and give
you a break."

"There, Joanie; I hope that puts you to shame," rebuked Julian.

"I suppose I shall have to turn up," grumbled Joanie.

"Certainly. Good child," encouraged Julian. "I, I'm afraid, shall be out. The Widow is not my meat at all. As far as I am concerned, anybody can have the old cheese."

Mr. Rostrum's spirits were still high, still effervescing, when the children had gone; but now there was no one except Mildred and Dudley before whom he could display them. "Well, old dear," he said, getting up, "we're in for it now. The Widow. General Inspection. You'd better begin putting the house to rights. You'd better clean it from top to bottom. Her eye won't miss a thing." And he rubbed his hands with delight.

"Oh, I *wish* she weren't coming. It's just the last straw. I've everything to prepare for the holiday. I've all Dudley's clothes to mend. Oh, *leave* that alone, I tell you!" Dudley had touched something on the tray which she was loading before carrying it to the draining board. "Leave it alone!" She stamped her foot at him.

"Oh, whatever *is* the matter with you," demanded Mr. Rostrum. At the touch of her ill-temper all his humour had turned to resentment. That fine fresh morning milk, receiving this spoonful of vinegar from her, had gone sour. It had gone exceedingly sour. "I come in all jolly, and I'm greeted with nothing but snappiness. What the devil's the matter?"

"Don't say 'what the devil' to me."

"I'll say 'what the devil' to whoever I like and whenever I like. Don't have any doubt about that. I have every reason to be angry. Why should you make my life miserable just because the little boy played you up this morning? I came in all jolly, and—dammit, he spoils everything. Everything. He ruins my life. I was feeling thoroughly happy; now I'm feeling depressed. I was feeling full of affection for everybody; now I don't care what happens to anyone. *Leave those things alone!*" He had followed her, the tray, and Dudley to the sink, so as to vent some more of his indignation over her; and now he was shouting at Dudley because he had knocked over some cups, trying to move them from the tray to the draining board. "Can't you do what your mother tells you? And don't look at me like that. He looks thoroughly malignant when he looks like that. *I* think he's a thoroughly unpleasant little boy. Nothing but rows and strain. I wish to God he'd never been born. I do, really. Nothing but trouble and quarrelling and strain. I don't even like him. I don't like him at all. And I don't pretend to." When in his heat Mr. Rostrum abdicated from rational thought, he would surrender at once to a secret idea, immured in a little dungeon of his mind that it was Mildred who had erred, and done him a wrong, by producing Dudley when she was forty-five; and he would feel driven to punish her by saying derogatory things about her production. " He's nothing but a trouble and a curse. I can't stand the strain of your incessant rows with him much longer. I don't wonder that men get out of their houses and sit in the pubs all night. I don't wonder they take to drink. I shall be doing it myself soon."

" Do it," shouted Mildred. " Sit in all the public houses you like. Sit in every public house in London." If ever she felt ready for a highly dramatic scene, she felt it now : a scene of fine, loud speeches, not one word of which she would believe, but all of which she would enjoy, as their creator, deliverer, and audience. " I don't want anyone to stay with me who finds me a strain. I've done my best ; that's all I know ; and I ask no gratitude. I don't expect gratitude in this world, neither from my children, and certainly not from my husband. Strain ! I should like to know how your strain compares with mine. Do *you* get up and dress him ? Do *you* have to fight with him to get every garment on ? Spoils everything !—and you see him once or twice at meals. I have him every minute of the day. And now someone's taken my mop. How in pity's name can I wash up if people take away and hide my tools ? Oh, it's enough to drive one mad the way you and the children take my tools——"

" I haven't touched your bloody mop," said Mr. Rostrum, surprised at his own word. It must be the influence of Julian—or Dudley.

" People take them and never think of putting them back in their proper place. I've said a thousand million times that if I'm to do the work of the house, people are to leave

82

my tools alone." At that moment she saw the mop where she had placed it, only a few seconds before, in the corner of the sink. Sure that he hadn't seen it, she immediately put the enamel washing bowl over it to hide it from the world's view. Her dramatic sense instructed her that a speech of mounting fury mustn't be ruined by an anticlimax. She turned on the tap and, while the steam rose from the bowl, matching well with her mood, she reverted to her former topic. " I've done my best for you and the children for thirty years, and if I'm a failure, I'm a failure. I can't help it. If you think that, I'm ready to admit it. No doubt other women could have done much more and much better. It's a pity you didn't find one before ever you met me. And if you can find one now, I shan't stand in your way ; I promise you that."

" Is Daddy angry, Mummy ? " asked Dudley, detached and unperturbed, but interested. " Has Daddy been rude ? "

" Yes. Everybody's rude to me. I do all I can for everybody and get little but rudeness in return."

Mr. Rostrum raised his voice. " I haven't been rude to anyone. I came in all jolly——"

" Move out of the way, child. How can I put things here if you're there ? " She shouldered Dudley away from the draining board and laid down a plate which she'd washed under the steaming, scalding tap just as if there were no mop beneath the basin ; just as if it had been shamefully removed from its place and her work made more difficult and more painful. " Let me get on with my work. It's got to be done whether it's appreciated or not. And now there's this woman coming to-morrow. Your Auntie Elizabeth. Her eyes'll be on everything, and she, like everybody else'll think that I don't know how to run a house and a family. She'll probably say so to other people."

" Who cares what she says or thinks ? No one's afraid of *her*. I'm not afraid of Elizabeth."

" Saying that I drive you to public houses and make you take to drink. Saying things like that. And saying that he's a thoroughly unpleasant little boy without a single good thing to be said for him, when there are times when he's quite good, and you know it. It's no way of talking, to my way of thinking, either to him or to me." Here was

83

the point for tears, and she provided them. They fell into the bowl or were brushed from her eyes with her sleeve. " Oh, no, no, no." The more she thought of it, the less it seemed to be any way of talking. " Oh, no, no, no, *no!* No, no, *NO!*" This was almost bellowed. " I've done all I could all my life—all my life. I've given up all my best years to working and slaving for you all——"

" Oh, God, I wish I were dead," announced Mr. Rostrum.

" So do I. So do I with all my heart and soul—sometimes."

" Mummy." Dudley, who had been studying his father with a calm, scientific interest as a specimen of a grown-up who'd been rude, was now moving in a different region of thought. " Ken's daddy isn't half as tall as my daddy."

" Isn't he ? " sobbed Mildred, as though, in these circumstances, this was something she wasn't anxious to admit.

" I'll go," said Mr. Rostrum, turning away. " I'll go and do my work. At least I'm happy in that. There are times when I thank God that I am an artist, if only a small one, because I can always escape into my art. It must be dreadful when your work's a drudgery, and you're as miserable in it as you are in your home. I don't know where you escape to then. The river, I suppose."

" Oh, *you* needn't go," she shouted after him, much as she had shouted at the woman in the shop. " If you're unhappy with me, I'll go. I've no doubt there's somewhere I can go to. I'll go and take Dudley with me."

" Yes, for God's sake, don't leave *him*," called Mr. Rostrum, as he went with an immense emphasis up the basement stairs.

§

Elizabeth Leicester, or The Widow Leicester, as it was Mr. Rostrum's pleasure, and the family's, to call her, was his elder sister. Ten years older than he, she would have held that this seniority alone justified her in tutoring and correcting him, his wife, and their children ; but what was worse, what invested her with the sacred pallium and its accompanying right to judge, pronounce and condemn, was the fact that she had been for sixteen years the widow of the Rev. Prebendary James Leicester, Vicar of St. Cuthbert's, Elliston Square. In addition to calling her the Widow and the Inspector, Mr. Rostrum would sometimes call her the Family Miracle, because she had been but a mild, obedient, and conventional young woman, a simple-minded churchgoer and Sunday School teacher at St. Saviour's, Upper Kilburn, until the curate married her. In those far-off days before they were married, fully fifty years ago, the Rev. James Morton Leicester had been as naïve and earnest as she, and, upon seeing her in the Sunday School, of which he was Superintendent, he had sought the guidance of God as to whether she would be a good, serious wife for a poor parish priest ; and God, in his view after much prayer and thought, had assured him that the marriage was in accordance with His mind, so he had asked for her hand, and she had willingly given it ; and thereafter, within the bosom of the Rev. James Leicester, she had changed completely.

For James may have been naïve and over-solemn at the beginning of his career, but he had a great reputation for scholarship. The son of a clerk in the General Shipping Corporation, who had but three hundred a year to bring up six children, he had been educated at a small grammar school in South East London and from there, being a studious and docile lad, he had won a Balliol scholarship ; which success he had followed up at the University by carrying off a Craven scholarship and taking his degree with a First in Classical Moderations and a First in Greats. With these distinctions behind him he did not stay long as Curate of St. Saviour's, Upper Kilburn : he advanced up the ecclesiastical ladder with the speed of a fireman, carrying his wife upward in his arms. From St. Saviour's he went as Vicar to St. Silas the Martyr, Maida Hill ; while here he was made examining chaplain to the Bishop of London ; and soon, being ever in the Bishop's eye now, he was preferred from the quite important cure at Maida Hill to the celebrated church and key position of St. Cuthbert's, Elliston Square. To be Vicar of St. Cuthbert's was to be a well-known name throughout the Anglican communion, and because of this, and because of his academic distinctions, he was offered and accepted various honourable chaplaincies, lectureships, and professorships. And as each rung of the ladder raised him higher above his colleagues and higher above the multitude, he shed all his naïvete and diffidence and put on instead, together with a fine covering of flesh and a ruddy dye on his cheeks, a manner so self-confident and commanding that some of his less successful and no doubt jealous brethren interpreted it among themselves as conceit. As he rose he enlarged like a prize crimson dahlia on its stalk ; he expanded alike in corpulence and in character, and deepened at the same time in colour, till at last he was such a royal bloom, such a heavy, imposing, and nodding flower, as few would have predicted when looking at the pale, closed bud of thirty years before. Everyone said of him that before he was full-blown he would put on gaiters and a pectoral cross, but he died of heart-failure in his desk chair when he was still but fifty-four years old.

But in the meantime Elizabeth had blossomed brilliantly at his side. She had not put on rotundity, for the Rostrums remained long and slight, but she had put on an enormous, an exorbitant authority. She had persuaded herself that by marrying a scholarly, brilliant, and dominating man she had become not only one flesh with him but also one brain ; which was absurd. The more self-assured, authoritative, infallible, and intolerant of criticism he became, the more self-assured, authoritative, and infallible she. Because James knew everything and was right on all points, so was she ; and it was ridiculous, it was insufferable, it was worthy of only an impatient " Pshaw ! " if less well-informed persons tried to contradict her. And this conviction that none of her pronouncements, whether on religion, politics, parenthood, or household management, was matter to be argued about, but rather the truth to be hearkened to and bowed before, was reinforced by the fact that, in addition to being the wife of a brilliant husband, she was also the mother of a brilliant son. It was not only hand-in-hand with her husband but hand-in-hand with her son, one on either side of her, that she had soared, a slight figure, into the empyrean. Or, as malicious friends amended, into the inane.

Herbert, well disciplined by his father, had run as strenuous a course in the academic field. From one of the cheaper public schools, Merchant Taylors (for James and Elizabeth were poor when he was young, and at no time rich) he had won a scholarship at Oriel and had crowned his university career with Firsts in Classical Mods and Greats, besides, winning the Hall Greek Testament Prize and the Passmore Edwards Prize. It had been his intention to take Holy Orders, urged thereto, or rather propelled thereto, by the firm hand of his father, but he had decided at the last moment when, somewhat late in the day, his manhood came upon him, to change direction left (as the sergeants say) and to march up the interesting avenue of art instead of up the straight, steep road of religion; and he had now a responsible and scholarly post in the British Museum, in the Department of Prints and Drawings. With a husband who had been to Oxford and become a prebendary, and a son who had been to Oxford and now sat in the British Museum, how was it likely that Elizabeth Leicester, in her widowed retirement, should meet many, or any, whose brains were equal to hers? Was it not natural that she should mutter "Pshaw!" and become a shade impatient when they lifted their light weapons against hers? Was it not most natural of all that she should find it difficult to suffer the opinions of a younger brother who had remained in a photographer's studio upon the Kilburn flats, and the opinions of his children who, though no fools, had been neither to public schools nor to university? Was it not inevitable that, when in their presence, she should be afflicted with an itching need to put them all in their place and, if necessary, to take down their conceit. If Alec was presumptuous enough to dispute her assertions, was she not justified in summoning up, like rocket-firing aircraft, the endorsements of James and Herbert? Were not the rulings of James and Herbert decisive? Did they not establish the truth on a plane above the level of argument?

Sitting within the warm glow of James and Herbert's success, she had ripened marvellously in appearance as well as in character. She was still thin, but who would have believed that that long weed of a girl, Elizabeth Rostrum, timidly teaching in her Sunday School, and flushing and faltering when the clergy spoke to her (even more so than Brenda did now) would have developed into this fine old fusilier of a woman with the imperial coiffure of white, waved hair, the strong-featured, over-powdered face, the diamonds on her strong old fingers, the harsh, hearty laugh, and the deep, masculine voice ?

Mr. Rostrum, it will be rightly apprehended, was not the man to bear with patience the dogmatic affirmations of his sister and her manifest feeling of superiority. We have said that he was as sensitive to correction as Mildred, Brenda, Joanie, or Dudley. We have said that the whole Rostrum family was a very sensitive family. He did not like it at all when a toss of the Widow's head, a tweak of her shoulders, and a most pregnant silence behind her lips made it plain that she thought it ridiculous for him to argue with her and to pit his opinions against those of James and Herbert. Let her run up this haughty flag and he was upon his feet and striding the carpet before her, with danger signals in his face. It so riled him, this attitude, that from the moment of her entry into his house he waited for it—waited impatiently, his guns at full cock and eager to fire. If she was lively and unprovocative for too long, he stirred her up to battle with a well-placed shot so that, battle joined, all his weapons could go off and be relieved of the charge that was in them. In his heart of hearts he knew that he had always been afraid of James, the brilliant prebendary, and anxious to escape from his company lest he should say something ignorant or unwise ; and that he was now uncomfortably conscious of the same feelings in the presence of Herbert, his scholarly and fluent nephew ; he knew that his fear of their learning was enough to upset his stomach and put wind in his throat, so that he longed to break from them and find peace for the inconstant stomach in loneliness ; but he knew also, and with a great certainty, that he had no such fear of Lizzy. No, and no desire to escape from her proximity, but rather a desire to board her and attack. Good God, did he not remember Lizzy in the days before James came upon her like the power of God and begat in her these mighty pretensions ? No, he was taking nothing from Lizzy. She wasn't putting over on *him* any of her highcockolorum stuff.

The opposite face of this determination that Lizzy wasn't going to put over anything on him was a compulsion to put over on her his own successes and those of his children. Mr. Rostrum had many cravings but none stronger than

88

this. Directly he knew that she was coming into his house, he was possessed by a demon of self-display. Everything about the house must be clean, from its doorstep to its bathroom basin and its lavatory pan ; anything that she might visit must be polished for her eye. It was a hawk's eye, and its sweep was catholic. The tea-tray must be furnished with evidences of culture ; his wife and children must be prosperously dressed, and so must the sofas and the chairs ; all his possessions must be decorated and deployed in the way that would most impress the Widow.

So this same evening, twenty-four hours before her arrival, he started upon the preparations. He sat in the kitchen with Mildred, their quarrel of the morning having been tacitly expunged like an incorrect sum from a slate, and, with his shirt sleeves turned back and his spectacles now on his nose and now on his brow, cleaned all the silver, polished all the brass, dusted all the best china, and gave to several pieces a second rubbing if they were not shining as he wished. Restless after finishing these tasks, he went alone into the drawing-room, swept its carpet, arranged the folds of the curtains, and shook out and smoothed the cushions. Stooping down, he tidied the pleats of the loose covers. Next morning at breakfast he importuned Mildred on the question of what she was going to wear, and what Brenda, Joanie, and Dudley were going to wear. He himself was already in his best blue suit. Before he left for business he swept the asphalt paths of the garden, clipped one or two of the shrubs, and with the same shears laid low a blade or two of grass that seemed too tall. These touches completed, he stepped out into the roadway to study the appearance of the house. Not wholly satisfied, he went back into the house to arrange the curtains of a bedroom window. In the afternoon, returning early, because he trusted nobody but himself to achieve the imperative perfections, he dusted and set the drawing-room again and carefully laid upon a table the best of the prints that he was sending to the exhibitions. Then he went downstairs to see if Mildred was dressed. She was not : she was still in the kitchen, preparing the sandwiches for tea. " Hadn't you better get dressed, darling ? " he asked. There was an hour before the Widow was likely to arrive, and he wandered about the house, unable to sit down for more than a minute or to read more than a paragraph. Once he went into the bedroom where Mildred was now dressing and asked, What was Brenda wearing at her school? And from what Mildred told him he came out satisfied that Brenda, when she returned from school, would not let the family down.

Four o'clock. He went into his study and stood by the window to see if the visitor was in sight. His legs ached with walking about and standing. Ten minutes he stood there and then saw her in the road. Yes, there was Lizzy, a study as usual in black and white : black hat lit up by a small bunch of white artificial flowers, silver hair, bleached skin, black dress, white pearls, pale grey stockings, and shining black shoes. Slipping back from the window he waited out of view, touching his tie into place and pulling down his cuffs. The bell rang, and he walked with un-hurried steps to open the door.

" Hallo, Liz. How have you come? Bus? "

" Haw, haw," she laughed ; and her laugh was always a loud guffaw. " What do you think? Walked all the way from Marble Arch. I never take a bus if I can walk. I'm seventy I know, and proud of it, but I'm still pretty active." Her conscious superiority to normal weaknesses sounded in every tone of the loud, deep, masculine voice. The voice was taking possession of the house. " Well, how's Mildred and the family? How's the baby? "

" Fine, thanks. Come into the drawing-room. Take this chair."

" No, no. I've little use at this time of the day for deep, easy chairs. I don't go to bed in a chair like you men do. I'll sit here. Ah ! " She sat on a small chair with a sigh that seemed to be in a different key from her protestations of vigour. And she stared at her brother as he stood before the fireplace. " Well, Alec, how are you? I don't think you're looking too well."

So ! The first prick of the candid sword.

" Thank you. I feel fine. I'm always well. I've hardly had a day's illness in fifty years."

" Aren't you looking a bit yellow? "

" Yellow be hanged ! " He had almost said " damned ". " What do you mean : yellow? " He pretended to laugh, for he must not quarrel at once; but "there's going to be trouble," he thought, "if she starts this game of speaking the unpalatable truth, which she thinks she does so much better than anyone else. There's going to be very serious trouble indeed." "I've been working very hard lately. That's all that's the matter with me. Working on some pictures I'm going to send to the London Salon of Photography. And to America."

"But I thought you were having some indigestion pains last time I was here. Pains in the chest."

"Was I? Yes, I believe I was. But that was nothing. There's nothing wrong with me."

"Aren't you stooping more than you did?"

"Stooping?" Hell! He braced back his shoulders. "I've never stooped in my life."

"Oh, yes, you have; and you do. You can't see yourself. All men stoop who are too thin for their height."

"Whad'you mean: too thin for my height? I'm not too thin for my height. I'm perfectly proportioned."

"Haw, haw, haw," she laughed; and her laugh was maddeningly full of good-humoured toleration. It was the laugh of one who looked down from an eminence upon the weaknesses of men. "Well, well, well! Really! The vanity of you men!"

Mr. Rostrum decided that he had said too much. "What I mean is, I'm quite satisfied with myself as I am, thank you."

"Good. Splendid. How are the children?"

"My boy's doing very well. He sits for his Finals in a day or two, and after that he'll be a fully qualified solicitor." Let her know that there were other successful children besides her Herbert. And a solicitor was as good as a British Museum official any day.

"And the little boy?"

"The little boy's terrific. He's a packet of bursting dynamite. I've never seen such a child. But I wouldn't have him different. I wouldn't have him different for a moment. And he's enormous. He's not four yet, and we have to get him clothes for a child of five. And I'll tell you something more: he's getting quite beautiful."

Again the smile of kindly tolerance.

"What are you smiling at?"

" I like it : your enthusiasm. But I wonder how many parents have said just what you're saying. He's probably just the same as any other child."

" I don't think he's the same as any other child. I don't think he's the same as any other child at all. I think he's quite beautiful."

" Well, let's hope he is. And what about the girl ? "

" Which girl ? "

" Brenda. Anyone after her yet ? "

" A man, d'you mean ? "

" Of course. What else ? "

" No. Not to my knowledge."

" I doubt if she's the sort to attract men. She's not to be compared, in that respect, with the other one."

" Brenda is a saint." His lips came sharply together, and he walked to the window and gazed out. " If we were all as good as her, the world would be all right."

" Is she still full of those High Church notions ? "

" She still goes to the same church, if that's what you mean. I don't discuss her religion with her. All I know is that it's made her good, and that, whether she marries or not, she'll be happy because she's good. I've no fears for Brenda. She's the best of us all. She'd do anything for anybody. Brenda is one who really knows how to sacrifice herself for others. I often think that something in me which I could never bring to birth, Brenda is bringing to full flower. I mean, I've often dreamed of giving up my whole life to others—I suppose most of us do, really—but I've never really done it. Brenda does it. And she'll always do it. She's the Real Goods."

The Widow's comment on this was never given, because at that moment Mildred entered, pushing Dudley before her, and followed at a trotting pace by Sankey. Mildred was ill at ease and gushing ; Dudley was ill at ease and not gushing ; Sankey was completely at ease and went up and smelt the Widow and then sat down in front of her, panting. Dudley had been washed and garnished for his aunt : his golden hair was precisely parted and brushed to a silky floss ; his cheeks were pink and carmine from the abrasion of a wet flannel ; his hands were sleek, limp, and clean (except for the finger nails which culminated in little arcs of black) ;

and he was wearing the clothes which became him best : a yellow shirt, pale blue shorts with straps over the shoulders, clean white socks and shining brown sandals. Mr. Rostrum looked upon him with the eyes of a creator and saw that he was good. He was beautiful. Mr. Rostrum turned towards his sister that he might enjoy his triumph.

" Well, my little man." The Widow put out both hands to him : she imagined that her way with children was a gift that approximated to genius. " Well, my young rapscallion. Coming to see your old auntie ? How big we're getting. We're no longer a baby but quite a little boy." (She really imagined that this was the way to talk to them.) " What ? You're not afraid of your old auntie ? Oh, come, come. Aren't you going to give me a kiss ? Go away, dog ; I'm not talking to you. I see that you've still got that extraordinary dog. Go away, animal. You're the ugliest dog I've ever seen. You're like a great black slug, and why haven't you got any legs ? Now then, young scapegrace, come and let's look at you. I don't bite. I've never bitten a little boy yet."

Dudley, apparently, was less sure that this was the way to speak to children. He turned shy and, putting his head on one side, pressed himself against his mother.

" Say good-afternoon to your auntie," encouraged Mildred. " Sankey, lie down, lie down ; you're a nuisance. Go on, Dudley. Give your Auntie Elizabeth a nice kiss."

But Dudley only pressed himself closer and began to climb up her as if he had climbing irons on his feet and she were a massive tree.

" Oh, come along, you little silly," rebuked Mildred. " Aren't you going to say good-afternoon to your auntie ? "

" Good morn-ang," said he, and climbed a little further.

" Haw, haw, haw." The Widow's laugh was like the cawing of a rook ; and this harsh, loud, unexpected sound brought him quickly to the floor again to study it.

She laughed again ; and when Elizabeth really let herself go in appreciation of a joke, and of her own sense of humour, she threw her head back and opened her mouth wide to emit the raucous noise ; and the effect of this was to reveal two sets of very regular and very white teeth. They were so regular and so white that Dudley's interest was immediately transferred to them. Working outward from them as a centre, he studied the whole of his auntie's face. He was fascinated by this assembly of different whites : silver-white hair piled up in an ordered array on the top of her head ; plaster-white powder on her large nose ; grey-white pearl in each ear ; and china-white teeth between her lips.

" Can you take your teeth out ? " he asked with interest. And he added, with pride, " My daddy can."

" Haw, haw, haw. That's all right, Mildred ; don't be angry with him. I don't mind what children say to me. I hope I've enough sense of humour for that. Children are always perfectly at ease with me. I can do what I like with them. But you're right, Alec. This young gentleman's no fool."

Dudley, encouraged by her laugh and this sensible opinion, decided to entertain her further. " Oh, damn and blast," he said.

" *Tst !* " Mr. Rostrum's pride leaked painfully away. Why must he do these things before his auntie?

" Oh, no ! Come, come," the Widow remonstrated. " Little boys mustn't use words like that." Evidently her sense of humour wasn't capacious enough to make room for this. " Little boys mustn't use naughty bad words. Oh, no, certainly not."

Dudley leaned forward to project another word at her. " Bubbly," he said.

" What ? What do you say ? "

" Bubbly," he repeated with zest.

She turned to Mr. Rostrum. " Why does he say Bubbly ? "

" I can't imagine," said Mr. Rostrum.

And just then Brenda came in. " Hallo, Auntie," she cried brightly ; and Mildred, much put about by the Widow's presence and Dudley's behaviour, seized the opportunity to " go and make the tea " and remove Dudley from the room. He was removed, saying " Bubbly."

" Well, Brenda, my dear ? " The Widow's eyes, the eyes of the Inspector, were roaming over her. " You look quite different. What's happened to you ? "

Instantly the crimson flux rushed over Brenda : it rushed up her brow to her hair and down her throat to her breast.

But she put laughter in her eyes that it might deny this treachery in her blood. "Nothing, Auntie."

"Oh, yes! You're quite different. Is someone in love with you?"

"No!" Brenda pretended to be still laughing, but the burning of her cheeks made a lie of the smile in her eyes. "No, of course not."

"I'm not so sure," said the Widow knowingly. "You look very different. You used to look a little pale, I thought, and sometimes a little sad. Now you look happy and blooming."

And the Widow was speaking the truth. Brenda was different. All the family had noticed it for days past and were teasing her about it. Her brown hair was still drawn away from its central parting and wound into a chignon at the nape, but whereas a few days since it had been done austerely and defiantly, it was now done lovingly and with care. Yesterday her hair was without light; now it shone like a lantern which had been lit. Her cheeks, when the hot colour flew home from them, were still pale, but they were now powdered and lightly rouged. Her mouth, once paler than pale coral, was now scarlet and carefully shaped with lipstick. Her long red hands were manicured, and the nails painted. Perhaps she was an inch too tall for a girl, but her face, to a man's eyes, if not to her aunt's—to her father's eyes, and even to the gasping Julian's—was beautiful. Warm colour and light had poured into it from somewhere as once they ran into the sculptured marble of Galatea.

The eyes of the Inspector dropped to Brenda's hands. "Surely you haven't taken to that dreadful habit of painting your nails?"

Brenda shut her fingers into her palms that the nails might be hidden.

"Don't adopt that nasty habit, Brenda dear. There's nothing beautiful in it. It's just revolting, I think. It's bad enough, the way you girls all paint your lips. I may be old-fashioned about this, but, if so, I'm not ashamed of it. I think it's extraordinary that ladies' daughters should go about with painted faces. In my day it was the mark of a woman of the streets."

Brenda kept her lips closed and her pain and anger behind

them. But Mr. Rostrum saw the pain in her eyes and leapt to her defence. It gave him an acute pleasure, singularly sweet, to be defending Brenda.

"I don't see what's so wrong with it. I don't see what's wrong with any young girl making the best of herself. They can be young but once. I think they do us all a kindness by making themselves as beautiful as they can. There are enough ugly things in the world."

"It's wrong because it's a lie; it's pretending to something you haven't got. Nothing that's false can be beautiful. That's what James always used to say. And Herbert says exactly the same. He dislikes heavily rouged cheeks and painted lips. And he's a young man of the present day."

"He's not the only young man. There may be others who think differently. I should say that the vast majority of them like their girls to be as beautiful as possible. And very sensible too, it seems to me."

"They may like it; I daresay they do; but they're not artistic experts——"

"I hope I'm an artistic expert——"

"Herbert is an artistic expert. He's dealing with beautiful things every day in the British Museum. It's his business to know what's beautiful and what isn't. And he knows and says—just as his father used to—that nothing that's false can be beautiful."

Brenda longed to say, "What about your hair, Auntie? How much of that is a lie? And the powder on your nose, which is not only a lie but a messy one?" but her conscience was ready, as ever, with an inhibiting quotation—this time, "Whosoever shall smite thee on thy right cheek (when it's rouged), turn to him the other also"—and she imprisoned her anger in a silence.

Mr. Rostrum was not visited by this quotation. "Damn it," he said—and at the word Elizabeth shivered away, "Your hair isn't exactly as God made it."

"That's different," she declared.

"Damned if I see why." Mr. Rostrum judged that "damn," having burst into the room, might as well stay among them. "You make your hair as beautiful as possible—and may I say I think you do wonders with it? She does it beautifully, doesn't she, Brenda? And what about your powder, Lizzy? That's telling a few lies, isn't it? What does Herbert say about that? Does he consent to it? I'm sure he does. Well, if one can use powder, why not paint?"

" I'd rather not discuss it."

This was infuriating. Infuriating, this method of dodging defeat. Mr. Rostrum felt blasphemous. " I'm sure you'd rather not. It's always much wiser to get out of an argument that's going against you. Like hell it is! Get out while the going's good. But the fact remains that if paint's a lie, so's powder. And so's false teeth."

" I shall never believe in girls who are ladies painting their lips."

" No? Well, I don't know what you can do about it. They'll go on doing it in spite of your disapproval."

" They should keep the lips they were born with."

" Oh, and is that so? Well, I take it you weren't born with pearls on your ears. I thought they were a disease of oysters."

" That's quite different."

" I fail to see why. If pearls on your ears, why not paint on your lips?"

Fortunately for the Widow, if not for Mr. Rostrum who was enjoying a tourney which he felt he was winning on points, Joanie rushed in at this juncture, her eyes alight. To Joanie any visitor, even her auntie, was exciting. She had a high colour in her rounded cheeks and a wind-blown freedom in her waved, abundant, and flouncing hair; and her breast was heaving as her eyes danced. If Brenda had looked rather beautiful before Joanie's entrance, her lamp, so newly lit, was quite outshone by her sister's natural radiance.

" Hallo, Auntie."

Her kiss, and her obvious excitement at this visit, allayed the displeasure which had begun to froth up in Elizabeth. She picked up Joanie's hand affectionately and inquired in the hearty manner which she deemed appropriate to young people, " And how's the young man?"

" Steve's all right. If he passes his Final B.Sc., we're going to get engaged."

" Good gracious! Is everybody sitting for exams just now?"

97

" Yes, both Julian and Steve. And they're both going to pass easily ; I know it."

" But aren't you much too young to be engaged ? "

" I'm eighteen next month, so it all fits in perfectly."

" Well, I'm sure I wish you all joy. And now, Brenda, we must do something about you."

" About me ? "

" Yes, isn't it time you had a young man ? "

The blood, so recently dismissed, rushed to its stations in Brenda's face. " It might be, if I wanted one," she said ; and, having said it, pretended to laugh that the words might not sound rude.

Mildred's entry with the tea-tray and with Dudley put the closure on this discussion. She set the tray on a low occasional table, and all leaned forward from sofa or chairs to receive their cups. It was Mr. Rostrum's ukase that when the Widow came to tea they must eat in this polite and uncomfortable way.

As Elizabeth masticated her potted-meat sandwich, which she was inclined to mill between her front teeth, her eyes roved round the room. They fell upon Mr. Rostrum's boat on a table in the window. He had placed it there the night before partly because, in his view, it lent distinction to any room, but mainly because he wanted Elizabeth to ridicule it so that he might convict her of ignorance and folly. He was exactly right in thinking that she would regard it as a good target for humour ; he knew his sister well. " Good gracious, Mildred," she laughed, gazing at the boat and milling her sandwich vigorously. " He doesn't still play with toy boats, does he ? Really, Alec, it's time you grew up. At sixty, really, you're old enough to know better "

" That's not a toy boat," said Mr. Rostrum coldly, his mouth full. " That's a perfect scale model of a ten metre yacht. And the sailing of it is a highly skilled business."

" I should have thought it was something on Dudley's level."

" No doubt you would. One's apt to be very badly wrong, and very dogmatic sometimes, about things one's never troubled to study. Model yacht sailing is a sport indulged in by people of the highest intelligence. They are intelligent enough to be fascinated by its technical possibilities and artistic enough to be thrilled by its sheer æsthetic beauty. Like fly-fishing in waders along a rapid stream the art itself is utterly beautiful and the places where it carries you are always lovely. It takes you into the trees and among the birds, and when you're alone with nature, and everything is silent, you're happy—happier perhaps than at any other time of your life. It's solitude and peace."

" Gracious me, what eloquence ! "

" It's not eloquence at all. It's just a statement of the truth. Perhaps you're not aware that there are Model Yacht Clubs all over England ? "

" I certainly wasn't, but I don't wonder at it. Men never grow up, do they, Mildred ? "

Heavens, the woman was a fool ; the woman was a fool and thought she was clever ; what was one to do ; what was one to say ?

" Have another cup of tea, Elizabeth," Mildred invited. " Do. Please do. Thank you very much." Mildred was always so nervous in the Widow's company that not only did she gush and flatter but her tongue became autonomous and uttered sentences that she had never told it to. She would be surprised and shaken by the things it said. It would persist, for example, in saying, when there was no occasion for it, " Thank you very much ; " and Mildred had the wit to perceive, and was vexed to perceive, that this leaping, ungovernable utterance was an expression of her sense of inferiority. " Pass your cup. Please do. Yes. I want you to have some more. You'll have some more, won't you ? "

" Well, I will if I may, Mildred."

" Thank you very much. Just pass the cup, if you don't mind." She filled the cup hurriedly and too full. " There you are. And there's the sugar in front of you. You've got everything ? Thank you very much." And Mildred sighed because the inapposite words had said themselves again.

" You'd be lucky if you could get that boat for thirty pounds," continued Mr. Rostrum, who didn't want the subject shouldered aside so quickly.

" Thirty pounds for that ? "

" Yes, certainly. And I wouldn't make it myself for fifty. The mathematics involved in building a boat like that would make my head ache. You've got to understand the First

Linear Rating Rule and the International Rule and the relation of Sail Area to Load Water Line, and how the Sail Area varies as the square of the scale, and the Displacement as the cube of the scale." He was piling up the technicalities for her overthrow. But she was no longer listening. She had withdrawn, as usual, from a contest in which she could not fight as a master. Her eyes were on a photograph standing on the mantelpiece. It was a print which he had placed there for her instruction and humiliation.

" Is that one of your photographs ? " she asked, fingering her pearl necklace.

" It is." He was delighted to be asked this. He'd been waiting to be asked it. " I don't want to brag, Lizzy, but I must say I regard it as one of my best. One of my triumphs. I'm hoping great things of it at the London Salon."

" You mean you're sending it to an exhibition ? "

" I certainly am."

She looked at it again ; and it was obvious that to her it was no more than the photograph of a country road such as a child might take with a five-shilling camera, but that she didn't like to say so, since there'd been arguments enough already. But Mr. Rostrum was most anxious for her to say so. He encouraged her to say so. " You don't see much in it ? "

" It's pretty enough."

" Pretty ! It's not pretty. I don't seek to produce pretty pictures. It just happens to be an absolutely perfect composition. I know it is, though I say it myself. I suppose to the ordinary untrained eye it's just a country road swinging past a clump of trees, but to a real judge of photography, it's—well, quite frankly—it's a masterpiece. You hadn't noticed, I suppose "—Mr. Rostrum stood up and, removing his spectacles, used them as a pointer—" that these clouds make a single splendid formation whose line exactly reproduces the curve of the tree-tops ? Nor that this point here, where the sky is visible between the branches of the trees gathers the whole picture together and concentrates its interest there——" He cupped his hands together as if gathering something within them and concentrating it there. " Nor that this weight of dark hedge in the right-hand corner exactly balances the weight of cloud on the left. Nor that, because of the absence of any distracting element, the eye is at peace everywhere. Or, again, that the curve of the road answers the curve of the furthest tree. These two receding curves, and the light in the sky behind the trees, give a wonderful depth pattern to the picture, I think. The flat pattern is perfect, and the depth pattern is perfect. I call it *The Road to Freedom*."

"Why that?"

"Well, one must call a picture something. It's the road we're taking next week, eh, Mildred? The road to Life. The road that's left the last of the town behind it and is going on and on, just round that bend there, into the clean, open country. I thought of calling it *The Road to God*, but Brenda wouldn't let me; she said it was high-falutin'. As a matter of fact, that bit of road is only a mile or two from Kilburn, but it leads to the North. The North!" He rubbed his hands together in his joy of the words. "Not that it matters twopence what you call a picture, really. The title of the picture is nothing, because the subject matter of the picture is nothing. Nothing at all." He overstated the case to provoke her.

"I should have thought it was everything."

Exactly what he wanted her to say. It would enable him to show her that she knew nothing about art and that it was as silly as it was impudent for her to argue on such a matter with him. "Yes, that's what all people think until—if you don't mind my saying so—they've had a little instruction."

"Instruction! I think I know as much about pictures as most people. James was devoted to pictures, and we've been to many picture galleries together. We've been to galleries in Vienna and at—at the Louvre. And I think you forget that my son is in the Department of Prints and Drawings at the British Museum."

For the moment he had forgotten it, and he felt as if his sword had been blunted in his hand. But when, in an argument, Reason is a casualty, Anger, and even Rudeness, will often leap into its place. "I can't help that. Anyone who doesn't know that the subject of the picture is not its subject—I mean—oh, you know what I mean—*you* know, don't you, Brenda?—that the pattern, the form, the organization, the mood, is the real subject, and not the subject matter—anyone who thinks that the merely literary interest of the picture is its subject is way back in Victorian times. They may still think it in the British Museum, for all I know."

"Don't be ridiculous, Alec. It's only men of the highest qualification who get into the British Museum. I think you forget that Herbert had a most distinguished career at Oxford. And so did his father before him."

"Oh, yes, I know that I didn't go to Oxford. But you can learn about an art at other places than Oxford—and probably much better. I'm not aware that Dickens went to Oxford. Or Turner, who was a haidresser's son. Or—or most of them. I'm ready to believe that James and Herbert learnt a lot more about Latin and Greek than I shall ever know, but when it comes to Art, I'll back my opinion against theirs any day. After giving forty years of my life to the study of Art—after thinking of nothing else for forty years—I'm afraid I have very little interest in the opinions of untrained amateurs."

"And I think that's very conceited of you, don't you, Mildred?"

"It *sounds* conceited, but I think I know what Alec means. Yes, I think I do. Thank you very much."

"Conceited! Would James have liked it if I, knowing nothing about Theology, had tried to teach him how to compose one of his lectures? Would a doctor like it if I told him what was wrong in the way he was performing an operation? Would he be conceited if he thought that I'd better stick to photography? No. It'd be mere sense. Well, in the same way I believe—I just *know*—that I know more about Art than either you or James—I leave out Herbert—have ever known. I've given a lifetime's apprenticeship to it, and I find I can still learn something new about it every time I make a picture. It's a highly specialized business. Do you suppose, then, that the opinions of people who've never had time to study it are of any interest to me whatever except in so far as it is always interesting to know the reactions of completely uninstructed people. If it's conceited to believe that, then I'm conceited. But if it's humble to know that I have never, and never shall, make a picture that even approximates to the perfect thing I can see in my mind, then I'm the humblest man in England."

Tears had jumped to his eyes, and he snatched at a chocolate cake to divert attention from them. " I'm humble before my Art, but, by God, I'm not humbled before the facile and cocky dogmatisms of the ignorant."

Elizabeth was chewing her cake fast and severely. " Well, well, I may be completely uninformed, but I still say I'm entitled to my views about a picture." She glanced round for an ally. " You think you're entitled to your own opinion too, don't you, Brenda ? "

" I'm afraid I agree with Daddy, Auntie," said Brenda, who, directly James and Herbert and Oxford were introduced, became hot for battle on the family's side. " Most people—I don't mean you, Auntie—*are* so intolerant about things they don't understand. They are, aren't they ? And usually their intolerance is in proportion to their ignorance —I feel. . . ."

" Of course Brenda agrees with me. Unlike some people she knows enough about Art to know how little she knows, and to be properly modest."

" Well, I still say that I'm entitled to have an opinion and to express it."

" Certainly you're entitled to have an opinion and to express it, but you're not entitled to think it's worth as much as you obviously do. Not unless you've given years and years of study to what you're talking about. For anyone who's given his life to his art to sit and listen to parsons and what-not laying down the law about it is like—well, it's like having a highly developed ear for music and listening to tone-deaf people condemning Bach and Beethoven. It's comic. They don't know how ignorant they sound. If they did, they'd keep quiet. It's nothing new that I'm saying about pictures. Why, Constable a hundred years ago laid it down—though I don't suppose you knew this—that the apparent subject of his pictures was never the real subject."

" Well, what *was* the real subject ? "

" Himself."

" But that's nonsense."

" There you are ! Nonsense. Constable talks nonsense about Art and you talk sense ! Now we know where we are." He was delighted that she should have dropped her guard and exposed her body to a mortal thrust. " And I may say that I'd rather talk nonsense by the side of John Constable than wisdom, or what they imagine to be wisdom, by the side of James and Herbert; because, you see, my dear Elizabeth, I have a fancy that he knew a little of what he was talking about."

The Widow bridled. She fiddled with her pearls. She laid her hand on her handbag which rested on a chair at her side. "You forget that Herbert meets the most distinguished artists of the day and talks with them. And James used to meet them too at his club. He met Herkomer and Sir William Richmond and John Collier——"

"Oh, damn James. And Herbert too."

"Alec! Alec!" protested Mildred.

"If he's going to be rude to me like this, Mildred, I think I'd better go after tea." And she laid her fingers again on handbag and gloves.

"Oh, no, no, Elizabeth. Thank you. . . . No, very much. . . . Yes, do stay. . . . *Please*. . . . Sankey, lie down, lie *down*, will you!" She half rose, because Sankey, in the general disturbance, had got up and gone to the Widow, apparently to help with the handbag and gloves. "Lie down, I tell you! That's right. Thank you very much."

"I'm not accustomed to having people talk to me like that."

"You attacked me first: you said I was conceited."

"And I still say so. I think you've been talking some of the most conceited stuff I've ever heard."

"Oh, do you? Well, you're not the only person who's entitled to call other people conceited. I say *you're* conceited too, about your James and your Herbert and their Oxford. I say that whenever you talk about them, you talk some of the most conceited stuff I've ever heard."

This time she really picked up the handbag and gloves. "I shall have to go, Mildred. I can't stay here to be spoken to like this. My husband is dead. I'm not having his name taken in vain like this."

"Thou shalt not take the name of the Lord thy God in vain," sneered Mr. Rostrum.

"Daddy! Daddy!" pleaded Brenda.

"No, Elizabeth, please, please sit down," begged Mildred. "Oh, I wish we'd never got on to this discussion. And,

Sankey, you lie down too. Yes, lie down. That's right. Thank you very much."

The Widow put back the handbag and gloves, but sat silent. Joanie kept her eyes on her plate. Brenda looked away towards the window. Only Dudley and Sankey stared at the guest, but neither of them seemed quite happy about the shape of events. And by now Mr. Rostrum was distressed too, not so much at what he had said, but because his temper could so ride and gall him. Sitting down slowly he mustered all the decency he could find at the moment and, when it was at fair strength and in good marching order, said gently, " I don't want to be rude, Lizzy. I was only trying to say that my own opinion on my own art was perhaps more likely to be right than the opinion of those who haven't had the opportunity to study it as much as I have. They've had other and perhaps more important things to do. That's all I meant when I said, ' Damn James and Herbert '."

CHAPTER SEVEN

It was the First Day, the morning of their first day at Callerdale, a day to be thought of with capitals, for the first day of a holiday is a little like that First Day when the world was newly created. Mr. Rostrum and Mildred walked arm-in-arm along the mossed and grassy path between a stone-walled meadow and a steep, wooded hill. Joanie was not with them this morning, because she had rushed into the market town to get some heavy shoes, having developed in the train a " state " about the thinness and frailty of all her footwear. Anxiety like an ichneumon fly had laid its eggs in her heart and left them to hatch out there and devour their host. The failure of her shoes would ruin her holiday, she had explained to her mother all the way from Preston to Lancaster, and from Lancaster to Kendal, and " I do so want to enjoy it," she said. There had been nothing for it but to let her anæsthetize the ache by a rush into Windham this morning and the purchase of a new pair of shoes. So Mr. and Mrs. Rostrum walked by the meadows alone. Mr. Rostrum was in his mustard brown golfing suit with a cap to match, and he carried a haversack slung on his hip and his miniature camera dangling on his breast. Mildred was in a tweed skirt, silk blouse, ribbed stockings, and thick brogue shoes. And the feel of these holiday clothes upon their bodies, and the feel of the ridged and stony path beneath their feet, were sensuous pleasures like the caress of the sun and the warm, soft blandishments of the breeze.

Mr. Rostrum gazed over the ambling wall at the plumped and fat beck meadows. These fields among their moss-creviced walls were green and not green ; they flushed crimson with sorrel and clover ; they turned yellow where the buttercups were high ; and they were white where the ox-eye daisies overtopped and outshone the grass. The smell of the cowpats came towards him like a tangible form of the joy he was drawing from the grass and the earth. He said only, " This is IT, Mildred."

And Mildred, nodding, pressed his arm.

The path led them on to a metalled road that ran for a mile between high hedges ; and the hedgebanks were starred with stitchwort and herb robert, speedwell and bush vetch, hare bell and campion ; and there were few of these tiny flowers that were missed by Mr. Rostrum's hungry and searching eye.

The road took them on to a humped stone bridge that leapt the narrow Caller stream. And they went to the grey parapet, and rested their arms upon it, and looked down upon the water. Coming from Kilburn, what else would they do ? The water was a sage-green liquid glass sliding over silver stones, where it was not a travelling froth or a tumble of cold, tinkling gems. An angler in long waders stood in the midst of this scampering water, casting his line ; casting it once and again. A dipper whirred through the tangled trees, perched on a stone, flirted its tail, and flew off into a spinney on the opposite bank. Mr. Rostrum drew in his breath with happiness, and that breath was almost pain.

The river was hurrying to the lake a half-mile farther on, so now Mr. and Mrs. Rostrum left the road and began to climb a long green hill that ran by the side of the lake. They went slowly, for Mildred was a heavy woman ; and

Mr. Rostrum, delayed by her slowness, looked down into the tight-woven turf for the tiny flowers that lived there : starry saxifrage and butterwort low down ; then, higher up, thyme and bird's-foot trefoil, tormentil and lady's bed-straw, meadow crane's bill and cuckoo flower and Alpine lady's mantle. He knew their names because he had learned and loved them on past holidays, and he rejoiced to call them out and display his knowledge to Mildred, as she came beating up behind.

The path burst into the bracken and became a thread through a ferny sea. For one second he looked back and saw that the lake was coming into view beyond the trees, but he quickly turned his eyes from it because he didn't want to see it till a greater height had unveiled its whole face from bank to bank. He climbed on and on without turning round ; and here, a few yards above him, was the ridge, the top, and he brandished a triumphant arm, as one who sees within his reach the top of the Jungfrau. And when he stood on the ridge, some minutes before Mildred, he turned to enjoy the vast outlay of hills and lake and rippled pastures, and with a quick intake of breath, spread his arms wide as if to embrace both earth and sky.

§

A few yards away there was a grey boulder like a slanting tomb. Its surface was as smooth and grey as a Quaker's frock, and you could see that the sun had been warming it for the last few hours. It invited them to come and be seated ; and they sat there side by side and gazed at the world below.

" Well, well, well," sighed Mr. Rostrum.

Here they were, far from Kilburn High Road, high among the curled bracken, and there beneath them was the lake with the trees crowding along its shores and its wooded islands afloat on it. There on the farther side was Cold Breath Bay, a half moon of slack water between its two little tree-crested headlands, Gull's Cape and Lord's Finger.

" This is the Real Thing," he said.

" Yes," she answered, and no more ; but he could feel that she was feeling it all too.

And in that moment of brimming exultation, as sometimes in moments of brimming distress, he knew how strong was the bond which, no matter how often Mildred and he might disappoint and fret each other, thirty years of life together had forged between them. He knew that he would rather be sitting here with this grey-haired, heavy-bodied woman, in this sea of stems and fronds, than with anyone else in the world. He was very happy in the knowledge, and he gave some time to considering the wonder of it.

"Glad I've been able to give you this holiday," he said, and laid a hand on hers.

She pressed his hand and smiled. "I hope Dudley's all right. You *do* think he'll be quite happy without us, don't you?"

"I should think he's paddling at this moment and has completely forgotten our existence."

"I think Sylvia'll look after him all right." None the less she submitted a few of the anxieties that had assaulted her since she waved good-bye to Dudley at Waterloo Station. Would he adventure too far into the sea, would the sea come in too quickly and envelop him, would he tread on broken glass with his bare feet, would he give up his toys to Ken, would he hit him on the chest in a quarrel, or, worse, would he hit Sylvia, would he behave so badly that the Trimmings would send a telegram saying they could stand him no longer?

And then he began to be impatient with her again for vexing herself and him with these worries, when he wanted everything to be perfect.

"Don't worry," he enjoined. "*He's* all right. Be happy. Be happy. This holiday has cost me a lot."

And for a few seconds, but not longer, he sat there disenchanted because it was so easy to be impatient with her. When he picked up her hand again and held it, he did it more for his own comfort than for hers.

A little dinghy had put out from the boathouse in the wood, and a man and a woman were gently rowing it towards the deserted jetty that thrust itself into the green lunulet of Cold Breath Bay. He gazed down at the lake's face, so wholly beautiful, and pondered on the mystery of it just as he would sometimes ponder on the mystery of little Dudley's face. Everything was wonder and mystery, when you began to think about it. And it was sad to be getting old and to know that quite soon now he must leave for ever this puzzling but often beautiful world without having been given one glimpse into the purpose and meaning of it all.

§

Next morning, immediately after breakfast, Mr. Rostrum went along this same route alone—resolutely alone. His haversack was slung under one arm with his lunch in it ; and under the other he carried his model yacht stowed and strapped in its canvas carrier. He walked much faster than he had done with Mildred ; his pace was as fast as that of a boy approaching an eagerly anticipated entertainment. He arrived at the boathouse in the wood, and here he hired a stolid and comfortable dinghy. Laying the yacht on the cushion of the stern-seat, he clambered in, shipped the oars, and sculled round the headland till he was out of the boat-man's eye and alone on the great sheet of water. Alone, in a great solitude, and with a great beauty. Unshipping the oars, he took the yacht on to his lap and, while the dinghy rocked beneath him, rigged the sails, trimmed them for reaching, and adjusted the steering gear. Satisfied with the trim, he unshipped his spectacles from his nose, stowed them in their case, and laid the yacht delicately over the boat's side, pointing her stem towards Cold Breath Bay.

" Now then, my beauty," he said. " Non-stop for the jetty, if you please. You can make it."

Taking his eyes with her, she drifted from under the lee of the dinghy, and instantly the wind, well channelled in this trough between the hills, swept into her sails, and she heeled over to screw into it, but her self-acting rudder worked, and, instead, she held her course and raced forward. Straight as an arrow, eager as a live thing, leaning over with a feminine archness from the rude male play of the wind, she cut through the spangled water, leaving an arrow-head wake behind to enlarge and enlarge in the sun.

" Gosh, she's a flyer ! " said Mr. Rostrum, watching.

Now, racing into mid-water, she felt the hardening wind but, like the perfect instrument she was, she converted the raw, crude energy into a clean and lovely motion and went scissoring towards the bay with a speed that was beyond anything (or so he liked to think) that she had achieved before.

" My God ! My hat ! " he exclaimed, hastily and clumsily shipping his oars to pursue her. " She travels ! She travels as never before ! She's doing five knots, every bit of it."

And he sculled excitedly after her. An unhandy oarsman, he had some difficulty in keeping up with her, and this pleased him, for he was as delighted to be defeated by her as a father would be delighted to be outpaced and surpassed by his son. But he pulled hard, because she must not foul the farther bank. And as he pulled, he thought, " A thousand times better, this, than doubling round the Model Yacht Pond to meet her on the other side." More than once, rough-handled by the wind, she tried to turn into it, and then he would shout at her desperately, " Hold it ! Hold it, my dear ! " and she held it ; she held her course ; and his pride soared into the upper air and into the sky. " My God, she's the best little craft ever."

He got himself abreast of her, to windward, and, sculling easily (for one improves quickly at this craft) kept pace with her and watched her. His body was in the dinghy, but nothing else of him : all the rest, heart and mind, was on her deck or in her sails or (anxiously sometimes) at the tiller. His whole conscious being was in her as an artist's in his picture, or a poet's in his lyric, when for once in a way the wind of inspiration really possesses him and the miracle is happening and he knows that he is creating something good. In these tense, exquisite, timeless moments Kilburn High Road did not exist for Mr. Rostrum, nor 25, Nunsbury Road, nor, it is to be feared, Mildred or Julian or Joanie or Brenda ; and, least of all, Dudley. Nothing existed but the grace of his yacht's motion and the swift and transient furrow that followed behind her. More real than himself or his children or his friends were the crew on the yacht—for there was a crew on board—a vaguely imagined but remarkably skilful crew—and the owner and skipper, who was a member of the Royal Thames Yacht Club and the Royal Yacht Squadron, Cowes. And as she ran triumphantly into the still water of Cold Breath Bay, having held her course all the way and beaten the record, there was a crowd to welcome her on the shore and music on board.

CHAPTER EIGHT

WHILE Mr. and Mrs. Rostrum were enjoying, for the first time in years, this holiday in a familiar country, Brenda had escaped, for the first time in her life, into a country that was wholly strange to her but quite as enchanting. No one was aware of this escape. In her reticence, her fear of failure, and her need to be sure of her triumph before she proclaimed it, she had told no one, in the family or outside of it, about Larry. Almost every evening before the family dispersed northward and southward she and Larry had met in the Underground train and walked along the High Road together and kissed in the church doorway before parting. Once or twice after supper they had snatched a meeting in Queen's Park and held each other under the trees. But she had not gone out for a whole evening with him, because she did not want to say anything about it to the family, and could not lie. " Wait till they've all gone," she said to Larry laughing. " There'll be plenty of time then. Only Julian'll be at home, and he'll ask no questions. He'll probably be out on the razzle himself."

She had been eager, breathless, for the holiday to begin, because she was now in love with Larry. He loved her, she believed, and her love had run out to meet his with open arms. She believed, and yet she dared not believe. Once in the church porch she had asked him if he really loved her ; and he had held her with both hands before him and, looking into her face with mischievous eyes, said, " What do you think, young woman ? "

" I don't see why you should," she had answered, gazing back into his eyes seriously.

" One reason might be that you're beautiful," he suggested.

" I'm not. I'm too big," demurred Brenda, who had no skill in this new game.

" Permit me, lady, to disagree. I thought you were rather beautiful the first time I saw you in the train. I think you are very beautiful now. You've got more and more beautiful these last few days. That's always the result of being loved."

Loved. He had said it, and she believed he had meant it. Believed, because she so needed to believe.

Probably she would have loved him for no other reason than that he loved her, but there were other things to swell the volume of her love : he was lively, witty, intelligent, interesting, and, with it all, so gentle. And so modest and frank. He was completely frank about being poor—and she was glad he was poor, because it made him seem easier to hold. He told her his whole life-story ; he seemed to like dwelling upon it, for he told it to her more than once and each time in almost identical words ; but that didn't matter at all, because she loved to hear it. They had been well off, he said, till his father died. His father had been the South of England Director of a large and famous firm of wholesale drapers, and they had lived, his father, his mother, his sister, and himself in quite a fine house in Bournemouth and owned a good car. But his father had died when he was fourteen, and his income had died with him. "That smashed up my future for me," said Larry. "That finished up my chance of going to Marlborough and Cambridge." His mother, a woman with plenty of vigour and go, had promptly put all the money available into starting a private hotel and, there being none left to spend on his education, she had apprenticed him to Beddington's, a firm of Outfitters, Drapers, and Furnishers, with a dozen shop-fronts in King Peter Street, Bournemouth. There he had worked as an assistant window-dresser. "But I was very unhappy in the job," he told her, his eyes averted and gazing into that unhappy past ; and after a silence he admitted that he found it hard to forgive his mother for having sentenced him, whom all pronounced ("if you don't mind my saying so ") to be a child of much promise, to such drudgery just for the sake of an extra ten shillings a week. "My father would never have allowed it if he'd been alive," said Larry. He went so far as to draw a likeness between himself and David Copperfield who, on the death of his mother, was sent, as Brenda would recall, to wash bottles in the dark warehouse of Murdstone and Grinby. Brooding on this likeness, he used much the same words to Brenda as David wrote for his readers. " A child of excellent abilities," wrote David, " and with strong powers of observation, quick, eager, delicate, and soon hurt bodily and mentally, it seems wonderful to me that nobody should have made any sign in my behalf. . . . No word can express what I suffered sometimes, when I felt all my hopes of growing up into a learned and distinguished man crushed, in my bosom." And thus, in words only a shade different, Larry to Brenda.

But there was a spirit in that unhappy child, he gave Brenda to understand. Young Larry Blythe had no intention of being smothered and stifled like that. He was not the sort you could easily suppress. He kept that job just as long as it suited him and no longer. All the time when he was working downstairs (like David Copperfield) distempering the back-drops and linings for the shop windows, his head was busy with his own ideas. He bided his time ; and, when the hour suited him, walked out of Beddington's and out of his mother's house. He told the old lady a few home truths in her bed-sitting-room and walked out. And like Dick Whittington and the other boys he set off for London. Risky ? Yes, but he didn't think he was the kind to fear risks. And he had never regretted it. He wasn't making much money yet (Larry was inclined to stress this) but he believed he was on the way to doing so ; and, anyhow, he was his own master ; he was not being ordered about by a lot of coves whose mental equipment, to put it frankly, he considered inferior to his own ; he could work when he liked and as he liked, and dress as he liked : he was nobody's drudge and, if he wasn't making much money yet, there was always the chance that he might make immense sums one day. He wasn't the sort who preferred a small steady wage and security to risk and adventure and the chance of a fortune. Arriving in London, he had gone straight to where the money was. And where was that ? Why, in Films, of course.

Larry was interesting about the world of the films, and Brenda could listen for hours to stories about an environment so much livelier, so much more amusing, so much more open and unfenced, than the fusty, straitened, pent-up world which was Kilburn. He admitted that at present he was only an " extra," but, then, he hadn't been at the game very long, and he was beginning to think—in fact, he had good reasons for thinking—that they'd got their eyes on him for something better. What exactly was an extra? Well, it was one who filled out the crowd scenes in a picture: he might be a guest at a Thé Dansant or a diplomat at an Embassy Reception or one of the young officers dancing on the quarter deck of a battleship. It was fun. But, mind you, you had to look the "officer type." They chose you because you were the officer or Foreign Office or University type. It was extraordinary—pathetic, really—some of the chaps you saw in the agents' offices who imagined they would do very well as naval officers or Austrian aristocrats or members of the old French nobility. The payment was a guinea a day—yes, it sounded good, but you had to pay ten per cent. of it away to your agent and of course you might not be required for the picture more than five or six times in half a dozen weeks. All producers were the same: they poured pounds and pounds away on flowers and fruit and furniture for their sets and tried to save money on the extras by paying them overtime instead of letting them do another day's work and earn another guinea. If you were lucky, you might be able to work on two pictures at once, but that wasn't always possible. Thus your income jumped up and down like the temperature of a patient in high fever, and you were lucky if it averaged out over a long period at more than two-pound-ten a week. He'd just picked up a pleasant two guineas from the Research Man who'd sent him off to do a spot of research work in the British Museum. The Research Man was a guy who hung about the studio and got bored, waiting to be told to go and find out something, and the other day, seeing Larry standing by the set, he'd offered him two guineas to breeze off and find out what sort of broadsheets they used in Charles the Second's time. That, by the way, was how he came to be in the Underground train on the celebrated, momentous, not to say fatal, occasion when he found himself sitting next to Brenda. The research work had given him an idea for a story outline of his own, which he was at work on now and going to submit to the producer. He had terrific hopes of it. And once get in with them as a script writer, and there was money to be picked up like buttercups and daisies.

All so open and honest and gay; and he was no less honest about the girls he'd been in love with; indeed, he gave them ample space in his zestful and voluble auto-biography. Brenda would rather he told her the truth about them, wouldn't she? But of course he couldn't really have been in love with them; he'd only imagined he was; to be quite honest, most of them had been more in love with him than he with them; but he was the type who was for ever seeking someone he could love properly—and here he squeezed Brenda's hand.

No one could argue better than Larry (not even Dudley) that what he had done, or what he wanted to do, was the only right thing. He would explain at length and with a persuasive laughter in his eyes that it was right—beyond question right. When he saw that his fine scene with his mother, that scene of spirited and splendid revolt, had provoked some doubts in Brenda, that it had not drawn quite the applause he expected, he was quick to deal with her hesitancies and to alter them. He was verbose in its justification. Unkind? Oh, no. It was kinder in the long run to let people know the truth of your thoughts. It was best for them to be brought up sharply against Reality. Didn't she see that? . . . Or it might be that Brenda would reveal some doubts, some scruples, some unexpressed anxiety, about the more ardent of his embraces. Did she think they were wrong? But why? Why? Why was she saying, "Don't darling," and "Not like that—*please*"? At what point did an embrace become wrong? If it was not wrong in a church porch, or sitting on a seat, why was it wrong lying under the trees? If he might stroke her cheek and press her waist, why might he not rest a palm upon her breast. If he might touch her lovely arm, why not her other limbs? Who was injured by it? It made him happy; it made her happy, didn't it? Well, then, where was there anything wrong in it?

Yes, it was a correct and agreeable picture that he drew of himself for Brenda's eyes. He liked it well and, had his intelligence not been as keen as it was, he might have believed in it. But all the time he knew it for an elegant composition in meretricious materials, and knew that this knowledge was a little focus of corruption in his character. Sometimes, when his intelligence and his decency met, he deplored the corruption. His father had not been the South of England Director of a famous firm but merely its traveller among the towns of the Southern counties. They had not lived in a large house but in a very small one. He had invented the fine house in Bournemouth to balance No. 25, Nunsbury Road. It was true that his father had driven a car, but Larry had avoided mentioning that it was less often occupied by the family than by samples of general drapery. There had never been any chance, or a single word said, about his going to Marlborough and Cambridge. There had been no question but that he went to a cheap private school in Bournemouth. Marlborough and Cambridge were latter-day garnishings of his own. At one time he had intended to say Eton and Oxford, but his artistry forbade it. It deleted Eton and Oxford. A feeling for moderation and restraint told him that the tale must not be over-written ; a desire for verisimilitude warned him that Eton, or even Harrow or Winchester, was a little too obvious ; a hunger for originality insisted that they'd been done too often before. Marlborough was more convincing. Who would say Marlborough unless it was the truth ? The same artistic conscience, the same avoidance of the cliché, had blue-pencilled Oxford and Balliol and substituted Gonville and Caius, Cambridge. There was enough of a poet in him to relish the music of Gonville and Caius.

His defiant departure from Beddington's he had pictured as the bright act of a bold, untameable Elizabethan spirit ; actually he had been a docile apprentice for several years, and it was not till he was twenty-two that the conviction descended upon him that he was too much the gentleman to be anyone's underling. Likewise the scene with his mother, before he walked out of her house and out of Bournemouth, had some points of difference from his dramatised version of it. It had been a very violent scene, and thoughts of kindness had not been in his mind as he spoke his lines. He had been quite unaware of any desire to do his mother good ; on the contrary he had been gripped by a strong desire to hurt her. He had told her that she had robbed him of his inheritance ; that she had appropriated for herself all the money his father had left and sent him out to work like a common board-school boy ; that he reckoned she owed him a third at least of his father's money ;

and that he had every intention of having it. He wanted a hundred pounds, he said, and he intended to have it while he looked for a suitable job in London. Either she gave it to him or he would consult lawyers as to whether she had misappropriated trust funds. She was so frightened of him —at one time, so fierce his eyes, so tight his fist, she thought he was going to hit her—and perhaps she was uneasy about her use of the money—that she gave him fifty pounds, which was twice as much as he expected. And with this in his pocket he had come to London, determined to have as little to do as possible, in the future, with the hotel in Bournemouth. He was rather ashamed that his mother should be running a hotel that was little better than a boarding house ; though he was glad she was making enough money to be independent of him. With Brenda he implied that the hotel was an establishment of some size. Finally, it was less than accurate to say that he had worked as a film extra for only a little while. He'd been doing it for fifteen months now, and in melancholy moments he would wonder if, like so many of the other extras, he would stay for ever in this crowd of the nameless and unsung.

And because he was earning, on the average, so little money, he was very well satisfied with Brenda as the easement for his immediate needs. In many ways she was lovable, unexpectedly lovable, and as entertainment she was certainly cheap ; almost, you might say, she was free. He could have his pleasure of her on the free seats in Queen's Park or on the free grass under the trees ; and soon, if all went well, in the free lodging which was her room. And she, having no previous experience of a man's generosity, was not in a position to draw comparisons. And now that, so obviously because of him, she was making herself as beautiful as possible, he really was getting no small pleasure from his embraces. The fact that no one else had approached her before him produced conflicting results : to one part of him it made her less desirable, but to another more so, because he found it an interesting adventure to be giving a girl these experiences for the first time, and one that appealed as well to something in him that was generous and liked to give.

The first night of Mr. and Mrs. Rostrum's holiday, at about half-past ten, when they, tired of their day on the hills and in the sun, had retired early to their bedroom in the farmhouse and fallen quickly asleep, Larry and Brenda, three hundred miles away, were walking home from the park ; and when they were some distance from Brenda's door, Larry stood and lingered with her, thinking his own thoughts, which he was too discreet and skilful to submit to her as early as this. She parted from him at last, and he stood watching her, as she slipped into her room by the basement door. After lingering a little longer he wandered back towards his own home.

The next evening, at about eight o'clock, when Mr. Rostrum had returned to his bedroom after supper to study again how far the sun on the lake had tanned his face, Larry was walking with Brenda, his arm around her waist, along the paths of the park and under a sky that was conveniently overcast.

" It's cold for June," he said.

" Yes. Poor Daddy and Mummy. I hope it's different weather up there."

" I wish we could go somewhere where we could sit in warmth and comfort and be really alone."

Brenda, guessing at once what was in his mind, and fearing it, did not answer.

" Is Julian out again to-night ? " he inquired after a pause.

" Yes."

" Well, couldn't I—couldn't we sit in your house ? "

" Oh, but—I don't know when he's coming back."

" Would it matter if he did come back ? "

" Oh, yes, I—you see, he knows nothing about you. I've never told him anything about you."

" No, what I meant was : need he know I'm there ? "

She looked up sideways at his face, frightened. " How do you mean ? "

" Couldn't I sit with you in your room ? "

Silence. She was seeing her room. If it had been merely

a sitting-room, this suggestion might not have troubled her, but she was seeing that old-fashioned bed of iron and brass and that old-fashioned Victorian dressing-table of chintz and muslin and that old brown chest of drawers. . . .

He smiled down at her; kindly, tolerant, amused.

"I wish I could ask you into our drawing-room, but——"

"But why not your own room? What's wrong with that? Isn't one room the same as another? If it's right to sit with me in the park, it's right to sit with me anywhere. And it's much more right where it's comfortable. You could lock the door, and even if Julian came back, he'd never hear us. I don't want to talk to you, my pet; I only want to hold you in my arms."

Still she did not answer, but he knew that this last sentence had breached her defences, old-fashioned as they were, and insecure.

"I know what you're thinking," he went on, with his amused and affectionate smile. "You're very sweet and silly, but I love you for it." And he squeezed her waist. "You ought to have lived fifty years ago. Nobody worries about that sort of thing now. Come along. We can be warm and happy and comfortable there."

A brief silence, and then Brenda said, "All right, darling, but I'll have to dash in and see if he's out."

"By all means. . . ." And, happy in her consent, he took her by the fingers and, gaily swinging her hand, led her towards her home. "Why have you never told them anything about me?"

"I don't know. Why doesn't one? Perhaps I will one day."

"I don't mind being a secret of yours. I rather like it." A sincere remark, for it suited him well that her old father and tall brother should be unaware of his approach. "I feel rather like a ghost—the ghost of someone who's not yet been allowed to live."

"You talk an awful lot of nonsense, my dear."

"I don't know that it's nonsense. It may be that one's reality is increased or diminished according to the number of people who know of one's existence. These are abstruse matters."

When they were near her house, she ran ahead and after a few moments returned. "It's all right," she whispered,

" there's no one in the house ; " and this time it was she who picked up his hand and led him towards her door. But as she did so, she looked up the road apprehensively, and across it, and up at the higher windows of her house, but the whole road seemed quiet and empty of eyes ; and a moment later she said defiantly. " I don't mind if anyone *is* looking. My life's my own.

" That's the spirit ! " he encouraged, as they went on.

Nevertheless it was very quickly that she led him through the gate and down the path to the door beneath the steps ; very quickly that she led him into her own room ; and very quietly that she shut its door. He heard her turn the key, though she had done it gently, as if ashamed that he should hear it.

Before he took her into his arms he walked around the room, looking at her pictures and books. He looked first at the large reproduction of El Greco's *Agony in the Garden*, with its distorted forms, melodramatic lighting, and tormented sky. He turned his eyes from this, for it was jarringly out of key with his thoughts and schemes ; and the eyes fell on her *prie-dieu* with its crucifix and vases and pile of black prayer books. They left this quickly too, for it was another discordant note, and travelled to the books on her white shelves. They rested particularly on the French poets. Théophile Gautier, Sainte Beuve, Baudelaire . . . Verlaine, Rimbaud, Laforgue. He took down *Les Fleurs du Mal* (the title promised well) and turned its pages.

> *Blanche fille aux cheveux roux,*
> *Dont la robe par ses trous*
> *Laisse voir la pauvreté*
> *Et la beauté. . . .*

" Crumbs ! " he exclaimed. " Can you translate this sort of thing ? "

" Oh, only after a fashion," she laughed ; and came at once to his side to display, if possible, her knowledge of French. And she translated for him, roughly, " White girl of the russet hair whose robe by its rents lets me see your poverty and your beauty. . . . For me, a lean poet, your youthful body, frail and full of freckles, has its sweetness. . . . "

"Well now, whad'you know?" he muttered. "Can you believe it? She speaks French like a native;" and he put the book back, impressed.

Her scholarship (for so it appeared to him), like the size of the house, and like her family's holiday in Westmorland, put a new desirableness into her body; and this desire was abetted by the words she had just read; so he snatched her sharply into her arms, and they stood there, breast to breast and mouth to mouth, for a long time. Then he sat her gently on the bed's edge and held and caressed and kissed her there. That she delighted in his kisses and did not want them to stop was explicit enough in the increasing passion of her response, and when he was sure that she was unable to resist him, he laid her gently upon the counterpane, and himself beside her.

"This is happiness," he whispered, drawing her close. "This is Paradise. This is the only perfect happiness to be found in this world."

"Yes," she answered in an even lower whisper. "I love you so. I love you as I never knew I could love anyone."

And they lay there together, unoffending, as they had lain beneath the trees. The sacred pictures on the walls watched this ready treason of Brenda's, and the highly sophisticated books on the shelves looked down upon her simplicity.

CHAPTER NINE

WHEN Mr. Rostrum returned from his holiday, he told Brenda and Julian and Dudley, and anyone else who would listen, that he'd never felt better in his life. He asserted this with enthusiasm, in part because it was nearly true, and in part because he wanted to think it. "I felt twenty-five before my holiday," he told the company at the breakfast table. "I feel eighteen now." The holiday had scattered like a covey of birds all the fears that his arches might be collapsing or osteoarthritis be settling in his members or one leg be getting shorter than the other. He had walked his ten miles over the hills on many a day, and once he had walked fifteen and called it twenty. He had eaten immoderately. The only pain that had troubled him during these vigorous days had been the faint niggling and stabbing in his breast after the excellent farmhouse meals. But this little ache had never been one which he had taken very seriously. It was not in a position which suggested aortic disease of the heart or congestion of the lungs; and he counted it no more than a tendency to indigestion which was always with him. He was, in fact, rather proud of his indigestion.

He had brought back on his face a fine coffee tan; and as this was a creation to which he had given much effort and time, he was anxious not to lose it, and on Thursday afternoons and Sundays he sat in his narrow garden, face to face with the sun; which was most uncomfortable, since it made it difficult for him to read his newspaper or his book, and toasted his eyelids behind his spectacles, but he continued in this posture because he hoped thereby to sustain the tan and even to nourish and deepen it.

Dudley was very well too after his holiday with the Trimmings. " Too well," Mr. Rostrum would sometimes lament. " He had quite enough vitality before. It was a mistake to send him to the sea. Children like that should be kept away from ozone." For long periods of the day Dudley would sing monotonously and unmusically but at the top of his pitch and power, and sometimes he could only give full expression to his *joie de vivre* by standing in the kitchen and emitting a continuous, high-pitched shout; not abating this fog-horn roar till his face was red with the strain of it and his eyes a-gleam as if the friction on his throat had raised a fire there. It tore Mildred's nerves and stirred in her a desperate apprehension about " the people upstairs ". Mr. Rostrum, his nerves in excellent condition after his holiday, only watched and smiled (as a rule), and Dudley, his eyes above empurpled cheeks perceiving that smile, would either prolong the performance or provide an instant encore. And Mr. Rostrum, as he stared at that super-abundant vitality issuing from his little boy like the super-heated steam from a locomotive, was thrilled by it. He sat and worshipped the mystery of incarnate and escaping Life.

" I'm liking him just now," he said. " I'm glad."

And the liking was mutual. Never did Dudley see him now, in a passage or on the stairs, without running after him and shouting, " Dad-eye, Dad-eye," whereat Mr. Rostrum decided that his vexation at this pursuit was a little less than his pleasure. Dudley never found the study door unlocked but he fumbled with the handle and came in and staged a clown's act for his father on carpet or easy chair ; and Mr. Rostrum, though he called in despair, " Mildred . . . Mildred . . . it's here again," was not at all sure that his gratification did not transcend, though only just, his despair. " He does love me so," he complained to Mildred when she came to fetch him away. " What in mercy's name am I to do ? " Sometimes the little boy, if he saw his father approaching, would rush to meet him and clasp him round the knees, and then Mr. Rostrum was quite certain that there was a small credit balance in this business of the production and possession of Dudley. " Yes, the profit is greater by a few points than the price," he told himself, " but thank God it can't happen again."

Sometimes, if Dudley saw his father walking away from him along the passage, he would run and thrust his round head between his father's legs and with his arms about his thighs run him towards his study door, Mr. Rostrum both liking it and hating it—and, occasionally, taken by surprise, swearing most damnably and doubting the credit balance. This was a trick, it seemed, that he had learned with Mr. Trimming—but Mr. Trimming was a young man, not yet thirty.

There were other occasions, of course, when the annoyance far exceeded the satisfaction. The young Trimmings were very genteel in their language and ways, and Dudley had learned to approve of this refinement and did not wish his father to fall short of it ; so he would now correct his phraseology much as Brenda was accustomed to do. " It's not a plug ; it's a lavatory chain," he would affirm ; and Mr. Rostrum, who had suffered quite enough of this kind of thing from Brenda, would bark, " Oh, don't *you* start now ! I don't want any corrections from *you*. As far as I'm concerned, it's a plug."

" It isn't. It's a lavatory chain," insisted Dudley.

" My dear child, do you really suppose the Trimmings know better than I do ? "

" Plug isn't a nice word."

It is. It's a beautiful word," declared Mr. Rostrum, getting angry. " Lavatory chain ! Whoever heard . . . ? "

" And, in any case," Brenda submitted, "etymologically a lavatory is a place where you wash, not where you——"

" Exactly," said Mr. Rostrum.

All keys, locks, bolts, and door handles were still of irresistible fascination to Dudley ; and, as likely as not, if he was let out of sight, he would rush into the study and turn or unturn the keys of his father's cupboards, till Mr. Rostrum, coming into the room and seeing a cupboard door ajar, or finding a lock jammed, shot up in flame like petrol fumes at the touch of a spark. Once, when Mr. Rostrum was trying to read in his chair, Dudley began fiddling with the key of his door from outside, and Mr. Rostrum, provoked beyond endurance, leapt up, ran to the door, flung it open and yelled to the experimenter outside, " You're *not* to break it, I tell you ! You're not to."

" I'm trying to not," explained Dudley reproachfully.

Another time, finding the key on the outside of the door, Dudley fumbled with it quietly so as not to enrage the lion within, and he had just managed to lock it when his interest was captured by something else, and he hurried towards this, not giving another thought to that locked door. In time Mr. Rostrum rose to go out and learned that he was a prisoner ; and this was one of the occasions when his pleasure in the little boy was hardly present in any perceptible degree. But the worst time of all was when Mr. Rostrum came into his room and saw Dudley twisting with some force the key of his photographic cupboard and heard him say, " Daddy, I'm afraid your lock's getting breaken." Mr. Rostrum rushed to the lock. It *was* broken. Dudley in these few seconds had broken it—and his father was almost glad that his worst fear was fulfilled and his worst temper justified. " Oh, my God ! " he cried to the household. " I can't go on like this. I can't go on. I shall go mad. Everything in my study's getting breaken—I mean, broken. It's heart-broking—oh, hell ! damn the child—it's heart-breaking, and I can't go on. This frightful baby. He's not only ruining my study, he's ruining my character. He's ruining *me*. I used to think I was fond of children. And once upon a time I was. Now I've learned that I dislike

them intensely. Do you hear? I dislike them intensely.
And it isn't just dislike: it's an eager, active hatred. The
lock's broken. He's broken it. Broken it."

§

Joanie was radiantly happy too in these sunny weeks of
July, and the ferment of her spirits was little less than
Dudley's. She was eighteen now; Stephen Emery had
passed the Finals of his B.Sc.; they were engaged; and
she wore a sapphire and diamond ring, and felt for it and
fingered it and looked at it a thousand times a day. Stephen
was getting a job as a junior designer in a firm of consulting
engineers, and though his earnings at first would be only
four pounds a week, they would rise quickly to eight, and
then he and Joanie would be married. She told this to
every assistant in her Library, every friend in the road, and
every friend who came to the door.

But it was Julian who introduced the greatest triumph
into the household at this bright and happy time. He rang
up his father in the shop one day, speaking from somewhere
in Chancery Lane, and told him that the results of the
Solicitors' Final were up in the vestibule of the Law Society's
Hall. "Yes, yes?" his father eagerly prodded.

"Well, believe it or not, Dad, I've passed with First
Class Honours."

"Say that again," said Mr. Rostrum, whose heart was
thumping as if he himself had just been awarded a Nobel
prize.

Julian said it again, and added that he had just rung up
his mother at home and Joanie at her Library and Brenda
at her ridiculous school, and that now he and all the lads
were going to adjourn to the Mitre to celebrate.

"Celebrate, of course," adjured Mr. Rostrum, trembling.
"And, my heavens, we'll celebrate this at home, old chap.
Look here: stand the lads a drink all round from me—anything they like; and listen, Julian, listen: a real bumper,
a double one, for the boys who've failed."

And he put down the receiver, conscious of an exultation
different from anything he had known in sixty years. It
is a fact that there were tears in his eyes. They subsided

quickly, and he ran from his "finishing room and office", where the telephone was placed, into the shop to tell Miss Fletcher at her reception desk. This done, he returned into the finishing room and rang up Mildred, still trembling; and while he waited for her to come to the burring telephone, he thought, "A fully qualified solicitor. 'My son who's a solicitor. . . .'" Having decanted his excitement into Mildred's ear, and received hers into his, he walked out of his shop, entered Truppy's next door, waited till Truppy had finished serving a young couple, and then said, "Well, young Truppy, I thought you'd like to know that Julian's passed his Finals with First Class Honours and is now a solicitor. Just heard." And Truppy said, "Well, I do congratulate you, Alec, old son. I feel as pleased as if it had happened to me;" and he called up the stairs to Mrs. Truepenny, who came hurrying down to hear the news. "You *must* be pleased," she said; and he answered, "Yes, it's times like these that more than justify all the years of trouble and expense that children cause you." And Truppy said, "He's a fine lad, our Julian;" and Mrs. Truppy added, "He's so nice-looking, I always think;" and Mr. Rostrum declared, as modestly as was possible, "Yes, I don't feel I need be ashamed of any of my productions."

From Truppy's he went out on to the pavement and walked along the High Road, hoping to meet other friends; and when he did meet them, he worked into their brief conversations, "My boy's doing well. I reckon he's got the ball at his feet now," and explained his reasons for this reckoning. And suddenly he saw something that must be done at once—why had he not seen it before?—and he hastened back to his finishing room and wrote the news to the Widow Leicester. He posted the letter at once and returned to the shop, calculating the hours it would take to reach her, and when she would be likely to tell Herbert of the British Museum. Then, though much work was awaiting him in his dark room—much developing, fixing, washing, and drying of negatives—he suddenly accepted the fact that his hand wouldn't touch it, and there was only one thing he wanted to do and must do. He left the shop to Miss Fletcher and went home to share his joy with Mildred.

Never had he walked faster between shop and home. He

ran down to the basement door and burst into the kitchen. Mildred was not there, and, after shouting for her, he learned that she was engaged on one of the most intimate tasks of a mother. Dudley had just decided that he could do some duty, and Mildred was lowering him on to his exclusive receptacle, a small sky-blue urn with a shield in front to annul any mishap that might result from a small boy's instability and unrest. At such times as these, when she had to return to the kitchen while he was held by duty to this exacting throne, she would let him sit in the middle of the doorway, so that the hinder half of him could be in the proper place and the front half in the passage, where he could establish communication with his mother in case of loneliness, sociability, or accidents.

When Mr. Rostrum came upon them, Mildred had just disposed him upon his cold blue vase in this *media via*.

" Well, old dear," began Mr. Rostrum. " Well, Mildred, my honey. Are we pleased or are we not ? "

" I think it's wonderful," said Mildred, straightening her back, her task done. " I can think of nothing else. There now, sit quiet, my pet one, and call me when you've——" she whispered the close of this sentence. " You're quite happy there, aren't you, my angel, my best ? *That's* right. He said he thought he'd passed, but he never gave us to understand that he'd done anything like this."

" He was keeping it quiet, I expect. He would. He's rather like me in that respect."

" It's so lovely. I keep remembering it as I get on with my work."

" So do I. Well, Dudley, old cock, you've got quite a distinguished brother. Did you know that ? "

" I want my lorry," said Dudley, completely self-centred on his seat.

" Daddy'll get you your lorry, I know," Mildred promised. " Get him his lorry, my dear. He likes to play with it while he's waiting, and I think it helps."

" O.K. There's nothing more to do now. He's a solicitor —d'you realize that ? He can be admitted any day now."

" Yes, isn't it wonderful ? "

" He should get a job as a managing clerk at about four hundred a year," explained Mr. Rostrum, raising his voice as he receded into the kitchen in search of the lorry. "Out of that, if he's clever "—Mr. Rostrum was now returning with the lorry, which he'd disentangled from a heap of toys —" he'll be able to save enough to buy himself a partnership. He could save a thousand, and a life insurance'd do the rest. Here you are, your Highness."

Dudley, from his lowly position, stretched up a hand to take the lorry. He liked to operate the lorry when he was seated upon this circular stool, because he could swivel himself, and sometimes the stool, round and round ; and for the first few minutes the lorry, in his fancy, was travelling along the High Road, when it went at a reasonable speed ; but later it became a vehicle on the children's roundabouts and so increased its velocity that there was some risk of the central pole of the roundabouts (which was Dudley) becoming displaced from its seating. He sang as he swivelled around and operated the lorry and awaited the main event. Dudley never forced nature.

"Heaven knows how much I spent on that boy, all told," said Mr. Rostrum, returning behind Mildred to the kitchen, "but it was worth it all to buy this moment. To-day I am justified. So are you for all your years of labour. We are both justified. 'Cast your bread upon the waters, and you shall find it after many days.' I've cast nearly all I've got on my children, but I must say it's coming back with interest." Mr. Rostrum was too full of his justification to trouble about his metaphors. He was following behind Mildred as she went from kitchen to larder and from larder to living-room, laying a light meal. "Extraordinary, isn't it, Mildred, that there's only one person in the world that one would like to see do better than oneself, and it's one's child. I'm a vain man, terribly vain, but I'd rather that Julian did well than that I did. I get a bigger kick out of it. Children may be a frightful curse sometimes, but there's no doubt they're a part of yourself, and the part that you really care about most. And, Mildred, I don't want to be coarse, but I do say, just between ourselves, that we must have been a good—well, how shall I put it ?—quite a good pair of progenitors. I mean, all the children are fine ; and Joanie's beautiful, everybody says so ; and Brenda's beautiful in her way too, and completely good ; and now it seems that

Julian's brilliant. Really brilliant. I mean, First Class is First Class : you can't get away from First Class. D'you realize, Mildred, to-day is a great day ; it is the end of something and the beginning of something ; to-day, as ever was, they are all provided for. At last they are all provided for. The job is done. We can sit back and take our ease. If I were to be called away to-morrow, I should go knowing that, at any rate, I'd completed my task as a father——"

" Mummy, Mummy ! Done some ! Done Big ! " Dudley proclaimed triumphantly.

And Mr. Rostrum remembered the existence of Dudley. Dudley would exact their labour and defence for another fifteen years at least, till they were both very old ; and it was unlikely that he himself would ever sit down for his final rest, his task laid by. Mildred ran at once to Dudley, and Mr. Rostrum was left with his pæan truncated and his jubilee in mid-air. Mildred always ran to Dudley on this call, because he was apt to get up and escape after a tedious session ; and before this escape she must attend to his toilet, which he resolutely declined to do. Mr. Rostrum, temporarily discarded in the living-room, heard the rendering of some perforated paper, and Mildred saying. " Stoop over, my blessing," and Dudley singing as he was purified.

§

The Family Celebration took place at the Grange Cinema, Kilburn High Road, and in its most expensive seats. This was no time to be thrifty with shillings. Before their arrival in the cinema they'd had a little dinner at Salvini's Restaurant, also in the High Road, Mildred having affirmed that if they wanted to give her a treat, they'd let her have a nice little meal somewhere that she hadn't cooked herself. The people upstairs had consented to watch over Dudley, who, by the way, was now sleeping again in his parents' room at the foot of the stairs, and Mildred, free for to-night from all household cares, had been able to give a long and secretly happy hour to arraying herself for the restaurant and the theatre. It was one of her keenest pleasures, though a private and unspoken one, to go out dressed up in her best, and she gave great pains at such times to her clothes, her hair, her face, and her hat. In the past she had always allowed herself a little powder, and to be sure her complexion, so shiny and brick-coloured now, needed it, but paint and lip-stick she had eschewed. In these last few weeks, however, Brenda having surprised them all by putting lip-stick on her lips, and putting it on quite brightly, Mildred had put a little quiet colour on her own ; and this evening, flurried by a sudden chorus of complaints in the hall that she was " taking all night about poshing herself up ", she put on a little too much, with the result that Julian, when she emerged from her room, fully dressed for the street, stared at her face and exclaimed, " My God, Daddy and Brenda and Joanie, this house is beginning to look like a brothel ; " which shocked Mr. Rostrum till he had adjusted himself to it, and drove Mildred back at a high speed to her dressing-table mirror to see if the matter was really as serious as that.

In the cinema Mr. Rostrum sat with Brenda and Mildred on the right of him and Joanie and Julian on the left. The chief picture proved to be a very affecting one, and it shook the whole family—except perhaps Julian, who sat back in the darkness and provided a cynical commentary for Joanie's ear. It always entertained him to spoil her film for her by a mutter of intermittent witticisms, dangerously loud. If everything was going awry for the lovers, as it usually did throughout the main body of the film, he would comfort her with the loud whisper, " It's all right, ducks ; don't worry ; they'll click in the end." If the heroine gave the hero a stinging slap on his cheek, as she always did once in the film, he muttered loud enough to be heard two rows away. " That's right. That means she's going to marry him. The point's settled. Is it worth sitting it out any longer ? " And Joanie would beg him to shut up, so that she might enjoy herself. To-night, as always, Joanie was much more demonstrative in her responses to this most moving and elevating film than the others of her family, though all of them were suffering. She screamed at alarming situations, gasped at unexpected ones, sighed like an escape of gas at disappointing ones, and let loose the loudest laugh in the house at farcical ones, flinging herself right forward in her seat ; and at such moments Julian, as he explained afterwards, leant away from her on the opposite arm of his chair, that no one might suppose he was in any way connected with her. Brenda was completely silent during the last pathetic sequences, because the swelling in her throat blocked all speech and sound. Once she managed to lean across her father and ask Julian, " What do you think of this ? " to which he replied, " Obscene ; " and she said, " Yes, I know, but . . ." and was in no condition to speak further. Mildred blew her nose as unobtrusively as possible, strove to control the quivering of her lips, and, when she was convinced that nobody was looking at her, knocked the moisture from her eye with a knuckle. Mr. Rostrum sat as upright as a statue and, so far as a man can be, was in a dreadful state.

CHAPTER TEN

THESE days of liveliness and content lasted for some weeks, but then a cloud came over one corner of the sun. In other words the beam that had rested on Brenda went out. Only her parents noticed it, but to them, to Mildred first and then to Mr. Rostrum, it was plain that her joking and laughter were forced, and that though she had not abandoned the painting of her face and the new dressing of her hair, she was attending to them carelessly and with little heart. She had always been prone to long silences, but surely she had never sunk into such silences as now. They did not dare to ask her why ; if they hadn't dared to comment on her silences, when she was happy, still less could they do it when she was sad. They didn't want to be snubbed. Not for a moment, or by any sign, did they let her guess that they were watching her. But in their bedroom, as they undressed for the night, they discussed her. Mildred at her dressing-table, letting down her grey thinning hair, asked, " What *is* the matter with her, Alec ; oh, what on earth is the matter ? I daren't say a word to her. I told her yesterday that she wasn't looking too well, and she nearly snapped my head off. And she *is* looking ill. Her face looks quite grey sometimes, and this morning I noticed a look like terror in her eyes. Oh, she might tell us what's worrying her. We only want to help her."

"It's quite simple to me," said Mr. Rostrum, tossing off his braces with an air of worldly wisdom. "She was in love with someone; that's certain. And now there's been a rift. They've probably parted. To a girl like our Brenda such a parting would seem like the end of the world, but it'll pass over."

"But why can't she tell us all about it like Joanie? Joanie always tells us everything. Joanie isn't happy unless she's sharing everything with us. But Brenda, no; never a word. Never a word to anyone."

"She and Joanie are as different as two peas," said Mr. Rostrum, getting his simile upset but not, perhaps, making it any the worse for that. "There's nothing wrong with Brenda. She's cast in a different mould, that's all. It's an heroic mould, and reticence and reserve are inevitable qualities of it. I've the utmost admiration for our Brenda. She's a much finer piece of work than I am."

"Well, I can't make the girl out sometimes. I give her up."

One evening Mr. Rostrum worked late in his study. He was sketching out the design for some pages of a store catalogue which was to be illustrated with his photographs. This was imaginative work in which he liked to think he excelled, and it held him as a canvas will hold a painter, or his first drafting of a play a dramatist. It was nearly midnight when he laid it by and crossed the passage to his bedroom. He didn't turn on the light, for Mildred was already in bed and, with her face to the wall, seemed asleep. He pulled up the blind a little way and undressed very quietly by the light of the lamp on the pavement. Before getting into bed he knelt at its side and commended all whom he loved to God. Then he slipped in beside Mildred and, turning his back upon her, drew his knees almost up to his chest and composed himself for sleep, with the bed-clothes half over his head. But that fascinating work was still alight in his brain, and he stayed wakeful. Everything in the house and street was quiet, for it was after midnight. He heard only a slow sighing in the trees and the constant and undulating murmur from the High Road. The only busy place, apart from that unsleeping High Road, was his brain. It formed and framed for him, and he lay considering them carefully, more and more original designs for successive pages of the catalogue. He turned the catalogue page by page. And suddenly he stopped thinking ; he stopped breathing ; he lowered the bed-clothes from his ear and listened.

Their bedroom, as has been told, was the front room on the right of the hall door ; that is to say it was immediately above Brenda's. Brenda's. Had he heard the sound of sobbing in Brenda's room ? Keeping his body still, he up-lifted his ear and strained to catch the sound again. And he thought he heard it—a low sobbing, fevered, impetuous, and past control. A few seconds of thought, and he slid from the bed—gently so as not to wake Mildred—found his slippers and dressing-gown, and tip-toed down the basement stairs. Hardly breathing, he stood outside Brenda's door. The door was firmly closed, but there was no doubt about the sobbing now ; that old-fashioned door, cheaply made for a basement room, was too shrunken and relaxed to im-prison the sound.

He waited, wondering, but at last he could endure the sound no longer. Pity, swelling intolerably, thrust his diffi-dence aside. He knocked tentatively on the door.

" Brenda ? "

Instantly a silence within that room, broken only once by a creak of the bed. A long silence, like the silence of death, as if no one were breathing in there.

Oh, well . . . perhaps he wasn't wanted . . . perhaps he'd only hurt her by going in. Softly he went up the stairs again, but at his bedroom door he stopped, hesitated, turned about, and went down again to Brenda's door. Again he listened. The same silence. An absolute silence.

He turned the handle and went in.

" Brenda ? "

She leapt up in bed, and sat up, either startled or feigning it. " Yes, Daddy ? "

" I thought I heard you crying."

" Crying ? . . . No. . . ."

This much had been by the light of the street lamp which shone through the bars of her window and the worn holland blind. Now he switched on the electric light, and he saw that her face was wrecked with tears and her eyes drenched and shining with them and her hair tossed like a mænad's.

133

He went to the side of the bed, sat there, and gathered her into his arms. "What is it, my Brenda?"

She dragged herself from him and flung her arm and her face upon the pillow.

Gently he laid his hand on her shoulder. "Tell me."

"Oh, I can't. I can't."

"You must tell me everything." Very gently he turned her round so that her eyes were looking up at him. And he knew that a moment ago they had been full of terror and that she could hardly hide the terror now.

"Come," he said, and he drew her up again and held her against him, very tightly, like a lover. He felt like a lover, and his love caused him to use, unwittingly, an endearment that he had never dared to use before. It was a phrase that Mildred used often with Dudley, and he was driven to echo it because these were the only words full enough and strong enough to give expression to his love. "Tell me everything, my lovely one."

This time she did not drag herself away but just held him closely and passionately, breathing heavily against him. Not for years had he found a wisdom to get through her palisade of silence, but now the simplicity of an outrushing and overwhelming love had broken it down.

"You're cold," he said and, tenderly disengaging himself, he found her slippers and put her feet into them, and took down her dressing-gown, and wrapped it about her shoulders. "Listen. You're going to tell me everything, and I'm not going to tell anyone else in the world if you don't want me to. Now look. It's cold here; put the dressing-gown on properly—there: tighten it up—and we'll go into the living-room where we'll be warm and comfortable, and no one in the world can hear us. Come, my pet."

Taking her fingers, he led her across the cold passage into the living-room and shut the door. He placed her in his own easy chair, smoothing the cushions for her; he switched on the portable electric stove and turned it towards her feet; then sat on the edge of a hard dining chair, close beside her, and, picking up her hand, said, "Now, there's nothing in the world you need be afraid to tell me. I'm with you in everything. I'm on your side in everything. Everything I have in the world is yours."

CHAPTER EIGHT

LARRY had come many times to Brenda's room in those holiday weeks when Julian was out with his friends ; and they had lain together as quietly and innocently as two lovers in the grass of an open common, when it is summer, and daylight, and people are abroad. He had longed for more than this, but had had neither the crudity nor the courage to tell her of his desire. Larry was feeling a real tenderness for Brenda at this time, and a real gratitude ; and because of these he was feeling also a little shame that he was not doing more for her and giving her more. To express the gratitude and relieve the shame he brought her more than once a little offering of flowers. One day it was a bunch of sweet peas, another day a sheaf of antirrhinums or a half-dozen of young red roses. And Brenda's " Oh, thank you. Oh, it *is* sweet of you. You really are an angel " was but a poor, inarticulate manifestation of what these flowers meant to her—she who had never received such attentions before. She would spread them about her room and then take Larry silently into her arms to say a better thank-you that way. And they were a joy to her in the morning when she awoke, and throughout the day whenever her eyes fell upon them.

And so the first half of the holiday passed, and the day drew nearer when the family would return and the house be closed to Larry and Brenda. Then it was that Larry, stuttering, blushing a little, and laughing to pretend that he wasn't, put a new suggestion before her. He had been lying beside her on the bed, and he rose upon an arm and looked down upon her. It was less than twilight in the room—almost dark—for night was nearly down in the road outside, and the street lamp was lit, and that was the only illumination visiting the room. As if to match his voice to this deep gloaming and perhaps as if a softness and lowness best suited his words, Larry spoke in a whisper.

" Brenda darling, we've so little time left, and I want to be with you as much as I can. Couldn't I come to you sometimes *after* Julian has returned and gone to bed ? "

"What?" Brenda looked up at him, her eyes startled and uneasy. "How do you mean? . . . I don't see. . . ."

"I mean just this, my sweet: you say he gets back from his dissipations about eleven o'clock. Well, couldn't I come to you, say, between eleven and twelve? Just for a little while. We've had such lovely times together, and we've only a few days left."

"Oh, no . . ." she stammered. "I don't think that would be possible. . . . Oh, no . . ."

"But why not?" His eyes smiled down on her tolerantly. His words were merry and fluent. "If it's all right from eight to ten, it's all right from eleven to twelve. If it's all right when Julian's out in the street, it's all right when he's in his room upstairs. What on earth has a clock to do with the rightness and wrongness of things? And what on earth has the geographical position of Julian to do with it? Our loving each other like this is either right or it isn't. Julian's nearness makes it no better or no worse. It's irrelevant—like the clock. I only mean for an hour or so, my silly but rather dear little prude. I'd go when you told me. You're safe with me, you know that, don't you?"

Silence.

"You trust me, Brenda, don't you?"

"Of course."

"And you like me to be with you?"

"You know I do."

"Well?" He arched his eyebrows to indicate an amused bewilderment. "Well, what's the difficulty?"

"Julian might hear us."

"Oh, no, no. That little argument won't do, my sweet. That little cock won't fight. Julian's room is too far away; he never comes to your room, you say; and if we spoke only in whispers, how on earth could he hear anything? Besides, I don't want to speak; I only want to hold you in my arms. I'd wait till you left some sign in your window that he was safely in bed and the coast was clear. Then I'd slip in by our own private door, and we'd have another hour or two of happiness. You said it was happiness. Let's seize all the happiness we can, while we may."

Brenda lay beneath his smiling, tolerant gaze and looked up at him. Yes, it had been such a happiness, such an unbelievable happiness, that like a drug which one had taken many times it was now beyond her power to reject it. And with this eager thirst went a fear lest she offended him and lost him ; and these two together forced her to answer after a while, and not without a defiance of herself and everyone else, " All right, Larry. . . . Yes, if you like. . . . Just for a little while . . . sometimes. . . ."

And so that same night he loitered for an hour in Kilburn High Road, coming often to the corner of Nunsbury Road and looking down it ; and soon after a church clock had chimed the first quarter between eleven and twelve, he strode quickly past her house, but there was nothing in her window ; so he walked the length of the road and turned round and came back, and this second time saw by the light of the street lamp a bowl of his flowers, sweet peas, carnations, and blown red roses, standing on the window sill beneath the bars. One quick glance up and down the dark road, and he turned in at her gate and walked down the path to the basement door. It was latched, but unlocked. He stole into the dark passage, and there was her door. It was latched, but unlocked.

Having yielded this first time, Brenda was not able to resist any more. He came every night. At first he did not stay long. After an hour or two she would insist that he must go ; and he accepted her command with a long fare-well kiss and went. But as the time drew near when the family would be home again and on guard around her room, he remained longer, loth to leave her, and she loth to lose him. And all these nights Julian slept easily above, unaware that there was a stranger in the house, lying in his sister's arms. When there were but three nights before the family returned and garrisoned the house again, she let him stay till the dawn was in the street beyond the blind. She had been unable to tell him to go. The words would not get past her desire to hold him. In these latter nights they had adventured far among the tender licences of love, even trespassing on the borders of the last licence of all, but always halting there. And they halted there till it was their last night together, and then, because of the iron barrier that was about to fall, because this seemed their last chance and it was passing away with every chime of the church clock, she did not, because she could not, withstand him. Her desires long repressed, her craving for knowledge and the fullness of experience, her thought that this perhaps was the only opportunity that would ever be hers—these were enough ; they carried her whither they would. She took her chance and when it was all over, when Larry had kissed her gratefully and slipped away, she could feel nothing but a sense of buoyancy and deliverance. Shattered by exultation and peace, she fell easily and at once into sleep. The heart had outworn the breast ; it must pause to breathe, and love itself have rest.

§

There were doubts and questionings in Brenda's mind the next day, but there was more of triumph and of the sweet peace of healing. Larry, secretly ashamed of his part, had surrounded it with words of passionate love, and when he was whispering his good-bye, he had tried to bury the deed beneath passionate kisses and to conceal behind the same kisses that he was weary and ashamed and anxious to escape into the street. And all this day as she taught in her school or sat alone at her meals or welcomed the family home Brenda was recalling those words and those kisses and believing in his love. The belief swelled her own love into something that was a kind of recurring and rhythmic ecstasy.

And Larry, feeling both gratitude and guilt, both a new tenderness and a new shame, brought her a gift of roses, larger and dearer blooms than any he had brought before, and twice as many of them ; and because, after an effusion of thanks, she said that she must put them in her class-room since she dared not display them at home, he brought her the next night a large, a too large, box of chocolates which had cost him, in his own rueful phrase to himself, the Earth. These gifts coming after his passionate words on that night of climax reinforced and enlarged her belief, and therefore her love and her exultation. Her fervour now began to frighten Larry, but he hid his recoil for her sake, and so it was that in the first weeks after the family's return she seemed as happy and high-spirited as the others and had the light and colour on her face that of late had so changed and beautified it.

And then, darkening a whole landscape that a moment ago was under the sun, came the fear. This fear had threatened her from the first, but she had thrust it aside; now it sprang up and quickly covered the sky. It was the time to suspect, and she suspected that she was pregnant.

There was no one to whom she could speak of this except Larry; and all that day when the fear first attacked her, she was impatient for the hour when they would meet. And in the evening she hurried over the pavements, between the faded but respectable homes of her neighbours, carrying her burden to their place of meeting in Queen's Park. And walking round and round the paths of the park, which make a huge figure of eight about the flower beds and the grass plots, she told him.

His alarm, at first shock, was almost as great as hers, though he did not let her see this. And in the next second he refused to believe in her alarm. He refused to believe in it because he dared not. He wanted to be happy, and this contaminated the whole of his happiness. "Oh, no, no, my dear. A false alarm. Almost certainly a false alarm. It's much too early to know anything yet. I don't mind betting what you like that you'll be laughing at this fear in a day or two. So come along; be happy; forget it. It's nothing."

"Oh, do you think so?"

"Yes, yes; forget it."

But she didn't forget it; nor did he; and it was a poor, dull evening they spent together, their talk forced and uneasy, their embraces formal and weighted with care, their affection feigned. And when they parted at a little distance from her house, Larry walked all the way home, because he wanted to be alone in the night with his fear. And the fear, walking with him, became an ever more hateful companion. If it was as she suspected—and it might be—then what? Her father? What was her father like? Her brother? That brother, Julian, whom he had never seen, but who night after night had been above them, somewhere in his room. Always the shadow of Julian, twenty-two and tall, had disquieted him more than any other, and more than he in his vanity liked to allow. Would they insist that he married her? God, no! He wasn't going to do that. And because there was this danger of her being forced upon him as a wife, all the tenderness and gratitude that he had felt for her in these last days drained immediately away. She had been pale and drawn to-night, and when she looked like that she was without beauty, and all desire for her died within him. More, it changed to a recoil. And now, determined not to have her forced upon him, he asserted this recoil with the harshest words he could find : " Drab . . . dowd . . . drab . . . dowd. . . ." No, thank you. He was not going to be linked for life to *that*. They couldn't make him take her, and he just wouldn't. After all, it was her fault as much as his, and he wasn't going to pay that price. " My God, if it only comes all right, I'll never take such a risk again. Yes, I think I'm glad it's happened—if it comes all right —because I know now what the price is. I don't want to go through this again. Like hell I don't. If only it would come all right, and I could be happy again as I was this morning ! "

He walked fast, as if his thoughts were riding him hard. And so he went on for some time. Then suddenly he began going slowly, and more slowly, as if the thoughts were reining him in. He was seeing something that he could do ; something that would make it all right, no matter what happened, so that he could, after all, be happy again. *It was only a matter of money.* If Brenda's fear was justified, well, somehow or other, he'd raise the money. Yes, he would be glad to do this for her ; to pay all the costs and look after her while the thing was being done ; he would feel generous, protective, and faithful—a man who admitted his obligations and honoured them ; and he would much rather feel like that than feel a cad. He would much rather be kind to Brenda than hurt her. Yes, everything would come all right, and he was feeling decent again instead of rather rotten, and glad to perceive that he so much preferred the feeling of decency to the feeling of rottenness : it showed that he was fundamentally a man of honour with a revulsion from caddishness ; and he walked the rest of the way in good heart. Everything was solved, and his step was speedy again because of the relief.

§

And next day he was quite eager to hear her news and to tell her of his happy decision and to stand before her as a man of the world who knew what to do in this matter and was ready to do his part honourably. By eight o'clock he was loitering at the corner of Salisbury Road in sight of the entrance to Queen's Park. But while he might be eager to talk to her, he could not feel, he could not make himself feel, any desire for her embrace or for the touch of her body against his; rather did he feel a distaste for it. Unreasonably, as he saw, but very surely notwithstanding, he felt angry with her for what had happened. He was angry with her because there was this danger that she might become a source of exasperation and discomfort to him. One was but human and, so far from loving that which frayed one's heart and nerves, one ran from the sight of it.

They met at the corner of the road and kissed, and he recoiled from her touch, though he did his best to save her from knowing this. And as they wandered along towards the tall, massed trees of the park and the lichgate entrance beneath them, he could not, for the life of him, avoid leaving a space between himself and her. They came nearer the entrance, and the irrational notion seized him that he must tell her his decision before they passed between the pillars of the lichgate " or everything would go wrong." If he spoke now, on the other hand, before the trees and the grass claimed them, " everything would be all right." So he spoke hurriedly, before it was too late : he told her that she mustn't worry in the least ; that he'd been thinking the matter over and saw exactly what to do if her fears were proved right ; and that she could be sure he'd make it his business to see that everything necessary was done and to care for her and help her through it all. And when she asked what he meant, as they were passing under the lichgate into the green light of the park, he expounded the situation fluently and with little pause, partly because he didn't want her to speak as yet, partly because he was covering his un-ease with talk, and partly because he enjoyed appearing worldly-wide and well-informed—though, behind the confident and copious words, he knew that in this hitherto unvisited and misty zone he was, in fact, little less than blind.

Brenda listened, sometimes turning up her face and looking at his in a way that discomposed and annoyed him. But she did not answer. She walked at his side without a word.

Was she sulking? If so, then, by God, he really felt angry
with her. That she might be justified in some displeasure
didn't lessen his anger at all. Sulkiness invited sulkiness.
"Why don't you talk? Why don't you say something?
It's not very cheerful for me."

Since he had asked her to speak, she spoke. Never would
she forget, she thought, this clear, bright evening in this
urban garden when her heart was a throbbing pulse of fear
and pain. On one side of her stood the summer-weighted
trees, the chestnuts, planes, and lindens, impressed together
and crowned with light since the sun was low; and on the
other the carpet of trim grass around a broken pattern of
flower beds, each bed a jubilation in colour among the
extending shadows. Here, as they walked, was a bed of
fiery red cannas, blue lobelia, and white alyssum; now
one of salmon-pink dahlias, mauve-pink dahlias, and tall,
scarlet pentstemon; now a low forest of fuchsia and helio-
trope; and now a long bed of blown and fallen roses.
Lovers, untroubled, sat entwined on the seats or lay together
on the grass; birds were chirping and whispering in the
flushed evening light; and over all was a sea-blue dome
mapped with continents of white cloud.

"I couldn't do what you're suggesting," she said. "I
couldn't."

"But why ever not? You'd have to——"

"I couldn't. Do you suppose the idea hasn't occurred to
me a hundred times in the last day or two? And I've only
to consider it to know that I could never do it. I just
couldn't and wouldn't."

"You mean that, if things are as you imagine, you'll make
no attempt to stop them?"

Brenda nodded once and nodded again; then kept her eyes
on the passing flowers. "I've thought it out, and I couldn't."

"You mean you'd go on with it and have the baby?"

"I should have to."

"Why?"

"Oh, I've just told you, Larry. Because I couldn't do
the other thing."

"But good lord——"

"Oh, no, *no*," interrupted Brenda, as she considered the
idea again. "There are some things one cannot do."

"I don't see that," he objected sullenly; and as usual he began to justify with many words the rightness of what he wanted to do. If it was right to prevent a birth immediately *before*, it was right immediately *afterwards*. Where was the difference? It was just sentimental to pretend there was any difference. What *was* the difference? Would she tell him, please?

"I don't know. I can't argue it, Larry, but to me it's not the same thing. It's just *not*. I know that if I were to do it, I should go to pieces. I could never go to church again. I could never say a prayer again. I could never tell a soul what I'd done, and because I could never speak of it, I should be haunted by it for ever. I know myself, and I know that I should be completely lost and rudderless."

"But that's nonsense. That's absolute nonsense." And no doubt it looked so to him.

"It may be nonsense, but it's me."

Larry walked on, staring before him; and the space between them widened. "I think that's just foolish . . . and rather feeble."

"It may be, Larry. I daresay I'm not being very wise about this, but I'm still only a girl. I've tried to be wise about it. I've thought and thought and thought, and the only thing that has become quite clear to me is that I could never do that. I could never end a life that has begun. Is it so silly? I love you, Larry . . . I love you only . . . but I couldn't do that, even for you."

"I can't understand it. You pretend to be so mighty intellectual and sophisticated and modern, and you talk such completely irrational, sentimental, taboo-ridden stuff. Your intellectuality's all a pose. Good God, surely the thing's simple enough, if you turn your intelligence on to it instead of an emotion that's merely a vestigial relic from some age and an environment that no longer exist: if it's right to control reproduction a minute before conception, it's right a month after. Obviously."

"I think I can imagine cases where it might be justified, but I can't believe, I really can't, Larry, that it'd be right to do it just to save you from worry and expense and myself from some shame."

"Well . . . I don't know. . . ." There was an empty

cigarette carton on the path, and he kicked it on to the grass. " I think it's all rather selfish. You're ready to make colossal trouble for yourself, for the kid, and for me."

At the word " selfish " her whole mood changed. There was always, deep down in Brenda, a powder-barrel of defiance, and the word was like a match laid against it. The fire appeared in her cheeks, and in her eyes as she swung them up to him. " I'm not going to commit murder to save you a little trouble," she said.

Her anger fired his. It brought his lips tight together. He told himself that he didn't like defiance from her at all. Not at all. And he wasn't taking any—he who had given her love when no one else would look at her. And a love that other girls would have envied her. " All right," he began. " All right . . ." but even in his anger he hesitated before saying the next words—hesitated till the thought came that she might be hoping by this refusal to force him to marry her, and then the words said themselves. " All right, my——" he had been about to say, " my dear " but found he could not—" but I think I ought to say—I think I ought to make it quite clear—that there's no possibility of my marrying you."

She stopped in the path. She looked at his face in that way that frightened him. He stopped too, looking at her. Then she walked on again and he with her. She spoke first. " I haven't asked you to marry me."

" No but——"

" I wouldn't in any circumstances marry you. I wouldn't do it in a thousand years."

" I only thought we ought to get things quite clear. You've said something very final, and I think I ought to do so too. It would be quite impossible. I have no money."

" Will you understand that the last thing I want is to marry you ? Please ! " She stopped and beat her foot on the path. " *Please !* "

" Very well. Only don't stand here and make a scene. People will see us. Come along, do."

They walked on again, in a charged and hostile silence. And before the silence was broken they walked past the place where they used to lie on the grass together, beneath the spread of a willow and a plane. There, in that narrow place under the lee of a shrubbery of sycamore and thorn, Brenda, lying face to face and breast to breast with him, had met for the first time an absolute of happiness. Each saw the place and pretended not to see it, as they passed it by and left it behind. Then, with eyes gazing hopelessly ahead of her, Brenda said, " Do you imagine I'd let anyone marry me who didn't love me and want me ? I'd die first."

" It's not a question of love."

' It certainly isn't." And she laughed rather loudly, for she meant something different from him. " We needn't talk about love any more, thank God, either yours or mine or any one else's."

" What do you mean by that ? "

" I mean that I'm seeing things clearly for the first time. Oh, I'm seeing what a fool I've been—what an utter, idiotic, mad fool."

" In what way, please ? "

" In believing a lot of fluent lies just because I so longed to."

" And I am the liar, I suppose ? "

" Oh, yes. Don't have two doubts about that. I wouldn't want you to think I wasn't quite clear about that. I was deluded at first but not at the end. Not now. I'm seeing you now exactly as you are. And oh, my God, my God, it's not pleasant ; it's not pleasant to wake up from a completely idiotic but completely lovely dream and see that there was nothing in it at all—nothing in what I imagined you felt for me, and nothing—certainly nothing—in what I imagined I felt for you. I didn't know anything could hurt so much."

" I don't want to hurt you. I've never wanted to hurt you."

" It's like coming back from drowning. I've always heard that it was agony to be saved from drowning and brought back to life, and I suppose it's rather like this. It's an extraordinary thing to love somebody one moment and to have lost it all—utterly—the next. I can't grasp it." She looked up at the sky and at the tranquil beauty of the evening, and wondered that it could insult her suffering so. " I loved you a moment ago, I loved you better than anything else in the world—only a moment ago—and now I don't even like you. I don't, Larry. I only dislike and despise you."

" Despise ? "

" No, it's not like coming to life ; it's like dying ; it's like waking up on the other side of death."

" You say you despise me ? "

" Yes. Strange, isn't it ? I can't feel any love at all. I'd much rather, but I can't. I don't care the least thing about you. You were a tremendous joy to me, a joy that was almost too much to bear, and now you're only an irritation and a pain. I don't feel that I should care if I never saw you again. I don't think I *want* to see you again. It's so extraordinary ; it's a terrible experience ; it's like being in hell. I can't quite get my bearings."

" I don't really see why you should despise me."

" No. You don't." Her words, like his, were saying themselves now. From brow to breast her skin was flushed, and any dignity which she had shown was being burned up in her anger. Like her mother, when the woman in the shop made an attack upon Dudley, she was ready, should he provoke her with one more word, to shout abuse at him in the voice of a fury and in the hearing of all. " You don't, and it's because you don't that you're despicable."

" Hell and the devil ! Look here, Brenda. It's not good enough, being talked to like this. I don't care for it."

" Don't you really ? Well, I can't say that that distresses me frightfully. It wasn't designed as a sweetmeat."

" But, good lord, it's no good putting all the blame for what's happened on me."

" Oh, my heavens, what've I been doing all this time but putting the blame on myself ? What else have I been saying ? Haven't I been saying that I've been a fool, a blind fool, to let myself love and trust a contemptible little trifler and liar ? "

" God and Christ, I'm not staying here to be insulted like this." He stood still in the path. " I just won't. Some time when you're behaving less like a child, we can talk seriously." And he turned sharply and walked from her.

Then it was that Brenda, her breast a furnace of wrath, defiance and despair, cried after him in a loud voice laden with tears—cried like a fury in the hearing of all, so that the people paused in their walking and the lovers lifted their faces from each other's lips : " Go. Go, if you like. And don't think I care if I never see you again. I *told* you I didn't just now. Good-bye. Good-bye. I'm going home. . . . home. . . ."

§

Larry hurried away along the path, his head dark and hot with resentment. And yet within the dark resentment there was a faint, diffused light like the grey halation at a tunnel's end. It spread as he looked at it, hurrying on. Look, did not this quarrel justify him in flight and escape ? Again and again in the last twenty-four hours he had been visited by the thought that if he considered only himself, the best thing to do would be to disappear for ever from Brenda's sight. To run somewhere beyond the reach of those shadows, her old father and tall young brother. Very pleasant looked the freedom, the old unworried freedom, yesterday's easy happiness, which then would be his again. That freedom and happiness beckoned like a paradise after a day or two in purgatory. And quickly came the arguments that excused his escape. If she flatly refused to do anything sensible, then there was nothing more he could do or say : it was *her* funeral. He'd made his offer, and she'd scorned it ; she'd turned it down finally. There was nothing else he was ready to do ; there was no advance on that offer ; the sin had been hers as well as his, and he certainly wasn't going to pay for it with a life-time of punishment ; his had been a good offer, and a fair offer, and she'd rejected it, and the negotiations were at an end. He wasn't coming back to be scorned and insulted. Not on your life ; that sort of thing wasn't in his line at all. She'd said she didn't want to see him again ; she'd shouted it after him like a street-walker in a slum ; and by the Lord in His heaven, she needn't see him again. She shouldn't. He wouldn't offend her with his presence at all. He was going. Yes, he was going. It would be easy enough to go. There was no need to live in his present lodging ; he was his own master and could leave it to-morrow. He'd disappear into some other part of London. Not *out* of London—oh, no, he wasn't going to be driven off his course by her whom he was beginning to believe he hated. A big place, London. The greatest and most

difficult maze in the world. Let him but disappear into some
other part of it, and would she or her family ever find him?
If they did, well, he could just deny it all. Say it was an
effort to foist a paternity on him. Swear this, if necessary, in
a court of law. And, for all he knew, perhaps it *was* that.
Perhaps he was not the only one who'd gone in by that
basement door. A girl who was such easy fruit, a girl who'd
yielded in a matter of days, a girl who'd just snatched and
devoured him—how was he to know that he was responsible
for her condition. Yes, think of that. Or perhaps the whole
thing was an invented story, a trick to jump him into marriage. It was a trick they often played. But not on him.

Wrathfully, sullenly, and pleased to be wrathful and
sullen, he walked out of the darkening park into the quiet
and silent streets on its western side, the side most remote
from Kilburn. And the great city absorbed him. Neither
Kilburn nor its neighbourhood saw him again.

CHAPTER TWELVE

LEANING forward in his chair and holding Brenda's hand, Mr.
Rostrum encouraged her to speak. " What is it, Bren? "

" You won't tell Mummy? Or anyone? "

" No one." And though he was suffering because Brenda
was suffering, her readiness to tell him and no one else in
the world was a small spring of pleasure. " No one ever."

Her eyes, large with anguish, were fixed upon his. " I
don't know how to tell you."

" Is it something you're ashamed of? "

" Yes . . . yes, of course. . . ."

" Well, I shan't blame you for anything. I made too
many mistakes myself when I was young." He paused,
patted her hand, and added, " And committed too many
sins."

And while he waited for her to speak, he wondered what
is could be of which she was ashamed. His mind, leaping
from guess to guess, even touched, without believing it, the
idea that she might have misappropriated some money entrusted to her by the school. Mr. Rostrum's moralism was

as intense as Brenda's, but so completely was it crowded into a corner now by the love he was feeling for her and the love he felt for the picture of himself as her father and rescuer, that he could almost wish she had stolen hundreds and hundreds, since it would enable him to say, " Everything I've got is yours. Why have you been worrying ? " His pity was real enough to be full of her pain, but with it dwelt a pleasure in being a man of power to-night and a man of means.

" Tell me. I don't mind what it is Brenda, darling. I'm just longing to do what I can to help. And I don't believe that there's much you can tell me which I can't put right for you."

" Oh, but there is."

He shook his head and smiled his dissent.

" I fell in love a little while ago, Daddy."

" I know. I guessed that."

She told him all that it was easy to tell. And because she was proud of the fact that someone had been attracted by her and sought her out and wanted to kiss her, it was easy to tell of the meetings in the train, the walks together, the embraces in the church porch, and the evenings of love in the park. He too was proud that someone had admired his daughter and wanted her.

" And you never told us anything about this," he chided her, banteringly. " Why not ? I should have so loved to know."

" Oh, I was silly : I didn't want to boast of it till I was sure that he really loved me, and nothing would go wrong. I didn't want to be pitied if anything went wrong. Everything about Joanie's love affair was going right. Oh, I'm so glad now that I didn't speak of it to a soul."

" It has gone wrong, has it ? "

To this she gave no immediate answer. Keeping her eyes on a far corner of the room, she began, " I got to love him a lot . . ." and then, feeling that this was less than the truth, she changed it to, " I let myself love him terribly. He could be very sweet, and it was so wonderful to have someone in love with one at last. And then you went on your holiday . . ." She paused, and Mr. Rostrum waited ; and then slowly she told him how Larry had come to her room, at first when Julian was out, and afterwards when he was upstairs and asleep. "I didn't like to refuse him, I so wanted him to love me, and I was afraid I might lose him. And the night before you came home—oh, it was as much my fault as his—but it seemed my last chance, Daddy . . . and I persuaded myself that if I really loved him, I must . . . I ought to. . . ."

He patted her hand. "I understand."

"Oh Daddy, do you think I'm very awful?"

Smiling, he shook his head. It was not the shock it might have been, because, before she in her hesitancy could arrive at this climax of her story, he had got there himself and was waiting with his answer. It was a quiet and confident answer and strangely different from the answer he must have given, an hour since, about another girl. But this was Brenda, and because he had filled up with love for her, he had filled up also with wisdom. "No, my dear, it's so easy to understand."

"But I don't want to lie. I don't want you to think I did it only out of love. It was more for my own sake that I did it—yes, I know it was—more for my own sake than for his."

"Very well, dear. Even so, I understand perfectly."

"You don't blame me terribly, then?"

"I can't."

"But, Daddy . . ." and now she told him what she feared, and why. And he only nodded in understanding, allowing no hint of dismay to appear on his face or sound in his voice. "I see. And Larry?"

"He has disappeared."

At this point his lips came sharply together. Taken unprepared, he let shock and anger be seen. "Oh, he has, has he?"

"I told him about it, and when I wouldn't do what he wanted, he just disappeared."

"Oh, he did? He disappeared. I see." His grasp of her hand had slightly relaxed and this was a symptom that he was losing his grasp upon wisdom. He was just an ordinary man now and creating for himself a fine part to play—the part of the father with the whip. By heaven, yes! There was not only the treatment of his daughter to avenge but the treatment of himself. This young Larry had dared to forget the existence of Brenda's father. Or he had rated it of no account. He should soon learn whether it was so easily ignored. . . . But Brenda's hand was still in his, and there was wisdom enough left in him, and love enough, to make him hide his own hurt. " Are you sure he has gone ? "

" Yes." Striving to tell only the truth, and the exact truth, she explained, " I lost my temper with him and told him I never wanted to see him again. And I suppose he took me at my word. It was partly my fault. I said some dreadful things to him."

" How long ago was this ? "

" Nine days."

" Perhaps he will return. He may be only sulking."

" Oh, no, he's gone. I know it. There are some things one just knows."

" He can be found."

" But how ? " And she pointed out that she knew nothing about him, except that his mother lived at Bournemouth and that he lodged somewhere in Kensal Rise and did occasional work in some film studios. She didn't even know the names of the studios. And in any case he might have given up this work and gone far away.

" I'll find him if I want to," affirmed Mr. Rostrum, and his lips shut together like the jaws of a trap.

" But what's the good of finding him ? I'd never marry him now. And I'm not going to ask anything of him."

" All the same he's not going to get off scot free. He's going to know you've got a father. Whether he hears from you or not, I can assure you he's going to hear from me. Oh, yes. He's going to hear a lot."

" No, Daddy, please. . . . Leave him alone. I don't want you to go near him. He might think I sent you."

" But, Brenda, listen : I don't blame him too severely for what he did. I've been a young man myself, and I think I can understand him as I understand you. And if you're right in saying that he loved you at first, I'll try to forgive him. I'm not taking the conventional line in this matter— I don't think I'm a conventional person—I try to think for myself—and it's a fact, isn't it, Brenda, that the more you think for yourself, the more you understand and forgive.

I'll forgive him for being carried away by his love for you, but I'm not forgiving him if he's run meanly away to save his own skin, and left you to face everything alone. Great Heavens, no. Not, at any rate, till he's taken his punishment. And a pretty severe punishment. From me."

" I know him now. I believe he would deny everything."

" We'll see about that. There are ways of bringing these things home to people. If necessary, I shall neglect none of them." Fine words, but Mr. Rostrum was thinking : a summons ; a hearing in court ; Brenda in the witness box ; no it would not be possible ; but it would be very possible to terrify the young man with the threat of these things, and he intended to do so. Young Mr. Larry Blythe was going to have one hell of a fright before he was through with this. " I'll see to that," said Mr. Rostrum to himself ; and the words were doubly satisfying : they satisfied his desire to see himself as the domestic Jove coming with thunder, and the impatience to avenge the wound to his own self-love. But then he looked at Brenda again and saw that, while his own words had made him feel rather fine, her words, " He would deny everything," had drained the blood from her face, leaving it white and dulled and drawn. And, ashamed of his self-regarding thoughts, he fled from them and tried only to share her pain.

" Tell me, my dear, do you still love him ? Are you very unhappy because you still love him ? "

" No." It was an instant answer, and an emphatic one. She had lifted her head haughtily as she said it. " But the extraordinary thing, Daddy, is that I'm terribly unhappy because I no longer love him ; because there's not a trace, not a single trace, of my love left. Loving him, or thinking I did, was the loveliest thing that had ever happened to me ; and when it all disappeared in a moment—in the moment when he said, ' Don't suppose I'm going to marry you '— the pain was something quite unimaginable. And it's stayed with me ever since. I can't think of him without an awful sick pain. I should never have believed that it was a more terrible unhappiness to lose your love than to lose the person you loved—but it *is*, Daddy. It's as if you'd put everything you are into something, and were quite unspeakably happy, because it seemed to fulfil everything in you, and then, suddenly, it isn't there. It's a most extraordinary experience; it's like absolute defeat; it's blinding. One's head aches all day with it."

"It will pass, my pet. It will gradually heal itself. Just think that with every tick of the clock it's getting easier to bear."

"Yes, and with every tick of the clock I'm getting nearer my disgrace and shame, before Mummy and Julian and Joanie and everyone in the world."

"No; listen, my dearest: it's not time to despair about that yet. It isn't really. You're quite unexperienced in these things, and you've begun to panic much too soon. This may be nothing."

"But do you really think so?"

"I do. I'm an old married man, and I know how often these alarms prove false. Many a time your mother and I have wondered if there was a child coming, and believed there was, and it turned out we were quite mistaken. Well, if this turns out to be nothing, nobody but you and I will ever have known anything about it. If, on the other hand——"

Here Brenda interrupted, and there was a bitter, hard look on her face, which frightened him. "If it turns out to be something, do you know what I'm going to do? I'm going on. I'm going to have my baby and let the world say what they like. I'm going to have it openly and in the face of everybody. Quite a lot of girls do that now. I'm going to say, ' This is my baby, and I'm not ashamed of it. I'm not married, but I chose to live my own life, and no one was able to stop me '."

"But, Brenda, how could you do that? How would it fit in with your church-going and your——"

"Oh, that's all over and done with. I no longer believe there's anything in the world but chance. I don't believe there's anyone who cares anything about any of us. How can there be if one's driven, just driven from within, to do something and then punished for it for a lifetime? Oh, no, I'm finished with all that. Finished with it for ever."

"No, you're not, Brenda. Not *you*. You're only thinking you are."

"Oh, yes, I am. Life doesn't care what happens to any of us. All it wants is to get its way with us, and if that means misery for us, well, what the hell? Who cares? It's all part of the fun. I think Life's an insult. It's a silly and, as far as I can see, meaningless trick played on us all. I'm quite ready to be done with it—or I think I am. It's funny: I want to die, and yet I don't want to leave you and Mummy and the family for ever. I suppose it's only that that's keeping me alive. I see no reason in the world why people shouldn't die when they want to. It seems the proud and decent thing to do, if you find Life an insult."

"Oh, no, my darling; no, no." He did not know what he meant by this " No, no "; he was patting her hand and gaining time. There was a fog before his struggling thoughts, and all he could see was that Brenda in her distraction and defiance was ready to turn her whole life into some new and sombre path, and that he, as her father, must save her from it. Mr. Rostrum, despite his boast of unconventionality, was a man who thought in commonplace phrases and was unashamed of them; rather was he proud of them; he thought them exactly the right words. And now he said to himself, " Brenda is at the cross-roads. I must save her; " and he prayed to God for wisdom. He was praying as he patted her hand.

But the only wisdom that came to him as he prayed and gently patted her hand was this—and it may be there was none better: the cruelty of the world had come close to Brenda and shown itself to her; very well, then, the love that was in the world must come close too and be felt by her; and it must seem as large. That was all. And yet it was probably an ultimate wisdom.

"No, no; that's not Brenda speaking. It's just that you're finding this too heavy to bear alone. But you're not alone. I'm with you, and we'll see it through together. I'm not going to let it hurt you. Nothing's going to hurt you. But I don't think we can do anything by just defying the world; if I thought we could, I'd do it with you to-morrow. But the world's too strong. It's useless trying to give battle to an army that's a hundred times stronger than you are. You can outflank it, though; yes, you can outflank it sometimes." The words were coming—in answer to prayer perhaps; and he was rather proud of them. " And if we have to, we'll outflank it together. I tell you what we'll do. If it's as you think, we'll tell your mother but nobody else, and then you and I'll go away together, far away from everybody—abroad somewhere. I have some capital and you can have it all. I can spend hundreds, if need be. And I will."

" Oh Daddy, you're wonderful, but how could I let you spend all your savings on me ? "

" How could you stop me ? Who else do you think I'd rather spend them on ? But I shouldn't spend them all, or anything like all. I was just talking big. It would only cost a hundred or two. But even if it did cost me all I'd got, don't you think I'd love to spend it all on you ? Of course I would." This was a completely true statement. Mr. Rostrum had discerned in this moment, and for the first time, the tremendous truth of the words, " It is happier to give than to receive." He who had loved to accumulate a capital for himself now saw a quite astonishing joy in the idea of pouring it all into Brenda's hand. " What I've got is yours, my dear. But, as I say, this is only a question of a hundred or two. And even the hundred or two we might spend I could replace in a few years. I'm going to work for a long time yet. I'm only just sixty, and what's that to a man with health like mine ? I guess I've got fifteen good years of work in me yet. And especially if we had a long holiday together first. Think how natural it would seem. What more natural than that an old boy of sixty should decide to fulfil a lifelong dream and take a holiday abroad with his daughter while he's still full of vigour ? We'd go off, saying we were going to visit half a dozen countries, and when the time came, we'd settle somewhere, and nobody in England would know anything about the birth of the . . . the little one."

" Oh, Daddy. . . ."

" And then—I tell you what ! " A fine idea had come to him, like the sudden answer to his prayer. " Your mother and I, the only people who'd know anything about it, could adopt the little one as a companion and playmate for young Dudley. Why, it all fits in perfectly ! Everyone knows we can't hope for another child ; everyone says he'd be less trouble to your mother if he'd a child of his own age to play

with ; so why shouldn't we adopt one and give it our name ?
—and you would be with us and your child all the time or,
if you got married, we'd keep him for you, and afterwards,
when we were gone, you could have him for yourself. There !
I said we'd outflank them together ! And we have ! So
you're not to worry about anything, any more. Is that
understood ? Everything's going to be all right for you,
whatever happens. *I'm* going to see to that."

" Daddy, you're wonderful."

It was plain that his words had comforted her, and he
led her back to her bed, tucked the clothes comfortably
around her, and kissed her before leaving, as he used to
when she was a child. Then he crept upstairs to his own
room, shaken, anxious, but in one part of his heart very
happy. A clock struck two, and Mildred was sleeping
quietly.

CHAPTER THIRTEEN

AND so Mr. Rostrum and Brenda waited through the days,
keeping their secret. Often she was very quiet in the house,
but she had always been given to quietness, and neither
her mother nor the rest of the family suspected the real
nature of the cloud that enveloped her. Sometimes she
laughed and joked and made puns with the others, and only
her father guessed what the effort must be costing her. For
his part he said no more just yet about their secret, but
he would leave the breakfast table to kiss her in the hall
and to convey by the kiss that he was with her in everything.
And she would smile and walk away as bravely as possible
to her work.

He might be sharing her pain but at the same time he
was happy in supporting her and ministering to her, and
happy in the dream of taking her away, if necessary, and
surrounding her with his protection. At times, standing in
his dark room or in his finishing room and letting his thoughts
stray into curious places, he would wonder if this feeling of
fulfilment was a father's equivalent of a mother's relief and
pleasure when she was nursing her child. It was a warm,

glowing satisfaction, as of a deep hunger appeased ; and
he would savour it and take stock of it, telling himself,
" This is my job, and I shall see it through."

Brenda, he saw, was trying to play her part and by keeping
a cheerful countenance to protect him from her heartaches,
but he knew that her unhappiness was all too little assuaged ;
and there was one night when he awoke as before and lifted
his ear from the pillow—and, yes, she was crying ; she was
crying to herself in her room below.

It was only in her room, then, and behind its closed door,
that she let her misery have its way. He lay listening for
some time and at last, unable to hear her any more without
action of some kind, he looked at Mildred, saw that she was
sleeping with her face turned from him, and, very carefully
so as not to disturb her, slipped out of the bedclothes and
knelt at the bed's side.

" Oh God, I cannot stand it," he said, pressing his face,
cupped in his hands, into the quilt, as he knelt just above
Brenda's head. " Help her. Please help her. Help me to
help her. I will do anything. Oh God, show me how I can
help her. Show me what you want me to do."

A man of simple faith, at least when he was defeated and
could not do without it, he rose from his knees and got back
into bed, persuaded, or almost persuaded, that God would
come to his aid in the morning.

But nothing remarkable happened the next day, nothing
that looked like a message from a watching and pitying
Father ; and the following day—well, at about three in the
afternoon of that day there happened something which
suggested that God, so far from aiding him, was going to
thwart him ; that his prayer had brought down upon him,
not kindly succour, but a malign thunderbolt, wholly mysterious ; that God was not on his side but most strangely against
him.

§

It was nearly three o'clock ; he was seated before his
typewriter in his finishing room, one end of which served
as his office ; he had been back from lunch about an hour
and a half and, forgetful for a while of Brenda, he was
composing with some pleasure a full, knowledge-displaying,

polysyllabic, and orotund letter to Garden Tanks, Ltd., who had written to him asking the cost of a series of photographs, for use as illustrations in a folder, of their canvas bathing tanks. Now this was the kind of inquiry that pleased him more than any other. It invited him to the work he liked best. It enabled him to exercise those talents which he considered his finest. Talents, in fact, that approximated to genius. It revealed him to himself and to his customers as a man of ideas. So, seated at his desk, his creative energy pulsing at full pressure, he was submitting to Garden Tanks, Ltd., that instead of a folder that merely described their products and illustrated them, they should embark upon one that would be a fine example of picturesque and effective salesmanship. He was " submitting for their consideration the following proposition " : that he should rent through a film agency a country garden with a handsome mansion in the background ; that he should engage through a theatrical agency some three or four actresses to pose as bathing guests, and a few other ladies and gentlemen to stand about and admire the bathing after their tennis ; and that he should hire from Cammle Coaches, Ltd., for whom he had done work in the past, and who knew him well, a small char-a-banc to convey company and properties to the " location ".

Such a letter seemed to change him from a portrait photographer into something like a film director ; and he was as happy writing it as a director engaged upon an exciting script—he was plunged above head and ears in it—when suddenly, sharply, without initial throb or warning of any kind, a pain like a burning knife shot through his breast. It was as if the knife-blade had entered under his breastbone and passed out under his left shoulder ; and as if the wound were on fire. He shot his hand to his breast ; tried with grappling fingers to grip the whole breast in his hand ; bent forward to double himself up ; and stretched out his other hand to gather the support of his desk. His spectacles slid forward and swung between his eyebrows and the bridge of his nose, but he had no hand to deal with them. His jaws drew in his lower lip and gripped it like pincers.

Gradually the pain subsided. It passed as if it had never been.

He stood erect, but very still; his only action to push the spectacles back. He was held where he was by fright. All his tendency to fear sickness or injury had rushed into this new fright and crystallized in it. And this time his reason endorsed his fear. It was no imagination this time. No self-suggestion here. Never in his life had he known such a pain. This was something real. This was something terrible.

Death?

He felt at once terrified and proud. He felt a longing for someone else to share his alarm and be impressed by his sudden distinction. Miss Fletcher. He ran out from the finishing room into the shop. She was seated at her reception desk, and he told her all about the pain. She was impressed. After Miss Fletcher, Mildred. He must hurry home and tell Mildred. He had a greater longing to tell Mildred than anyone else—Mildred and the whole family. Seizing the letter and his black hat, he got as far as the door on this thrilling errand—and then he remembered. Brenda.

Brenda. He walked slowly into the road with this new thought. Brenda mustn't think he was going to be ill. He was her only prop and crutch just now. She mustn't think he was going to be seriously ill and perhaps die. That would knock away all the help and hope he'd been able to give her. No, he must say nothing about this, and Miss Fletcher must say nothing about this, till he knew the truth about Brenda. " I daren't be ill—just yet. Perhaps it was nothing. Just heartburn. Yes, it was only a worse attack of indigestion than usual . . . I suspect. They can be very bad sometimes, I've often heard. . . . But whatever it was, I must keep it to myself. And I'm going to keep it to myself for Brenda's sake. She's not going to be given this new fear just now. She's suffering enough."

Yes, that was settled; and if he had been proud of the extraordinary pain and longed for an audience to hear about it, he was yet more pleased with this act of self-denial which he was performing alone and without an audience.

And all that evening, though he was shaken by the memory of that sword-thrust through his breast and fearful of its return and thinking of little else, he laughed with the

family, or tried to ; he talked merrily with Dudley and
smiled in the presence of Brenda ; and he drew some happiness from the effort and from a certain amount of self-
esteem which he felt was justified.

§

But next afternoon, in the same place and at about the
same time—about two hours after his mid-day meal—the
sword-blade pierced through him again, and he bent double
with the burning pain of it and pressed a hand against his
breast. With clutching fingers he tried to grip the breast.
A slow lessening of the agony, while he remained quite still
and it was gone. Peace. A lesser attack than yesterday's,
he thought, but it left him quivering and breathless. The
door of the office was shut, and he stood there alone with
his enemy. This enemy within his breast. The longing
to go home and tell Mildred was almost irresistible, but the
memory of Brenda and of his pleasure in self-conquest remained strong enough to proscribe it ; and he shook his
head at the bare office wall. "No. No, Brenda, my dear.
If I tell your mother, she'll insist that I do something about
this at once, and then I shall have to tell her all about you.
I shall have to tell her that I'm not going to remove from
you just yet the promise of my support. It's your only
comfort that, if necessary, I can take you far away. You
must keep that comfort a little while longer. What God is
about, trying to prevent me helping you, I don't know ;
but I'm not going to let Him. I promised you I wouldn't
tell your mother anything unless we have to, and I'm going
to keep my promise. Yes, whatever happens."
And the spiritual comfort of this was more than the mental
anxiety or the bodily pain.
All the same, to live quite alone with the anxiety, to live
in blind doubt with the fear of death, was not possible. He
must tell *someone*. He must have someone's advice and
sympathy. Who ? The doctor, of course ; and he could
swear him to secrecy. He would go to the doctor this
afternoon. The time now ? Nearly three. Dr. Soden's
surgery hour was from five to six. Two hours to wait.
Those were two hours in which he did no work at all.

He just sat in the finishing room or walked up and down it, or wandered into the dark-room and out again, like a prisoner in the cells below the court, awaiting the summons to his trial. A hundred times in that hundred and twenty minutes he looked at his wrist watch. And all the time he was wondering if the pain would come back and almost hoping it would, so intense was his interest in it. In the same way this restless anticipation of his visit to the doctor was as pleasant as the prospect of drink to a parched throat ; and his walk to the doctor's house, when the time came, was not unlike the eager walk of a man to an entertainment. He arrived at the tall, double-fronted house in Priory Road fifteen minutes too soon, as one arrives at the door of a theatre. He was obliged to walk up and down the pavement till a clock struck the hour. Several other people, driven no doubt by a similar anxiety and interest, had been equally premature and were waiting near the doctor's steps ; and since most were women, and all were poorer than he, he let them go before him up the steps. A maid opened the door, and they all filed into the large, bare waiting-room. Here they all sat around the wall on the heterogeneous parade of chairs and kept a suitable silence. If anyone spoke, it was in a whisper.

Mr. Rostrum was the only one who was unaccompanied. There were two old men, one who coughed and retched as he bent over his stick ; and each had his old wife with him. There was a young, sallow, haggard mother with her little girl at her side who sat overawed and staring. There was an old lame woman with a rubber-ferruled ash stick, and a young woman with her who might be her daughter. There was a young working man and his wife, little more than a schoolgirl, and Mr. Rostrum, remembering Brenda, could guess what advice they were needing. He himself, feeling full of vigour and wisdom, as he saw their slackened postures and wan, dull faces, sat rigidly upright on his hard chair with his hat on his knees and considered them one by one, these strangers whom the eddies of life had tossed for an hour around him. There was not a trace of pain in any part of his body. There never was, once he had made his appointment with doctor or dentist. If to be greatly interested in what you are doing, and impatient for its outcome, is to be happy, then he was happy as he sat by the wall.

In their turn, singly or in couples, those whom he had let enter the house before him passed from this ante-room to the doctor's consulting-room across the hall. And now he was next in the order, and after what seemed a great time the doctor came into the passage, said good-bye to his patient, and called, " Next, please."

Mr. Rostrum rose and with a heart that was less beating than bubbling, but with an outward display of *sang froid* and self-possession, designed to show that he was of stronger fibre than the others, walked across the hall into the presence of the doctor.

A large, old-fashioned, bay-windowed room, twin sister to the one he had left; a desk in the middle turned towards the door, and the young doctor seated at it; a chair this side of the desk for the patient; a couch against the wall—so much Mr. Rostrum apprehended as he entered, smiling.

" Well, Mr. Rostrum, what can I do for you? Sit down." Dr. Soden, without rising, pushed back his own chair. He leaned back in it and sighed.

Mr. Rostrum, a sensitive man, immediately noticed the sigh, and it disappointed him and perturbed him. It made him feel a nuisance. It confined and obstructed the channel in which he would pour forth his story. It showed him that the doctor was weary after a dozen previous interviews, and it made him wonder why God should punish him like this for having let all the poor people enter the house before him, instead of rewarding him.

" I won't keep you long," he began.

The doctor did not demur at this; he did not smile and say, " Oh, don't mind me," or " Please take your time; " he just bowed as if grateful for the assurance; and Mr. Rostrum felt more than ever a nuisance. He didn't want to have to hurry over the question whether he was going to live or die. He sat down before the doctor sadly, and in a deep disappointment.

Dr. Soden was a tall, slender, lissom young man who didn't look a day more than twenty-one. He was possibly twenty-five. It was not two years since he had been house physician and house surgeon at Kilburn General Hospital; not a year since he had acquired this practice from old

Dr. Westerham The first thing you observed about him was that he was exceedingly well dressed, in a dark suit and shining collar ; and the next that he kept his voice, consistently and studiously, as soft as a zephyr at twilight. The clothes were right and apt, no doubt ; the voice was a few tones too soft. You suspected that he was very conscious of these clothes and this voice ; that, in a word, he was dressed for his part both visually and aurally. You deduced from the clothes and the voice that he was very proud of his new position as a man seated in a chair of knowledge and authority. A house physician in a great hospital is a small, subordinate figure ; a general practitioner on his own ground is a Regius Professor of Medicine. Dr. Soden, this newly vested young doctor, was as pleased with his learned-sounding medical terms and his fluent and polysyllabic vocabulary as Mr. Rostrum was with the polysyllables which he could produce in his business letters and in his discussions on art, photography, and sailing. Just as a young clergy-man, newly priested, is proud to be called " Father " for the first time by people old enough to be his parents and is pleased (unless he has the humility of a saint, which is unusual) with his seat of authority in vestry or confessional, so young Dr. Soden, yesterday a schoolboy, sat with no little self-satisfaction at his surgery desk in this large room ; and just as such a young clergyman's manner will be more priestly than the Pope's, so Dr. Soden had a correctitude of dress, voice, and deportment above that of the President of the Royal College of Physicians. Indeed, having pierced with your keen eye to his ever-present awareness of his dress, voice, words, and bodily movements, you began to suspect that his young, pale face was worn and racked with it.

As Mr. Rostrum's story poured from him, and it was racing forth now because of the obstacles in the channel and the shortness of the time, Dr. Soden offered no resistance to the flooding tide but, leaning back, wrote a few notes on a case card or just considered his visitor while his fingers twisted his pencil round and round like the blade of a propeller. " Phew ! " he thought. " How these old birds do blow off when they get into the presence of a doctor."

" I see. Thank you." The record was over at last ; and he asked his questions ; and, as he did so, he was hardly more conscious of Mr. Rostrum's answers than of the softness of his own voice and of his manner, so quiet, controlled, and unrevealing.

"Very well. Let's examine you. Just strip to the waist, if you don't mind, and lie down on the couch."

His lean old patient obeyed, and he felt his pulse and pulled down the lower lids of his eyes and looked at their lining. Then, with searching fingers, proud of their skill, and, for that matter, of their appearance, he felt his abdomen. He stayed the fingers at a spot beneath the breastbone.

"Some tenderness there?"

"Yes. Yes, that is where . . ." and the old gentleman began again, too enthusiastically, his description of the pain at this point.

"Yes, yes . . . I see . . . I quite see. All right, Mr. Rostrum, you can dress up again." And he himself went back to his desk and wrote on the case card his diagnosis— or, rather, a good guess with a query mark before it.

"Sit down," he said to Mr. Rostrum, when the old gentleman was dressed and buttoned up.

His patient sat down humbly and waited, eyes fixed on him. Plain from his face and eyes that he was waiting like a prisoner for the verdict; and Dr. Soden, like many a judge on his bench, felt simultaneously a pity for the man before him and a pride in his own position of power. He twisted the pencil round and round, round and round. "Well, quite definitely, Mr. Rostrum, I think you ought to have a far more thorough examination than I have been able to give you."

"Yes. . . . What does that mean?"

"I think you ought to go to the Out-patients Department of Kilburn General Hospital and see my old friend, Sir Joshua Dymote. He's quite the best surgeon in England on this sort of thing."

"Surgeon? Do you mean an operation?" The old man's face had blanched.

"I don't know, Mr. Rostrum. We can't say anything about that till after the examination. But I must be frank with you and tell you that—well, I think we ought to take this seriously."

Old Mr. Rostrum said nothing, but just stared at him,

164

looking even older than he had done a minute ago; and he, the doctor, explained with his studied quietness and what he imagined was an admirable tact, the processes of a test meal and an X-ray examination, drawing pleasure meanwhile from the learned terms in his exegesis, and from its precision and lucidity. No judge, at the end of the day, could be more pleased with the phrasing of his Charge.

When he had finished, old Mr. Rostrum nodded, but to himself rather than to him. And after a pause he asked, "When do you say I ought to go?"

"Just as soon as possible."

It was at this point that anything like humility, anything like hesitation or uncertainty, dropped from his patient's face. He who had seemed a meek and worried listener was now a man of decision and resolution. "I can't do that."

"Why not?"

"I can do nothing about it for some little time."

"Not even if I say to you that every day is of importance."

"No."

This irritated him. Obstruction in patients always angered him because it spoiled his picture of himself as the man of knowledge, wisdom, and authority. Conscious of his youth, he suspected that, because of it, they were not taking him as seriously as they took older men, whom he did not consider half as well instructed as himself in modern medicine. And because he was thus irritated, he persuaded himself that it was his duty to "come out into the open with this old boy," even if it hurt him.

"But, Mr. Rostrum, you appreciate, I suppose, that if it's serious, and surgical treatment is advised, the chance of success may depend almost entirely on the stage at which the operation is performed?"

"Yes, I appreciate that. And you think that they might recommend an immediate operation?"

"I certainly do. My experience is that time is everything in these cases."

That had shaken the old boy, palpably; but he quickly recovered a stable attitude and, merely lifting his eyebrows and shoulders as if in acceptance of the statement, inquired, "Are you suggesting cancer?"

Now the doctor lifted *his* shoulders, but this was a shrug

of helplessness. He opened the palm that had held the pencil and displayed it to the ceiling, empty.

"Don't be afraid to tell me, Doctor. I'm one of those who prefer the truth."

Offensive, this suggestion that he was afraid to do something. "I cannot tell you what I do not know. I should need a far more careful examination before I could make any final pronouncement. All I feel disposed to say, and I say it very plainly since you ask for it, is that I'm not prepared to take the responsibility of letting you wait."

"I understand your point of view."

"It's more than a point of view. It's a very grave conviction. I tell you here and now that you should see Sir Joshua at once. I can fix it up for you : he's an old friend of mine ; and, if I may say so, you're lucky to have the chance of his advice."

There were some seconds of silence while Mr. Rostrum thought this over ; then another shake of his head. "No. It can't be done."

"But, if I may say so, this is rather absurd. Why can't it be done ? "

"I haven't the time . . . just now."

The doctor tossed his head to one side in a gesture of impatience. "Why ? Doesn't this sort of thing take precedence over everything else ? "

"No."

The word was firm ; and its firmness increased the doctor's anger. He heaved a sigh ; and this obstinate patient, hearing the sigh, as he was meant to, affirmed with a slight asperity, "There are domestic reasons which I do not care to enlarge upon."

"Very well." Firm words these, too. "But, Mr. Rostrum, you asked me to be frank ; and may I say that sometimes you patients make things very difficult for us doctors ? You only come to us when the pain has become so insistent that it can no longer be tolerated, and then you merely decline the advice we give you. But, believe me, when the pain is reaching that pitch, time is getting late." Having been a student under Sir Joshua, he considered cancer to be a subject on which he had specialized ; and he felt driven, accordingly, to exhibit his knowledge. "Do you realize

166

this : it's estimated that of the cancer patients in a London hospital not one person in five among the well-to-do has come for treatment in time, and, among the working classes, not one in a hundred."

" What do you mean : 'not come in time'? Do you mean there's no saving them? "

" Of course." He saw that these ruthless thrusts had transfixed his opponent, and he felt some shame for them. Bad doctoring, this, but he was a man as well as a doctor, and a tired man ; and a tired man's vanity is easily hurt and his temper easily frayed. It was his vanity and temper that were speaking now instead of his professional virtuosity ; and he pitied his victim even as he stabbed him. " We patch them up sometimes for a little, but if they'd come earlier and done what we told them, it might have been a very different story."

Obviously the old man resented his tone. " It's possible that doctors don't always know all the circumstances of their patients. It is just possible, I imagine, that a patient may be right sometimes, even if his doctor can't see why. One is entitled to choose whether one will undergo an operation or not."

" Most certainly you are, and it's the doctor's business to leave you in no doubt about the consequences of your choice."

" But, Doctor, I can't believe I'm really ill. Apart from this little pain I feel perfectly well. I've never felt better in my life. I've just come back from a holiday, and I walked my fifteen or twenty miles without turning a hair. I can't believe it's as serious as you suspect. No, quite honestly, I don't believe it. I know my constitution. I'm never ill. I'm sixty now, and I've never been really ill in my life. I'm the only one of my family who never has to go to the doctor at all."

" All right, then. If that's what you think and believe, there's not much more I can say. It's for you to decide." All too plain that the old man was doubting his judgment because he was young. He was pitting his uninstructed views against his, a highly qualified doctor's, expert knowledge. Dr. Soden felt as exasperated with Mr. Rostrum as Mr. Rostrum would feel with the Widow Leicester or Truppy when they scoffed at his doctrine on art. " But let me tell you this, sir ; it's perhaps my duty to tell you this : good health proves nothing where cancer is concerned. The great majority of cancer cases are among those who have enjoyed excellent health all their lives, most of them having had no serious illness since their childhood. They may even have no history of pain. None at all. Pain is a usual but by no means necessary symptom of cancer. Cancer can come suddenly, out of the blue."

" Can it really ? "

" Yes. There are such cases."

" I didn't know that. I never knew that."

" No." The old man was looking stunned ; and the doctor wondered where his irritability was carrying him. But though he might disapprove of the methods he was using, he could not arrest them. More compelling than anything else was his need to justify himself as an authority. And at the same time the fixed, staring interest of this uninformed man increased his temptation to bedazzle him with scientific terms. " It's a strangely mystifying disease because of the utterly contradictory ways of its incidence. Scarcely two cancers are alike That's why our knowledge of its incidence, which is considerable, helps us hardly at all towards an understanding of its ætiology——"

" Ætiology ? "

" Yes. It's cause Even after centuries of investigation only one thing is really known about it."

" And what is that ? "

" That excision is the only remedy. Though remedy is hardly the word. It is the only effective *treatment*. We have been doing research on this disease for Heaven knows how many years, and we still stand where our forefathers did. All that they knew was that the best thing to do with a cancer was to cut it out. All that we know is to cut it out. We do it with less pain than they, thanks to anæsthetics ; we do it with greater safety than they, thanks to antiseptics and aseptics ; we do it with less probability of its return than they, thanks to better technique ; but we still do nothing to cure it."

Dr. Soden was not a little impressed with the clarity and balance of this statement, and he felt that Mr. Rostrum must be impressed too. Mr. Rostrum, however, was obviously more impressed with the substance of the statement than with its form.

"But, Doctor, if it turns out to be cancer, what can have caused it? I've always led an abstemious life. I've never been one to indulge myself immoderately. I've never been a drinker, for instance. And I've led on the whole a fairly easy life. I've always been able to, because I've made quite good money in my time."

"And I'm afraid you can't base much hope upon any of that. I'm sorry, but there it is. In the first place, only about five per cent. of cancer patients have a history of alcoholic excess. And, as regards your second point, that you've always had a pretty easy life, never knowing want or under-nourishment or anything like that, well, I'm afraid the answer is that cancer is what we call a prosperity disease. By that I mean that it is as seldom found among primitive peoples as it is rampant among the civilized, and especially among the well-to-do. If you ask me why, I can only say, Who knows yet? My own view, for what it's worth—and I may say that I've made a considerable study of the subject— is that it is caused by a slight but steady poisoning over a great number of years. It may take twenty or thirty years to mature. Just as some animals come to maturity in a day or two and others take many years, so do some diseases develop in a matter of days, while another, like cancer, requires twenty or more years of incubation." Another shapely exposition. Dr. Soden picked up the pencil, which he had dropped, and played with it again. "And that also shows, in my view, why it is almost exclusively a disease of the elderly."

"What do you understand by 'elderly'? Am I elderly?"

"I mean that it usually appears in the fifties and sixties."

His patient, being sixty, heard this in silence. He did not seem able to move from his chair, or move his tongue; and at last Dr. Soden, fretted at a new point, glanced at his wrist watch as a hint that other patients were waiting for him.

Instantly Mr. Rostrum rose. Even though this was a conference dealing with his life and his death, he could not continue in it, feeling an encumbrance. "Well, I won't keep you any longer. I mustn't inflict my woes on you any longer. Thank you for all you've told me. I wanted to know everything. I——"

"And you're still determined not to act upon my advice."

"Oh, yes. I have told you I cannot."

"Very good then." The doctor rose too, that he might strengthen Mr. Rostrum's willingness to go and to take up no more of his time. But he saw that the hint of despairing and despising resignation in his "Very good then" had been resented by this rather touchy old gentlemen. The old boy's underlip was protruding, and his eyes were sullen. And when he spoke, it was to say tersely, "I cannot do what I cannot do, Doctor. I know how I am situated, and I alone know. That is all I can say. If the consequences of waiting a bit longer are serious, I shall have to take them. That's all."

The doctor bowed slightly. Considering himself the aggrieved party, he liked this tone no better than Mr. Rostrum had liked his ; and he felt a compulsion to fire a parting shot from a very heavy gun. "All right then, Mr. Rostrum. It's for you to say. I can only repeat—and I feel I should be doing less than my duty if I didn't repeat—that every year hundreds and hundreds of lives are lost—*lost*, Mr. Rostrum—by the procrastinations of patients, and all of them might have been saved if they'd listened to their doctors."

"That may be," said Mr. Rostrum. "I can't help that. I . . . I shall wait. Good evening, and thank you very much ; " and he went from the room somewhat slowly ; and Dr. Soden heard him fumbling his way out of the house.

§

"I don't believe it. I don't believe it. He was trying to frighten me. He's the type that gets a certain pleasure out of frightening people. I can always see through such people. Just because he was tired he worked it off on me. I don't believe a word of it." Mr. Rostrum was going down the steps slowly—as slowly as if he were one of those old men in the waiting room—because he felt benumbed and stupefied, and the street at which he was looking—indeed, the whole world—seemed unstable and hazed and oscillating. His confidence in his body's balance was disturbed. Slowly, and sometimes blinking his eyes, he walked along the street, his mouth open ; and the thudding, jarring Kilburn High Road, when he turned into it, seemed a strange place, and slightly distorted, as if it stood in a new light ; as if he were looking back on it from the frontier of another world. " No, no. I must wait. I'm *going* to wait." And he walked yet more slowly, as if he didn't want to arrive at his home. " I shall wait till Brenda knows more. It's only a matter of weeks ; and if a few weeks can make all the difference between life and death, well, they must make it. That's all."

He turned into his own road, alone with his knowledge and his fear. They made up a dull weight in his heart, and the weight was very heavy when he saw his tall grey house standing behind his own tall trees ; but when he thought, going slowly up the steps, that he was carrying it for Brenda's sake, it was lightened a little by his pride.

CHAPTER FOURTEEN

But if there was no one in the house to whom he could speak of his anxiety and relate the magnificent story of the doctor's diagnosis, if he must smile with the family and listen to their jokes and appear happy, there was one outside to whom he could turn, and he turned to him the very next day. The next day, first thing in the morning, he walked to the front of Truppy's shop, dawdled about the threshold till it was empty, and then went in and said, " Well, how's young Trupps ? Everything fine ? "

" Can't grumble, Alec, old man. And how's things with you ? Everything all right ? "

" Well . . . yes . . . at least, p'raps they might be better. S'mattrafact, that's what I've come about. How about coming for a walk with me this evening ? There's something I'd like to discuss with you. In absolute confidence."

This is an invitation few can refuse, and Truppy was not one of them. His eyes, behind his gold spectacles, lit up with interest, and he put a fitting sympathy into his voice. " Of course I'll come along, old man."

" Yes, you'll find it interesting, I think. Definitely interesting."

" Why not come here for a chat, and the missus'll make us some tea ? "

" No, I'd rather we were quite alone. It's something I can't even tell the family. In fact, I shan't tell anyone else but you, and I don't want you to breathe a word about it to a soul."

Truppy's eyes looked more mystified and interested than ever. He was flattered and made happy by this confidence. It was something to be a man's best friend.

" Well, you know, old boy, I'm at your service whenever you want me. I'll wait for you in here, shall I ? "

" That'll be fine, Truppy."

" S'mattrafact, I was going to look up Young Beechy about some printing he's never done, but I can easily put that off."

" Well, if you can . . . it's rather urgent, in a way."

" You bet I can. I'll be waiting in here for you."

And they met at the door of Truppy's shop that evening and, turning southward this time, walked for miles together, side by side, Truppy in his bowler and Mr. Rostrum in his narrow black hat, talking with much animation and more than a little pleasure, along the broad and noisy High Road, the broader but quieter Maida Vale, the populous and clanging Edgware Road, where all the lamps were alight in the shimmering dusk, and so up to the very gates of Hyde Park. Then back homeward along the same pavements, but with their faces to the north and nothing but the night before them.

Truppy, a considerate and conscientious little man, did not ask for the confidence ; he waited for it. And they had not gone far before Mr. Rostrum, after speaking of general things, introduced it. " Truppy," he said, " promise me you won't breathe one single word of what I'm going to tell you to Mildred or any of the family. Or to anyone else in the world."

" Of course not. Not if you tell me not to."

" There are reasons, old man, why I can't tell anything of this to the family. Reasons that I can't disclose to you. You must just trust me that I know what is best. And, by the way, if anything goes wrong, you're never, never to say to the family that I told you all about it before I told them. I don't want the children—Julian and . . . and Brenda . . . to think that I had a reason for not speaking. I must leave it at that, old man. I can't say more."

" Yes, yes." It sounded very mysterious and alarming, and one part of Truppy, and indeed one part of Mr. Rostrum, was enjoying it.

" Well, it's this, Truppy. Putting it quite simply, I may not be long for this world."

Truppy shot up his little face at Mr. Rostrum's, and he saw that Mr. Rostrum's sharply pointed profile, under the narrow black hat, was staring before him into the evening light at the end of the long broad road. For a space he said nothing ; then managed to answer. " Don't be silly. You're good for twenty years yet and more."

" No . . . I doubt it. . . . I used to think so, old man, but I went to the doctor yesterday, and he took a very grave view."

" Grave view of what ? "

This opened the floodgates for Mr. Rostrum, and he let the waters pour through. No obstacles in the channel, no constraining shortness of time, no fears of being a nuisance, with little Truppy. He told his story from its beginnings in the small, niggling pain many months ago to its majestic climax in his finishing room the day before yesterday. He told it in full detail and with a fine, rich texture all the way from the close of Kilburn High Road to the close of Maida Vale and the busy thoroughfare of Edgware Road. It was almost worth having had that ghastly attack in his office for the pleasure of describing it ; almost worth having been nearly wrecked by the doctor's words, now that he could relate them in all their drama to Truppy. His last summing-up, offered with a laugh, was, " Yes, he as good as said, Truppy, old son, that if I didn't have an operation at once, I'd make a nice little job for the undertaker. And I just *can't* have an operation at once—for a certain very private reason. So what, young Trupps ? So what ? "

" Alec, old man ! I didn't know anything like this was in the wind. But if the doctor says you must have an operation, you must have it, and no nonsense. Life's more important than anything else."

"Oh, no, it isn't," said Mr. Rostrum.

"Of course it is, you old ass. Your family depend upon you, don't they?"

"My family'll be tolerably well provided for when I take my leave of them, but let's not go into that. I told you I couldn't go into my reasons. My mind's quite made up, old man. I know what I'm doing, and I know that I must stay as I am for a little while longer."

"Well, I don't think you ought to. I don't really. You asked my advice as a friend, and I should be a poor friend if I didn't tell you that you ought to obey the doctor and go to the hospital to-morrow. If it's cancer—but I don't believe it's cancer. I just don't. Cancer can't suddenly assert itself like this."

"Oh, can't it?" interrupted Mr. Rostrum triumphantly. "Cancer can come out of the blue. Click! Like that. It's a completely mystifying disease. It's got the doctors beat. They know everything about its incidence but nothing at all about its ætiology."

"About its what?"

"Its ætiology. That means its cause. All they know is that there's only one thing to do with it, and that's excision."

"Cutting it out, you mean?"

"Exactly. Cutting it out. They do it better than they used to, and with a better technique so that there's less chance of its returning, but that's still all they know about it : cut it out."

"Well, then, Alec, go and have it done, if it's got to be done. Go at once, I beg of you, as a friend. As your closest friend."

"I shall go just as soon as I can, you bet. But I must wait a little longer. For a strictly private reason."

"Well, you know, old man, don't you, that whether you go now or later, we're with you in this, Florrie and I, right up to the hilt. We're with you through thick and thin. If there's anything on earth you'd like us to do for you, or any way at all in which we can help, there we are, in the little old shop."

"Yes, I know that. And I shall call upon your help, I feel sure. When the time comes. And it's because the time *is* coming that I wanted to feel you knew about it. You've already done me a great service in letting me tell you all about it—I daren't mention it to anyone at home just at present. It's good to feel that someone knows. And "—he looked ahead of him to where, beyond the lines of traffic and the stream and counter-stream of pedestrians, the glamorous evening lay low upon the gates of the park—" I shall like to think that if anything happens, you'll be there to keep an eye on Mildred and the children. Especially the little boy."

" Nothing's going to happen to you, you tough old thing. Not for years yet. I'm five years older than you, and it's you that'll stand by my grave and look in—that's to say, if you care to come to the ceremony. I hope you'll be there, supporting old Florrie, and feeling good for another dozen years yourself. *And* you will. You're the sort they can't easily kill."

" Yes, I'm pretty tough, I think. That's my one hope."

§

He waited through the days with his fear. The fear walked always at his side and stood with him in every room ; it sat with him at his desk in his office and in his chair at home ; it sat with him at meals and lay with him in bed ; and the doctor's words were ever in his ears. He was frightened of what he was doing by waiting, but he waited. There were more spasms of agonizing pain, but, though bad, none of them seemed quite as bad as that first attack in the office. They were oddly irregular in their onset, and there seemed to be no mathematical progression in their intensity. Another odd thing was that if the pain wasn't too bad, it was accompanied by a longing to eat, and the eating would end it, but only for a time ; after a time he would realize that he had only made it worse by eating ; and thus he was forced, day after day, to pace his office arguing the question, Shall I eat or not eat ? He ached to tell it all to Mildred, to present to her, with a multitude of words, the twin horns of this dilemma, but he couldn't, he mustn't, so he went once and discussed it with Truppy in his room over the shop, and, having gone to him once, didn't like to go again. Sometimes when the pain was nearly as bad as that first time, he would stand bowed over his desk or over a chair, the sweat bedewing his brow and his hands, and the doctor's words sounding in his head, "Not one person in five comes for treatment in time. And then there's no saving them;" but he bit obstinately upon his lip and swore that he would not give in. Once or twice he thought that he would have to give in; but he didn't.

There was a mirror in his office, because he liked to examine the set of his hair or his hat before he went out; and now he would go and peer into it to learn if he was looking ill. And he saw, or thought he saw, that his features were thinning and his skin yellowing, and then perhaps this thought would be eclipsed by the question whether his face wouldn't be improved by a beard like Joseph Conrad's or Edward VII's. He'd often thought that since his nose was a fine one and his chin wasn't, a neat, pointed beard would be just the thing for him, but he had never grown it for fear of its coming in greys or whites and turning him into a grandfather. At home Mildred would suggest that he was looking poorly, and he would laugh the suggestion away, saying, "*I'm* all right. It's only the old indigestion. I've been having a few twinges of it lately."

He was impatient for a word from Brenda, and when he thought it was time for her to know more, he asked her if she had anything to tell him. She looked at him with frightened eyes and said, "Nothing yet. . . . Oh, Daddy. . . ."

And he comforted her. "Never mind. Don't despair. It's possible your very terror is preventing things from happening. I know only too well myself that the fear of something going wrong will often start it going wrong. It's not time to despair yet."

"Oh, but it is, Daddy, it is."

And though he shook his head and patted her shoulder encouragingly, he believed it was.

And so they waited, walking and working apart from each other, she with her fear and he with his.

He was waiting for something else beside the word from Brenda. Every morning and evening he looked first among his letters for one with a certain postmark. That young man. That young Mr. Blythe. He wasn't going to escape as easily as he supposed. And a few days after his midnight talk with Brenda he had asked her in a low voice as he kissed her good-bye, " Anything more been heard of the young man ? " And when she answered, the dismay having leapt into her eyes, " No, Daddy," he had said, " I see," and said it with a crisp significance.

And he had turned from her into his study. This was intolerable. Precisely, literally, intolerable that this puppy should treat her father as a nonentity or imagine that he would not be clever enough to find him. " All right. All right. I'm waiting no longer for you to turn up, young man. Instead I'm coming to you. I suggest you have quite underestimated Brenda's father, Mr. Blythe. If necessary, I shan't hesitate to employ a private detective to run you to earth, but I rather fancy I shall manage without that. I rather fancy myself as a private detective."

And he found it pleasant, playing the detective, as he walked to the shop that morning. What had he to go on ? What were the data so far ? That the boy's name was Larry Blythe ; that he lodged, or had lodged, at Kensal Rise ; that he worked for various film companies ; that his mother ran a hotel in Bournemouth—ah, an idea ! It quickened his step. It drove him, before he entered his own premises, into Truppy's shop next door. Truppy, being a stationer, might have an *A.B.C. Railway Guide.* He had, and Mr. Rostrum borrowed it, and hurried with it, as enthusiastically as a child with a new purchase, into his office and, sitting at the desk and whipping on his spectacles, opened it at the advertisement pages. " Bourne-mouth." One full page after another of hotels in Bourne-mouth. Wetting his thumb on his tongue, he turned one page after another. Now half-page advertisements of smaller hotels . . . private hotels. " Mrs. Lawson, Manageress . . . Miss P. Crosse, Resident Managing Director . . . H. L. and D. Savory, Resident Proprietors . . . Major and Mrs. Ling, Resident Directors . . . Mrs. Colin Blythe, Resident Proprietor."

Mrs. Blythe.

Ha ! It was a sharp, exulting laugh. Mr. Rostrum stood up from the desk. He had seldom known a better moment. " Ha ha, Mr. Larry. I think it hasn't taken me long. Precisely fifteen minutes. Now we know a thing or two.

This is Mummy, I suspect. This is our dear Mummy, unless I'm much mistaken. If it isn't, we can ask her to guide us to another Mrs. Blythe who keeps a hotel. I suggest you never made a greater mistake than when you wrote the old man down as a factor of no importance. You probably think that everybody else besides yourself is a fool, but they're not, you see, they're not. Now we'll write a little letter."

And for some minutes he walked up and down the room, enjoying the delights of composition. The composition complete in his mind, he shot again into his desk chair, as if the chair had been suddenly magnetized and drawn him into its grip ; he pushed the spectacles well into position ; took paper ; and wrote. " Dear Madam, I should be very grateful if you could favour me with the present address of your son, Lawrence. He has been a frequent visitor "—no, guest —" he has been a frequent guest at my house of late, as no doubt he will have informed you, but we have not seen him for some days and I have some information of much interest which I feel sure he would wish to have . . ." Very good, that. " You will readily appreciate my desire that he should be advised of this at his earliest convenience. Thanking you in anticipation of an early reply, I am, Madam, Yours truly, Alexander Rostrum."

Much pleased with this creation, he thrust it into an envelope, licked down the flap, and went out forthwith to post it. He might expect an answer when ? In two days ? Three days ?

But no answer came on the second day or the third, or in the days that followed ; and he began to think that the message which he had sent out so confidently would never be heard of again. It had gone to the wrong woman and been disregarded. A damned discourteous woman, that Mrs. Colin Blythe, whoever she was. Might at least have acknowledged the letter. How long since he had sent it ? Eleven days. No, it had proved a damp fuse, that little letter. What next ? The film studios ? Visit each of them —Denham, Elstree, Welwyn, Ealing, Islington—and inquire about a Mr. Blythe ? Perhaps that would be the way ; but since it was a strenuous and uncertain business, he postponed it from day to day. Sometimes when the pain trapped and tormented him, and he wondered how near he was to death, he would tell himself that perhaps he ought to forgive the young man and spare him. But no : the idea that a young man could get away with this sort of treachery without a word from Brenda's father amounted to another stabbing pain ; but this was a pain in his mind and one that could quickly be healed by an operation and must be. A few words to that young man, and the pus would be out of the boil. Besides, it was his duty—it was his duty to other men's daughters—to give that lad such a fright as would make him mind his step in the future. It was his duty to do it even on the brink of the grave . . . a duty to the world before he went hence and was no more seen. Oh, yes, surely.

And when the letter came, on a Saturday evening, fifteen days after he had written to Bournemouth, he persuaded himself that it was a sign from God. It was God's ratification of what he had done and His command to him to go on. The letter was a full, galloping, careless document : the letter of a woman who was ready to dilate upon her worries and grievances to a complete stranger. " I am sorry not to have answered your letter before but I have had my sister very ill nearly dying in fact and at one time we were in doubt as to whether she could possibly pull through but I am glad to say she is better now and I have been able to get back here, I have been away for more than a week twelve days in fact right in the busiest season and things are at sixes and sevens here but she has no one else and she was really very ill, I only got back the day before yesterday and of course there was any amount of business to be attended to, Servants are not to be trusted with no one to look after them and my daughter refused to give up her holiday so as to help, I have not heard from Larry for some time he writes very seldom but you know what children are I wrote to him about his auntie's illness and he has not even answered about that, His last letter was only a card telling me that his new address was 210, Munster St., S.W.1."

Munster Street, Pimlico. Mr. Rostrum knew the road and saw it in his mind's eye. Triumph surged in him. " I think I have him. Yes, I think I have you, Master Larry." A quick, clean, neat piece of detection. " I got him without help from anyone else, and it didn't take so very long, either. No fault of mine that it wasn't all done in three days. And now he's got a pleasant little surprise coming. He's going to meet Mr. Rostrum, Brenda's father. He's going to learn that some fathers are not quite the mere ciphers, not quite the mere jokes, that he supposed." 210, Munster Street. He burned to act upon his knowledge. How soon could he present himself before the young man, like Justice on the threshold? Not to-night. No, on a Saturday night he would almost certainly be out. Probably flirting with some girl somewhere. Planning a new seduction. Well, not much more of that, young man. We're coming, and we'll frighten you out of that. Enjoy yourself to-night, because it'll probably be your last night of pure, unalloyed pleasure. There's going to be a bitter taste in your apple after to-night. To-morrow I think we'll come and see you. An idle young loafer, you'll probably sleep late on Sunday, and we'll be there in the pride of the morning before you're ready for the street. We, Brenda's father, shall be standing in the passage between you and your little games.

Meanwhile there was nothing he could do except stride up and down his study, packing his mind with whip-lash phrases for the young man; but this was an engrossing occupation, and not once in these intervening hours did he have any pain, because his mind was filled with a different excitement.

He arrived in Pimlico at about half-past ten the next morning, just as the church bells were beginning their appeal to the empty streets. The effect of the appeal seemed to be exactly nothing: the streets remained empty with nothing in them but the morning sunlight, the wind-lifted dust, and the sound of bells. Munster Street was a long road, half a mile long, and built of block after block of substantial houses, each house a cake of thick yellow brick iced with stucco and ornamented with architraves, cornice, and pillared portico. These solid and stilted houses, designed for large, prosperous families and obedient, parasite servants, were now in the hands of absentee proprietors who had sliced them up into small cheap flats, or of resident landladies who let them off in furnished rooms. 210 was a high number and must be at the far end near the river. Mr. Rostrum, no memory in his mind of his pain or of his fear of death, primed only with charge and fuse for this raid on No. 210, marched to his objective as fast as the youngest man. 210. Heart fluttering, but lips firm, he walked up the steps, examined the three bell-pushes, perceived that only the lowest of them was in order, and pushed that. It rang in the kitchen places below.

Steps approached, and the door was opened by a tall, big-bosomed, black-haired woman whom he judged, because of her dark brown eyes and old-gold skin, to be Spanish or Italian.

" Is Mr. Blythe still here ? "

" Please ? What name ? "

" Blythe."

" Oh, Mr. Blythe. *Si*, he lives here."

" I should like to speak to him, if I may."

" I don't know if he's dressed yet, but I shall see. What is your name ? "

" Rostrum."

" Please ? "

Instantly he saw that he had committed a tactical blunder by giving his name ; he should have concealed it ; but it was too late to retreat now. " Rostrum."

" Ros-trim. Thank you. I shall go and see what he is doing. Excuse."

And she walked away, along the passage, to the door of the back room and knocked. Oh, so the young man lived there. He was as close as that. He was in that room at this minute. Good. It might have been difficult to come upon him if his room had been at the top of this lofty house. With some notion of preventing the door being shut in his face, he placed a foot on the threshold between the jambs.

He could hear voices in that back room.

" Who ? " A young man's voice. Strange to hear his voice for the first time.

" Mr. Rostrum." If one catches no other words distinctly, one can always hear one's own name.

A silence ; and then the young man's voice again, but the words not distinguishable.

" I cannot verra well say that to him." The woman's voice, her words easily heard because she was near the door.

The young man's voice again ; the door closing ; dimmed

voices behind it ; the door opening again and the woman returning along the passage. " I am afraid you cannot see him, no. He is not up yet."

Immediately a rising of Mr. Rostrum's temper. " I can wait. But tell him he's got to see me. The matter is urgent."

" Please ? "

" Tell him the matter is very important. I will wait."

The woman went back with this message ; and in a few seconds returned. " He says he is sorry, but it ees quite impossible."

An insult, this ; the temper rose higher ; and Mr. Rostrum, speaking very deliberately, said, " Would you kindly tell him, Madam, that I'm not going till I've seen him." The temper swelling, he did not mind what he said. " Tell him that it is a legal matter."

He saw that the word had frightened the woman. She was an Italian, he guessed, and probably a refugee from the Fascists. To her a visit in the name of the Law might imply much trouble for herself and her house. He drove home his advantage. " Tell him it's a legal matter and must be attended to at once." She gave him an unhappy glance and turned and went back to the room. Mr. Rostrum took the opportunity to step into the passage. And there he stood like a bailiff in possession.

" Wait—wait a minute, Mrs. Parini, please. Wait while I close the door." The young man was speaking, and the door closed, and Mr. Rostrum extended his ear towards it, but he could hear only voices in argument, not their words, except at one time when the young man's voice said loudly, " I will not."

" I think you will," muttered Mr. Rostrum to the closed door.

The door was opening, and Mr. Rostrum's head sprang back into an innocent position. He gazed at a hat-stand in front of him. The woman was returning. " I am afraid it is notta possible. He says he will not see anyone this morning, no."

The temper, which had been smouldering, wanted only this puff of wind to blow it into flames. " I'm very sorry, but then I'm afraid I shall have to take the Law into my own hands. I've got to see him, and I intend to." And before the woman knew what he was about, he had walked past her and was entering the room.

The young man was not in his bed. He was standing in a beige dressing-gown by a table under the window ; and on the table were the remains of a breakfast and an ash-tray with some ash and the stub of a cigarette. A Sunday newspaper was in one of his hands, and a second cigarette in the other. With threads of grey smoke issuing from his fingers he gaped at this visitor who had walked in so unceremoniously. For a second Mr. Rostrum was interested in the appearance of this young man who had lain with Brenda in his house, and surprised, irrationally, that his face should be so ordinary and agreeable. At the moment his face was frightened, even terrified, but there was nothing malign or evil in it. He was cornered now, but in happier times, for nine-tenths of his days he would be just a lazy, amiable, pleasure-seeking lad, no different from a million others, no different, in fact, from Julian.

But the shock of this entry had struck all liveliness from him now and banned all dignity. His face was hardening. " Here ! What the devil ? You can't come into my house like that. Would you mind going out again ? "

" I am Brenda's father."

The young man's eyes were those of an animal trapped. It was clear that the brain behind them was struggling against time with the question, how to bear himself, what to say. He gained time with a word. " Really ? "

" Yes. And I am not leaving this room till I've said to you what I've come to say." Mr. Rostrum too was fighting time : the landlady and her husband might be upon him at any minute. Had he not heard her hastening with her story down her basement stairs ?

The young man's brain was recovering its equipoise. " This is an extraordinary way to behave, but if you are Brenda's father, I don't want to be rude to you. How is Brenda ? "

" I think you know how Brenda is."

" I'm afraid I don't. I haven't seen her for some weeks. Your manner suggests that there's something the matter with her. I hope not."

Now it was Mr. Rostrum who stared, his thinking disabled and his speech struck from him. " I—Brenda has told me everything," he stammered, " and I—I am here to tell you that you're not going to escape a single one of your responsibilities."

" Would you mind shutting the door ? It invariably swings open."

Mr. Rostrum moved towards the door, but decided immediately that he wasn't going to obey him. " The door will do very well as far as I am concerned."

" Very well." With some dignity the young man pressed out his cigarette in the ash-tray, tossed his paper on the bed, walked to the door and closed it. " There are other people in the house, who won't be interested in all this. ' Responsibilities,' you said. I'm afraid I don't understand."

" Oh yes, you do. Did you really imagine you weren't going to hear from me ? Did you really think I should have the least difficulty in finding you ? You're not dealing with fools, you know. You don't just run away from your obligations when a girl has a father and a brother. Next time I should pick your victim more carefully."

" I wish you'd make clear to me what you're talking about. I'm unaware that I have any obligations. I went out with her for a little while, it is true—I don't deny it—but if you think that involves me in any serious obligation, aren't you —aren't you being rather old-fashioned ? Things have changed quite a lot, you know, since Victorian times when, I imagine, you were young. What happened was that Brenda and I quarrelled, and she was very rude to me, and we agreed to part. In point of fact, she told me she never wanted to see me again."

" And that's the whole story, is it ? "

" Certainly."

" You merely walked out with her ? "

" Yes."

" Just up and down the streets or in the park ? Just looking at the flowers, I suppose ? "

" Yes. . . . No, let me be quite accurate. I went to your house once or twice and sat in her room. While you were away, I think."

" And yet "—deliberately, to strike alarm into his heart,

184

Mr. Rostrum stated as a fact what was still only a fear—
" and yet Brenda is expecting a child."

A bewildered silence from the young man ; and Mr.
Rostrum had no doubt what was happening within that
silence : the young man was deliberating whether to admit that
Brenda had told him of her fear and to assert that he had denied
all responsibility then, or to pretend that this was the first
he had heard of it and to deny all responsibility now. Either
lie was so tremendous, so unlikely to be believed, that they were
hanging like impediments upon his tongue. Mr. Rostrum felt
that he was his master now and had him against the ropes.

" I repeat. And yet Brenda is expecting your child ? "

" *My* child ? "

" Yes, sir, your child. And I've come to assure you that
it shall receive every support from you throughout its life.
Every support that the Law enjoins. Perhaps you don't
know that my son is a fully qualified solicitor ? "

When selfishness is driven into its last corner, it turns
to venom. It is converted from a mere absence of good
into living evil. There was a poisonous and malignant
hate in Larry's pale face now. " That's all very fine, Mr.
Rostrum, but there's just one little error, and a basic one.
It is not my child."

Mr. Rostrum met the envenomed look with a smiling and
nodding contempt. " Yes, you're a nice little cad, aren't
you ? If you live till your dying day "—words might get
badly mixed, but what did that matter ?—" you'll remember
how you behaved this morning and sicken at yourself. Or
if you don't sicken with shame at the memory, you'll know
that you're completely bad. You'll know it, because you've
got plenty of intelligence, I can see. I want you to remember
this day. It's a Sunday and the sun's shining. I hope it
sticks in your heart for ever. I hope you remember it when
you're an old man, as old as I am, and when you're dying.
My God, I can almost feel sorry for you, because I don't
think you're really bad, and therefore you must be seeing
at this moment what a noisome little mess you are and be
feeling pretty nauseated with yourself. I hope you are,
because then there's some hope for you. *You* know it's your
child, and we know too. Brenda doesn't lie. And we shall
have no difficulty in proving it." The wind was in his

sails, and he was scudding before it, no matter into what wild waters it drove him. All that mattered was to frighten him—to leave him with such a fright in his heart that he would suffer day and night something of what Brenda had suffered. "There are those who knew you were in my house for whole nights through. You forget that my son was there too. He wanted to come with me this morning and tell you what he knows, but I wouldn't let him. I was afraid of what he would do to you. You forget that there were people in the upper parts of the house. And we have friends across the road ; don't forget that ; we have friends across the road. We know how much they saw, and we shall know when to call upon them. My son and I will know how to deal with the evidence we have, and we shall use it ; we shall deal with you by every process of law. We shall pursue you, if necessary, through every court in the land. You may think that I have not the means for this, but let me tell you I have ample means, and I can think of no purpose to which I would rather devote my capital than bringing you to justice. I know all about you. I can find you at any time. I have made it my business to learn your home address. I have been in communication with your mother——"

"I wonder if you realize "—Larry's gaze was like a poisoned javelin aimed at Mr. Rostrum's eyes ; his hands were trembling—" how unpleasant it is to see an old man giving way to a vulgar, hysterical exhibition——"

"And that, I imagine you think to be clever. You think that hurts me." It did. It hurt him poignantly. "No doubt I seem to you old. I *am* old. I admit I am old, and it may be thanks to that that I haven't indulged in something vulgarer than words. My son may not content himself with words, I fancy, when he meets you. And if it's a vulgar exhibition to let a little rat know the truth about himself and hear what he's got coming to him, then this is certainly vulgar. But I'd rather be vulgar than be the little gentleman that you've been in the last few weeks. I've no doubt the sight of me is singularly unpleasant to you—it was meant to be—but I wonder if you realize how revolting is the spectacle of a slippery little worm twisting and squirming when it's caught and trying to escape with lies——"

Voices outside the door; and the handle turned. A round-bellied and unshaven little man in trousers and shirt, with braces festooned over his hips, his black hair disordered, and his black eyes glittering with the delights of outrage and rancour, entered the room, followed by the large, dark woman, who was tall enough to stare over his head at the scene.

"You cannot walka into my house like-a this. *Dio Santo*, you cannot do it. It is trespassing. It is against the Law of England. Not even the police can do it without they have the search-a warrant. My wife did not know this. She is not a woman who understands politics. But I happen to know that it is the Law in this country that you cannot force-a your way into an Englishman's house, and I am an Englishman, I am a naturalized Englishman. *Si.* So you get outa my house dam queek, ess? You no get outa, I calla da policeman. You may getta past my wife, but notta past me. This is my dam house, and this gentleman is my guest. You go, ess? You go, or I calla da policeman?"

Mr. Rostrum turned to the little man, glad to be able to be polite to someone, liking him (because he had no quarrel with him) in proportion as he disliked Larry, and drawing a subtle pleasure from the prospect of admitting with admirable frankness that technically he had offended.

"I am very sorry, sir. I have no quarrel with you, and I agree that my method of entry was not strictly justified. I apologize to you. I apologize unreservedly to you and to your excellent wife. But it was imperative that I said something to this young man, and I have said it. Yes"—he turned to Larry—"and let me now repeat it in the hearing of these good people. I repeat that you have behaved insufferably and as no man with a shred of decency could possibly have done, and that you are, in my view, a noisome little mess. I have nothing further to add this morning. You will hear in due course from my legal advisers. . . . Thank you, sir. If you will let me pass, I will now get out of your house. Thank you, Madam. Good-day to you both."

§

Mr. Rostrum's heart was hammering and his hands trembling, as he walked into the street. His lips were muttering some of the phrases with which he had scourged Larry, reiterating them automatically, because he was proud of them. He longed to tell someone, Mildred or Julian or Truppy, of the splendid punishment which had come from his lips, and to strengthen the tale by incorporating phrases which were only now occurring to him and inventing others which he might well have used, such as, " I have called you a noisome little mess, and that is a description which I do not feel the passage of time will cause me to revise ; " but he quickly saw that he could do none of this because to do so would be to divulge Brenda's story. And he would never do that. Never. She had entrusted her secret to him, and it would be safe in his heart for all time. It was a minor triumph, this resolution, since it is not easy to keep one's conquests hidden from the world, and he was pleased with it as well as disappointed.

He had not walked far along the street, shaken and breathless—he was not two hundred yards from that house —when the most violent pain shot through his breast. It was the worst that had attacked him in all these weeks. It made him stand still on the pavement and bend forward with his hand pressed against his chest ; and in that long minute of agony, as he always remembered, the church bells ceased ringing, and the clocks struck eleven. He thanked heaven as, still stooping and clutching, he took a few despairing steps along the pavement and halted again, rubbing the seat of the pain, that there was no one in the street to stop and stare at him. The agony lasted till he was able to void wind and then, like an abscess that had burst, it eased. It eased and ended ; but the relief, as when the smoke of a conflagration clears away, found him a shattered ruin, a gutted house, empty even of hope.

In a complete despair he walked on, having no purpose for the present but to get out of that street lest anyone had seen him and to hurry home as a wounded dog slinks into his kennel. Not till he was there, and the door of his own room was shut on him, would he be able to deal with this despair. Alarm had forced the sweat on to his brow, neck, and breast, and he knocked it from his brow with his sleeve and wiped it from his neck with a handkerchief. In Buckingham Palace Road, near Victoria Station, he found a taxi. Telling the driver to drop him near the entrance of Nunsbury Road, Kilburn, he flung himself on to its seat and wiped the sweat again from forehead, ears, and neck. And as the taxi trundled on, he prayed to God. There was nothing else to do, and his lips would have prayed even if his heart was not with them.

" Oh God, not yet. Help me to be with Brenda a little longer. Oh God, what are you doing, striking me down like this when I am only trying to help her. Why are you trying to force me away from her. She is my daughter. I do not understand. But you cannot force me away from her, however much you try. I'm not going while she needs me. You can do what you like to me, but I shall go on as I have been doing, no matter what happens. The pain is bad, but I can endure it. I can stick it out. Oh God, help me. Help me to help Brenda. It is not much to ask. I have not much faith now—I can't feel it, however much I try—but if Thou art there, forgive me that, and help me a little."

His elbow on the window ledge of the taxi, and his chin in his hand, he looked out at Hyde Park and Edgware Road and Maida Vale and wondered if these were his last days for looking on them. Was he killing himself by disregarding the doctor's advice? Was he choosing death as he sat here in this musty and vibrating taxi?

" Well, if I am, I am."

Maida Vale ending; Kilburn Park Road and Brenda's church; Priory Road where he had seen the doctor; Kilburn Empire where he'd often enjoyed an evening's show with Mildred and the children; Kilburn High Road and his own shop-front with his pictures in the window; Nunsbury Road a little way on . . .

" Here you are. Stop here, please."

Tapping on the driver's window, he told him to stop and let him get out before they reached the corner of Nunsbury Road. He paid the driver, tipping him a shilling with the vague idea that he might not have many more opportunities of being generous.

Then he walked slowly into and along his own road, and up the steps of his house, and into his room, shutting the door quietly. There was no pain in him now; only fear;

only despair. As he had not been able to kneel in the taxi, and this might have lessened the value of his prayer, he threw himself upon his knees against his table, thrust the magazines and papers out of the way, and sank his head in his hands. " Oh God. . . ." He tried to remember the words he had used in the taxi. Lifting up his face and gazing at the ceiling—gazing through the ceiling—he tried to repeat them. " Oh God, don't strike me down till I can safely leave her. That is all I ask. Oh God, look down upon us both and help us both. Nevertheless, not my will, but——" no, he couldn't, he wouldn't, say it. He could not suggest that, if it was God's will, Brenda should be deprived of her one support and hope. If that was God's will, he was not associating himself with it. In that case he was on the opposite side from God ; he was fighting Him. He'd stay where he was and be loyal to his own, God or no God. If it was God or Brenda, he knew which side he was on.

" But oh God, help us all if you can, in spite of what I am saying and thinking now. Surely my vision of what is right must come from Thee. . . . Help me. Help me."

As he said these words he heard feet running towards his door. He leapt up from his shameful position. He picked up from the table the *Miniature Camera World* and pretended to be reading it. Sometimes one knows a thing ahead of its happening ; and he knew now that these were Brenda's feet.

His door opened.

" Is that you, Daddy ? " It was Brenda, and her face was illuminated. She was happy. She had not looked like this for many long weeks. " Oh Daddy, where have you been ? Why weren't you in when I wanted you ? "

" Oh, I just went out for a bit. A bit of a walk. I felt like it after breakfast." Should he ask her what had happened ? No : she would tell him. Instead, he tried to be facetious. " How is it you're not at church ? This won't do. We can't have you shirking your duties like this."

" Oh, but you've been gone such ages. You've been gone *hours*. And on the one morning I wanted you to be here. Oh Daddy, it's all right. Can you believe it ? It *was* a mistake, after all. Oh, why is one made to suffer weeks and weeks of agonizing panic about nothing at all ? And

I've worried you so terribly. I've pushed it all on to you."

"My dear, my dear, I'm so glad."

"Oh, is there any joy in the world like the sudden end of a ghastly worry and pain?"

"Nothing." He put an arm round her shoulder and gave her a kiss. "I'm as happy as you."

The unutterable relief of it. It was a joy almost as racking as the pain had been just now; *his* great panic was gone; he would not fail Brenda now; he was free now to go to the doctor at once; perhaps it was not too late; perhaps this was a reprieve from death; perhaps this was a promise of life. . . . And among these greater joys there was a smaller but a very real one, or Mr. Rostrum would not have been Mr. Rostrum: all his capital was saved. . . . But how he had lied to that young man! Never mind, never mind, he was glad of it. He was glad that he had had his fright.

"I want to shout for joy," exclaimed Brenda, rising up and down upon her toes as she stood before him. "I've been *dying* for you to get back. I had no one else to tell. Oh, why in Heaven's name did you have to go out? There was no else in the world I could speak to about it, and it's as necessary to have somebody to pour one's joys over as it is to have a tame somebody to inflict one's pains on. One needs at least *one* person."

He smiled. "I'm sorry if I let you down."

"Oh, I think I can just manage to forgive you, because you've been so wonderful, so absolutely wonderful, these last few weeks. I don't know what I should have done without you. I don't think I could have endured this business quite alone."

"I didn't do much. I was just there when you wanted me. Just standing by with the fire-escape."

"And that was everything. That made it just bearable, knowing that if the worst came to the worst, there was a way out. Oh Daddy, thank you so much."

"Nothing much to thank me for. And now—well, my dearest, that little trouble's all over and done with. Dead and buried. No one need ever know a word about it, and no one ever shall."

" No, and now we can all be happy again. Happy as we used to be."

" Yes. . . ."

When she was gone, he knelt again at his table and, with his face in his hands, thanked God for the miracle.

CHAPTER FIFTEEN

Now he could tell Mildred all about the pain. An ache of weeks could be gratified. He could tell her everything about it from that first attack in the office many weeks ago to this last attack in the street this morning. He could let her know that he had kept silent about it during many weeks, though he mustn't give the real reason for this silence ; he must pretend that he had said nothing for the sake of the whole family. What with his pride in his pain, his pride in his silence, his longing for sympathy, his longing for praise, and the fact that these longings had been repressed for weeks, there was a steam pressure within him that sent him immediately down the basement stairs. It was only Mildred he could tell : the news must be kept a secret from the children, lest Brenda observed a coincidence between his illness and her deliverance, and guessed the reason for his silence and delay. Some days must pass before his examination at the Radiological Department of the hospital could be completed, and the results given them, and if the results were unfavourable and the doctors insisted upon an operation, it would be time enough to speak to the children then. They need never know, and certainly Brenda must never know, that he had been suffering seriously for a long time.

As he went down the stairs, he heard Brenda talking to her mother in the living-room, and sometimes breaking into song ; and he loitered near the door in the dark passage, hoping she would come out and go into her own room. She did not, and, disappointed, he went slowly up the stairs again. But he did not return into his own room ; he waited near the head of the stairs listening to Brenda's voice.

Brenda, in her happiness and gratitude to God, was eager to help her mother or anybody else, and he heard her bustling around and chatting brightly and singing. It was a long time, and a fretting time, before he heard her ask, " What can I do now, Mummy ? " and Mildred answer, " It's half-past eleven, and our bed's not yet made, nor Julian's. We do get so late on Sundays. Would you like to nip upstairs and make them ? "

" Right-ho, Mum. Of course I will. But why, when someone asks somebody else to do something, do they always suggest that it's only a matter of ' nipping ' ? I'll nip."

Mr. Rostrum dodged into his study. The living-room door opened, and Brenda came singing up the stairs and along the passage. She went into their bedroom opposite, and his lines of communication were now open. So he came singing out of his own room, since everybody else was singing, and went down the stairs again. Mildred, having caught Brenda's tune, was humming it over her work, and Dudley was chanting a song of his own, and sometimes shouting advice and instruction to himself. Mr. Rostrum felt a pity for Mildred who was so unaware, as she sang at her work, of the consternation he was bringing to her.

He went in. She was at her ironing board, holding up a pair of Dudley's underpants to the light, before she laid the iron to them. A pile of his vests, shirts, and corduroy shorts lay on a chair at her side. Dudley was lying on his stomach on a toy trolley and, with the toes of his sandals for pro-pellers and his hands for steering purposes, was circling round and round his mother (and under the flex of the electric iron) with engine noises and appropriate orders and interpolated music. Sankey, as pleased as he with this operation, and with the music, was either trotting round with him, like a shining black engine-boiler on paws instead of wheels, or standing at Dudley's arrival station and barking a welcome, while he wagged his whip-like tail.

" Hallo, Daddy," Dudley greeted him, without ceasing to circulate.

" Hallo, Dudley, old pal. . . . Mildred, there's something I think I ought to tell you, dear."

She glanced up, for the words carried a hint of alarm.

" Is something the matter ? Oh, what is it ? "

"It's nothing very much—at least I hope it isn't—but, understand, you're not to breathe a word of this to the children. Promise."

"Look, Daddy!" shouted Dudley, as he propelled himself under the flex and round the kitchen table like an aircraft taxi-ing round the perimeter track.

"Yes, dear, that's fine. . . . Promise you won't say a word to them. Not a word . . . even to Brenda."

"Of course I promise. Oh, what is it?"

"Well, some time ago I was sitting in the office. I was writing a letter to Garden Tanks, Ltd. I was just writing the last words when——" and he told her the whole fine story, from that first assault to the torment of this morning. He told it with swiftness, clarity, picturesqueness, and power, the words coming easily, because his interest in the theme was high enough to amount to inspiration. To dramatize his weeks of silence, and his triumph over himself, he had to paint the background of pain in tints sufficiently dark—his artistic conscience would suffer no less. His moral conscience told him that he ought, for Mildred's sake, to minimize the doctor's words, but the artistic conscience, strongly supported by his longing for sympathy, drove all scruples from the field, and he gave the words their full power. In fact, he spared Mildred as little as he spared Brenda much. His child was something to be protected ; his wife was his natural victim and burden-bearer.

"I had to come back in a taxi," he concluded with pride. "All the way from Victoria Station." It was always a small pride to him if he had taken a taxi ; and he would hope that his neighbours were seeing him if he got out of a taxi at his garden gate. "I stopped the taxi at the corner because I didn't want you to see it and start imagining things. I didn't want you to be worried."

"But, Alec!" Mildred had laid down her iron, as if all ordinary life were suspended. "What can it be? Oh, for mercy's sake mind the flex, Dudley, and keep quiet. What do you think it is?"

"I'm afraid I know what it is. I'm afraid I know only too well." And he explained, trying to be gentler now, the real meaning of the doctor's words.

"Alec! Oh, it can't be that. Why in the world haven't

you told me all this before? Why have you kept it all to yourself? It's not like you."

"What do you mean by that?" Now he was angry with her. Was she suggesting, after his really rather splendid self-martyrdom, that he was one who talked easily about his ailments? She who, if she only realized it, was for ever talking about hers? "I'm not one who likes to talk of his aches and pains to other people. I try to keep them as far as possible to myself. I hate people who are for ever inflicting upon you their latest potty little aches and pains. I dislike them so much that I tend to do the opposite myself. It's what you call a reaction-formation, and I'm very conscious of it. It's extraordinarily strong in me. I've kept lots of pains to myself in my time. More than you know."

"But not if they're serious."

"Yes. Sometimes if they're serious. Certainly if they're serious, sometimes. I've known this was serious for weeks, and I've said nothing about it. I didn't even tell you that I'd been to the doctor about it. And that was weeks ago."

"Did he really think it was serious?"

Did he really think it was serious! Mr. Rostrum was just about to quote the doctor's words, "I'm not prepared to take the risk of letting you wait another day," when he saw that Mildred's eyes were full of tears, and knew that he had struck her a merciless blow. Her eyes might be gazing at him, but really she was looking at Death. At Death and an End. She was thinking, "A few days, perhaps, and he will be gone. He will not be there." In those eyes he saw, as never before, the loneliness and fear of women when they begin to be old. She looked down at Dudley who, his stomach having protested against the trolley, was now sitting on the floor and building a rococo pavilion with his bricks, and instructing himself in his task with shouting, or lightening his labour with song. In that look he saw the fear of a mother who might soon have no man to fight for her child. He saw that the walls of her keep, which a minute ago she had thought to be stable and strong, were falling about her.

He felt guilty and ashamed; and they stood in silence together, looking at the possible End. An end after thirty years. Against that threat the meaning of those thirty years of mutual support and fellowship revealed itself in clear outline and in depth. Never had they known their unity as now. With his pity there mingled pleasure and pride that she should feel helpless without him.

Dudley's pavilion crashed down. "Oh!" he cried. "Damn and blast! I've fallen it all over."

"Do be quiet, darling," begged Mildred, "please, *please!*"

"Damn and blast," said he.

"That'll do. That'll do. Your daddy and I are talking."

"All right. I won't sturb you." And he began to re-build, singing.

"That's a good lovey-boy. That's my precious heart. . . . Oh, well. . . ." And she put on the whole armour of her courage. She held the iron to her cheek, as if picking up the daily duties of life again. Satisfied with its heat, she applied it to Dudley's garment. "I can't think why you didn't tell me. You ought to have done. I wouldn't have let you wait a moment."

"I felt I ought to hold out, if I could, for all their sakes. And Dr. Soden didn't know anything for certain. He said I should have to have an X-ray examination before they could know anything for certain." Now he was minimizing the doctor's words, now that it was too late. "It may be all right. You mustn't worry. Please don't worry."

"Worry? Of course I shall worry."

"It may be nothing. I have long periods when I feel perfectly well, and then I wonder if there's anything in it."

He began to prowl, and his boot came near to Dudley's building works. Dudley shouted to him to keep away.

"Mind! Mind, Daddy. Don't—*don't*, or it'll all come awfully down."

"Sorry, darling."

"Daddy nearly felled it all down, Mummy."

"Did he . . . ?"

"Oh, hell, it keeps undone-ing."

"Don't use words like that, dear. Don't say 'hell'." She laid down her iron. She had come to a decision. "I'm going to get the doctor at once."

"Oh, no, you're not. I can walk round to him if necessary. I'm not on my last legs yet. Perhaps I'll stroll round and see him this afternoon. No, I won't, though. It's Sunday."

"You won't delay another day. If you don't go, I shall."

"All right, then. I'll go if you insist." He was glad she had insisted. "But, remember, there's not to be a word of this to the children. We shan't know anything definite for some days, and if it turns out all right, it'll be a pity to have frightened them unnecessarily. Not a word—and especially not to Brenda. I feel, somehow, that she's the sort who would suffer most. And if we have to tell them in the end, let them think it's only become serious in the last day or two. Perhaps it hasn't been anything so very much, really."

§

Mr. Rostrum went to the doctor that Sunday; and, since we feel kindly disposed to those who admit their folly and our rightness, and since the doctor's conscience had not been happy about his irritable treatment of an elderly patient, he was as kind and encouraging with him that Sunday afternoon as he had been brusque and punitive before. To-day, even though it was a Sunday, he placed his time at Mr. Rostrum's service as generously as the other day he had stinted it. To-day he spread his knowledge before his patient even more fluently, sonorously, and gracefully than on that earlier visit. To-day, in short, he liked Mr. Rostrum as much as the other day he had disliked him.

Under his instruction, armed with his counsel, and with his path made easy for him by the doctor's efforts, Mr. Rostrum went to the hospital. He went four times in the space of eleven days, and all those days he was hoping, hoping, that the doctor's suspicions would be proved wrong; that he would be told to go in peace for there was nothing within him that diet and medicine wouldn't heal. After all, Brenda's alarm had been a false one—God had been good to him in that—and perhaps his alarm was another of the same kind. He prayed each night that God would forgive him his many sins and vouchsafe, if He saw fit, this second mercy.

His first visit to the hospital was for a preliminary consultation with Sir Joshua; his second for a test meal; his third for an X-ray examination; and his last—the last act and climax of this four-act drama—to see Sir Joshua and hear the verdict.

It was half-past ten in the morning when he came for the verdict, and he sat on a bench in the spacious Waiting Hall of the Out-patients Department among sixty or seventy other people, all of whom were awaiting their turn to go through that narrow brown door into the Consulting Room. The brown benches were set like pews, and Mr. Rostrum sat in the fourth of them, in the very midst of the assembled congregation. All of his companions seemed very poor— bent old greybeards; tired old grandmothers; sallow, weedy, hollow-cheeked youths; jaundiced and houseworn young women with squalling babies or scampering children —and he felt extraordinarily gentleman-like as he sat among them. His consciousness of social superiority, and of his best blue suit, white collar, and cuffs, caused him to sit erect and elegantly, like a king granting audience, his umbrella aslant between his knees and his right hand touching it like a sceptre. Perhaps his black hat, which he had removed out of respect to all these poor people and laid upon his opposite knee, might be regarded as the balancing orb. Looking round upon them as he waited, he recalled the words, " Give me your tired, your poor, your huddled masses yearning to breathe free; Send these, the tempest-tost, to me; " and, though he could not remember where they came from, he was proud of having found so apt a quotation.

But as the long minutes built up an hour, and the first half of another hour, he lost all interest in his fellow out-patients, these fish caught up in the same net with him; and he kept his eyes on that Consulting Room door, impatient after eleven days of consultation, examinations, and suspense, for the last act to begin.

" Alexander Rostrum, please." A nurse had appeared in the door.

He stood up and walked towards her.

" Come in, Mr. Rostrum," she said kindly.

All the staff of the hospital were kind, but this long, lofty Consulting Room was not. It was harsh, unemotional, and cold. With a blatant light from its tall windows shining upon its stained and peeling walls, its scratched brown dado, and its scanty furniture, it appeared worn, overworked, and perfunctory. The only furniture was the doctors' table islanded in the sea of bare floor and looking small in so large a room ; a long brown bench similar to the pews outside, standing against the wall ; a weighing machine between the windows ; a sink in one corner with a table of dressings at its side ; and a cubicle in the opposite corner, screened with green curtains. It was, he suddenly thought, remarkably like the Charge Room of a police station. That closed door into the Examination Room might well have been the door into the Detention Room or the way to the cells.

There were two doctors at the table in long white coats, and one of them was Sir Joshua. A young man in a short white jacket, perhaps a student, stood at Sir Joshua's side, bending down to look at some papers, and talking with him. Two nurses were working and whispering at the sink in the corner and at the laden table beside it.

Nervously Mr. Rostrum went towards the empty brown bench, but Sir Joshua called out cheerfully, " No, Mr. Rostrum, come along here, please. Come and sit by me."

So he diverged abruptly and went to the table's end, where he sat by Sir Joshua's left elbow. He saw some large X-ray photographs on the table and a Report from the X-ray Department signed by the radiologist. He tried to see what was on that report, like an examinee cribbing from a better informed candidate, but the writing was not large enough, and his reading glasses were in his pocket. The writing was a blur.

Sir Joshua looked at him with a smile. Sir Joshua Dymote, the Senior Honorary Surgeon of the hospital, was a tall, portly man with a bald head, long nose, merry, mobile lips, and merry little eyes. Lips, eyes, and portly frame proclaimed a man of genial and jovial habit. This smile which he now played like a beam-ray on Mr. Rostrum's features was designed to encourage ease and allay fear.

" Well, Mr. Rostrum ? How've we been feeling since we were last here ? Not too bad, eh ? We're still looking pretty good. Still dodging the undertaker ? "

Mr. Rostrum responded to this kind and encouraging inquiry with a flow of information.

Sir Joshua nodded understandingly as he listened. Then,

the narrative at an end, he said, after a pause, " Well, Mr. Rostrum, you want us to put you right, don't you ? "

" Of course, Doctor."

" O.K. Right-ho, sir ! Then you've got to come in here, and I think we'd better get you in soon. At once."

" Into hospital, you mean ? "

" That's it."

" For an operation ? "

" Right first time."

" Is it—is it cancer ? "

Sir Joshua picked up one of the X-ray photographs and looked at it, but Mr. Rostrum did not believe he was really considering it. He believed he was considering his reply. Apparently absent-mindedly, but probably on purpose, he turned over the radiologist's report so that it was face downward on the table. And he looked up and smiled. " We shall just have to open you up and see. That's all I'm going to say. But even if it is a cancer, we can take it away from you, you know. That is, if we act promptly. But if you wait, it'll spread, and then there's not much we can do. No more waiting, *if* you please." He put on a chiding but forgiving smile. " It was very wrong of you not to do as Dr. Soden told you and come along at once and see me. Soden's a good lad—an old pal of mine—he was a student under me only a little while ago—and I can tell you he's a good doctor, with a real eye for illness." Was he covering a retreat with a smoke-cloud of words ? " You remember all he said to you, don't you ? Or perhaps I should put it : you remember what your desire to procrastinate forced him to say. One just mustn't wait with this sort of thing. One just mustn't."

" Directly I felt free to come, I did," said Mr. Rostrum, and an obstinate sense that he had behaved well compelled him to add, " I might have had to wait much longer."

" Yes . . . well, all I can say is, I'm glad you didn't. I think I must tell you frankly that quite enough time has been lost already, and we're not losing any more. We must operate at once. I will operate on you myself."

" That's very kind of you. Thank you. And may I ask —it's rather important, isn't it ?—may I ask—— ? "

" Ask anything you like."

" What are my chances ? "

Sir Joshua looked at him with a long, teasing smile. " Well, sir, now that you've reconsidered your obstinacy and are doing what your doctors tell you, I think I can say that we've probably taken it in time. Yes. . . . But whether you deserve this gracious and forgiving treatment instead of having the fear of God put into you, I don't know. But no more delays, please. No more family reasons. I never heard such nonsense. The best family reason is to get you right and to send you home to them fitter than you've been for years. Though whether you're half as important to them as you imagine, I doubt. We none of us are. My children don't take me the least seriously. And they don't do anything I tell them, either. They might be temporarily disorganized if I went and died on 'em, but a week after the funeral they'd be quite cheerful again, and probably much better off because they'd have to start fending for themselves instead of having me to do everything for them and keep 'em sitting warm and pretty. Don't you agree ? "

" Yes . . . perhaps. . . ."

" Yes, of course. Certainly. It's enervating for children, all this parental care and protection. There's a lot to be said for letting the old central-heating furnace (that's you and me) go out, so that they've got to get up and light a few fires for themselves. Oh, but you've got a small baby, haven't you ? Well, perhaps on the whole we'd better let you keep him warm a little longer. Just for a year or two. Yes, we must patch you up, I think, for *his* sake, Mr. Rostrum. You go home and tell your wife that when we've decarbonized you and re-bored you, you'll run much more sweetly than you have for years. Tell her she won't know you after we've done with you. Tell her you'll be offering to take out the baby. And add that if you start waiting about again, I shall come round and talk to her myself. *Then* you'll get your marching orders."

Mr. Rostrum tried to smile at the raillery. " How soon shall I have to come into hospital ? "

" Just as soon as we can get you in."

" I shall have a few days to put things in order, shan't I ? "

" Not one more than I can help." But, seeing that this

firm utterance had startled him, Sir Joshua added, " That'll be all right. Don't worry. There's sure to be a day or two before you're written for." And, gathering up the photographs, he packed them together as though the interview were finished.

Instantly Mr. Rostrum's diffidence forced him to get up and prepare to go, though there were many more questions that he would have liked to ask, and that seemed important. But he was always afraid of being a nuisance, and he remembered that crowd of sickly and anxious people waiting on the benches outside.

So they exchanged smiling good-byes, he, Sir Joshua, and the student, who had been listening ; and he walked out of the Consulting Room and through the Waiting Hall and out into the street. Those who watched him go by saw that his long face was so pale as to be almost grey and that there were diamonds of sweat upon his brow. They saw his brow, and the red ring round it left by the pressure of his hat, because he was still holding the hat in his hand out of respect to these poor, suffering people and to the nurses and doctors who were good to them. He kept it in his hand till he was out in the street. He himself saw nothing of the Waiting Hall, nothing of the corridors, and little of the street, because he was seeing all the time that Consulting Room and hearing again Sir Joshua's words. He was reviewing them again and again. " Put you right." He had certainly said that. " Want us to put you *right*. . . . Even if it is a cancer, we can take it away from you, you know. . . . Tell her that when we've done with you, you'll run much more sweetly than you have for years. . . . We'd better let you keep him warm a little longer." But : " Quite enough time has been lost already . . . I think I can say that we've probably taken it in time." Only " think " ? Only " probably " ? Plainly there was urgency. And didn't urgency mean doubt and fear ? " Not one more day than I can help." Was there not more doubt than assurance in these doctors ? Wasn't all the rest only lies to keep up his spirits ? Didn't they always lie because it was bad psychology to tell the truth to patients ? If it was a matter of days, how much damage had he done by waiting all this time ? " As good as new." He had certainly said that at one point. " As good as new—or almost." What was implied by that " almost " ?

He walked home, his mind heavy with doubts and dim with want of knowledge ; but there was one bright glow in the heavy twilight, and this was the prospect of telling Mildred, in a few minutes now, the exciting news and, later on when the children came home, telling them for the first time of his illness and distinction.

§

When he had told Mildred, and they had made their plan for telling the children in the evening, he was restless to tell someone else. And after lunch he went round to see Truppy. He walked quickly, and with some enjoyment, his pains and his fear of them temporarily forgotten, because the interest and excitement in his head were a perfect prophylactic against pain in his body.

It was early closing day in Kilburn High Road, and Truppy's shop door was locked. Mr. Rostrum rang the bell at the side door, and Truppy opened to him.

" Hallo, young Truppy."

" Hallo, young Alec, what now ? "

" I happened to be passing, so I thought I'd pop in and tell you the latest."

" From the hospital ? "

" Yes."

" Well, what is it ? "

" It's a True Bill, old boy. I'm committed for trial, and the case will be tried in the next day or two." And, seeing that Truppy looked confused by his wit, he explained, " Got to have an operation at once, old son."

" Good lord, Alec ! "

" Yes. Thought you'd like to know, so, as I was passing——"

" Heavens, Alec, old man, I don't know what to say, except that—well, here I am, and anything I can do for you and Mildred—Lord love you, I'll shut the shop up if necessary, so as to be at your disposal any minute of the day."

"I know you would, old thing; and thanks very much; but I don't know that there's much I need ask you to do. Not yet. At present I'm fit for most things. I can do whatever's got to be done. But if things go badly, why then . . ."

"They aren't going badly, Alec, old man. Don't you believe it. Doctors can do marvels nowadays. They can take all your inside out and look at it and pack it all back again, and no one any the wiser."

"Sir Joshua didn't seem too gloomy, certainly."

"No, of course not."

"And he's the greatest authority in England on the subject."

"Well, there you are! Don't you worry any more."

"He's going to do the little job himself, which is something of an honour, I understand. He doesn't operate on anybody."

"Well, he wouldn't do it unless he believed in it, you bet. It's like a Defending Counsel with a great reputation to keep up. He doesn't take on a case unless he's got a pretty good chance of winning it. He doesn't want to be associated with failure. If *he* says *he's* going to do it, that's O.K. *I* shouldn't worry. Don't you worry, old man."

"He said I should be almost as good as new after it."

"Fine. He probably saw at a glance that he'd a tough old sinner in you, who could stand up to anything."

"Yes, this is the first time I've ever been really ill—if you can call it ' ill '."

"When does the great event take place?"

"Any day now. To-morrow, perhaps, for all I know."

"Well, look here, old thing: I'd like to go along with you to the hospital when the time comes. You must let me do that." And as if ashamed of the sentimentality of this, he justified it. "Mildred'll probably be rather upset after she's said good-bye to you—not that there's any reason to be really anxious, not in the least, but you know what women are when someone of their own is ill; and hospitals and operations always frighten them much more than is necessary—she'll probably work herself up a bit, if I know her; she may even raise a rare to-do, and then I could be of some support to her as she comes away. I could bring her home."

For a second Mr. Rostrum saw a picture of Mildred, half a head taller than Truppy and twice his weight, being led home by him in disarray and general dissolution, but he put it aside at once because he preferred to be greatly moved by this offer of his friend ; and he *was* moved—moved to tears. He turned away that Truppy might not see him in his weakness. " Thank you, old man. I shall be glad to think of her being looked after by you. I'll let you know when I get my summons."

" You won't come in and see Florrie ? "

" No, *you* tell Florrie. I mean, it's not a subject I like talking about much. It always embarrasses me to talk about myself and my troubles. To you, I don't mind ; that's a different thing. I've told you most of them, haven't I, in my life ? No, *you* tell her. Besides, I've a great deal to do —a very great deal—I've all my house to put in order in case . . . the worst happens. A good workman always leaves the place clean behind him, doesn't he ? And in the old war we always left the field absolutely tidy when we struck camp, didn't we, Truppy ? Yes, I've a lot of work in front of me and I'd best be getting down to it. So cheerioh, young Trupps."

" Good-bye, old man ; and good luck."

" So long."

And Mr. Rostrum strolled away along the pavement wondering whom else he could tell about his interesting condition and about Sir Joshua ; and Truppy shut his private door upon the street. The door latched, he ran up the steep, narrow stairs to tell Florrie, who was in the sitting-room immediately above the shop. He was shocked by Alec's news, but within the shock, like a vein of shining silver in a lump of heavy rock, there was an element of pleasure. He was pleased to have this alarming news to carry to Florrie ; and he was happy as he ran, because he was designing for himself, in these melancholy circumstances, the part of a perfect friend. An earnest and sentimental little man, he loved and admired his friendship with Alec as much as Mr. Rostrum admired it ; and he was glad that it was now going to be put to the Test. He assured himself that it was going to pass the Test with distinction. Truppy never heard over the wireless, in his room above the shop

a song like " Mate o' Mine " without a swelling of the throat
and a secret pleasure in applying the word to Alec and
himself. " We wended road and hill, mate o' mine." They
had not wended the hills together, but they had wended
pavement and High Road many a time, confiding in each
other and supporting each other with sympathy and counsel.
" And if you should be late returning home, I'll greet you,
mate o' mine." Was not that how the words ran ? He
was not quite certain what they meant, but they sounded
beautiful, and he applied them now, the lump swelling in
his throat, to Alec and the darkness that had gathered
around him. The song, " I'll walk beside you," in the minds
of other listeners, might seem the song of a lover to his
beloved : to Truppy it was always the song of a friend to
his friend. " I'll walk beside you through the passing years,
Through days of cloud and sunshine, joy and tears ; And
when the great call comes, the sunset gleams, I'll walk
beside you through the land of dreams."

If this was the great call for Alec, he'd walk beside him.

Meanwhile Mr. Rostrum was daundering along the High
Road in the hope of meeting someone else to whom he could
unfold his stirring tale. But the shops were all shut, and,
though he walked a considerable distance past the doors
of his neighbours, and came back the same way, he met
nobody. So he fell to wondering whom he could tell by
letter and in less than a minute he was hastening home,
as eager to write to one person as he had been to visit
Truppy. He composed the letter as he walked. Delightful
work, because he was feeling like one who'd had a great
success ; feeling much as Julian felt when he heard that
he had passed his Finals with First Class Honours. And
he justified this urge to write immediately by telling himself,
" Yes, she ought to know. She's my only sister."

§

It was quiet in the house that night after the family had
been told. And this quiet, this almost tangible sobriety,
made him feel both sad and happy : sad because he was
sorry for them all and because their anxiety made him
anxious ; and happy because of the handsome cloak with

which the threat of death had invested him and because of the tranquil, modest, and dignified way in which he was wearing it. He could not but feel that his bearing in this somewhat tragic atmosphere was good.

The bearing of the children was most praiseworthy too, he thought; they were fine children that he had produced. Julian was not fooling to-night. On the contrary he was either keeping silent or jumping up from his chair and offering to help his mother. " O.K., Mum! *I'll* do that for you...." Joanie was frightened, chastened, and tongue-tied, but in her too the danger had quickened a new considerateness. " O.K., Daddy, Brenda and I can do that." To which Brenda would add : " Yes, *you* sit down, Daddy. What's the good of being the family's little invalid if we don't all wait on you? Make the most of it, *I* should." But Mr. Rostrum could not help wondering what were the real thoughts of two, at any rate, of these children : Julian and Joanie. They were young ; and were their selfish thoughts stronger, perhaps, than their compassion? Was Julian thinking, " If Daddy dies, I shall have to help support Mother ; " and was Joanie thinking, " How will this affect my marriage to Steve ? " Probably they were thinking these things and trying not to ; and he did not blame them. He could understand the burden of parents to young people who longed to rush out into the lively world ; and all he wanted to do was to live and be healthy and preserve them from any such burden. Of Brenda he had little doubt but that she was thinking only of him. Ever since she had been relieved of her dark anxiety—until to-night—she had been radiant with happiness, and as between herself and her father all barriers had been dispersed like vapour on the wind ; she had been a daughter as demonstrative as she was devoted, and as close to him as a wife ; so that he had been telling himself, " At least I shall have known this happiness before I die." And now, her mother having told her the news when she came home from her school, she had run up to him in his study, put her arms around him, and said, " Oh Daddy, it's going to be all right ; I *know* it is—and, do you know—it's very wrong, I'm sure—but a bit of me is almost glad that you're not as well as you ought to be, because now I can do everything for *you*. You will let me, won't you ? " And that evening after supper Brenda slipped from the house. There was a week-night service at her church.

Only one of them, Dudley, was completely indifferent to the atmosphere in the home and as happy as ever. " Quiet, *quiet !* " Mildred begged of him more than once, but Mr. Rostrum said only, " No, no, let him be happy. I like to hear it."

§

The next day he spent some time in his finishing-room at the shop, arranging with Miss Fletcher for her to carry on in his absence, writing to customers to postpone or cancel engagements, and setting his papers in order lest he should return to this room no more. After he had sat at his desk for a couple of hours, writing the letters and arranging the papers, he got up and walked about thinking, " Is there anything else I ought to do ? My will is made ; I have nothing to add to that. My papers are now in order : there is nothing that Julian cannot handle if I'm no longer there. Is there anything I have left undone ? "

He looked at his long working-bench against the wall, with prints and designs laid upon it. He looked at the shelves and pigeon holes above, holding plates, films, printing papers, dry mounts, catalogues, directories and old copies, ten or a dozen years old, of the *British Journal Photographic Almanac*, the *Miniature Camera Magazine*, and the *American Annual of Photography*. He looked at the table against the opposite wall, on which stood his retouching desk, his guillotine, his dry-mounting press, and some prints which had yet to be mounted. Those prints held his eyes. He would mount them now. A good workman, as he had said to Truppy, left everything well completed, and swept and dusted and tidy, before he went from the house.

Taking the first of the prints and some shellac mountant tissue, he placed the tissue behind the photograph and with the top of his hot mounting iron touched the tissue at one or two points so that it adhered to the photograph. Then he put the photograph, with the tissue adhering, into the guillotine and trimmed them—a neat, nice, delicate operation and one that filled him with a sense of power ; a satisfying operation in every way. Next he prepared the art mount, laying upon it black edging paper and Japanese tissue, both trimmed to fit the print. When all this—print, tissue, and edging paper—had been precisely centred on the mount, he loosely fixed it with his iron. Now came the most satisfying moment of all because it brought the neat task to completion : he unscrewed the dry-mounting press, put mount and print within it under a sheet of zinc, and swung the press home, holding it down for some five seconds.

To this pleasant work he gave the best part of another hour, and since it was largely mechanical, his thoughts wandered far from this room, and far from Kilburn, as he manipulated guillotine, iron, or press. They wandered to Callerdale and its lake with the wooded islands afloat on it ; to the Yacht Pond at the base of the green heath ; to London-grey streets he had lived in as a boy and to the church with the tinted and chequered windows where he had attended afternoon service on dusky winter Sundays. From that church, and from the sermons that he had heard there and the prayers that had risen in unison from its brown, ranked pews (" Forgive us our trespasses as we forgive them that trespass against us ") his thoughts strayed into the narrow path, " Is there anyone with whom I ought to make my peace ? " And as he asked that of himself, unscrewing the press, he remembered the young man in Munster Street. He lived again through that violent scene in the ground-floor room. And once again his mind threw up a text that he'd often heard from pulpit or lectern, " Let not the sun go down upon your wrath."

He laid a well-completed print upon the table, joined his hands behind his back, and gazing down at the old linoleum on his floor and the patternless track which his feet had worn in it after thirty years, he considered a chain of new ideas. Often, because his head was bent, his working spectacles, which he had not removed, slid forward on to the bridge of his nose, and he pushed them back into place. That boy. He had behaved abominably, but in terror ; and he was young. Death, coming close, so close as to be perhaps only a day or two away, made one feel very gentle towards every-body, and especially towards the young. He was not wholly bad, that boy—no one was wholly bad. He might grow into a very decent man yet, and especially if someone showed him an example of generosity. No man, young or old, had ever been helped or healed by hate, but only by forgiveness. Did punishment ever help or heal anyone either? He doubted it. Sometimes it might do a little, but unless it was gently done, it was far more likely to harden the offender and teach him violence and vindictiveness and contempt. Anyhow, the boy'd had his punishment : one could imagine his daily and nightly fear since Mr. Rostrum had visited him nearly a fortnight ago. And one knew what it was to walk with fear ; Brenda knew, and he, Mr. Rostrum, knew. It would be a good and right thing to try to help that young man by an example of forgiveness, and he would like to do a good thing before the end—if the end was really at hand.

" Yes, he's only young, after all, and he was very much afraid," said Mr. Rostrum, measuring the room with even tread. And he recalled many weak and contemptible things which he himself had done when he was young and hungry and afraid. And some of these, indeed most of these, as he reminded himself, had never been punished at all.

" Yes, I will do it. All's well that ends well, and I don't want him to suffer any more. Brenda has been set free from her fear. Let him be set free too."

Leaving guillotine, press, and prints, forgetting them, he went straight to the desk and gave himself to the joy of framing a letter in well-trimmed and well-mounted phrases. And just as the last acts of mounting a print were the most satisfying of all, so it was pure joy when he was penning his fair copy from the mangled drafts at his elbow.

" DEAR MR. BLYTHE,
" You will remember my visit to you some days ago when we discussed certain obligations which, in my judgment, devolved upon you. At the time we were both a little heated——"

No : " heated " was crude ; it lacked dignity.

" We were both somewhat incensed, and you were not prepared to admit the existence of those obligations ; but I cannot, I do not, doubt, that in the end you would have acknowledged them. I am confident that the behaviour for which I censured you, and the manner in which you

210

saw fit to address me, taunting me with my age, were not a true expression of yourself, and I readily concede that my asperity at the time was such as to provoke you to reprisals which later your kindlier and more generous side weighed at their true value and regretted. Unless I am quite mistaken in you, you will have suffered much apprehension and distress in these last days, and I am genuinely glad to be able to relieve you of any further anxiety. It has transpired that the particular event which we anticipated is not, after all, to come about. As often happens in such cases, our apprehensions were not justified, and I feel it only right, therefore, to assure you that you will hear no more of me and my family ; and I take this opportunity of wishing you well.

> " Believe me,
> " Your sincere well-wisher,
> " ALEXANDER ROSTRUM."

When he had written this, a quite extraordinary happiness suffused him, so that he knew as surely as the wisest man that what he had done was good. In a mood so happy one cannot work, and Mr. Rostrum, unable to turn again to his prints, sat at the desk for a long time, thinking of dead loves and old sins.

§

It was about four o'clock when he arrived home ; and at thirteen minutes past four a taxi came sighing up to his gate. From his chair in his study he heard it stop at the gate, and, since only the double knock of a telegraph boy is a more exciting sound than this, he leapt up to see who it was who had come to see him. It was the Widow Leicester. She stood on the pavement by the taxi door, a splendid assembly of blacks and whites : black hat with a single black and white feather, white waved hair, black coat with a black fur over one shoulder, grey-white stockings and black high-heeled shoes. On the pavement at her side stood a black gladstone bag, and on one elbow, as she fiddled in her purse, was a cone of white paper from which there peeped, shaggy as sheep dogs, the heads of some massy chrysanthemums. He heard her loud, deep, manly voice in a humorous and patronizing argument with the taxi-driver.

"No, I can carry that, haw, haw! I'm old, I know, but I can still carry a gladstone bag up a few steps. Well, if you insist, but I don't mind telling you that if I hadn't been in a hurry, I shouldn't have taken a taxi at all, haw, haw. I flatter myself I can walk to most places, and you're mostly rogues, you taxi-men. There you are: there's what the taxi-meter says, and a shilling over, and I suppose you'll say it isn't enough. No? Well, I'm agreeably surprised; I fully expected to be insulted."

Now they were coming up the steps, the taxi-man following behind her with the bag.

"Thank you; that'll do. I'll look after it now. You go off and earn some more money. Good afternoon."

Mildred, who had been in the front bedroom and run to the window as speedily as Mr. Rostrum, opened the door promptly and was at once greeted by the loud, manly voice.

"Don't worry. Don't worry. Don't be alarmed. I haven't come to stay. I hope I've too much sense for that. You've troubles enough without an ancient aunt in the best bedroom. I shall find a room somewhere: simple as A.B.C. I never mind where I sleep: travelled too much in my time. I flatter myself I'm a bit of an old campaigner, that way. I've just come to help you all I can; not to be a nuisance. How is he? Hasn't gone to the hospital yet? Good. No, I've just come to do all the chores while you look after him. You'll need to be free of all household worries. I remember what it was when James was so ill. I take it those girls will have to go to their work as usual, and you'll need someone to clean the house and do the shopping and cook the meals. I'll be head-cook and bottle-washer. I never mind what I turn my hand to. James used to say that I was the best cook of all those that he'd employed. And most of all, if I know anything of the young man, you'll want somebody to take Master Dudley off your hands. I'll take him out. All day if you like. Children are always good with me. I thought I'd take him to the Zoo and Madame Tussauds. And then there's that dreadful dog—Sankey, or whatever you call him—what a name for a dog!—he's got to be taken out for exercise and other small matters twice a day, if I know anything about a dog."

Mildred's voice, stuttering but pleased : " Oh, it *is* good of you. It is, really. Yes. Thank you very much. No, really, honestly, I *am* grateful," she insisted, as though normally, in the presence of the Widow, her " Thank you very much " meant something else. " It's most terribly good of you. It has solved all my difficulties. It *is* good of you."

" Not at all. Nothing of the sort. What else should I do ? He's my only brother, isn't he ? I got his letter this morning, and I was packed up and out of the house in two hours. I'll stay just as long as you need me and disappear directly I'm *de trop*. I've nothing to do for the next week or two : just an old horse out to grass and quite glad to be put in the shafts again. And, by the way, I brought a few flowers to brighten things up a bit. I thought he might have gone to the hospital, and you'd like something to cheer you up. These hospital businesses are always depressing. Ah, here he is."

Mr. Rostrum had gone out to meet her, but before he could say a word she was disburdening him of all fears with an upraised palm.

" Don't worry. Don't worry. I haven't come to stay. I'm just the char. Under Mildred's orders for ten hours a day. I'll turn up at seven in the morning, if you like, and cook the breakfast, and fade away in the evening when she wants to be alone with the children. Aunts can be an awful nuisance, I know. Don't tell *me !* Figures of fun. But they have their uses if only they can be persuaded to stay in the background. But what do you mean by saying that you're ill ? I've never seen you look better. You look better than you did last time I was here ; I thought you were looking very much under the weather then, and rather yellow. He's an old fraud, isn't he, Mildred ? There's nothing the matter with him at all. And there's the little man. How are you, Dudley ? Coming to the Zoo with your old Auntie ? See the lions ? And have a ride on the elephant ? "

The sight of his aunt stirred a pleasing reminiscence in Dudley.

" Bubbly," he said, thrusting his head forward.

" Haw, haw, haw ! Why does he say Bubbly ? What an extraordinary child ! He really is a Cure, isn't he ?

Yes, well, I'll sit down for a bit, and then go out and look for a room. No, nonsense. I'm adamant. I'm not going to turn anyone out of their room and make more work. Besides, you can't have the char living in the house."

§

Next morning, at half-past ten, the whole family, with the exception of Dudley, came out of the front door of 25, Nunsbury Road to start upon their walk to the hospital. Mr. Rostrum was in his best hat and best black coat and striped trousers. He had put on these garments because he wanted the nurses, patients, and porters to realize that, though he was in a public ward, he was a man of some substance and paying for his bed. Mildred had given some pains to her appearance too, and her hat was her best ; after all, visiting a hospital was not unlike going to church, and she would have to walk before the eyes of a considerable congregation. Brenda and Joanie were there, both having been granted compassionate leave ; and Julian was with them, carrying the suit-case ; he was his own master now, and had not hesitated to grant himself compassionate leave. Truppy came out of the house just behind the others ; he had arrived a quarter of an hour before, in accordance with his promise to go with Alec to the hospital and to look after Mildred, and when he found that Julian and both girls would be going too, he felt, as he said, " something of an also-ran," but all were pleased that Truppy should be with them, and he was proud to be there. The Widow in an apron and holding Dudley with one hand stood on the step and waved them good-bye, while she propelled Sankey back into the house with a foot. She had arrived at the front door like a charwoman at nine o'clock, and had been cleaning the house for some time, Dudley helping her. " You take yourselves off, you people," she had said, " and leave it all to me, and to this young man, who appears to be my mate." As Mr. Rostrum went down the steps, he turned to look back at Dudley, and he thought, " I'd like to be spared to provide for him. It was pretty good, that day when we heard that Julian had passed with honours ; in fact, I've had few happier moments. I should like to see some such day with the Little Boy. I should like to set

214

him on his path like Julian. Another fifteen years would be enough. He'd be nineteen then. And I did my job by Brenda too. I should like to do it by him." And he waved to the little boy.

Dudley waved back with a humorous vehemence, and then Mr. Rostrum turned his face to the road and did not look round again.

They passed through the gate on to the pavement. And on the pavement Truppy, not being one of the family but only a friend, walked a little to one side of the others and said nothing. (" I'll walk beside you.")

It was no distance to Kilburn General Hospital, and soon they saw its vast grey blocks, barrack beyond barrack, many-angled against the sky, above the Kilburn villas.

" Quite a nice little pub," said Mr. Rostrum. " Seems roomy."

" Looks like the Ritz to me," said Truppy. " What are you having here, young Alec ? A suite ? "

" The Ritz ! More like Rowton House."

" What on earth's Rowton House ? " inquired Brenda.

" Rowton House, my dear, is a home for down-and-outs. Good, clean beds for destitute old gentlemen. An excellent institution. I've long had it in mind as a place where, if necessary, I could spend my declining years."

Julian was staring at the grey, massive, many-windowed buildings. " You're allowed visitors after the first few weeks of your sentence, aren't you, Dad ? " he asked.

" If you behave yourself and earn the necessary remission marks, I think so . . . yes."

" And if you refrain from assaulting the warders."

" That's right."

So, joking rather weakly, they passed into the forecourt, and up the fan of white steps. Mr. Rostrum made another joke here, concerning the steps of the scaffold ; and the joke was a screen for the thought, Would he ever see those steps again ?

Now they were in the Main Hall, spacious, empty, and echoing. Long corridors branched from it, to left, to right, and straight ahead. The one straight ahead was so long that it seemed to go on and on into the dark abysm of future Time. It reminded Mr. Rostrum of the last shot in a film, when the central character is seen going away from the audience, down an endless vista, getting smaller and smaller, while the curtains close slowly across the screen.

An enormous hall porter, chosen perhaps to be in scale with the enormous hall, stood in a glassy office by the main doors, and Mr. Rostrum went to its open window with the printed form which had summoned him to the hospital. He felt a little ashamed before this uniformed official of being a patient, an inmate, and not a visitor of distinction.

" I—er—I have to report to the George Hoskin Ward," he stuttered. " Can you tell me where it is ? " and he thought, " If he says, ' To left,' or ' To right,' all will be well ; but if he says, ' Straight ahead down that long corridor there,' then . . ." but he left the alternative unstated.

" Yes, I can," laughed the porter, studying the document. " Yes, I can manage that for you ; " and Mr. Rostrum was not sure that he liked this easy badinage ; he suspected that, as the George Hoskin was a public ward, he was not being accorded the respect that a private patient would have received. " The George Hoskin Ward is straight on and up the stairs at the end. When you've gone up the stairs to the first floor, take the corridor to the right, and you'll come to it."

" Thank you," said Mr. Rostrum, politely but a thought coldly.

" Git up them stairs," whispered Julian, as the whole family started upon its journey along that far-stretching corridor. In the mists at the end they found a wide, central staircase, and they went up it. They passed a half-landing which had corridors branching from it, and arrived upon the first floor. Here they took a corridor to the right and walked on and on but came to no George Hoskin Ward. They turned at right angles and went along another corridor, and at right angles again and along a third, but nowhere did they see the name " George Hoskin Ward." They turned about and strolled back. Mr. Rostrum, as the natural leader of the party, walked a few paces in front of them with a quick step and peering anxiously, unwilling to allow that he was lost. The family, and Truppy, trailed behind. Nurses in crisp uniforms hurried past him ; doctors and porters in white coats walked past him less briskly, but quite as deliberately; and they all seemed too preoccupied, too set upon their present course, to suffer with any kindness a sudden stoppage and interrogation. He was rather afraid of them. They, for their part, seemed quite accustomed to the sight of a family wandering in some strength along the corridors at eleven o'clock in the morning.

" I suggest, but it's no business of mine," submitted Julian, " that we must have got a few points off our course. I suggest an S.O.S."

" No, I shall find it in a minute. I don't want to ask any of these nurses."

" I've seen one or two I should very much like to ask. There have been others, I confess, towards whom I haven't felt driven at all. But I'm sure they're doing an excellent work."

" Well, don't ask *any* of them. I've set my heart on finding the place."

" O.K., Boss. You're in command of the convoy."

" It must be somewhere here."

" Oh, yes, it's in the hospital all right."

" He said the first floor, didn't he, that porter? "

" Yes, but perhaps he isn't clear himself where it is. Should I go one way, and you another, and then we could meet somewhere and report? "

But Mildred wasn't having any of this. " No, for heaven's sake let's all keep together, or we shall all lose each other."

" Oh, well," sighed Julian, " *solvitur ambulando*, which, as our Brenda will tell you, means, ' The problem will solve itself if we go on walking long enough '."

" As if I didn't know that," protested Mr. Rostrum. " I don't need Brenda to tell me that. Of all Latin tags, that's about the most overworked."

" Sorry," Julian apologized.

And they walked on, Truppy trailing one pace to the rear, because he was not quite sure of his *locus standi*—if such a term can be used of a place with a peripatetic family.

Suddenly Mr. Rostrum remembered the half-landing and the corridors down there. " Perhaps that was what he meant by the first floor."

" If he meant that, he can't speak English," said Brenda.

" Why should he? " demanded Julian.

" I should call that a mezzanine floor," continued Brenda.

" Yes, you would," agreed Julian.

" Well, wherever it is," said Mildred, " let's go and see if this place is there."

So they went back to the stairs and down to the half-landing and along the corridor to the right. But down here, no matter how many corridors they turned into—and they turned into many—they came upon no wards at all. Nor did they meet any people.

" Do you think we've got into the Underground by mistake ? " asked Julian.

But just then a young probationer with black hair, round red cheeks, and large childish eyes, eighteen years old and looking fourteen, came running out of a door, and Mr. Rostrum, suddenly aware that she was the first person in the hospital of whom he wasn't afraid, accosted her in mid-rush, so that she screamed and laughed and apologized.

" Oh, no, you're all wrong," she said, when she'd heard his inquiry. " It's up here. I'll show you."

And she led them up the stairs again.

" Perhaps we've got to get on to the Piccadilly Line," mumbled Julian.

The young probationer led them, as it seemed, along exactly the same corridor as they had examined before, but this time there was a George Hoskin Ward on the left of it.

" It wasn't here when we came this way before," objected Mr. Rostrum.

" It's come back since then," suggested Julian.

" I think you must have been in a different corridor," smiled the probationer ; and with a further smile she left them by the entrance of the ward and went posting away on her present errand.

" Well, that's a mystery I shall never understand," said Mr. Rostrum. " What do we do now ? "

" Search me," answered Julian.

" Wait for the next probationer," suggested Brenda.

Looking through the swing doors, they saw that there were two small halls, separated by swing doors, before they came to the real entrance of the ward. These two halls were empty.

" Do we go through ? " asked Mr. Rostrum of the family in general.

" Why not ? " asked Julian.

" We can but be driven out again," agreed Brenda.

" Well. . . ." Indecisively, falteringly, Mr. Rostrum led them into the first hall and through the intervening doors into the next, but did not like to go any further. To go further would be to step into the ward. Pulling at his lip in doubt and meditation, he looked through the glass of the doors and studied the ward. It seemed almost as long as another corridor, but it was as full of people and activity as the corridors, for the most part, were empty. Every bed seemed occupied by a male patient, either lying down or sitting up in a red jacket. A doctor, old and grey-haired, with a dozen young men and women, the whole company in white coats, was moving among the patients, presumably on a teaching round. Probationers were pushing trolleys with cups and saucers along the feet of the beds. A sister, or senior staff nurse, with a mask over her nose and mouth, was pushing a dressing trolley down towards the doors. Nurses came hurrying out through the doors, nurses went hurrying in ; a young doctor, his steps as unhurried and calm as the nurses were rapid and obedient, went in, spoke to the sister, and came out ; but none of these people took any notice of the Rostrums. Again it looked as if they found nothing more natural than that a family group, father, mother, three grown-up children and uncle (?), should be standing at the entrance to the ward, silent and inert except that now and then they looked wistfully in.

At last a tall young nurse came out and, so to speak, really saw them ; really saw a body of dark-clad, waiting people. She could not help seeing them because they were standing in strength before the door of the Clinical Room, which she wanted to enter. She stopped, as if the realization of their concrete reality was a shock ; a blow between the eyes.

" Is there anything I can do for you ? "

Mr. Rostrum explained his position, feeling that the explanation was not uninteresting, but she was unmoved. She answered only, " Oh, yes. Would you wait in here ? " and opened a door on the opposite side of the hall. Obeying with the immediate subserviency, the over-stressed thanks, and the sycophantic smiles of the humble, they flowed into a small side-room, where she left them, shutting the door.

The room was empty except for a wheeled stretcher or trolley piled with pillows, some wheel chairs, a shelf littered with old library books, and a few bedside chairs.

" Now they've put us among the junk," said Julian.

" Hope they won't forget us," said Brenda. " This doesn't look like a place that's often visited. Do we sit down ? "

" Why not ? "

So they sat themselves on some of the chairs and waited. No one said anything more ; even Julian lapsed from the effort to be funny. They just sat listening to the sounds in the vast building that encompassed them : the purr of ascending lifts, the clash of lift gates, the ringing of a telephone, the voice of the nurse answering it, and the whispering and giggling of some other nurses in a neighbouring room.

After ten minutes the tall nurse swept in again and said, " You can come now," and " No, you only, please," to Mr. Rostrum, as all his family rose. The family sat down again promptly and with some shame. Julian had picked up the suit-case and sat holding it on his knee. The nurse took it from his hand before he knew what had happened to it. He looked down at the hand so suddenly evacuated. Mr. Rostrum, jerked into instant obedience by the nurse's brisk movements, followed her without word or question from the room ; and it was only in the hall outside that he remembered he had lost sight of the family without taking any farewells.

" Do I—do I see them again ? " he asked.

" Oh, yes, we'll let them come in and see you before they go," she said ; and there was a sharp relief at his heart.

Now they were through the swing doors and he was being led along the ward. She seemed to be leading him the whole length of it to the swing doors at the other end, while the eyes from every bed followed him on his long walk. He was vaguely aware of men with bed-cradles over their legs to keep the bed-clothes from touching them, men with wasted faces lying still, men with fractured legs strung up to beams, men in red flannel jackets sitting propped up with pillows, and convalescent men in dressing-gowns standing or walking about the ward.

The nurse led him into the bay between the tenth and eleventh beds. Here she sat him, baffled and obedient, on the bedside chair; set down the suit-case; fetched screens from an alcove and arranged them around him and the bed; wrote down certain particulars in the admission book including the name, address, and telephone number of his nearest relative (the significance of which he did not miss); took his pulse, temperature, and respiration and charted them; helped him undress; packed him up in the bed; and whisked through the screens to fetch the family.

A few seconds, and the family came threading into the privacy behind the screens. Truppy came a pace or two behind the others. " You can stay for five minutes," said the nurse, and she beamed once on them all, and was gone.

Since no one spoke, Mr. Rostrum plunged desperately into humour. " Well, this is Something Like. A Bit of All Right. What do you say to this, Truppy ? "

" I say it's a scandal. Going to bed at eleven in the morning. *I've* got to go back and work."

" Wish *I* was ill," said Julian.

" Wish I *were*," corrected Mr. Rostrum. " That's right, isn't it, Brenda ? Brenda keeps a very sharp eye on the family's grammar, Trupps. She's very stern. More than our life's worth to make a mistake."

" *He* isn't ill," scoffed Truppy. " He looks much better than I do. Old Malingerer. It's when you see him in bed that you realize what a humbug he is. Medicine and Duty is all I'd have allowed him." Twenty years before Truppy had been in the army for a few months when the nation was in peril, and he couldn't forget it.

" Well, don't think I approve of it, old boy. It's the first time I've done anything like this in sixty years. Spoiling my record."

" My only comfort is that they'll wake you up at about four in the morning. Lord knows why, but they do. I know. I've been in hospital."

" Well, I dunno. Feels funny in bed at this time of the day. ' I'll go to bed at noon.' Who was it said that ? "

" The fool in *Lear*," provided Brenda, who could never resist a chance to display her knowledge of literature.

" Oh, yes, of course. We saw it together, didn't we, at the Royalty. Brenda insisted on us all going. *Some* play, Truppy." And he suddenly remembered that " I'll go to bed at noon " were the last words heard from the fool before his death, but he decided not to remind them of this, though he was no less eager than Brenda to display knowledge.

Mildred was saying nothing. She was arranging on the locker at the bedside the comforts which she had packed for him : a jar of jam, a small tin of sugar, a box of sweets, some cartons of cigarettes, some notepaper and a half-dozen books. These in order, she arranged his shaving tackle beside the soap dish, prayer book, and Testament, which were already on the locker. When there was nothing more in this kind that she could do, she laid her finger on his hand which rested on the coverlet. That was to say enough.

Their embarrassment was dispersing, their conversation becoming less forced, when, all of a sudden, one of the screens left them, propelled by a new nurse who said, " Sorry. Must have these ; " and, smiling apologetically upon them all, she removed the two screens to another bed at the other end of the ward. The Rostrums were left to say their good-byes in public.

" Oh . . . well. . . ." Mr. Rostrum waited till the second of the screens had rolled away. " Well, there we are," he said, when he felt adjusted to this nakedness. " Julian, I leave it to you to see that the Awful Little Boy doesn't bully your mother. He's not to knock her about. At least, not more than he can help."

" I'll biff his behind if he does."

" Don't be too severe with him. He ought to be allowed to do a little in that line, if he wants to."

" Oh, no, he oughtn't. I intend to establish some discipline while I'm in command. Any monkey-stuff, and he'll be out of the house on his ear."

" And Brenda and Joanie, you will try to be polite to the Widow. She's behaving very well, and, remember, she'll probably be worn to a shadow of herself to-night after a day with the Little Boy."

" She'll probably give us notice to-night," said Brenda. " ' One day in our courts is better than a thousand,' as the psalm says, in a singularly unfortunate phrase."

" Well. . . ."

It was none of it any good. Their incipient ease had been destroyed at a breath, their current of persiflage cut off at the source, by the departure of the screens. Mr. Rostrum strove to rebuild the ruins.

"Eleven o'clock. I suppose it'll all be over this time to-morrow. I shall have been nicely filleted."

"*Don't!*" pleaded Mildred, disliking the joke.

"It's nothing," Truppy comforted her. "Just a little bit of plumbing. Personally I should have thought the suction pump would have been enough. That's all I use on my bath waste when it gets a bit corroded. That, and a pint of spirits of salts."

"I'm rather looking forward to it," said Mr. Rostrum. "In its way it's going to be quite an interesting experience. And quite a new experience for me."

"That's right, Alec. And when it's all over, you'll have nothing to do but lie here and be waited on, hand and foot. Wish I could go to bed for a month. Tell you what, old boy : I'll keep you supplied with reading matter. What's the good of being a stationer, if I can't do that ? Send you all the stuff I can't sell, ha ha ha."

"Thank you, Truppy. I——"

He was interrupted by the reappearance of the tall nurse. She beamed on them once and said, "I'm afraid that's five minutes."

"You mean they must go ? "

"I'm afraid so."

"Ah, well . . . can't be helped . . . there it is, children. Hop it. You heard what the lady said."

They didn't dare disobey her. Truppy, feeling that he, who was no more than a friend, ought to be at a distance when the family said its good-byes, was the first to leave. He shook Mr. Rostrum's hand. "Well, all the best, old bean. I'm off. I never disobey the Sergeant Major. Not on you life. So long. I'll keep an eye on 'em all for you and see that they behave themselves." ("And if you're late returning home, mate-o' mine. . . .")

"Thank you, Truppy."

Julian just touched his hand. "Well, good luck, Dad." Brenda kissed him gently and smiled ; this was a time when she kept silence ; but her smile said a good deal. Joanie, who had said nothing all the morning, suddenly kissed him passionately and said, "Good luck and get well, Daddy,"

223

in a way that jumped the tears into his eyes. Mildred passed her hand over his forehead and imprinted there a long kiss.

Then they walked away; and he watched them going. At the doors Truppy lifted a hand to him as he went out. The children turned and smiled, and Mildred waved, but he saw by her tremulous lips that she was battening down her tears.

The doors swung behind them; they looked back at him through the glass; Julian waved; Brenda waved; and then they were all gone.

Had he—had he seen them for the last time? Had Time already withdrawn them from memory?

All tracks end at the fringe of the desert. In the desert there is neither house nor family nor friend.

CHAPTER SIXTEEN

MR. ROSTRUM looked round upon the population of the ward. The men in their beds or wandering about in their dressing-gowns; the nurses in their crisp cotton uniforms; the young probationers in uniforms that were similar but less neat and well-fitting, their dresses too large and bunched about them, their aprons too long; the ward sister in her navy blue dress, blue belt, and small cap, the most impressive figure of all and monarch of this place of his exile—such were his new associates for—how long?—for the rest of his life perhaps; which was to say, for the rest of to-day and a part of to-morrow morning.

A voice broke in upon this thought. " Well, 'ow are you, ole cock?"

Mr. Rostrum was somewhat shaken by this mode of address. He was not at all sure that he liked being called " old cock ". Did this neighbour on his left, whose voice it was, think that because he, Mr. Rostrum, was in a public ward, he was only a working man and rightly addressed as " old cock "? But, much too courteous to let his displeasure be seen, he put on a smile and turned towards the voice. The smile was small, and it encountered a very much larger smile, a grin most deliberately placed beneath a stubbly white moustache and most deliberately accompanied by a twinkling of two small, moist, red-rimmed eyes. The face about this amiable grin and these faded eyes was round, weather-ruddy, marble-veined, scored and trenched with little lines and wrinkles, and crowned with sparse white hairs. It nodded cordially. " Pleased to meet you."

" Thank you," laughed Mr. Rostrum.

" I'd better introduce meself if we're to be mates for the next week or two. Meet Mr. Harry Burnaby. That's me."

" Oh, yes ? " It seemed strange to hear this very old man call himself Harry. " And my name's Rostrum."

" How do, Mister ? And what have they jugged you for ? "

" Pardon ? "

" What've they got you in 'ere for ? "

Mr. Rostrum explained. And, not without pride, hoping that it would put him back on his proper social level, he stated that his operation to-morrow was going to be performed by Sir Joshua Dymote, the Senior Honorary Surgeon.

" Yeh . . . I see. . . . Wurl. . . ." Mr. Burnaby, having listened with fixed, interested eyes, offered his comfort. " You'll be all right, mate. There's nothing to it. Don't you worry about it. Leave it to the M.O.'s. Yeh, leave it to the M.O's. They know what they're doing, and they're as clever as a cage-load of monkeys. I don't mind telling you that, the day before I had mine, I had the wind up good and proper. Law blimey, I've never been so frightened in my life, and that's the truth—though I didn't let on, mind you. I don't think anybody knew I was feeling like a bloody bag of wind and nothing else. They didn't need to give me any blooming aperients, I don't mind telling,you ; really I thought they'd be giving me something to stop it. Blue funk, that's what it was. I was never so frightened before, not even when they were dropping bombs around me 'ouse in the old war. But there was nothing to it. Gah ! " His large nostrils almost snarled in contempt for it. " Nothing at all. You always think you're going to die under the operation and never wake up again, but you jest don't. They put you aht and before you know you're aht, you've come rah'nd again and are spewing like a cat. A few 'ahr's go by, a cuppla nights, say, and you're setting up in bed, watching other poor blokes coming in with their bellies somewhere in their mouths and trying to pretend they ain't afraid ; and you're telling them there's nothing to it, absolutely nothing at all, just as what I am you, see what I mean ? "

" What was yours ? "

" They give it some long bloody name, but actually it was me little ole prostate. You know : couldn't when I wanted to, or else couldn't stop ; if you see what I mean. Very awkward, sometimes, especially for a dustman like me, out all day ; not but what I gave up being a dustman some time ago and retired on me pension. I'm a gentleman now. Don't work for me living at all."

" Oh, yours was a prostatectomy," Mr. Rostrum informed him, proud of knowing the word, and thinking that this exhibition of knowledge might help to place him in his right social plane. He knew the word because he had so often, behind his closed study door, given an intensely personal interest to the consideration of the symptoms and treatment of an enlarged prostate.

" That's it," confirmed Mr. Burnaby, with all the pride of possession. " Something like that. Gawd knows where they get these seven-and-sixpenny words from, but what it means in plain English is that me little ole prostate was getting a bit above itself. Getting a touch of swelled 'ead, if you like."

" And it had to come out ? "

" That's right. 'Ad to come 'aht. And, law love you, the tricks they 'ave to get up to after they done it, you wouldn't believe ! It don't 'alf make me laugh. I say to these nurses, ' Blimey, you young girls can't do that there to me,' but they just tell me not to be a silly old man, and they get on with it without turning a hair. They're good kids, you know ; I'll say that for them ; good kids."

Mr. Rostrum was much interested. He forgot his present condition and impending operation, as he inquired about Mr. Burnaby's symptoms and in his private mind compared them with his own. Mr. Burnaby described them in detail and with the enthusiasm of a proprietor ; and when the full tale was told, he asked Mr. Rostrum, feeling that the word should now be his : " And what's your job, mate ? "

Not quite liking the word "job," Mr. Rostrum repeated it. "Job?"

"Yes. Or have you too packed up and taken your pension?"

"Good God, no! I'm only just sixty."

"Is that all?"

This, for Mr. Rostrum, was a mental pain almost as acute as one of his bodily ones. "I'm a photographer."

"What? Press?"

"Oh, no," Mr. Rostrum hastily corrected. "I have my own studio in Kilburn. But I prefer commercial photography to portraiture. There's more scope in it." And he was beginning to speak of his work for famous commercial firms when Mr. Burnaby, discovering that he took much less interest in Mr. Rostrum's daily labours than in his present disease, looked right across him to the next bed.

"Meet Young Arthur there," he interrupted. "He's a nice lad. Been through the 'oop too."

Mr. Rostrum turned towards his other neighbour and saw that he was a boy of about twenty with a white face and tumbled brown hair. The boy, who was reading a book, smiled awkwardly· over its top at this introduction. Mr. Rostrum, liking the shy smile, gave him one in return and inquired what had been *his* operation.

"An appendicectomy," said the boy. "Nothing very startling." And by his voice Mr. Rostrum knew that he was a lad of education : probably a gentleman. He felt glad to have a gentleman on his other side to talk to. He would now show him, and Mr. Burnaby too, who would certainly be listening, that he also was a gentleman of some culture. His question elicited that Young Arthur was a student at London University, and he hastened to explain that one of his daughters was engaged to a graduate of London University, a B.Sc. (Engineering), Stephen Emery. Did he know Stephen Emery by any chance? No?

"Nice gurls, your gurls, chum," interrupted Mr. Burnaby, listening and feeling deserted. "I didn't butt in on your family party, but I see'd they were your gurls. There was enough daddying and kissing going on. One of 'em's pretty."

"I think both of them are pretty," said Mr. Rostrum ; "and you're right, they're two of the best," and, most un-expectedly, most disconcertingly, he felt a strong desire to

227

cry. Instead, gulping back the silly and shameful tears, he bragged about his children. "You saw the elder one, the taller one. Well, I'm not just trying to blow off when I say that she's Goodness Itself." (Steady! What about that young man? Well, never mind him. He quite understood how that affair came about, and if Brenda wasn't good, he didn't know the meaning of the word.) "She's a perfect Saint, in her way. For ever trying to help and serve other people. I don't know where she gets it from. Lord knows I'm no saint; and though nobody could have had a better wife than mine "—(Wasn't this rather like talking on the other side of the grave?)—" she's never set up to be a saint. But Brenda gives her whole life to other people. And what's extraordinarily pleasant is that she's quite devoted to her father. She takes me into her confidence about everything and seems to value my advice and help. There's none of the usual father-daughter opposition and antagonism between Brenda and I; on the contrary, there's what you might call a Unity. We understand each other absolutely. It's been a very pleasant experience in my life, that; on the whole, the pleasantest thing that's happened to me. Yes, I've been lucky in my children. I'm glad you liked them. The boy's a good piece of work too. He's a solicitor."

"*Is* he?" Mr. Burnaby opened his eyes wide. "A bleedin' lawyer?"

"Yes." Mr. Rostrum wondered if he liked Mr. Burnaby's surprise. "I've made fairly good money in my time and been able to start my children pretty well. He took a First Class in his Finals, and I reckon he's got the ball at his feet now."

"A bleedin' genius, in fact."

"Well, I wouldn't say that, but bright, I think, very bright. And they're not my only children. I've got a little boy just on four. He's at home now with his auntie."

"*You* got a boy of four?"

"Yes, certainly. Why not?"

"Crikey, you're a trier, aren't you?"

Crudely expressed, thought Mr. Rostrum, but he was proud of the achievement and pleased with the remark; and he began to trumpet the little boy's prodigal and turbulent vitality and to flaunt his impudence and his mischief.

" He's a proper little tough, and no mistake. Not the least afraid of me or anyone else. I get as good as I give if I try to throw my weight about with Mr. Dudley. And as for his poor mother, he's got her exactly where he wants her. He obeys me, occasionally, but her, on principle, never."

" Wurl, I reckon it's good going for an ole cock like you to have a kid of four."

" Confound it, I'm not as old as all that."

" Why, you must be nearly as old as I am, aren't you ? "

" I told you I was sixty." It was said sadly, not to say sulkily. Mr. Rostrum's heart had sunk like dead lead into the region of his stomach. Did he look as old as this old man ? Did this old white-haired grandfather with the red-rimmed eyes delude himself into thinking that he looked as young as he ? Or did he, Mr. Rostrum, delude himself into thinking that he looked at least fifteen years younger than this hoary, damp-nostrilled, cobwebby old man ? " How old are you ? " he asked, from his sickened heart.

" Sixty-eight."

Was that all ? Only eight years older than he ? Would he look like that in eight years ? Was he as near to the End as that ?

" And who was the little moke who come with them ? " asked Mr. Burnaby, unaware that his words had inflicted a deep and throbbing wound. " The little cove with the gold spectacles ? "

" Oh, that's a very old friend of mine—Truppy, we call him. A friend for thirty years. He's stuck to me through fair weather and foul, has old Truppy ; been with me in all my troubles and sorrows and all my joys. Yes, a really good friend," repeated Mr. Rostrum, who at this moment felt in need of one.

Mr. Burnaby in his turn bragged about his girls ; almost as if, thought Mr. Rostrum, they could be compared with Brenda and Joanie. One was married to a milkman in Gulliver Street, he said ; and one to a stevedore foreman ; and both of them had nice little homes now. And nippers. Chrissie had three of them, and Ethel four. " I was able to surprise 'em when they got married," he bragged, " be-cause I had a tidy little bit of money put away, and I said to Chrissie, I said, ' I shall be able to stiffen you, my gurl.

I'll stiffen you and Ernie quite a bit,' and they 'ardly believed me at first, because they didn't know that I had a terrible lot o' money sitting snug in the post office. But *I* did, and I thinks, ' Why shouldn't I give some of it to them, to start 'em up ? ' You see, I don't want so much meself nowadays : just the rent of me room, which I don't mind telling you's never once been owing, and me insurance, which I keep fully paid up, and me pipe—can't stand fags ; not strong enough—just me ounce of Nut Brown a day, and me glass of Mild and Burton now and again— that's the lot, Mister. That's all I want. I don't suppose I live like you, but I got all I want ; and I was glad to be able to give the gurls a start."

" I'm sure you were," agreed Mr. Rostrum. " It's curious, but there are few things quite so satisfying as starting your kids off well—as I know from my own experience ; " and in his mind he was comparing Mr. Burnaby's " terrible lot o' money " with his own capital, and wanting to mention that it was a matter of thousands, but having too much taste and pity to do so. " I'm glad you gave some to the girls."

" Yurse, they're good gurls. They come along each visiting day, bringing their flah'rs. You'll see 'em on Sunday." (But would he ?) " They can't always get away on a Saturday, but they never fail to come along on a Sunday afternoon. *Ere !* " He had called this out, looking right across Mr. Rostrum's bed, because the tall nurse was now tidying Young Arthur's bed, and to do this she had lifted him up with an arm around his neck. " *Ere !* What's he got that I ain't got ? Did jever see the like of that ? 'S'all my eye. Does she put her arm round my neck ? Never, if she can help it. Nah, they don't embrace us old men like that, do they ? Wurl, we've 'ad our day, I suppose, eh ? What do you say, chum ? Gaw, it's a game, isn't it ? That lad was perfectly comfortable. None of that there was necessary ; don't you believe it. She only done it because she likes doing it."

" Don't be a silly old man," rebuked the nurse.

" And don't you give me any of your sauce. There's a hospital up the road."

" Is there ? Well, why didn't you go there instead of coming to us ? We shouldn't have broken our hearts."

"See? See, chum? That's all I get. No embraces, and not even respect. And I really do want my bed seeing to. It badly wants setting to rights."

Smiling, the nurse came to his side and tidied his bed for him in the same fashion, her arm supporting him ; and he pillowed his head on her breast and pretended to go to sleep there ; but she slapped it away and went off laughing.

Mr. Rostrum had turned to Young Arthur. "What are you reading ? "

"The Oresteia of Æschylus."

"Pardon ? "

The young man repeated the title. "The Oresteia of Æschylus."

"Oh, yes. Is it good ? "

The young man smiled. "Well, it's endured over two thousand years."

"Has it ? Why ? It's Latin, is it ? "

"No, Greek."

"Oh . . . I see. . . ." Mr. Rostrum, who had intended to establish a relationship as of social equals with this young man, but one in which he would be pleasantly patronizing, since he was so much older and wiser, felt suddenly like a balloon deflated ; and Young Arthur, to ease his palpable discomfiture, added at once, "But I'm not reading it in Greek. This is a translation by the Professor of Classical Literature at King's College."

But this did nothing to recover Mr. Rostrum. He turned slowly away from the young man, afraid of him. He was afraid of him as he had always, in truth, been afraid of Prebendary Leicester, his sister's distinguished husband, and of Herbert, her scholarly son. He turned back to Mr. Burnaby, because with him he felt at ease. With him he was a superior and not an inferior : better educated, better placed in the world, of wider experience, and wealthier ; and in what might be his last hours he wanted the ease of being looked up to and possibly envied.

§

Mr. Rostrum looked at his watch. Seven minutes to three. Four hours had passed since the family left. He was four hours nearer the ordeal. Time seemed to be passing at two different speeds as he sat upon his bed, reading, or lay back for a while, thinking. How slowly time moved: still only three o'clock, and there was nothing to do. How fast it moved: this was perhaps his last day in the world, and it was passing. And you could imagine, as you lay here, a third time in the ward: the time of the nurses who were for ever hurrying on to the next task, hurrying as if *their* time was against them, from bed to sluice, from ward to passage, from the centre desk to the Clinical Room, from the table by the doors to the ringing telephone in the hall outside.

Always, as he lay, he was seeing his house in Nunsbury Road, its broad grey front on the street, its passages and stairs and rooms. He was seeing Julian's room and Joanie's room and Brenda's room. He was seeing Mildred in the kitchen. He was seeing his study and thinking how yesterday he had wandered up and down it with his question, " Is it the End ? I feel so vigorous and young, and yet— is my life over ? " *Was* it the End ? Until he knew the answer to this question all his prospects and hopes were snapped-off things, with jagged edges ; and there was nothing to do but lie and wait till he knew if he could repair and extend them again. If it was the end, what on earth did it all mean ? Why had he been born ; why had he endured for a while, and then abruptly been extinguished ? One went on experiencing and learning as if one had Forever, and then : " That's all, Alec. Time now." And no explanation. Not a word. Fancy going out of life and never knowing why one had lived. No answer out of the everlasting silence. Only the wide sky stretching like Time from one end of the world to the other. Of course there were all the things that religion said, but one couldn't *know* that they were true ; they were just hopes to which men clung like shipwrecked seamen who could not know whether there was land beyond the mist.

" You'll be all right, mate. There's nothing to it "— that was what he had said. But was *his* operation a really serious one ? " You always think you're going to die under an operation, but you never do." But some did. Mr. Rostrum could remember friends who had. There was Jerry Westcott, the butcher, and he was only fifty. The time was passing, and Mr. Rostrum knew that, like Mr. Burnaby, he was very greatly afraid. Probably far more afraid but, like him, pretending not to be. Lying here, without the family, without Truppy even, he felt forlorn and at the mercy of these confident and level-voiced doctors and these brisk and able nurses. So quiet and confident, the doctors ; so untroubled and efficient, the nurses. The only ease for his fear was his faith in them.

He felt like a prisoner in a huge prison. He lay listening to the sounds of the prison, and then to the sounds of the free world outside, which seemed very far away. Listen as you lie : the muted singing in the headphones above your bed, the scrannel of a screen's iron wheels as the nurse draws it away from a bed, a coughing into a sputum mug, the clink of the mug on the locker, the snores of a lad who had fallen asleep, and, loud, persistent, unremitting, the tearing breaths of that man who lies so torpid by the doors. And beyond the doors : the tink of the telephone as a nurse replaces the receiver, the ever-recurring purr of ascending lifts, the clink of metal instruments on dishes in the Clinical Room, and a clatter of tea cups in the kitchen to remind one of home. And listen to the sounds of the outer world. They are remote and dim, and one's only contact with them is by this straining of the ears, but one can just hear them : the diminishing sigh of a train, the labouring of a lorry, the interwoven voices of a hundred children on the harsh asphalt of a school playground, the broken drone of pigeons, and—yes—far away, like the plucking of a high, tuneless string, the cries of gulls scavenging above some London waste or railway bed.

But now he lifted his head. He had become conscious of a tacit but fluttering excitement in the ward. All eyes were directed towards a corner by the swing doors—all eyes except those of the men who slept. Nurses were standing by the bed of the unconscious man who had been breathing so heavily and so hoarsely. The ward sister, newly summoned from without, was looking down at him. She was saying something to a young nurse. The nurse went to the oxygen apparatus in the centre of the ward and dragged it on its wheels to the bed's side. " Fetch the screens, nurse." It was said sharply but not loudly. The ward hushed. Probationers rolled the screens around the bed. The sister told one nurse to stay within the screens and went out into the hall with another. The telephone tinked.

The ward began to whisper. Mr. Burnaby, propped up against his pillows, removed his head-phones and laid them on the blanket. He watched for a while and then turned to Mr. Rostrum. " That's the lot," he said.

" What do you mean ? "

" He's packing up."

" Dying ? "

" That's right. Yepp . . . been obviously going for some time. He was on the D.I. List."

" What's that ? "

" The Dangerously Ill List. I knew he was *for* it directly they moved him this morning to the bed by the door. Yepp, I knew he was done for then."

" Why did they move him there ? "

" You'll see, mate."

Mr. Rostrum stared at the screens. " What was the matter with him ? "

" He ? He's 'ad a—I don't rightly know what was the matter with him."

" Had he had an operation ? "

" An operation ? Oh, yes, yes," Mr. Burnaby admitted brightly. " He'd 'ad some sort of operation. Yes, that's right, mate."

" What for ? "

" *I* dunno ! All I know it was a very bad one ; *you* know, something quite out of the ordinary. Pretty 'opeless from the start. He looked more'n half dead when he come in, didn't he, Young Arthur ? "

" Yes. It was a partial gastrectomy," Young Arthur supplied.

" Something like that. Yuss, he'd let hisself go too far. He should'a come in early like you and me, and then he'd 'a bin all right for a cert. There'd 'a bin nothing to it."

" Do they tell you when they know you're going to die ? "

" I dunno. I shouldn't think so."

" How old was he ? "

" Somewhere about fifty. A bloody dangerous age. All my pals died in their early fifties. It's best to be old like us, or young like Young Arthur there. I always say, Get

234

past your fifties, and you can look forward to a nice long spell. You're all gristle then."

All the business of the ward was going on as usual. Once the screens were round the dying man, his dying made no difference. The nurses, moving this way and that to their heaping tasks, did not even speak about him ; except one who murmured to another in Mr. Rostrum's hearing, " I hoped he'd wait for the night staff." Some twenty minutes of this normal, unexcited activity, and then the sister came in with a heavy-bodied, grey-haired, middle-aged woman and a tall youth (as it might be Mildred and Julian). She was obviously doing all she could for them ; talking to them in kindly tones and a low voice, and faintly smiling sometimes to help and encourage them. She fetched a second chair for the young man and put it within the screens. She gently drew the screens together and came quickly away. And the business of the ward went on.

Mr. Rostrum gazed at the screens and thought of the miracle that was happening within the small cubic space they enclosed. There in that narrow space, shut away from this large, man-made, populous ward with its clean, shining, cream-painted walls and clean, hygienic, sea-water smell, a God-worked miracle was in hand ; the miracle which was the opposite of creation, because that which had been was ceasing to be, and something was being changed into nothing. Wife and son were there, watching it.

It was done. God had created nothing out of something. The woman and the youth came away from it, back into the man-made world, their faces pale but their eyes dry, either because they could not weep or because they would not before an audience of strangers. The sister walked with them out of the ward, her hand resting gently on the woman's back.

" That's the lot," said Mr. Burnaby.

And immediately some nurses went to the screens and so arranged them that they made a continuous curtain covering the bed and the way to the door and the door itself. Then there was a rumble and mewing of bed-wheels as, unseen by the patients, the bed with its sheeted body was wheeled from the ward. Almost at once a new rumble and a new intermittent cry of wheels, as of a bed being brought through the door and pushed to the wall ; and then, in no time, the nurses were rolling the screens away, and Mr. Rostrum saw a new bed there, made up and ready ; smooth, clean, and shining. The afternoon sun poured its moted beams through the high windows, as it must have been doing all the time, though one had not noticed it. The clinking sounds from alcove, sluice, and dressing trolley, reasserted their presence. The noises from the yards and courts of the hospital visited Mr. Rostrum's ears again, including the liquid and low ululation of the pigeons and the happy cries of some young nurses playing tennis in the bright afternoon. Beyond these, just audible, the world went humming and murmuring on its way.

§

He could not sleep, though the ward had been quiet for some hours. There were no sounds now in the long room, except the heavy breathing of sleepers and the lowered voices of two night nurses who sat by a shaded lamp at the centre desk, making wool swabs and gauze dressings and packing them into drums. The lights that hung from the ceiling, those globes of white light, were dimmed, and, apart from the nurses' lamp, the only illumination in the room was the shaded lamp over the bed of a man who was very ill. A church clock far away struck the first bell of midnight. To-morrow was now to-day. To-day was here. The day on which, perhaps . . .

Perhaps here in this bed he would die. In this room. Difficult to believe, difficult to accept, because he was quite empty of pain. He had felt hardly any pain in all the dozen hours he'd been in this bed. Was this because his mind was fully engaged with his thoughts of loneliness, his wondering and perplexed meditations, and his expanding fear ? Sometimes he could wish that the pain would return because, when it was at its worst, why, then he was quite ready, he wanted, to die. All was simple then ; problems and love and fear were no more.

A woman's shriek from some ward above—all sounds were dramatic in the quiet and the dark. No doubt a woman was in labour up there in the maternity ward. Her pains were mounting, and a birth was at hand. She cried again

—and again—and it reminded him of the mad wife in *Jane Eyre*; but now all was silent; they had put her to peace for a little. In a ward on the other side of a quadrangular court a man was coughing and coughing. Probably he was coughing his way out of the world. Somewhere a telephone was ringing with a muffled persistence under the duster which a night nurse had placed over it. Listen: a rattling of a trolley in the corridor, and an accompaniment of voices as loud as the voices of daylight. Clash of lift gates, and purr of lift ascending. An emergency case, perhaps. All sounds were dramatic in the quiet and the dark.

Another hour of tossing and listening, and he was asleep; asleep and dreaming of his family and his home. They were all there about him: Mildred and Brenda and Julian and Joanie and the small boy; and he was walking his familiar rooms again. They were laughing together because he and Julian had been teasing Joanie over the breakfast table about Stephen Emery; and now he was in the High Road talking with Stephen, and Sankey was leaping up at them both, while the crowds on the pavement went streaming by. Joanie joined them, and together they walked along the High Road, Sankey following, and opened the door of his shop. In the shop stood his mother and his sister, Elizabeth, a tall, timid girl with her prayer books in her hand, because they had just come from Morning Service at St. Saviour's, Upper Kilburn. He himself had just come from his school in Elmsleigh Road, and he couldn't understand why, since he was now forty-five, he should still be at school and learning arithmetic and history and bookkeeping by double entry. Surely the teachers and the boys must see that he was thirty years older than the oldest pupil, but they didn't seem to notice it or wonder about it. He was glad to be home with his mother and sister; they were his home, they were everyday ease and shelter and the end of anxiety and strain. It was warm, sweet peace at home.

Oh, but he was awake again; yes, awake in the hospital ward, because its lights were fully on, and there was a bustle and stir in it, though the darkness, untinted by daylight, still filled the world beyond the windows. It was half-past four, and the day was beginning, or, at any rate, the hospital's day; and the nurses were taking tea to the patients.

237

One must just wait. He had five hours, perhaps, to wait. Nothing to do but watch the grey dawn-light invading the dark beyond the windows and slowly defeating the bright opalescent globes that lit the centre of the ward. At about five o'clock one of the nurses, the plump and rosy one, brought a bowl of water to his bed and told him to wash himself all over in readiness for the theatre, and he wanted to make a joke about preparing the lamb for the slaughter, but decided that it was not very good, and she had rolled the screens around him and was gone before he could think of a better. While he was washing, she came within the screens again, bringing his operation gown and a pair of white woollen bed-socks. " Ah ! " he said. " The sacrificial robe ! " and he examined it with interest : a long coat of white flannel with a high collar. He put it on. It was meant to be calf-length but was too short for him, and he felt a little ridiculous and very self-conscious in it, and clambered quickly back into bed. The nurse reappeared, wearing her mask now, and said she was going to " prep " him ; and he laughed and said, " Oh, yes ? It's all very interesting." And as she rubbed the operation area and the whole front of him with ether soap and methylated spirit and the surgeon's special preparation, he said, " You'd make a good cook, I can see that ; you prepare the old joint so skilfully." And when Mr. Burnaby called over the screen, " Don't let her get too tough with you, mate," he called back, as she bandaged the sterile towels around him, " But what can I do ? She's got me at her mercy, and I'm terrified of her." " Sock her one," recommended Mr. Burnaby ; and she, as cheerful as she was brisk, enjoined Mr. Burnaby to keep quiet because nobody wanted to hear anything from him.

" Caw, they've got a sauce ! " said Mr. Burnaby's voice, beyond the screen. " Talking to an old man like that. And one who's lying on a bedda sickness."

" There ! That's fine," said the nurse, as she tidied the bed. " All quite comfy ? "

" Perfectly. Thank you very much. Thank you, nurse. And what time's Zero Hour ? "

" What time's what ? "

" When will it be ? When do we go over the top ? "

" Oh, about half-past nine or ten. You're first on the Man's List."

" Am I ? " He felt rather proud of this. " Why's that ? "

" Oh, I don't know. Perhaps because the Big Noise himself is doing you."

" I'm top of the bill, eh ? "

" That's it." And she rolled away the screens, gave him a smile, and left him.

Seven o'clock, and the day staff arrived. They went to their work like a relieving army. They snatched basins away, seized screens, washed patients behind them, scrubbed their hands in the alcove, dressed patients, took temperatures, made beds. The two ward charwomen arrived, in their pink overalls and mob caps. They went to the end of the ward and, each taking one side of it, began to sweep it with their wide brooms and their tea leaves, pulling out the beds as they did so. Mr. Rostrum's bed was the third from the end on his side, and when the charwoman, a short woman with a cast in one eye, drab wisping hair, and a body that seemed half as long again as her legs, came to its foot and pushed it away, she asked, " Well, how are you, Dad ? "

The " Dad " hurt. It hurt a lot. " I'm feeling fine," he said.

" That's the spirit. They're doing you to-day, aren't they ? " There was a keen interest in her eyes, but kindliness too ; and the kindliness quickly outstripped all else. " When are they doing it ? " she inquired as she swept.

" This morning. Soon now."

" He's first on the Man's List," pronounced Mr. Burnaby, who had heard this fact through the screen and was proud of it.

" Yes, I'm top of the bill."

" Well, there's nothing to worry about," she comforted him. " There's nothing they can't do nowadays. It's no more to them than what putting my old sewing machine to rights is to me. A cuppla minutes' work on it, and the old dear's going better than ever. It's just the same with them. I seen enough since I been coming here to know that. I always say I shouldn't mind what they did to me. I should say, ' Let 'em get on with it '." She pulled and

239

pushed the bed till it was in place again. "After this you'll never look back, you mark my words. There's a lady lives two doors from me, and she got worse and worse with something inside her till she was as thin and stringy as a scullery rag what's on its last legs ; and they got to work on her and took her to pieces and put her together again, and now you'd never know her. You wouldn't, straight. She's fat and bouncing and bonny. She looks a sight better'n I do. I said to her, I said, 'If that's what they can do to you, I'm having sixpenn'orth. The place is a blooming Beauty Parlour.' And it was here too they done her. Or look at *him*." She was now pushing Mr. Burnaby's bed out of her way ; pushing it with a feigned anger, as if it was a nuisance because it contained a bad old man. "It ain't hurt *him* much, has it ? Personally, I think it'd'a bin better if they'd let him alone. He was perky enough when he comes in, and now there's no holding him. Gawd knows what games he'll be up to when they let him out."

"I never pay any attention to this class of woman," said Mr. Burnaby.

"Oh, you don't, don't you ? Well, p'raps we're none the worse off for that. I wouldn't say as your attentions weren't best avoided. You don't look to me the sort that it's nice to know."

"I don't want you to get the wrong impression," pursued Mr. Burnaby, explaining his view to Mr. Rostrum. "I don't want you to make no mistake. It's not that I don't think they're good-'earted enough sometimes. It's just that they're no class. As a good, honest dustman I got my position to consider."

"Oh, that's what you think, is it ? Well, p'raps we're particular too who we associate with. You and your old dust-cart ! I wonder you don't get in it yourself. They'd never notice you among the rest of the rubbish."

"Gaw ! J'ear that ? Gaw lummy, I arst yer ! " Mr. Burnaby tut-tutted behind his teeth, as she pushed his bed into position. "Is that any way to talk to a sick ole man ? And who are you shovin', anyway ? "

"I'd shove you somewhere if it lay with me. That's the last of you this morning, and thank the lord for that. I can't stay here listening to your sauce, while you lay there doing nothing ; I got something better to do." She looked back at Mr. Rostrum. " He's always got a sight too much to say for hisself ; though I expect you've found that out by this time. I wouldn't say as you were lucky getting put next to 'im. He don't make for peace and quiet, to my thinking. But don't you worry about this morning, love. *You*'ll be all right. Not a doubt of it. When next I see you, it'll be all over and you'll be wondering why you ever thought there was anything to it. Good luck, and all the best."

" Thank you. Thank you very much."

So she passed ; and though she was no celestial visitant, Mr. Rostrum did feel strengthened by her passing.

Eight o'clock. The church clock in the distance struck eight. The day was fully alive now, and he could see the September sunlight lying aslant on the walls of the opposite block, and hear the brief, cheery, syllables of the sparrows and the easy voices of people in the yard below, who had no doubt that they would be alive to-night. He looked round upon the nurses, the patients, and the charwomen, who would all be alive to-night.

A staff nurse, older than most of the others, with a thin, pointed face and bronze hair, came to his bed, bringing a syringe on a small glass tray.

" Suffering any pain ? " she asked with a smile.

" Just a little this morning. Not much," he answered, trying to be a good patient.

" Well, this'll stop all that. This'll make you nice and comfortable."

" What is it ? "

" Just a little hypodermic injection. It won't hurt."

" Oh, well, plug it in."

" Let's have your arm."

And with the brisk indifference of one whose brain and hand had done this a thousand times before, she swabbed the skin of his forearm with a spirit and jerked the needle in.

" What is it ? " he asked, looking down upon the syringe. She whispered the answer. " Morphine and atropine."

" It doesn't put me out, does .it ? "

" Oh, no. Dear me, no ! *I'm* not the anæsthetist. Now lie back and be comfortable."

A few minutes after the injection he began to feel, or to imagine that he was feeling, drowsy. The pain, which had probably been caused by apprehension, and the apprehension itself, faded away. His mouth went dry, as the atropine cut down its secretions. He lay there thinking; and it seemed but a little while before the church clock struck nine.

Soon they would wheel him to the Anæsthetizing Room, and there the world would be extinguished for him, as they sent him into the dark. "The bright day is done, and we are for the dark." He could not remember who had said that, except that it was in some Shakespeare play to which Brenda had dragged them; but he said it again and again to himself because it pleased him with its melancholy. Other quotations kept appearing from nowhere and forcing him to repeat them ten, twenty, and thirty times, monotonously, rhythmically, and senselessly. Once, when there came upon him in its fullness the sense that it was he and he alone, not anyone else in the ward, not anyone else at home, not anyone else in Kilburn High Road, who was in danger of death, he found himself repeating dully, emptily, but with a compulsion to continue, an old negro spiritual which he had not heard for years.

> It's not my father, it's not my mother.
> It's me, Oh Lord,
> Standing in the need of prayer.
> It's not the deacon, it's not the leader. . . .

He wished he could stop saying it, and he tried to turn his thoughts to other things. He tried to centre them on an obstinate certainty that he was going to live.

"I'm going to live. I've made up my mind to it. I'm going to get back to them all. I believe that if I'm sufficiently determined about this, if I'm finally and absolutely convinced about it in my own mind, nobody and nothing can prevent me doing it. Nothing can be stronger than my will if I choose to make it strong enough. I believe one can do anything by sheer will-power, even to the point of refusing to die. One can say when one's ready to die and when one has no intention, not the slightest, of doing so. One dies in the end because one is willing to; and I'm not in the least willing to. Not in the least. Oh, no, I'm not dying.

They don't get me this time. I laugh at the idea. You've come to the wrong shop if you think you're going to get me. We'll see. We'll see. Nothing is perfect in this world, but I know this : I've only to face the thought of never seeing Mildred again . . . or Brenda . . . or the little boy . . . or any of them . . . to know that it's not something I have the least desire to do. In fact, it's an idea that I find quite unimaginable. And what one can't even imagine doesn't easily happen, I fancy. ' Never ' . . . ' for ever ' . . . oh, no, it's just impossible to believe. There's a great deal I want to do yet in life and have every intention of doing. There's the small boy. I've a fancy to do my job by that small boy, whether he deserves it or not, and little devil though he is. That means that I've got to live at least another fifteen years, and I hereby record my immutable resolve to do so. The point's settled. There may be those who'd say I can't settle it for myself, but I say I can."

Then there were the places that he loved, as well as the people. Spread before him now he saw the Callerdale lake with its pine-tree'd islands sleeping on it, and the ferny hills marching at its side, and the footpaths, thin as veins, weaving their way up the flanks through the swarms of high-branched bracken. "And I'm going back to it," he said. "Just you make sure of that. I'm going back to it after all this is over. I shall need a holiday to put me right, and I can well afford to take a nice long one, because I've saved all the money I'd resolved to spend on Brenda. Yes, I shall go back with Mildred and walk again with her up that path through the bracken. We'll sit on that grey stone where we sat before. . . ."

But what of God ? At this point he remembered that he was a churchgoer of fifty years standing and that he believed, or tried to, in God. Supposing God's will was the opposite of his own ? Well . . . yes . . . he found that in his own case he could say what he had been unable to say in Brenda's ; and he said it. "Nevertheless, not my will but Thine be done."

Then his teeth set and one fist clenched again. That homage paid, he was going to believe that God's will was his will, and to fight the better, to be unconquerable, for that belief. " I shall win."

And as he vowed this to himself, the swing doors of the ward were pushed open and the theatre trolley came through them into the ward. It was wheeled by the theatre porter in a white skull cap and white overall. The ward sister, seeing him, went to meet him. She summoned a probationer and she, he, and the probationer, brought the white trolley to the foot of Mr. Rostrum's bed. They set a screen between his bed and the entrance to the ward. "Now then," said the sister to him with her heartening smile; and she, the porter, and the probationer slid their arms beneath his body to lift him on to the trolley.

"Here!" he protested with a laugh. "I'm not dead yet. Why can't I get on it by myself?"

"Don't you do anything that they're ready to do for you, mate," enjoined Mr. Burnaby's voice from beyond the screen. "You let 'em do it. They love it. What I say is, if women want to do something for you that you could perfectly well do for yourself, let 'em. That's what I say. It suits them and it suits me. I never interfered with my old woman if she wanted to do the work. Jest you fold your 'ands and let 'em get on with it. Now, easy, girls! Easy! Gently does it."

They had laid him on the trolley and were covering him with some blankets already on it. And now they were strapping him down, the straps passing over his chest and his thighs.

"Well, well." Mr. Rostrum smiled at this treatment. "Is this to prevent me putting up a fight?"

"Nah, they're going to swing you up on a crane, mate, when they get you outside."

"That'll do from you," said the sister to Mr. Burnaby, too busy to match humour with humour. She went to the head of the trolley. The porter went to its side. And together they pushed and pulled it along the gangway.

"Hold tight, please," advised Mr. Burnaby. "Hold on to your hat."

"Well, here we go," said Mr. Rostrum, as the procession began, the probationer walking ahead to open wide the doors.

"Up the Reds," said Mr. Burnaby, much pleased with the procession. "All the best, chum. See you again soon."

And he began to sing softly, " Any ole bones ? Any ole bottles and bones ? "

" Good luck," called Young Arthur. " You won't have any pain."

" You'll be all right, mate. You're only young."

" Good luck to you, sir."

" There goes the dinner trolley."

" Cheerioh. Thank you for calling. Come and see us again."

" There's nothing in it. I've been through it myself."

" Keep smiling, pal."

" Good luck, chum."

" Good luck, sir."

" Good luck."

From every bed, as he passed on his triumphal litter, came an encouraging word, or a facetious word designed to keep his heart light, or, if the patient was too ill to give more, a wan smile and the lifting of an emaciated hand. He acknowledged each of the courtesies with a smile.

The trolley was passing through the doors, held wide by the probationer. " . . . all the children are provided for now, except Dudley, and I've no real fear for him in life. I can't see *him* being a failure in life. And, anyhow, there's enough money to send him to school for some years, and there's always Julian to help him. . . ."

The doors swung behind him.

The trolley and its attendants went swiftly along the corridors, and the people stared. That is to say, the strangers and visitors stared ; the doctors, nurses, and students did not turn an eye as they strolled or hurried to their next occupation. A party of visitors, reminding him of himself and his family yesterday, stopped to gaze. " I feel like the world's treat," he said. He also felt, but did not say so, very small in the vast spaces of the hospital and the white, re-echoing corridors.

Never . . . for ever. . . ? The fetters that bound him to Mildred . . . or Brenda . . . snapped for ever ? Oh, no, it was too shattering in its finality. Mildred : never to be seen again ? Or Brenda ? He saw Mildred in the kitchen and Dudley playing about her heels, and Brenda teaching in her class-room, and Joanie sitting at her issuing desk in the Lending Library. He did not see Truppy, or the Widow, or Miss Fletcher, so different are the household ties from any others. He saw only those who lived with him in his grey corner house, and he saw Mildred most often. And all the time the trolley went on—not waiting for him to give a satisfactory shape to his thoughts. It seemed to go faster than his thoughts.

Into the lift. The trolley just fitted into the lift, and as the gates clanged, he felt shut in, and a small gripe of claustrophobia constricted his breast. Up, with the too familiar purr ; up, past the confining walls, past unregarded gates ; up to some unknown floor—and the lift halted uncertainly at the sight of some new gates but, when its mind was made up, stood still. The new gates clashed open, and now they were wheeling him the last few yards to the Anæsthetizing Room. He had just time to think of a criminal making his last, quick, unwilled, but externally impelled journey to the execution shed, and then he was in the Anæsthetizing Room. He was in a long, clean, white cell, and an odour of chloroform and ether surrounded him, and a strange new warmth. The anæsthetist was there in white gown and full mask. A nurse was with him in a similar mask. These hood-masks, going right over the head and leaving only the eyes exposed, reminded him instantly of the Klu Klux Klan, and he exclaimed, " Good lord ! " The anæsthetist, a tall man in early middle age, smiled. " You don't think we're beautiful, what ? "

" Oh, I don't know," demurred Mr. Rostrum, who didn't want to hurt anyone's feelings, even in his last moments.

" Perhaps some of us are better-looking with our masks on than without. That goes for quite a few anæsthetists I've known, believe you me. But not, I'm glad to say, or only very seldom, for the anæsthetic nurse. Eh, nurse ? Some anæsthetists, I've always thought, were enough to anæsthetize their patients without recourse to drugs or anything else. Well, now, sir, how about you ? How are you feeling ? "

" Not too bad."

" Good."

And while the anæsthetist was feeling his pulse and listening to his heart with his stethoscope and talking softly but cheerfully, Mr. Rostrum glanced round the room. He saw a shining trolley against the wall, with instruments and rubber masks laid on its top and gas cylinders attached to its side. He saw an array of white gowns on a line of white pegs, and two white chairs, and a brilliant white light in the midst of the ceiling above him. And then he saw, flush with the lustrous white wall, a pair of smooth brown double-doors. He heard footsteps and voices behind those doors and asked, " Is that the theatre ? "

" That's it," said the anæsthetist with an encouraging smile.

And, desiring to make a last joke, and because the thought needed to express itself in speech, Mr. Rostrum suggested, " The execution shed, eh ? "

" Well yes, if you like. We certainly execute something in there, but it's not you, you know."

" Quite sure ? "

" Yes, it's the little brute of a tumour that we put out of business, and a good job too. Ready ? "

Mr. Rostrum nodded—what else could he do ? He was not going to ask for a little longer, or appear to be afraid. " O.K., Doc. Get on with it."

" All right then, sir." The anæsthetist smiled. " Good-bye."

And he put the mask over his nose and mouth, slowly at first so as not to frighten him, then pressing it firmly. " Breathe deeply," he said.

Mr. Rostrum smelt the rubber of the face-piece and heard a hiss of gas. He smelt a tang of ether vapour. " The bright day is done, and we are for the dark. . . . But I'm not going to die. I've made up my mind to that. I'm not giving in. I'm not giving in. Nobody can kill me if I'm determined to live. I shall live. Ha, try what you like, you can't defeat me if I do not believe in defeat. We'll see whose will is strongest. My will is set. If they think they're going to get me this time, all I can say is, they've come too soon. Too soon. Much too soon, but . . . Oh God, forgive me my many sins, and into Thy hands . . ." The wheels of the train were hammering and banging, and a dark tunnel was rushing towards him. As it enveloped him, the world became a roaring vortex ; it went round and round in ever larger and larger circles—and ended.

CHAPTER SEVENTEEN

AT home, where the family had been told they could ring up the hospital for news at one o'clock, the hours loitered by. All the family was there except Joanie, who would return for lunch and in time for the news. Brenda had been granted a holiday to-day as well as yesterday. Julian, his own master, had not been less generous to himself. He had granted himself another compassionate holiday. The Widow Leicester had arrived soon after breakfast, bringing new flowers to add to, or replace, those she had brought two days before, and, when she had arranged these blooms, she donned her apron and helped Brenda wash up the breakfast things, helped Mildred make the beds, and helped Dudley tidy the house. To-day even her loud voice was subdued and her loud, guttural laughter chastened, though she made a joke now and then and accorded it a sober " Haw, haw " just to keep the hearts of all from sinking too deep.

The house in good order—in better order than it had been for days, because she was a splendid charwoman and gave Dudley high praise as a " handyman "—the house swept and pushed and dusted and left spotless, she declared, " Now, Mildred, my dear, the best thing I can do is to take out the brat and the sausage dog. I'll keep Mr. Dudley away from you all the morning, while you and Brenda do the shopping or anything else you fancy. He'll be quite happy with me. Children are always good with me. . . . Come on, Dudley. Come out with your ancient aunt ; " and thereupon, brusquely, but with bluff jesting, she attired him for the street, and summoned the dog, " Come on, ridiculous dog. Come on, Sankey, or whatever your most inappropriate name is," and accepted with as much equanimity as possible the sight of the tricycle which Dudley was disentangling from the kitchen, and drove them all before her—dog and Dudley and tricycle—into the garden and on to the pavement. Dudley sat astride his machine, and she, in obedience to his instructions, pushed it along the pavements with the ferrule of her umbrella.

It was a clear September morning, a morning, even in

London, of pearl and pale gold, and she pushed him, in such times as she kept pace with him, towards the bronzed autumn trees of the park where they stood in their masses beneath the iridescent sky ; and Sankey, as though he too perceived the park and all its bright promise, ran with leapings and rejoicings at their side. They went through the lichgate into the flower gardens, and she found a seat, hard but clean of bird-droppings, and sat down on it, with her face towards the dahlias and the gladioli and with the weak, diluted sunlight warming her folded hands and laying its sheen on her black clothes and the folds of her black umbrella. The dahlias, well trained, held up their heads, and their faces were scarlet and crimson and gold. It was pleasant, this first cold of the dying year, when the sun was still bright, and the world around her looked like summer and felt like early winter. A robin was singing on a branch in the shrubbery behind her, but his song, like the sunlight, had the touch of autumn in it. It was tempered to the morning, soft and infrequent, like her laughter in her brother's house to-day.

Dudley pedalled along the paths on his tricycle, and there was no moderating of *his* voice and song. Sankey, after gambolling after Dudley, had deserted him for his aunt, this new figure in the social picture, to whom, it seemed, he was much attracted. He was bringing twigs or sticks to her feet and standing before her, his legs tense with anti-cipation, his eyes eager and beseeching, his jaws parted, and his bosom palpitating. She picked up the twig and flung it on to the grass for him, and he chased after it through the grass like a galloping slug. Retrieving it, he brought it back and laid it again at her feet. Impatient at this solicitude, but unable to resist the appeal of his eyes, in one of which was a permanent tear, she picked it up again and threw it, and so forcefully this time (the im-patience acting like a charge of cordite) that it shot into a shrubbery and was lost to sight there, among the branches. Sankey searched and searched for it, nosing and scraping and burrowing ; but all his enthusiasm was bootless, an expense of spirit in a futile cause ; so, philosophically accept-ing frustration, he gathered up a fallen branch, twice as big as himself and gay with September leaves, and brought it across the lawns to his lady's feet. Thus did a soldier of Macduff's host bring his share of Birnam Wood to Dunsinane.

The Widow sighed, as he deposited the branch in all its glory of golden leaves at the right distance from her black, shining shoes, and she sighed again as he looked at her with his petition in his eyes and on his panting tongue and in his tail which wagged behind like a short black whip. "Dudley," she called. "Dud-*ley!* Can't *you* come and do it for him? You're younger than I am."

Dudley was delighted to help, so he left his tricycle in the middle of the path for anyone to fall over, and, running towards them, picked up the branch and hurled it; but when a small boy throws an object it usually travels along a different trajectory from the one he had in mind. The branch went vertically into the air and fell on the grass-patch behind the Widow's seat. Sankey rushed round to recover it, gathered it up at the point of balance, and, returning like a long black cylinder through the grass, laid it at the Widow's, not Dudley's, feet, preferring her artistry.

"No, no," she objected irritably. "I can do no more. You're not my dog. Run away. Run away. Take him away, Dudley. I don't love him. You're an ugly dog. You're like a long, silky black bolster. You're like some awful animal with the body of a miniature bull and the face of a terrier. It's revolting. You're a mistake in nature, and I don't like you."

In answer he laid the branch six inches nearer her feet. Such patience and such forgiveness were not to be withstood, and with the heaviest sigh of the morning she picked it up, broke off a manageable portion, and hurled it for him again. It fell on to a patch of untrimmed grass, and he went rocking after it, through the breast-high grasses, like a ship in a swell.

From ten till the approach of one she stayed in the mild sunlight and the soft milky air, looking often at her watch but determined not to weary of well-doing and return to the house, where Mildred and the children would wish to be alone. She would return in time to hear the news from the hospital. Sometimes as she helped Dudley in his play or stroked the long ears of this affectionate dog and told him she'd have them made into a purse after he was dead, she thought of Alec as he was when he was four years old like this young Dudley and she was a schoolgirl of fourteen and given the task, on a Saturday afternoon, of taking him into this same park to play. She looked at places on the grass where they had played together, that lank schoolgirl and that small, shouting boy. And, being a good church-woman and a prebendary's widow, she said more than once a prayer for him, as she played her part in a game with Dudley or threw a stick for the dog.

§

At home Mildred was looking often, far too often, at the clock, but not once did she ask Brenda or Julian the time or mention its passing in any way. She had gone out to the High Road and done some shopping as usual, Brenda accompanying her, and neither alluding once to the subject uppermost in their minds. Mildred, indeed, spoke of hardly anything, she who was usually so garrulous. When she was home again, she found little tasks to do about the house—not many, for the Widow and Dudley had done most of them—and if she passed the children in the passage or on the stairs as she went about these occupations, she smiled at them gently. Unable to do more in the clean and tidy rooms, she found some stockings to mend and some shirts of Dudley's that needed buttons, and took them down to the living-room, where she sat to work on them, her sewing basket on the table beside her. The children came in sometimes, and she greeted them with the gentle smile, but didn't say anything. She didn't let them know that, as she plied her needle or pushed her spectacles back into place, she was staring at a black emptiness before which she felt, for the present, baffled and lost. "What are we going to do? I don't know. I don't know." Whenever she thought of him as dead—and from ten o'clock onward she was telling herself that he might be lying dead at this moment—she filled up with a compelling desire to go upstairs to her bed-room and throw herself prone upon her bed. That part of her which was histrionic urged her to do this. But not

251

this morning ; no ; not before the children who were as anxious as she ; she must maintain a composure before them ; to-day she must not be the ship's mercurial first mate but its unruffled captain, whose calmness sustained all ; so, instead of rushing upstairs, she threaded her needle again and every time the children came in, smiled at them comfortingly. But she promised herself one thing : if at one o'clock she heard that he was dead, she would go into her bedroom (their bedroom) and throw herself upon her face and give in for a little.

The time ? Only six minutes to twelve ; and it was twenty minutes to, when she last looked. An hour and more to wait. Well . . . she rolled up a pair of socks which she had finished, and, taking another pair, touched the spectacles into place, and began work on them.

But if, because of the dignity of the time, she was staging no dramas before the children, it was very different in the private theatre of her mind, where she was the only audience. On this stage she was witnessing a train of affecting scenes and sometimes listening to a recital of words that fetched the tears into her eyes. He was dead, perhaps, and it was too late to express her contrition for the times when she had been resentful and sour and cruel. " When I am dead, my dearest, sing no sad songs for me. . . ." " Come not when I am dead to drop thy foolish tears upon my grave. . . ." She could not remember where these quotations came from, but the past presented them, one after another, to her mind. She saw the funeral service in their church, where the whole congregation was assembled to do honour to her family ; she heard the organ playing softly beyond the chancel arch as she walked behind the coffin on the arm of her tall son, Julian—not sobbing, but bearing herself with dignity . . . like a queen ; she saw Julian guiding her gently into the foremost pew of all and taking his place at her side. She heard the huge congregation behind her singing some of Alec's favourite hymns, which she and the children had chosen for the service. " Father of Heaven, Whose love profound," they were singing ; and " The day is past and over." So appropriate were the words of this latter hymn that their memory forced the tears into her eyes and she had to take off her spectacles to wipe them.

The toils of day are over ;
I raise the hymn to Thee,
And ask that free from peril
The hours of dark may be.

And now the service was over and she and her children,
Julian, Brenda, Joanie, and Dudley, were going out from
the church, while the congregation sang the last hymn—
another of his favourites, and appropriate enough to thrust the
tears into her eyes again : " Grant us thy peace upon our
homeward way ; With Thee began, with Thee shall end
the day."

She rose from the needlework to prepare a meal for the
children. Joanie would be back soon ; Julian was a boy
and might be hungry ; Dudley must be fed. And then
there was Elizabeth, who'd been so good ; there must be
a meal of some sort for her. Going into the kitchen, she put
some potatoes in a bowl and began to peel them. The
thought occurred to her that if she was good, if she just went
about quietly, doing unselfish actions, God might save him.
And as she peeled the potatoes, she watched a new drama.
She had died a few hours after him—not that she felt the
least like dying ; on the contrary, she had only to think
of dying to feel the stubborn health in her body—but it was
sweetly flattering to dream of dying and to imagine the two
coffins being placed side by side at the foot of the chancel
steps. The congregation would be one of the largest the
church had seen for years. Indeed it was the largest in its
history. The sidesmen were bringing in extra chairs from
the vestry and the parish room ; the reporters from the
Kilburn Times and the *North London Chronicle* were standing
at the back of the church by the west door, writing a
description of the scene ; the whole choir, men and boys,
was in attendance ; they had left their places of work on
this moving occasion, even though it was a week-day ; and
there was hardly a dry eye in the church, even among the
men, as choir and congregation sang the first hymn, which
would be—what ? Passing with the potatoes from sink to
cooker, she chose, and was most pleased with the choice,
" O perfect Love, all human thought transcending." The
kitchen was empty ; there was no one to see her ; and her

tears gushed over the saucepan as the huge congregation sang the hymn, and the reporters, perceiving the appropriateness and the story-value of the words, scribbled them down :

> O perfect Love, all human thought transcending,
> Lowly we kneel in prayer before Thy throne,
> That theirs may be the love which knows no ending,
> Whom Thou for evermore dost join in one.

§

About fifteen minutes past twelve Truppy walked slowly up the steps to the front door and knocked indecisively. He had known that the operation would be at about ten o'clock, and he had supposed that the family would learn at once of its success or failure ; and in either event he was longing to enter upon the service and obligations of a friend. By mid-day he could contain his uncertainty no longer. It was a heavy matter to think of losing his friend—" easily my best friend ; my one *great* friend "—but there was a small compensating pleasure to be got from the picture of himself saying to Mildred, " I'm at your service in everything, Mildred dear ; I know you've got your Julian, but he's had no experience—fortunately—of death, whereas I have buried father, mother, and one dear child. He and I'll do everything for you ; " and then printing a kiss on her forehead like his seal of friendship ; and thereafter, with lowered voice and quiet feet, Julian at his side, going about the sorrowful business of bringing Alec from the hospital to his home, visiting the undertaker and the vicar, and arranging the service at church so that in every detail it was perfect, like a warm and comforting cloak about the shoulders of Mildred.

Brenda opened the door to him, and he was quick with his apologies. " I don't want to be a nuisance, Brenda dear. Don't disturb your mother. I just wondered if you'd heard anything. Just tell me on the quiet, and then I'll slip away."

" No, we haven't heard anything yet. They said we might telephone at one o'clock."

"I suppose there's nothing Florrie and I can do. We should be so much happier if we had something to do."

"I don't think so. Everybody's being very kind. My auntie's here."

"That's good. Well, you won't want me hanging around. But don't you worry, Brenda dear. I feel everything's going to be all right. No news is good news. One o'clock : well now, I'll tell you what I'll do. I don't want to be a nuisance, and I won't come into the house, but I shall be outside in the road at one o'clock, and perhaps Julian or Joanie could nip out and tell me the news."

"No, you come in. We shall like to have you with us when Julian rings up."

"I don't want to intrude, you see. . . . I'd ring up the hospital myself, only I don't want to worry them more than is necessary."

"*You* won't intrude. We shall love to have you there when we hear. I think you ought to be there. You're one of the family, aren't you ? "

"Well, I like to think so, after all these years. But I'm not coming in now, dear. As I say, you won't want me hanging about the house. I'll come back just before one o'clock. Perhaps you'd like to leave the door on the latch, so that I could just slip in without troubling anybody. I should like to be with you then, I must say."

§

Towards one o'clock the Widow left the park with Dudley and Sankey. She too thought she ought to be with them when they heard their news, lest it should be alarming or distressing and she could be of help. So she came back along the pavements, pushing Dudley's tricycle from behind with her umbrella when she caught up with it, or when he halted it with a scrape of his feet and, lifting the feet in the air, demanded this service. The dog trotted errantly and intermittently at their side. As she approached the house, she saw Truppy going up the steps and trying the latch of the door and, when she was at the gate, she heard him saying to Brenda, " Are you sure it'll be all right if I come

255

in? I don't want to be a nuisance." She did not herself go up the steps, nor let Brenda see her; she went very quietly down the path to the basement door and, shepherding Dudley and the dog into the empty living-room and following them herself, shut the door on them all. She guessed that the family was now in Alec's study just above, where the telephone was; and she liked to think that she was there beneath them if she was wanted. The dog, supposing she had come into the house to play, barked enthusiastically.

"Keep *quiet!*" she hissed at him. "*Lie* down! Lie *down*, I tell you! Idiot dog."

It was a command that the most disobedient dog would have obeyed, and Sankey laid himself down and panted.

"Another word from you, and there'll be trouble," she warned him. "Have you no sense at all? And don't look at me like that. I'm too old a hand to be softened by looks like that. Now, Mr. Dudley, we'll play, shall we? We'll build something together, shall we, young man?"

"Oh, yes! *Yes!*" Dudley skipped at her side.

"Very good. But hush, hush, hush. This is a very secret game. *Tsh!* Let's see who can be the quietest. Now then, what have we here?"

She found a box of bricks and, sitting on the edge of a hard chair, built upon the floor a Greek temple and a Nelson's column and, with him as chief architect and surveyor, a tunnel for his engine and a garage for his motor car.

In the room above, unaware of this support beneath them, forgetful of the Widow's existence, Mildred, Brenda, Joanie, and Truppy were likewise seated upon the edges of chairs, and Julian was standing by the telephone. Truppy, in his modesty, was sitting apart from the members of the family and by the door. His bowler hat was on his knees as a kind of hint that, if necessary, he would go quickly and leave them to themselves. Julian's eyes were on the clock. Two minutes to one. One minute to one.

"I shouldn't ring up *just* at one o'clock, Julian," Mildred advised. "It would look a bit—oh, I don't know. But we don't want to seem a nuisance."

"O.K., Mum. If you like."

So Julian stood there and waited till two minutes past one, and then dialled the hospital.

"Hello? Is that the Kilburn General Hospital? Oh, this is Mr. Rostrum's son speaking . . . Rostrum . . . I was just ringing up to inquire how my father was We were told we might ring up at one o'clock . . . The George Hoskin Ward . . . Yes, Alexander Rostrum . . . He was operated on this morning by Sir Joshua Dymote . . . Thank you. Thank you *very* much, if you wouldn't mind."

Closing his palm over the mouthpiece, he turned to the family. "They're putting me through to the ward, I think. . . . It was a good touch, mentioning Sir Joshua. Unless I'm quite mistaken, they jump to it when you mention that name. . . . Something's happening."

Mildred sat staring at him, her fat hands on her knees. The blood had flowed from Brenda's face. Joanie's colour, always full, had not changed, but her eyes were round and stilled in suspense. Truppy, eyes lowered in modesty, fingered his bowler hat.

Julian kept the receiver at his ear and beat his fingers on the telephone's shelf. "There's nothing happening now. I can hear some nurses chattering their heads off somewhere, that's all. God, how these girls can talk. There's another telephone ringing in the distance. I can hear feet going to and fro—nurses' feet—they never stop ; you can always tell nurses' feet somehow. As far as I can make out there's a whale of a conference going on not far away : men and women's voices . . . Ah ! . . . Hello? Yes . . . I'm sorry. I can't quite hear you properly . . . Alexander Rostrum. He was operated on by Sir Joshua this morning . . . Yes . . . His son speaking. Yes . . . I see . . . Thank you very much. And what does that mean ? . . . Oh, I quite understand."

Slowly he put back the receiver.

"What did they say?" demanded Mildred in a hard, peremptory voice.

"They said, ' He's doing as well as can be expected '."

"Oh ! . . . What does that mean ? "

Julian, seeing a terror on her face, lied. "But that's good, Mum. When I asked them what it meant, they said, ' The operation passed off very successfully, and he's doing as well as can be expected '."

"Oh, but you didn't say they said that."

257

"Didn't I? Well, that's what they said. 'Very success-ful.' So far, so good. I think it's good."

"Oh yes, that's good," declared Truppy from behind.

§

But Julian told Brenda and Joanie that he had invented for his mother's sake the words "passed off very success-fully" and that all the nurse had really said was "doing as well as can be expected." He told them in part because he wanted to share the truth and in part because he was rather proud of his wise, prompt lie.

And the three children sat wondering what this formula might mean; what it was worth. "Doing as well as can be expected." Brenda's face was still drained white; and Joanie's eyes were full of doubt and fear, the eyebrows often coming together in a bewildered frown; so Julian, feeling a masculine obligation to sustain them as he had sustained their mother, added, "After all, I don't see what more they could have said. They can't expect more than they expect, so it really amounts to 'Quite satisfactory,' doesn't it?"

"Does it?" Brenda queried. "There's such a thing as euphemism."

"It depends on the tone in which it's said," suggested Julian.

"Exactly," he agreed. "And the little party who answered me sounded cheerful enough."

"Could we get someone else to ring up and see what they say to them: Truppy, for instance?" asked Joanie. "And you know how Truppy'd love to have something official to do. It's almost a shame not to let him. And they might tell the exact truth to someone who was not the family."

"No." Julian didn't think they should do this. Neither did Brenda; nor, after discussion, Joanie. All, and the tall Julian not least, were a little afraid of the hospital.

"We can only wait," he concluded, "and as long as we hear nothing, we can know that things are O.K."

But Brenda was driven by a quenchless hunger to hear more. She was fearing most because now she loved most.

258

During a perfunctory meal she laughed and made some jokes for her mother's sake, but directly it was over and cleared away, she went out into the street. She was not certain where she was going; she knew only that she must go somewhere and talk to someone and find out something. To the hospital? No. What would be gained by that? They were busy with a thousand patients, and she was only one of five thousand relatives; they had answered the family once and might resent her importunacy; almost certainly they would only give her the same formal answer. To Truppy? But he would have nothing to say. He would only try to comfort her as Julian had tried to do. His words would be medicine, not fact. To—ah, she was at the corner of Nunsbury Road and, as she looked southward down the High Road, she thought of Priory Road and the doctor's house. Oh, yes, Dr. Soden. Dr. Soden was at least an individual, a single human being, not a vast incorporation of human cells like the hospital, an enclosed and throbbing industry, high in purpose but formal and cold. Moreover he was young—not much older than herself—and always very nice to her, almost as if he admired her; and she did not feel afraid of him. Her steps quickened as she thought of his house and himself in Priory Road. Oh, if only he was at home! It was still early, and he might not yet have started out upon his afternoon visiting.

But when the doctor's door was opened to her, she met a barrier that discomfited her and shamed her cheeks and sank her heart. The maid's manner was discouraging; she said, " Oh, I'm quite sure the doctor can't see anyone now, miss; " and before either Brenda or the maid could add a word, the doctor's voice came from his consulting-room, irritably : " I can't possibly see anyone now, Rose. Tell them my surgery hour is five o'clock ; " and, as Brenda did not immediately go, but halted there with a dying hope, he came out angrily to assert his right to some system and peace. " I have said I can see no one——"

But then he recognized Brenda, and his manner changed at once. He was no longer an affronted disciplinarian but a smiling friend. " Oh, come in. Come in, my dear. *You* can come in—I didn't know it was you." He always liked to hear himself saying " my dear " to the women of his practice, alike to the old and to the young ; and he drew a particular pleasure from saying it to such as Brenda. " Of course I can spare you a minute or two. I'm sorry if your reception was somewhat chilly, but Rose has the strictest orders to try and protect me from visitors at this time of the day. You know how it is with a doctor. Now come in here and sit down. The operation seems to have passed off very well."

Brenda sat before his desk in the chair in which her father had sat. But she only just sat on it, as if to show him that she wasn't going to stay. He stood opposite her. And with much stammering and many hurrying words, she apologized for her visit at this hour, assured him that she wouldn't keep him a second, and explained her anxiety and asked if he could possibly tell her what " doing as well as can be expected " might mean.

Dr. Soden repeated the words. " Yes, they always say something like that. It's not much comfort to anybody, is it ? ' Doing quite nicely ' was what they said to me."

" Oh, did they ? That sounds better. That's good, isn't it ? "

" I think so. I hope so."

" Tell me—please—and then I'll go "—she rose from her chair as if this was her last word—" is there any danger of his dying ? "

The doctor walked to the window, looked out, and walked back. He came back with a smile, and the smile was intended to soften the impact of his words. " There's always some danger, my dear, after a serious operation, and especially if it's been at all delayed. And some patients *will* postpone and procrastinate and think that they know better than we do. But I think, I do really, that we got your father to see some sense in time. I don't mind telling you now that there was a time when I thought that if he didn't soon take my advice, we'd be in for trouble." The old grievance insisted on being vented this much. But that it might not appear as a grievance, he put on a mien of archness, his eyebrows lifted and his eyes lit in a kind of tolerant amusement. " He *wouldn't* do what he was told, you know. It was very naughty of him. But after a few weeks he came to his senses and obeyed me. Even so, I could wish he'd gone to the hospital directly I told him to."

" But "—Brenda was moving towards the door to assure him that she would keep her promise and go quickly, but in her surprise at the doctor's words she was compelled to work in a few more questions while there was a chance— " didn't he obey you at once? I knew nothing about this. I didn't even know that he'd had any really serious pains till about four days ago, when he told us that he'd been having X-ray examinations at the hospital and Sir Joshua had said that he must have an operation. That was the first any of us heard about it. I imagined that it had all come on very suddenly. When did he first come to you? "

" Oh, quite a long time ago. Early in August. He came when he could stand the pain no longer—as they always do."

" Early in August? "

" Yes. If you like, I can tell you exactly. I think it was the twelfth or thirteenth of August."

" Do you mean he was really suffering then? "

" I do. He was suffering very badly. And when I told him he must go to the hospital at once, he said he wasn't going to." Dr. Soden smiled at her as one does when describing the behaviour of an untractable child. " He refused flatly. I tried to be as severe with him as I could, for his own sake, but there was no moving him."

" But why? Why didn't he want to go? "

" I don't know. He said something about ' private reasons,' ' family reasons '."

As when the sun breaks cloud at last and the whole landscape is revealed in a clash of full daylight, so Brenda saw now the real pattern of the last few weeks. A hundred small incidents, such as her father's inquiries of her in the privacy of the passage, " Any news yet, darling? " took on their true shape and their right shade of meaning. " And when did he finally consent to go? When did he first go to be properly examined? "

" About ten days ago, I should say."

" Yes." It was the answer she expected; the answer she knew would come. " Thank you. Yes, I see now. Well—oh Doctor, he *will* be all right, won't he? Please tell me that he will be." The fingers of her clenched fist pierced into her palm as she stood there. " Please say you think so. He *must* get all right."

" I do think so, my dear. He had the best man in London to do the operation. I was able to work that for him, I'm glad to say. And he seems to have stood up to it quite well. I have every hope that everything will be quite all right."

" How soon can I know ? I'm so sorry to bother you like this. I'll go now. But Doctor, how soon can I know ? How soon can I know for certain ? Oh, you *will* forgive me for worrying you like this ? "

" I quite understand your anxiety, my dear, and I'm very glad you came to me. Please be sure of that. I'm pleased and flattered that you came at once to me ; and now I'll tell you what we'll do. Give me a little while longer, and I'll ring up the hospital myself. They'll tell me things they won't tell anyone else. I'll get on to the house surgeon early this evening. That'll be the best time. Would you like to come and see me again at about five o'clock, and I'll tell Rose to show you in before anyone else."

" Oh, thank you. Thank you. It *is* kind of you."

She put out her hand, and he pressed it so sympathetically and said so comfortingly, " Don't worry," that it lifted the tears into her throat and precluded an answer. She just nodded with a tight, shaking mouth and went from him, and from the house.

And where now ? Half-past two. Not home. For some reason not clear to her she did not want to go home. Nor to walk aimlessly about the streets. There was one place only to which she wanted to go, though there was no purpose to be served when she got there. But her will and her feet carried her there, none the less. She walked to the hospital and stood outside its railings, looking up at it. After looking up at it, she walked to and fro before the railings. For some time that afternoon she might have been seen, standing still in front of the hospital with her hands behind her back, or walking up and down the quiet street with her eyes on the ground. She did not go up the steps of the hospital to make any new inquiry, preferring to remain between now and five o'clock in her fool's paradise of hope, if fool's paradise it was. "Oh, he mustn't die. I couldn't bear it; my darling father. I'm outside here, Daddy, praying for you. Oh God, make him get well; don't make it that I killed him." With that she remembered her church, and hurried there to spend an hour alone on her knees.

§

His eyes were open, and he was looking at the ward. Yes, it was the ward. But the people in it and the furniture in it were blurred, and even though he blinked his eyes and knit his brows he could not pull them into focus. His bedside locker and the bed beyond were doubling their edges and oscillating, as he looked. Once they seemed to be coming towards him. But it was the ward. There was Mr. Burnaby, propped up in his bed and reading a book. There was the avenue of beds stretching away to the swing doors. A nurse was coming through the doors, and another nurse was scrubbing her hands in an alcove before dressing a patient. He was hearing the sounds of the ward: nurses' feet, a patient's cough, a sleeper's stertorous breathing, and the buzzing of music in the headphones over the beds. And in the distance he could hear the hum of the world, the old familiar human world. Its sunlight—the sunlight that shone only on this side of death—splashed the walls and floor.

It was over then. Apathetically, with little interest, he realized that it was over and he was alive. Alive and without pain, except for the tightness of the bandages round his body and some twinges in the wound beneath them and a sour taste in his mouth. He was lying on his back, his head turned to one side, and a bowl under his cheek. Thus his face was turned towards Mr. Burnaby; and Mr. Burnaby, as if he had heard him open his eyes, turned his own eyes in his direction and addressed towards him a wide smile, a single wink, and a small bow of salutation.

"Well, how are you, ole cock? Meet Mr. Burnaby again." And he looked round for a glass of something in which he could drink a toast of welcome and congratulation to Mr. Rostrum. Finding only his sputum mug, he lifted that high. "Here's how." And he pretended to quaff deep from it. Then, laying it back on the locker, he held his linked hands high above his head and brandished them, as a boxer does after he has triumphed in the ring. " Told you so, ole cock. Told you my money was on you. Now there's nothing to do but get well. Hatterboy ! "

Mr. Rostrum managed to smile an acknowledgment.

" Feeling rather lousy, eh ? Well . . . yes . . . you're not looking too grand, I must say. Gaw, it's a game, isn't it ? But they didn't get you that time, mate, did they ? I told you they wouldn't. Nah ! 'S'all over ; and there's nothing more to worry about now except that you won't be able to laugh for a fortnight. Your stitches 'urt every time you laugh, eh, Young Arthur ? Going to sleep again ? Good. That's the idea. 'Ave a nice long sleep, and you'll wake up feeling like a two-year-old. Good night." He turned to his neighbour on the other side. " My mate's come round. But he's not, as you might say, chatty yet. He don't love any of us yet. In fact, he's shutting his eyes because he can't stand the sight of us. Wurl, I don't wonder, on the whole. I've seen a better looking lot in me time. *Tsh !* He's going to sleep again." And Mr. Burnaby returned to his book.

He was alive and without pain ; he had achieved what he had willed to achieve ; the battle was won and the day was his ; and the fact was of little interest. He could take no pleasure in it because, though alive, his body was like a vessel empty of all strength except for enough to open his eyes. He tried to remember those for whom he had wanted to live, and to whom he had wanted to return, and it was an effort to recall them ; an effort that he hadn't the energy to pursue. Would it trouble him if he heard that he was never going to see them again ? Hardly : hardly at all. They seemed very far away, and he indifferent to them. One needed life to love, and he had only enough life to open his eyes on the ward, smile at Mr. Burnaby's greetings lest he hurt his feelings, and wish to sleep again. Perhaps, after all, he hadn't won his battle ; perhaps this was just a last glimpse of the old world ; a last return to it before he died. If so, he didn't greatly care ; he hadn't the energy to care. He closed his eyes on it and slept again.

Voices. A man's and a woman's. Just above his head.
He opened his eyes, and the flakes of sunlight on the walls
told him that it was now late in the afternoon. The young
house surgeon, in his white coat, a short, fresh-complexioned
young man, was standing by his bed with the ward sister
at his side. He felt a little better than when he woke before,
a little more alive, and a little—but not much—more interested in the things of the old, known world.

"Well?" The house surgeon was smiling down upon
him.

Mr. Rostrum smiled weakly back.

"Sleepy, eh?"

"Yes." He was unable to think of any other words.
The effort to think induced a dizziness.

"I should think you're quite a lot pleased with yourself,
aren't you?"

"Why?"

"Well, by gosh, you did jolly well. We're all very proud
of you, aren't we, sister?"

"We certainly are."

"You're pretty tough, you know."

Mr. Rostrum felt the prick of an old pleasure, but it was
a prick and no more.

"Old Josh did a marvellous job of work on you, and he
knows it. He's well up in the air about it. Is that right,
sister?"

"I think so."

"Think? You *know* he is. He's purring like an old cat
after a really satisfying meal. I've just been talking to
him."

Josh? Oh, yes : Sir Joshua. "Is it going to be all right
then?"

The doctor smiled down on him again, lips pressed tight,
as if impounding a secret behind them. "I expect the old
boy'll want to tell you that himself. How much can we tell
him, sister? What can we say to him without getting ourselves into trouble?"

"Spill the whole beans, mate," recommended Mr. Burnaby,
who had laid down his book that he might join the gathering

as a most interested member. "Let him have the whole can while you're about it."

"You keep quiet," commanded the ward sister, turning her head. "Nobody's talking to you; and you're a bad old man."

"That's right; but, leaving aside that that's no way to speak to me, I still say, If you've got any good news for my pal here, for Christ's sake—begging your pardon, nurse —for the Lord's sake, let him 'ave it. It'll do him good. I'm taking a great personal interest in him, and I want to see him get well quickly. 'Oo's to know what you tell 'im, anyway? *I* shan't split."

"Well, I'll tell you this much," said the doctor to Mr. Rostrum. "A minute or two ago Dr. Soden rang up and asked me to tell him anything I could. He said your daughter—your elder daughter, I think—had been round to see him, and——"

"She's a nice gurl," commented Mr. Burnaby, that most interested listener.

"——and he wanted to give her something a little more definite than the usual ' Doing as well as can be expected ' which doesn't mean much, does it? And do you know what I told him? "

"No."

"I told him he could tell her that we didn't think there was much more to worry about."

Mr. Rostrum stared at him, trying to take this in.

"I never did worry," said Mr. Burnaby. "I told 'im so."

"Well, are you satisfied? " asked the doctor, still smiling down on him. "And I expect she's hearing that this very minute. Dr. Soden said she was coming round to hear what he had to tell her——"

"Nice gurl ! " breathed Mr. Burnaby, richly appreciative.

"——and she'll be hurrying home to tell the whole family. So now, for Heaven's sake, get properly well, and don't let me down."

With his reason, if not with his feelings, which were so leaden and inert, Mr. Rostrum knew that he was being told a tremendous, a transcendent thing. He was being told of his reprieve. He was being presented with life. His reason,

266

faintly reinforced by his feelings, instructed him to thank the young doctor.

" Thank you, Doctor. How soon can I go ? "

" Oh, come, come ! Good lord, sister, he wants to get up and go home now. No, not for three or four weeks. We're going to do this job properly while we're about it, and get you really well. So just you stay there in your bed and, if you can, go to sleep. Come along, sister, we won't talk to him any more."

They were gone, with friendly, parting smiles, and as he lay there, reiterating the doctor's words, " Not much more to worry about," their meaning was breaking upon him like the wide glow of dawn along a dusky sky. The day, the sunlit human day, was being given back to him. His home in a Kilburn Road, and all that made it his home, were being restored to him. His joy in the restoration rose within him and began to warm his heart. Only think, only think : all his troubles at an end ; Brenda's great fear and, after it, *his* great fear ; both over and done with now and receding into the past ; their darkness disarmed of all power except to heighten this gathering glow of relief and peace. There was nothing but peace in the world. Soon he would be able to believe it ; to possess the knowledge in its fullness. Meanwhile let him lie there and allow the happiness to gather around him.

§

Some days later Brenda stood in the hall outside the swing doors of the ward. It was half-past twelve, and nothing could make it a visiting hour. Rather did she suspect that a visitor at such an hour would be more unpopular with the nurses than at any other time. And because she suspected this, she was standing there, hesitant, frustrated, uncertain whether to speak to anyone, fearful of a rebuff. She had longed to see him alone ; her dinner hour was her only free time ; so she had suddenly called up all her courage and hurried from her school to the hospital. Her courage had got her to the very doors of the ward and there, promptly, given out. After getting her, with some signs of failure, up the stairs and along the corridors and into this outer hall, it had here, ten yards from her goal, just ceased to play any part in the episode. It had left her naked, exposed, and immobilized on the wrong side of the glass doors, while her hands clutched the few presents she had snatched from the shops on her way to this point : some cigarettes, some sweets, a magazine, and a book.

She stepped a little closer to the glass doors and looked through them. Where was his bed ? Oh, there ; and there were screens around it. What did that mean ? A nurse with a mask on came from behind the screens, pushing a dressing trolley. Had he had a relapse after doing so well ? Had something gone wrong ? Now two other nurses were taking the screens away, and she could see him lying there, propped up with pillows, but very still. Oh, had he taken a turn for the worse ? Oh God—and if he had, they'd never let her see him.

A harassed probationer came running through the swing doors. She was young, with a face like a pretty cat's, broad at the brow and narrow at the chin ; and such a probationer as this, short, pink, and younger than herself, was the only functionary in the hospital of whom Brenda was not afraid. She stepped into her path, and her unexpected appearance stopped both the rush and the breath of the young nurse, so that she was as flurried and agape as Brenda was embarrassed and apologetic. She flushed, and Brenda flushed, and there was little to choose between the shades of crimson on their faces.

" I'm so awfully sorry to have come at this time, but *do* you think I could see my father just for a minute or two ? " Brenda was effusive. " I know it's not the right time, but I had no other time in which to come. I'm his daughter. It's my only time. I've hurried here from my school which is a long way away, and I shall have to hurry back very soon. Do you *think* it would be possible ? Not if it's any trouble. I *should* be so grateful."

" I don't know," said the child ; and from her fluster it was plain that she didn't. " I'll ask Sister." And she who had appeared to be running from the ward on urgent business now turned and ran back into it on this new errand.

Through the doors Brenda saw her go to the centre desk

where the ward sister stood by the side of a young doctor who sat in the desk chair examining some notes. The probationer, as diffident and apprehensive as Brenda would have been, halted a little to the side of, and a little behind, the ward sister. She halted and stood there, but certainly not " at ease " or " easy ". It seemed a long minute before she dared interrupt the sister and deliver Brenda's request. Brenda, watching and dreading a refusal, suspected an impatience in the sister's manner and immediately sank into a deep of discomfort and shame, her heart pulsing with a sickly rhythm as she sank. The probationer went from the sister's side towards the far end of the ward—on a third errand ?—and the sister stayed in her place, talking to the doctor. Brenda waited. She beat her foot anxiously and unhappily, for she had to be back in school at half-past one. She looked at her watch. A quarter to one. Oh dear, oh dear. And the sister had not moved.

But now she and the doctor were coming out of the ward, laughing together. They walked right past Brenda and through the next swing doors into the next hall, where they stood talking. But now the doctor had gone, and the sister was coming back. She saw Brenda and appeared to remember having heard something about her from a probationer. " Oh, yes ? " she asked. " Yes ? "

Her blush mounting and her tongue stumbling, Brenda repeated the rapid and wordy explanation she had given to the probationer.

" It's not the proper visiting hour," said the sister. " Is it impossible for you to come at any other time ? "

" It is, really. I'm teaching all day."

" Aren't you free on Saturdays ? "

" Oh, yes, I can come on Saturdays, but there's something I particularly wanted to say to my father."

" Wouldn't a message do ? "

" Oh, no, no . . . but it doesn't matter if it's impossible. Not if it's any trouble. . . ."

" We like people to keep to visiting hours if they can."

" Yes, I quite see . . . I quite understand . . . I'm so sorry to have worried you. I'll come on Saturday."

" Which is your father ? " The sister had not said this unkindly, but rather as a first step towards helping her ;

but no words could have put Brenda more completely in her place as one of a nameless and shadowy multitude.

" Mr. Rostrum."

" Oh, yes."

" He's not *worse*, is he ?—I'm so sorry—I won't keep you —I'm sure you're busy—but I noticed there were screens round his bed."

" Oh, dear me, no. He's doing quite nicely. His dressing had slipped : that was all." And she added another of the stock formulæ, as if answering the telephone : " He's quite comfortable."

" Oh, *good !* "

That word of relief escaped from Brenda with such power that it found its way to the sister's heart. " You can go in and see him just this once. For about ten minutes. Not more, if you don't mind."

" Oh, thank you, *thank* you. I shan't have time for more."

" Come along." The sister went before her into the ward. " There he is. Over there." As if Brenda didn't know ! " Go and cheer him up, but don't excite him. Your news isn't very exciting, is it ? "

" Oh, no, I won't excite him. It's nothing very much. It's just something I wanted to say to him. Oh, thank you most awfully."

The bloom of shame on her cheeks, Brenda walked towards his bed, and the eyes from all the other beds swung with her as she walked. Her father's eyes recognized her and smiled in surprise.

" Hallo, dear," said he, as she reached his bed.

" Hallo, Daddy. I've only got a minute or two."

" Here she is, come to see the ole man," said Mr. Burnaby. " He's doing very nicely, miss. He's looking a fair treat now. I'm completely satisfied with him. Yurse."

" I'm so glad."

The sister, liking Brenda and Mr. Rostrum now because she'd just been good to them both, and glad to sip further the sweets of kindness, wheeled up some screens herself and arranged them round the bed that father and daughter might be alone.

" 'Ere ! " Mr. Burnaby objected. " Don't screen me out. I'm one of the family now."

"Rubbish," laughed the sister. "They don't want you." And she closed the screens and walked away.

"He's my mate," Mr. Burnaby protested bitterly to her departing back.

Within the screens Mr. Rostrum accepted her gifts with a profuse gratitude, and she said they were nothing, and then he, trying to make conversation, asked, "Well, how's everybody? How's the Awful Little Boy?" and Brenda, also making conversation, gave a favourable account of the family; and for some time both talked, rather awkwardly, of small commonplace things, Brenda quite unable to say what she had come to say. The ten minutes were sliding away. When by her watch there were but three minutes left, and she feared the sister might approach at any moment and sound the retreat, she plunged desperately into it.

"Daddy. . . ."

"Yes, darling?"

"There's something I want to say."

"Yes?"

"Dr. Soden told me you first went to him early in August, and that you were suffering a lot then—so much so that he told you you ought to go at once to the hospital for an examination."

"Oh, *did* he? He'd no business to."

"It just slipped out. He was being very nice. And then I asked Mummy when she first heard about your pains, and she said she didn't know anything about them till a Sunday in September, when she made you go and see the doctor."

"I expect that's right. But what's all this arithmetic about?"

"It means that you were suffering horrible pains for weeks and telling nobody about them."

"Well, what of it? I hoped there was nothing to them."

"In spite of the fact that the doctor had insisted that you ought to go to the hospital at once?"

"Certainly. I don't always believe what doctors say."

"Daddy, I'm not a fool."

"No, dear, I don't think you are. No, on the whole, I should say not."

"The Sunday in September when you told Mummy and

went back to the doctor was the day I told you that everything was all right with me."

"Go on? Was it! You don't say so!"

"You know it was."

"Dear me! What a strange coincidence!"

"And I know why you refused to do what the doctor wanted."

"That's very interesting. And why did I refuse?"

"For my sake."

"Fancy that! So that's what you think, is it?"

"That's what I know, Daddy. And I want to thank you; that's all." She rested her hand on his. "But I'd never have let you do it if I'd known."

"Don't be ridiculous, child. Whatever was there in it? A few weeks, that's all. You're being very silly." But this insincere protest covered a great pleasure. He was pleased, now that all was safe, and she would have nothing with which to reproach herself, that she should know. He was not of the pure metal which desires that its good deeds should be hidden. At least, he was only ready for that extremity if it was absolutely necessary, and then only for so long as the emergency lasted. "There's nothing to make a song about. Should we talk about something more sensible? How are Joanie and Steve?"

"You were suffering all the time."

"Oh, no, I wasn't. Only off and on."

"And telling nobody. Having no one to comfort you."

"Don't you believe it. I worked off quite a lot on old Truppy, and wasn't he pleased with his job as confidant? I didn't tell him anything about you, of course, but I got rid of an awful lot of superfluous steam on him. Believe you me, everything has worked out splendidly for everybody."

"But it might not have done so. What should I have done if you'd died?"

"I never believed for a moment that I was going to die. I resolved firmly that I wasn't going to, and I flatter myself that will-power had a lot to do with the result. The doctors practically said it did." He patted her hand. "All's well that ends well. And now I want to ask you something else. Have you heard anything more from that young man?"

"No, Daddy. Nothing at all. And I never shall."

" And what do you feel about him now ? "

" Oh, I've got it all clear in my mind now. I've thought it out, and thought it out, especially in church sometimes during the services. And I saw that there were only two courses : either to be bitter about him or to understand and forgive."

" That's right. That's exactly right. And you're not being bitter ? "

" No. I saw that he'd only done just what I did, so I ought to be able to forgive him."

" How do you mean, darling ? "

" Well . . ." She blushed, looked down, and then looked up but not at him, and spoke. " I yielded to an irresistible temptation to escape from something, and that's just what he did, isn't it ? Some temptations *are* almost irresistible, and one's ever so much happier when one understands that and forgives."

" Good. Good. I know you're right. I knew it one day just before I came here." And he told her about the letter he had written. " It's better like that, Brenda ; better for you and better for him. One is happy again, when one forgives. In fact, I was surprised to discover, after being a Christian of sorts for fifty years, that there were few happinesses quite like forgiving. I shall try it again one day."

" Time now." The sister, smiling pleasantly on both, removed the screens. " We mustn't tire him, must we ? "

" Oh, no . . . well . . ." Brenda rose at once, bent over him, and kissed him. " Thank you again, Daddy. I think you've been wonderful, and I can't ever forget it."

He smiled deprecatingly ; and she scurried from the ward as if in shame, turning only once to wave at him, but leaving him happier, perhaps, than anyone else in that huge and swarming building. No joy so exultant as a love enhanced and secure.

CHAPTER EIGHTEEN

IT was a windy afternoon in October ; the wind had scoured the sky above Kilburn into a steel-blue reflector for the falling sun and now was sheering the yellow and brittler leaves from the trees in Nunsbury Road and moaning at times in the garden of No. 25, the tall, grey, corner house of the Rostrums. Behind its screen of wind-worried autumn trees, and under the oblique sunlight, the house stood very quiet; its door was firmly shut against the world; and you could imagine that it was keeping a secret, at any rate for a while, from the few who passed along that gusty street.

And, behold, that is exactly what it was doing. The house, No. 25, Nunsbury Road, was, as it were, in secret conference. Behind that closed and inviolate front door, immediately behind it in the narrow passage, Julian, Brenda, Joanie, and Dudley, and, for that matter, Sankey, were hard at work. They were disposed on or about a step-ladder in the form of a pyramid: Julian high up on the ladder with a hammer in his hand and drawing-pins, string, and scissors on its top rung; Brenda standing on one side of the steps and handing up certain articles as he called for them; Joanie standing on the other side and handing up advice and criticism which he was not calling for; and Dudley now standing on the lowest step and crying, "Let me, oh, let me," and now getting off to drag at a bundle of multi-coloured material on the floor. Dudley was working harder than any of them. Sankey either sat on his haunches and watched them, panting, or he joined Dudley in the business of making a selection among the brightly coloured articles on the floor.

There was no one else in the house.

"This was a brain-wave of mine," said Julian, lowering his arm from the ceiling. "Brenda, hand up some more of the doings. Joanie, hold this string. Dudley, behave yourself. We're getting on fine. It's a bit vulgar, I admit."

"It's vulgar in the extreme," Brenda amended.

"I know. The point is conceded. Don't labour it."

"Oh, but I like a spot of vulgarity." Joanie rose up and down on her toes, and worked her half-closed fists up and down, to express her delight. "Let's be thoroughly vulgar while we're about it."

"My dear child, I intend to wallow in it," said Julian. "All the same, I still think it should have gone over the front door."

"No," said Brenda emphatically. "I'd have died of

274

shame. I should never have held my head up in Kilburn again. It's what they do in the slums."

" Exactly. They have a heart in the slums."

The articles which Brenda was handing up to Julian, and which he was affixing with a dresser hook and drawing-pins to the ceiling, were a festoon of red, white, and blue bunting and a shield with the red lion of Scotland on its field and all the flags of the Empire radiating from its top. These decorations, faded and soiled now, were those which the family had hung over their front door on the occasion of King George V's Jubilee. A few minutes ago, directly their mother had gone from the house, the children had dragged them from their dusty sleep in the junk cupboard under the stairs. It was not easy to suspend a shield and seven branching flags from a ceiling, but Julian was determined that nothing of a festal character which the junk cupboard contained should be left out.

" I don't see what the flags of the Empire have got to do with it," objected Joanie.

" They've everything to do with it," declared Julian. " It's an imperial business, the Old Man coming home."

" Well, all I beg," pleaded Brenda, " is that you don't allow the taxi-man to come into the house and see it. Let the disgrace be kept among the family."

" Yes, I agree with that. I don't think the taxi-man had better see it. In fact, I don't think anybody except the family had better see it."

" Nor do I. It was a clownish idea from the first."

" Oh, granted, granted," Julian agreed. " But, like me and Dudley, the Old Man enjoys a bit of clowning. It's one of his more amiable characteristics."

" I can't think why you didn't get a choir of school-children to sing hymns of welcome."

Julian paused in his work, lowering his hammer to his side. " Now why ever didn't I think of that ? It would have pleased the Old Man no end."

" You don't think that the sudden sight of all this'll give him a relapse ? " suggested Joanie.

" My God ! " Julian turned to her as if the idea had only just struck him. " Do you think it will ? Do you think we'd better take it all down ? "

Brenda looked at her watch. " No time for that now. He'll be here any minute."

" Hell ! Will he ? Damn ! I've not finished yet."

" Yes, it'll only have taken Mummy ten minutes to get to the hospital and ten minutes to get him away, and then five minutes in the taxi."

" Don't you kid yourself. You know what the Old Man is. He'll want to say good-bye and thank-you to everyone in the hospital. But, for the love of Mike, let's be quick. The electric lights, please."

Brenda handed up a long flex from which small electric lamps of all colours hung at intervals like single fruits on a leafless branch. Julian festooned the flex over the shield and plugged one end of it into the lamp that hung from the ceiling. " No, don't turn it on yet," he shouted to Joanie, who had rushed to the switch. And he stepped quickly down from the ladder, treading on Dudley's fingers, who was just mounting. " Oh, damn the child ! Why is he always where you want to step ? Oh, shut that row. Call it off, pal. I didn't hurt you."

When his mother was out, Dudley received small quarter from Julian, and no excessive commiseration from Joanie, so, taking his injured fingers to Brenda, who would certainly stroke and kiss them, he lifted his face towards Heaven and yelled thereto ; but, after a while, Julian and Joanie being unimpressed, he abated the yelling, because he had found a new interest in what Julian was doing now. But he did not wholly stop it. His indignation would not allow him to do that.

Julian had shifted the steps to the side wall and was fixing up the strings of bunting and the flex of the electric lights so that they made a skeleton canopy with the shield and flags as its apex.

" Now switch on," he commanded Joanie, as he stepped down.

Joanie obeyed, with promptness and fervour, and the coloured lamps sprang into light. " Oh, Boy ! " she exclaimed. But somewhere among them there was an unhappy contact, so that, instead of remaining constantly alight, they went off and on in alternating spells and seemed likely to continue in this mutability till the current was cut from them.

" Well, that's pretty," said Julian, watching. He watched and waited, and they persisted in their rhythmic wink. " We'll pretend we meant them to do that. Now for the real climax."

He picked up a roll of cardboard and, opening it up, spread it the full length of his arms. In large red and blue letters on a white ground it said, " Welcome Home."

" Just the sort of thing little Truppy would have in his shop," he said. " Cheap and nasty." And he mounted the steps again to hang it from wall to wall.

When he had done this, he stepped down to survey the flags, the bunting, the lights, and the hanging legend.

" My God ! " he said. " It's awful."

Brenda agreed. " You're telling *me*."

And Joanie said only, " It stinks."

" Still, it's meant well," he submitted somewhat sadly, and, turning towards them a countenance that lacked conviction, asked, " You do think it'll give him more pleasure than pain, don't you ? "

They said that they did think so, and he was comforted.

Besides this business in the hall Brenda had another interest in the room on the right, her parents' bedroom. Now and then she had gone into this room to look at her handiwork there. She had lit a fire in the grate, placed his slippers before it, and arrayed on the bedside table a vase of chrysanthemums, a dish of grapes, a box of cigarettes, and a cluster of books. She went into the room again now to see that everything was still in order ; though how anything could have moved, or lost any quality that it had possessed a minute ago, it would be difficult to say. The fire, perhaps : she knelt down and poked it to keep the flames dancing. The wind was keening plaintively beyond the wide window and fingering fitfully its unsecured sashes, and she drew one of the curtains a little way to shut its cold breath from the bed.

Returning into the hall, she saw that Julian had the front door slightly open and was looking along the road for the taxi. Joanie was begging him not to open it too far ; begging him earnestly, because she was now having a " state ", a really terrible state, about the exhibition in the hall. She was seeking his assurance that they hadn't made fools of themselves over it; that their father and mother wouldn't suffer vicarious shame at the sight of it; that the people upstairs wouldn't come downstairs within the next ten minutes; that the taxi-man wouldn't force his way into the house with the bag to see it; and that the door wouldn't be opened wide enough for the Misses Mullard across the road, one of whom would certainly be watching, to see it.

"Oh, for heaven's sake forget it, forget it," urged Julian. "I wish I'd never built the beastly cathedral. The Old Man will love it, and that's all that matters. Now I'll tell you what we'll do. The door must stay shut. I'll run out and pay the taxi and bring in the bag and the parents. You two will stay behind the door ready to open it—to unveil the Albert Memorial, as it were."

"Not on your life," Brenda demurred. "I'm going out to meet Daddy as well as you."

"So'm I," declared Joanie.

Julian reflected. "Yes . . . well . . . mm . . . perhaps it would be better if we were all disposed around the gate. Yes, I approve of that. We'll leave the door on the latch, and you, Joanie, will rush up and open it."

"I *won't*. The thing's too shame-making altogether."

"Oh, well, I will, if no one else has got any courage——"

"There's a motor," shouted Dudley. "Did you heard it?"

§

Down Shoot-up Hill and under the spans of the railway viaducts, travelling with the rest of the traffic, came the car, and now it was in that broad and drumming thoroughfare, the Kilburn High Road, which all his life had run like a noisy diameter through the centre of his world. The low sunlight struck the upper parts of the houses, above the sunblinds of the shops, turning their dark red-brick into a bright terra-cotta under the blue of the wind-glazed sky and setting their windows on fire. And the long road with its buses, lorries, cycles, vans, and drays, its roar and sigh and drumfire beat, went on and on, straight as a ruled line, into a mist of pearl and watered gold above the wraith-like

278

mansions of Maida Vale and the unseen basin of the Park. There was the red Baptist chapel with the sugar-loaf spire; there was the Grange Cinema where he had so often been with Mildred and the children for an evening's entertainment; there was the Gaumont State Cinema with a tower like a campanile; there was his shop and Truppy's beside it, their sunblinds down—yes, it was strange and good to have come into this living street, bright with the good human sun, after going so close to the timeless and uncreated dark. He sat with Mildred at his side, looking out at the substantial road and the living people.

Mildred was as silent as he. Once, twenty years ago, she had thought that he was straying from her to another woman who had wanted him; and she had said nothing but had suffered many weeks of pain and anger and renewed love; and then one day she had known that it was all over and that he had come back to her. He had explained nothing to her, and she had said nothing; but his kiss had said all. Now he had nearly gone from her to another Lover, and she had suffered pain and anxiety and renewed love, but she had got him back. He had come back, and she did not know how to say—she was too shy to say—one word of what she felt.

But now, as he looked out of the window, he said, "It's good to see it all again. I've only been about four weeks and one mile away, but it feels rather like coming back from the other end of the world;" and he turned towards her and smiled; and she smiled too; and suddenly he took her in his arms and kissed her. For a second or so in the privacy of the taxi they were lovers again, even passionate lovers, as they used to be, thirty years before in fusty old four-wheelers when he was escorting her home. A second or so, and that cup of old, well-matured wine was drained to the lees, and she was rearranging her blouse and hair, and he was looking out of the window again.

Nunsbury Road. His own road. One by one he looked at its houses as they passed the cab windows. And here was his own house; and there by the gate were all the children, Julian grinning, Brenda smiling, Joanie's hair ablow in the wind, and Dudley swinging on the gate and singing. They rushed forward, Sankey with them, as the taxi veered

to the kerb, and Julian opened its door like a footman.
Joanie flung herself into the opened space and said, " Hallo,
Daddy." She said nothing more, but her eyes were alight
for the occasion and happy. Brenda stood behind her and
said nothing ; but there was no need for Brenda now to
show by act or word her feeling for her father.

" Hallo, Joanie. Hallo, Bren," was all that Mr. Rostrum
said.

The only two who were unafraid of being demonstrative
were Dudley and the dog. Dudley had not seen his father
for four weeks, and though he had been quite content not
to do so, it was exciting to see him again, and as Mr. Rostrum, aided by Julian, stepped out of the taxi, he rushed
forward, shouting the word " Daddy " twenty times in what
he held to be humorous fashion, and tugged him round the
thighs like a bear cub. Mr. Rostrum, pinioned in this tight
grip, wondered why he had so often doubted his pleasure
in the possession of a young child. And at the same time
he regretted that he would certainly do so again.

" And here's the Awful Little Boy," he said, that no one
might suspect the depth of his appreciation.

Sankey just stood and barked and barked, but probably
he meant this for a welcome.

Mr. Rostrum kissed Brenda. Joanie said, " Oh, Daddy "
again ; and when he kissed her, she hugged him appropriately. Joanie, after all, was not much less of a child
than Dudley.

Meanwhile Julian, with a managing and competent air,
had pulled out the bag and paid off the taxi-man and was
ready to mitigate any uncomfortable excesses on the pavement with some astringent humour.

" Do we have to carry you in, Dad, or anything like that ? "

" Carry be damned ! I've never felt better in my life."

" But aren't you weak on your pins ? "

" Not now so much. I was at first. I felt like cotton
wool at first, from my waist to the floor."

" But surely you're still a little drunk down there ? "

" A little, perhaps."

" O.K. Well, what about taking my arm ? " He asked
it awkwardly, because it is an embarrassing thing to offer
an arm to a father.

Mr. Rostrum was as shy of taking his son's arm as he of offering it, but he decided that it might be wounding to decline it and said, " Well, thanks, old man, thank you," and laid a hand within the crook of Julian's elbow.

" Joanie, you take the bag," commanded Julian. " You're a powerful child. And, Brenda, you go ahead and open the doors. And, Dudley, you behave yourself." Dudley was not within his purview at the moment, but this seemed a safe remark.

The family went up the steps : the girls in front, Mr. Rostrum on his son's arm, Mildred on his other side, and Dudley, who had stayed behind to watch the taxi turn about, running after them through the gate and proclaiming indignantly, " I'm all by myself alone."

When they were on the threshold, Brenda, the blood scalding her face, pushed open the door. She pushed it with an unhappy and irresolute hand.

And Mr. Rostrum saw the bunting and the lights (which were still winking) and the cardboard banner swinging like a punkah in the brusque, intruding wind : " Welcome Home."

" Good gracious ! " he exclaimed. And he bit his lip and blinked his eyes once, to catch and stay the tears.

" Oh, children ! " exclaimed Mildred. " Oh, what have they been up to ? "

Julian pretended to notice nothing unusual in the hall.

" Vulgar, isn't it ? " said Brenda.

" Is it ? " said Mr. Rostrum.

" Oh, yes," Julian maintained.

" It was Julian's idea," Brenda hastened to tell him. " You know how childish he is."

" Don't you believe it, Dad. Brenda and Joanie are just as responsible as I am. They aided and abetted like billy-oh. And the Awful Little Boy put in a lot of work on it."

Mr. Rostrum had thrust back the obstruction in his throat, and his voice was in control. " The idea, I think, was delightful ; the execution, perhaps, is a trifle vulgar."

" Oh, definitely," allowed Julian.

" Now then, children, your father has to go straight to bed," reminded Mildred. " The doctor said so. Come on, dear."

"Yes, put him to bed," assented Julian, "and we'll get all this down before anyone sees it."

"I like it," said Mr. Rostrum, as he went into the bedroom.

In the bedroom he saw the fire flickering, the bed turned down, the clean sheets shining, and the bedside table bearing its array of flowers, cigarettes, books, and grapes. The children followed after their parents, and Dudley began on the grapes.

"This was Brenda's effort," said Mildred, as he glanced round the room.

"Yes," said Julian, taking a grape. "She's been messing about on it all the afternoon."

"Thank you, dear. It's all very nice. It's very nice indeed."

"I think it's slightly better than the business in the hall," said Brenda.

"Oh, yes," agreed Julian.

"I like them both," said Mr. Rostrum.

A little later, when he lay in the bed, the family having withdrawn that he might try to sleep, he thought that, though no man was completely happy, he was a happier man than many.

In the hall Julian, whistling softly, began to lower the flags. Brenda went to his side to help him, in response to a whispered but emphatic statement that he wasn't going to do it all himself and he needed a mate. Joanie ran to the door and, opening it a little way, called to her dog to come in. She called quietly but impatiently, " *Come* in, Sankey. Come in, *will* you ? " Sankey went in at once, doubting whether he had sinned by staying out ; and she shut the door, latching it softly, as soon as his long black tail had whipped through.

And the house looked out upon the wind-blown road and the dwindling trees, a massive, grey mausoleum, silent, withdrawn, and unrevealing, though it had added a few more to its memories.

Portway Reprints

The following titles have been reprinted at the request of the
London & Home Counties Branch of the Library Association and
can be obtained from Cedric Chivers Ltd., Portway, Bath.

Non-fiction

Craddock, Joseph	HAUNTED HOUSES
Cardus, Neville	DAYS IN THE SUN
Cobbett, William	COTTAGE ECONOMY
Dearden, Harold	THE FIRE-RAISERS
Edmonds, Charles	A SUBALTERN'S WAR
Gibbs, P.	FROM BAPAUME TO PASSCHENDAELE
Grant, I.F.	ECONOMIC HISTORY OF SCOTLAND
Harris, John	RECOLLECTIONS OF RIFLEMAN HARRIS
Hitchcock, F.C.	STAND TO: A DIARY OF THE TRENCHES
Hole, C.	WITCHCRAFT IN ENGLAND
Jones, Jack	GIVE ME BACK MY HEART
Jones, Jack	UNFINISHED JOURNEY
Jones, Jack	ME AND MINE
Lowe, George	BECAUSE IT IS THERE
Price, Harry	THE MOST HAUNTED HOUSE IN ENGLAND
Quigley, Hugh	PASSCHENDAELE AND THE SOMME
Pain, Nancy	THANK YOU, NELSON
Stamper, Joseph	LESS THAN THE DUST
Tangye, Derek	TIME WAS MINE
Tangye, Derek	WENT THE DAY WELL
Thompson, P.A.	LIONS LED BY DONKEYS
Villiers, Alan	SONS OF SINDBAD

Fiction

Ainsworth, W. Harrison	GUY FAWKES
Ashton, H.	THE SWAN OF USK
Barke, James	THE END OF THE HIGH BRIDGE
Barke, James	THE SONG IN THE GREEN THORN TREE
Barke, James	THE WELL OF THE SILENT HARP
Blaker, Richard	MEDAL WITHOUT BAR
Broster, D.K.	SHIPS IN THE BAY